THE ANCIENT HOUR

EAGLE BROTHERHOOD SERIES

KAT LE VEQUE

Copyright © 2010 by Kathryn Le Veque

This title was previously published as Lady of Heaven and Sands of Time

Cover design by Kim Killion

Published by Oliver-Heber Books

0 9 8 7 6 5 4 3 2 1

AUTHOR'S NOTE

They call themselves the Eagle Brotherhood.

We've all got 'that' group of friends. People we've bonded with that just 'get' you and you get them. Whether you bond over common interests, or a job, of even just mutual friends, we've all found that connection at one time or another.

Same with the Eagle Brotherhood.

It started with five Americans. They were young, brilliant, idealistic, and met during a semester abroad. When I first wrote this series, many years ago, it was originally called the American Heroes series. It was supposed to be about guys who knew each other as young men, but who went on to live their own lives and have their own adventures. Ordinary guys in extraordinary circumstances was how I described it. There were only five in the beginning, but somewhere along the line, we added two Brits as 'honorary' members. There are actually more books slated to be written, but I just haven't gotten around to it yet. One of the Eagle Brotherhood — Nash Aury — even has a sequel mostly written to his book, so this is really a series that has a lot of growth potential. And why not? It centers around men who are honorable, chivalric, and end up facing some really stressful and, in a few cases, dangerous situations. Some explainable, some not. That's the fun of it.

But it all had to start somewhere.

Each Eagle Brotherhood book starts out with the same *"How it began"* preface so you, as the reader, knows where these guys connect because they don't appear in each other's stories. It's a rather interesting connection, but one that opens up the hero of each tale — and eventually the heroine — to one heck of a story. These guys are connected to me as much as to each other.

They really are a true brotherhood.

I hope you enjoy the stories in this series because they were a labor of love to write. You don't have to read them in any particular order:

The Burning Hour
The Sunset Hour
The Secret Hour
The Unholy Hour
The Devil's Hour
The Killing Hour
The Ancient Hour

Happy reading,

AQUILA FRATRUM

Seven men.
Each with a story to tell.
Welcome to the world of the Eagle Brotherhood.

Years ago, five Americans on a semester abroad met at the home of their sponsor in Yorkshire, England. They were taking the same course at the University of York, including the son of their host. But it wasn't the course in International Law that bonded them. It was an incident from that time, something that happened on a dark and stormy night in an alley behind a bar in York called *The Calcaria*.

It is something that changed their perspectives forever.

These days, the men who once called themselves the *Aquila Fratrum* or the Eagle Brotherhood — a name based on the Americans who were military-based at that time — have gone forth in their lives. They are men in normal, everyday professions who succeed in extraordinary things. Their paths aren't smooth, and they aren't perfect, but they understand more than most that life is never about the smooth or the perfect. It is about

the imperfect and the difficult. It's even about the unex-
plainable.

And, above all else, light overcomes the darkness.

Aquila Fratrum.

Ordinary men who have lived extraordinary circumstances.

And the women who love them.

HOW IT BEGAN

MORE THEN TWENTY YEARS AGO, THE CALCARIA, YORK

MICK MCCONNELL, PROPRIETOR

"Beck." A big man with a crown of auburn hair spoke with a drunken slur to his words. "Beck. *Seavington!*"

The blond Californian on the other side of the table, who had been half-lidded as he watched a group of women across the darkened room of the pub, jerked at the sound of his name as if he'd just been slapped.

"What?" he said, looking at the man with the auburn hair. "Christ, Phipps. Can't you just leave me alone for a minute?"

Archer Phipps struggled not to laugh. "Why?"

"Because you're breaking my powers of concentration, you ass."

That broke the table out in snorts of laughter. The man seated next to Beck, big and blond and with a mega-watt smile, put a hand on Beck's shoulder.

"What in the hell are you concentrating on?" he said, leaning over to see what Beck might be seeing. When he spied it, he gestured. "Over there?"

Beck full-on pointed to the women across the pub. "There."

"Those?"

"*Those.*"

"Well… what are you trying to do by staring at them? Just go talk to them."

Beck scowled at the man. "Because I'm trying to lure them with the power of suggestion, Trevor," he said. Then, he looked around the table and pointed. "It works. Colt over there has a laser stare. He doesn't even have to say anything — women know what he's thinking just by the expression on his face. Isn't that right, Sheridan?"

Colt Sheridan, clean-cut and square-jawed, waved an annoyed hand at the man he'd spent nearly every day with for the past six months. "Some of us don't have to be obvious," he said. "Look at Nash. All he has to do is give them one of those sexy, down-home expressions and they're falling all over themselves. I don't have anything on him."

Across the table, Nash Aury, the quiet and diplomatic sort with a Louisiana drawl, laughed softly. "It's all in the face," he said, gesturing to the big dimples in each cheek. "I don't have anything y'all don't have, but we don't have anything that Serreaux has, so maybe we should just give it up and let him take the lead."

The group looked over at Ethan Serreaux, a man with a French parents even though he was born in America. Dark-eyed and dark-haired, he looked like he'd just come off the pages of a men's magazine. When he saw that the entire table of semi-drunks was looking at him, he smiled lasciviously.

"*Belle fille,*" he said in his best Maurice Chevalier impression. "*Asseyez-vous sur mes genoux et dites-moi à quel point vous me voulez.*"

Everyone burst out laughing except for Beck, who slowly banged his forehead on the table. "You sound like Pepe Le Pew," he said. "Shut *up!*"

More laughter, most especially from Archer and the last man of their group, a giant of a figure who wasn't part of their academic group. Fox Henredon was in the process of obtaining his Ph.D. in Archaeology with an emphasis in Egyptology from Oxford. In fact, he'd come back a few months ago from a dig near Aswan and when he visited his best friend from grade school, Archer, he'd come across the Americans temporarily housed in Archer's pad. He'd gotten on so well with them that they'd made him an honorary member of their group. But not just the group — of their secret society, as well.

Aquila Fratrum.

The Eagle Brotherhood.

The whole secret group was really meant as a joke, but the basis of it — the honor, the patriotism — they took seriously. Three out of the five Americans had come from Annapolis and all five of them were majoring in International Law, hence the purpose of the semester abroad course. Archer was taking the same course, and he'd been the host house, and given that they were all within a few years of each other age-wise, they'd all bonded over common likes, common dislikes, and a passion for adventure.

It was a guy gang like no other.

But tonight, they were drinking to the group that would soon be separating. The course at the University of York was finished and the Americans would soon be heading back to their native lands, but promises of reciprocal visits had abound all evening. Nash, in particular, had invited everyone to New Orleans for the holidays because his family, having made their money in sugar, had a massive house that could accommodate everyone. Beck, Cord, and Colt had already committed to it, but Ethan had family obligations he needed to get out of. Archer was trying to figure out how to break the news to his parents, who were possessive of his time, while Fox was on the verge of committing. He'd never been to New Orleans and a street named after liquor intrigued him. As the Brotherhood planned their next gathering, Beck stood up from the table.

"I need to find the loo," he said, looking around. "Where is it? Back behind the bar?"

The problem was that he was drunker than the rest of them and probably not in great shape to find anything, so Cord stood up next to him.

"Back in the corner," he said. "Come on, little brother."

He had Beck by the neck, pulling him back behind the bar where there was a dark corridor that led to bathrooms and the kitchen. The term 'little brother' was essentially referring to Beck's age because he happened to be the youngest out of their group. But he was also the toughest. Beck Seavington could out-fight anybody, Fox included, and Fox had participated in under-ground fight clubs during his earlier college days. He'd won money at it, too.

But Beck's fists were quite lethal.

The Navy wanted him that way.

Cord went with Beck so he wouldn't get into any trouble. Cord was an enormous man, having played football, and the rumor was that he was being scouted by the NFL. He wasn't a fighter by nature, but no one was going to test of man of that size. He'd just push the scrapper, Beck, in front of him, anyway, and let the career Navy man do the damage.

Every group had a scrapper.

It smelled like stale booze and bleach back here and the door to the men's room was locked. Beck rattled it but it remained fixed. With a heavy sigh, he looked at Cord.

"I can't wait," he muttered.

Cord tipped his head in the direction of the door to the alley out back, which was next to the kitchen door.

"Outside?" he said.

Beck nodded, which nearly threw him off balance, and charged through the back door. Cord followed him and they ended up in the dirty, damp alley behind the bar. It smelled worse out here, like garbage and animals. There were crates against the wall, broken down cardboard boxes, and little else. There were two ends to the alley, but they were standing closer to the end that dumped out onto the street where *The Calcaria* was located. Beck was looking for a discreet place to relieve himself when the back door smacked back on its hinges again, spilling forth the rest of their group.

"I think we're done with this place," Archer said, rubbing his eyes because the alcohol was messing with his vision. "There's another pub down the way called Valhalla. Let's go there."

Beck had found a spot behind some crates. "Are the women more proactive there?" he asked. "I mean, will they actually come up and talk to you? I don't think my mind control is working."

Archer grinned. "Do you seriously want a woman that approaches you?" he said. "The wooing of a woman is an art, Beck. You don't want some nervy woman up in your grill, do you?"

The others snorted in agreement. Ethan and Nash were by the back door, leaning back against the wall, as Colt went to stand next to Beck. Fox went to stand with Cord, maybe as a lookout since they really shouldn't be pissing in an alley, when three men suddenly appeared from what was a small walkway between buildings. It was dark, so no one really noticed, until one of the men walked up behind Colt and put a knife to the man's back.

Then, everything changed.

The drunken, happy mood was gone.

"Easy, big man," the man said. He was short, with a dirty

jacket, but the knife he'd produced was quite large. "If you want to keep your kidney, you'll relax, mate."

Everyone froze — Ethan, Nash, Archer, Fox, Cord, Beck, and most of all, Colt. But his features never changed expression, even as he felt the prick of cold steel against his right kidney.

"If you're looking for money, you're too late," he said steadily. "We're coming out of the bar, not going into it. We've spent our money."

The man in the dirty jacket grunted as his friends also produced big knives. "Somehow, I doubt it," he said. "We were watching you inside. I think you're from money, so you've got more where that came from, Yank. I think all of you have more."

With that, his friends began to move. One of them was heading for Ethan while the other one was heading for Archer. The group, as a whole, instinctively started to back away from the men approaching, but Fox refused to budge. At seven inches over six feet, he had that luxury of being stubborn.

"You blokes really think you're going to rob guys who are twice your size?" he said incredulously. "You're either incredibly stupid or way too overconfident."

"I'll go with stupid," Cord muttered.

Fox quickly agreed with him. "Stupid, for sure," he said. "There are seven of us and three of you. You may be able to take out a couple of us, but there are five of us left who will break your fucking necks. Are you ready for that?"

That brought some pause to the man's companions, but the man in the dirty jacket poked Colt enough to draw blood.

"Give me your fucking money!" he hissed. "Another word and I'll cut a hole in this man big enough to stick my hand through!"

Colt didn't even flinch when the man jabbed him. He kept his right hand up while his left once reached into his pocket for his wallet. But as he was doing that, and the other two men with knives were advancing on Ethan and Archer, no one happened to be watching Cord.

And that would be their fatal mistake.

"*Quaere ferro scopum tuum*," Cord suddenly mumbled. "*Oboedite mihi!*"

Inexplicably, the man holding the knife to Colt's back jerked. He jolted. His hand flew up and the big blade he'd been forcing on Colt flew up and into his own throat, straight back through so that the tip came out of the back of his neck. It went through him like a bullet. As he staggered back and fell to the ground, his friends were momentarily startled and that gave Cord the opportunity to turn against them.

"*In molles venter it ferrum*," he growled, lifting a big fist as if to punch the men straight in the face. "*Utrumque vestrum!*"

The men screamed as the hands holding the knives came up and plunged the blades into their bellies as if they had a mind of their own. They went down as Ethan, Nash, Archer, Fox, Beck and Colt made haste to back up, away from what was evidently going on. No one knew what was happening and it was best to get clear considering knives were slashing all over the place.

At least, everyone but Cord backed up. He pointed a finger at the men who had just stabbed themselves in the belly.

"*Ferro ad carnem, ferrum ad os*," he said in a low tone. "*Collum secari debet.*"

The men with knives in their bellies suddenly withdrew those knives and stabbed themselves in the neck, three or four times, until they could stab no more. They simply lay there and bled as Cord turned to his stunned group of friends.

"We need to get out of here," he said quietly. "Before the cops come. *Quickly.*"

No one moved. They stood there, eyes wide at what they'd just seen. Colt, who was the closest to Cord, grabbed him by the arm.

"What in the hell just happened?" he asked in awe. "What did you do?"

Cord looked back at the men bleeding out on the alley floor. "I protected us," he said simply. "We really need to go."

"Protected us *how*?" Fox was at Cord's side, his handsome face seriously. "What did we just see, Cord? Hypnosis of some kind?"

Cord scratched his head. "No," he said reluctantly, looking at the curious group. "Can we just get out of here, please?"

"Not until you explain," Fox said.

He was serious. No one was moving, not really. Exasperated, Cord sighed heavily. "Fine," he said. "I did it to save Colt's life. That guy was going to kill him."

Colt, who had blood running down the right side of his torso, stepped forward. "He probably was," he said. "Nobody is disputing that. But *what* did you do?"

Cord looked at his friend. "It's not something I really talk about," he said hesitantly. "I haven't... I haven't done that stuff since I was younger, but you all know I'm descended from Abigail Williams. When we all talked about our families and stuff, I told you guys that I was descended from one of the chief accusers of the Salem Witch Trails."

"You did," Colt said as his gaze moved to the men on the ground. "But what does that have to do with it? And done *what* stuff?"

Cord was clearly reluctant. "My dad likes to call us Casters," he said. "Abigail Williams was an accomplished witch and that trait is passed down in my family, like red hair or freckles. Only it's some kind of power we can summon. What you saw was a spell. I turned their knives against them."

"You're a witch?" Colt repeated in shock. "Seriously, Cord? Like — magic?"

Cord didn't answer. He just started walking, very quickly,

and the others instinctively followed. They came to a walkway that led out onto the street and, nearly running, they headed up towards the main road.

"Yeah, like magic," Cord finally said as they came to the main avenue. "You saw it. I can't explain it more than that, but I wouldn't have done it if I thought we could have gotten out of that without Sheridan missing a kidney. Just... do yourself a favor. Forget you ever saw it."

"Wait," Ethan said as they began to walk, very quickly, towards the area with the car park. "We can't just leave. No matter what happened, or how it happened, we have to call the police."

"And tell them what?" Cord said. "That we got attacked and that I used a spell to turn the weapons against the guys who attacked us? They would think we were nuts."

As Ethan shook his head in disagreement, Archer grabbed him by the arm and pulled him along. "They would want to know who stabbed those guys," he said. "They'd take our finger-prints and find out that none of our fingerprints were on the weapons. How in the hell are we going to explain that?"

Ethan wasn't sure, but he didn't like running from a crime scene. "Guys, we can't leave," he said, trying to drag his feet. "We were witnesses to what happened. We have to..."

Cord suddenly came to a halt and grabbed Ethan by the shirt. "What do you think is going to happen?" he hissed. "Ethan, I don't want to run any more than you do, but I'm the one who killed those guys. That's the bottom line. And I'm not doing time for it and I'm not going to show the York Police how I turned those weapons against them, so forget it. We're not calling anyone. We're getting out of here and you are giving me your word that you'll never repeat what you saw. I need you to swear that to me."

Ethan could see how upset Cord was and he put up his

hands in a gesture of surrender. "I swear that I'll never repeat it," he said. "Don't worry about that. But if anyone else saw us..."

"Who is going to see us?" Cord said, letting go of his shirt. "No one saw us. We're going to fly home tomorrow, anyway, and we'll be out of here. Done."

Ethan nodded, but he wasn't happy about it. Even if he wasn't happy, at least he understood. The entire group began walking again, very quickly, with the car park in sight. Beyond that, freedom.

Freedom from something they hoped wouldn't come back to haunt them.

Cord most of all.

"You... you really *did* that?" Beck finally said. He was still astonished by what he'd witnessed. "How in the hell did you learn how to cast spells?"

Cord school his head. "I told you," he said. "It's in my blood. But I don't like talking about it, so let's just drop it... okay?"

"But we saw it."

They had reached the car park by now and Cord came to an abrupt halt, facing the group. He was normally a congenial guy, but the event had him spooked.

"I know you guys saw it," he said. "But you need to swear that you will never repeat it. You will never tell anyone. Because if you do, I'm going to be in a shitload of trouble. How in the hell am I going to explain to anyone that I used witchcraft to kill some criminals?"

"But it was in self-defense," Ethan stressed. "No one is going to convict you, or any of us for that matter."

Cord's frustration bled through. "But we would have to explain *how* it happened," he said. "Don't you get it? One question would lead to another, questions you don't want to answer. Trust me."

Nash, who had been silent for the most part, put a hand on

Cord's shoulder. "Cord, where I'm from, voodoo and witchcraft are part of the culture," he said quietly. "I've seen things I can't explain, so I believe what you're saying. I know what I saw. You have a gift, but it's a gift people don't understand. We've all witnessed something tonight that was... well, pretty damn amazing."

Cord registered some relief as he realized he had the support of Nash. The guy wasn't going to hound him. After a moment, he looked at the rest of the group. "You know, we've joked about calling ourselves the Eagle Brotherhood, but I think we really *are* a brotherhood now," he said. "We've experienced something that could have cost us our lives. It was small, but it happened. You saw something you shouldn't have seen because I did something I shouldn't have done. But to protect you guys... I'd do it again. I hope you know that."

"I feel like I owe my life to you," Colt said, reaching out to shake Cord's hand. "You were brave to do what you did, Cord, knowing... well, knowing that it wasn't something for all to see. But you did it and I'm grateful. I'll take an oath of silence on the Eagle Brotherhood if that's what it'll take. To protect you because you saved my life, I'll do anything. And if you ever need me, no matter where I am, I'll come. That's a promise."

More hands began shooting out, covering Colt and Cord's hands. It was a vow, a promise, not to discuss the event that bonded them more than a school or allied nations could. It was a bond that went deeper now because they harbored a secret. More than that, they had crossed into the realm of a brotherhood that would protect or kill for one another.

The true test of a brotherhood.

It was an oath that would take to their graves.

Wherever life would take them.

TEXT OF THE LADY OF HEAVEN PAPYRUS

Oh! Isis, Lady of Heaven, Favored of the Gods,
may she be given eternal life by the Gods who love her.
May she find peace within the bosom of the Most High,
from the Claw of the Ape,
ten days as the sun sets to the Holy City of Ranthor
which lies deep to the east in the arms of the Syene,
to the Fingers that Reach to the Sky.
May she know grace and divine protection,
our Holy Mistress, foremost Lady of the West,
as she Rests in the Shelter of the Sun.

Cairo at last!

Dear Louis and I have been on the boat for seventeen days from Southampton but fortunately the weather has co-operated. My dear husband wants to make sure our honeymoon is a journey to remember. We were met at the Cairo docks by our "dragoman", or translator, Mr. Arak. Louis does not trust him but I think he is fascinating. We are soon to begin our adventure!

~ From the Journal of Lady Frances de Lara Sherburn

ONE

BOLTON MUSEUM, BOLTON, LANCASHIRE, U.K.—
PRESENT DAY

IT TOOK two knocks on the old plywood door before he lifted his head to see who was there. The office door was open and his assistant, an older woman with curly brown hair and teeth that were in need of a cleaning stood in the archway, knocking again even when she saw that he was looking at her. It was an annoying habit she had.

"Dr. Henredon," she said in a strong Manchester accent. "Your one o'clock meeting is here."

Dr. Fox Henredon gazed at the woman as if he had no idea what she meant until, a split-second later, realization dawned and he sighed heavily. Eyes the color of obsidian glimmered, recollecting the meeting while simultaneously reflecting on the workload facing him.

He didn't usually deal with the public; he left that to those better suited. But this meeting had been different. He'd been virtually forced into it thanks to his assistant who had been a fixture at the museum for over thirty years. She knew the names, the people, their backgrounds and their connections. The subject of this meeting had all of that and more, and she had set it up without asking him. She simply told him about it.

Flicking the pen from his fingers and watching it clatter on the desk, Fox sat back in his chair, listening to it groan under his weight as he pulled off his reading glasses.

"God," he groaned softly, rubbing his weary orbs. He had a hint of the same Manchester accent that his assistant had. "I'd forgotten. Who is she again?"

The assistant wriggled her eyebrows. "Her name is Morgan Sherburn. She wants to talk to you about a relic she found in her great-grandmother's house."

He began nodding even before she finished her sentence, waving her off as he rose to his feet. The chair popped up and smacked him in the rear and he shoved it away as he made his way around the desk.

As he moved, he tried to stretch out the kinks in his big body. He'd been sitting in the same position for hours and had lost track of the time. But maybe it had just been wishful thinking. Maybe if he'd stayed still long enough and not utter a sound, Mrs. Moberley, the assistant, would take the meeting for him. But he knew that was too much to hope for. He could hear his spine cracking as he twisted and stretched.

"All right, all right," he snapped softly. "I really don't have time for this. Besides, any mention of a private party trying to sell a relic makes me nervous after what happened a few years ago with that old man trying to pass off a forged statue. The museum got into a hell of a lot of trouble for that."

The older woman nodded patiently. "I understand completely, but this woman comes from a very old and very good family. I would think anything she has would be authentic and worth a look-see."

He snorted. "Whatever you say. Get her in here and let's get this over with."

She got a grip on his elbow. "You're coming with me to get her."

He looked confused. "Why?"

"Because you've been sitting behind that desk for six hours. You've got to move around or you'll get the bends. A walk out to the lobby won't hurt you."

Fox knew better than to argue; he let her pull him along. Mrs. Moberley let go of him by the time they hit the reception area; the hallway leading to the lobby of the museum was dead ahead.

"Doesn't the name Sherburn mean anything to you?" she asked as she led him into the corridor.

Fox made a somewhat impatient face and scratched at his dark head. "No," he said flatly. "But I know it probably should. What about it?"

"Really, Dr. Henredon," the assistant sniffed as if he were in need of an education. "Sherburn is an old name in these parts, one of the oldest in Lancashire. They have a manor house just north of Bolton called Heaven's Gate. Surely you've heard of it."

He stopped scratching his head and looked at her. "I have."

"Then you'll also recall that the Sherburns were very close to the Barlows."

"The family that founded the museum?"

"The same."

He lifted an eyebrow at her. "I don't remember that part."

"I tried to tell you."

"I guess I forgot."

The assistant shook her head as if he were an imbecile. Even if the man was the Director of Egyptology Collections for one of the world's finest natural history museums, he could be rather singularly focused.

Fox Henredon was something of a legend in the British museum circles. He was a young man who was blindingly brilliant, acing his A-Level exams and earning his doctorate in a little over six years. He'd graduated Eton and even did a stint as a rugby player before transitioning to civilian life as an assistant museum curator. Eight years later, following a scandal involving forged Egyptian artwork that saw the head of the Egyptian Collections ousted, Fox ended up with the job.

He'd led an interesting life, no doubt, and Mrs. Moberley had known him since he had started at the museum, treating him as somewhat of a wayward son. She was the only woman in the museum who could handle him, mostly because all of the other women went to pieces at the sight of him.

Not only was the man brilliant, but he was extraordinarily handsome and he knew it. At six feet plus seven inches and around two hundred seventy pounds, with dark hair and nearly black eyes, he was an enormous man that reeked of comeliness, intelligence and intimidation. The women around the museum agreed that his birth name also described him; the man was indeed a fox.

But his handsome features were darkening by the minute as he made his way out of the administrative offices and into the main bulk of the museum. It was lunchtime and the museum was busier than usual with people visiting during their lunch hour. The entire museum was part of Bolton Civic Centre and housed, among other things, one of the oldest aquariums in the world. Busy workers loved to make the museum part of their lunch break. It was a popular destination.

Fox ended up dodging a couple of small children, moving around them with polite impatience as he followed Mrs. Moberley towards the information desk. It was busier than normal at this time of day and he could see several people crowding up around the modern information kiosk. Mrs. Moberley went directly to a woman seated near the desk, pulling Fox along with her.

Fox almost didn't see the woman at first; she was seated between the information kiosk and the wall. He was focused on the old ladies bickering with one of the museum docents when Mrs. Moberley's voice caught his attention.

"Miss Sherburn?" she gestured to the woman rising from the guest services chair. "This is Dr. Henredon."

Fox's dark eyes focused on the woman and, for a moment, he was actually speechless. A strikingly beautiful blond with exquisite features and wide brown eyes gazed steadily at him. She was petite, no more than an inch or two over five feet, dressed in a clinging gray sweater, slender blue jeans and flat black slippers. Although she had one of those curvy figures that made him take a second look, it was her face had his instant interest. He'd never seen anything so sweet or lovely. Fox suddenly wasn't so resistant to the meeting as she extended a slender hand at him.

"Dr. Henredon," she spoke with an American accent. "I'm Morgan Sherburn. Thank you for taking the time to meet with me. I know you're really busy but I didn't know who else to go to with this."

Her voice struck him first, like the cascade of sweet, cool water. He could have listened to that voice all day and it was a struggle to overcome his initial shock. He took her outstretched hand, dwarfing it.

"No problem," he said, feeling her soft flesh against his. "What can I help you with?"

Mrs. Moberley already had them on the move. "Let's get out of this crowd and go someplace where you can talk." She began to lead them across the busy museum floor, back in the direction of the offices. "Can I offer you a coffee, Miss Sherburn?"

Morgan shook her head. "No, thank you."

Mrs. Moberley smiled thinly in reply, her gaze inspecting the beautiful young woman, and continued leading the charge across the museum's main lobby and back into the administrative offices area.

Morgan followed, walking very quickly because the older woman seemed to be; carting her heavy purse and a portfolio-like briefcase, it was becoming an increasing struggle to keep up with the pace. Her clear brown eyes moved over the lobby of the Bolton Museum, which very quickly disappeared to become a hallway leading into the administrative offices. The entire place had an old smell to it mixed in with the modern elements that had been added, just like most historical buildings in Britain.

But the architecture of the building and oldness of it had not prepared her for the introduction to Dr. Fox Henredon. In fact, she had to take a second look at the man to realize he wasn't some old relic of an archaeologist buried back in the archives of a dusty museum. That's exactly what she had expected. But instead, Dr. Henredon was a very large, very handsome man with a deep voice that bubbled up from his toes. He looked like a movie star with his granite jaw and neatly combed black hair. Rip off his shirt and there would be a big "S" underneath. Now, her trip to Bolton wasn't such a boring chore after all. At least she had some eye candy to look at while discussing her business.

The dim hallway opened up into a reception area and the older woman again turned to Morgan, indicating a small alcove off to the left and a doorway beyond. Clutching her purse and her briefcase, Morgan followed the gesture and ended up in a big, cluttered office.

"Have a seat." Fox came in behind her, moving to take the chair behind his desk. "Are you sure I can't get you some coffee or water?"

Morgan shook her head. "No, thanks very much," she said, setting her purse down as she took position atop the fake leather chair. She held out the big, flat briefcase. "Do you mind if I put this on your desk?"

At least she wasn't going to waste his time with a lot of idle chatter. The woman was focused on her purpose and Fox appreciated that. He settled his bulk back in his chair, nodding to her question.

"Sure."

She noticed that he didn't move to clear away the disorder on the desktop. "Do you want to move your papers first?" she suggested helpfully.

He shook his head. "No need."

With some uncertainty, she carefully set the briefcase down and began to unfasten it.

"Seriously," she said quietly as she unfastened the ties. "I really want to thank you for your time. Maybe this is nothing at all, but given my great-grandparents' history in Egypt, I really can't be sure. I thought I'd better show it to an expert before I did anything with it."

Fox sat back in his chair, alternately watching her face and her slim, lovely fingers as she messed around with the briefcase. He noticed she wasn't wearing a wedding ring, which thrilled him. More than that, he was seriously trying not to gawk at the woman because it would have been damn easy. He was captivated by the pouty, lush lips and long-lashed brown eyes. So he labored to switch his focus to the business at hand.

"No problem," he replied. "But why me?"

She paused, looking rather confused by the question. When she answered, it was almost in the form of a question, like he was trying to trick her. "Because you were the closest."

"Closest to what? Your location? You're not British."

She smiled weakly, flashing great big dimples in both cheeks. "No, I'm not," she finished with the fastens and opened the top of the case. "When I called to set up this meeting, I explained everything to your assistant. Didn't she tell you?"

Fox was fascinated with the dimples. "She did, but all I remember is that you found whatever this is when you were cleaning out your great-grandmother's house."

Morgan nodded, carefully easing back the top of the case. "Sorry," she said apologetically. "I didn't want to waste your time with a big explanation if you already knew the story."

"Tell me."

"Well," she cocked her head, looking at whatever it was in the case. "My great-grandfather passed away in June and my mother and I were cleaning out the house and came across a lot of Egyptian artifacts."

Fox lifted an eyebrow. "A lot of Egyptian artifacts?"

She nodded. "I know it sounds crazy, but there's a room in their house with a bunch of Egyptian relics in it. My great-grandparents were quite the collectors."

Fox sat forward in his chair and waved his hands at her. "Let's start from the beginning here," he told her, indicating the chair. "You need to sit down and tell me everything from the start. Doesn't your family own Heaven's Gate Manor?"

Morgan did what she was told and planted her bottom back on the chair. Dr. Henredon had a manner about him that suggested complete obedience was wise. Besides, she didn't want to offend the man since she was here soliciting his pro bono opinion. She took a deep breath to slow her rush.

"I'm sorry," she apologized yet again. "It's just that I know you're really busy, I'm really busy, and I'm trying to get through all of this before I have to leave for home next week, so I'm just kind of rushing around like a chicken with its head cut off."

He regarded her a moment; it seemed all he was doing was regarding her. "Where's home?"

The man had amazingly intense eyes. There was warmth there and interest, but there was also hardness and doubt. She could sense it.

"Los Angeles," she told him. Then she full-on smiled, a flashy brilliant smile with big baby-doll dimples in both cheeks. "Couldn't you tell? Don't I talk like a movie star?"

He met her grin, his teeth straight and white with a slightly impish tilt to his lips. "Sure you do," he replied. "And you look like one, too."

She smiled bashfully, a very lovely smile that had Fox utterly captivated. "I'll bet you say that to all of the Americans."

He snorted. "Hardly," he replied. "At least not the ones I know. I've never been to Los Angeles. I'd like to go someday."

"If you do, don't miss Disneyland or the Hollywood Strip," she gave him some quick advice before veering back to the subject at hand. Dr. Henredon's compliment had her off balance somewhat. "Anyway, like I said, my great-grandfather passed away in June. My grandmother and grandfather are too old to really do any good, so the duty of cleaning out the manor house fell to my mom and me. My great-grandparents were avid collectors of Egyptian artifacts and since you're the department head for Egyptian Collection at the Bolton Museum, I thought you'd be the person to ask about the authenticity of the relics."

Fox watched her as she spoke, both because he was fascinated with the shape of her mouth and also because he was digesting her words. He wanted to slip another well-timed compliment into the conversation but he wasn't sure she was too receptive given how she had dodged his first one. When she was finished, he nodded faintly.

"Heaven's Gate is a very old estate," he replied, eyeing the now-open case. "I have also heard that your great-grandparents were friends with the Barlows who founded the Bolton Museum."

Morgan nodded. "They were. My great-grandmother, the Lady Frances de Lara Sherburn, was a friend of Annie Barlow. Annie was the daughter of the founder."

"I know who she is," he was looking up at her now, studying her face, and there seemed to be something on his mind. He gestured at the case. "You said that there is an entire room full of Egyptian artifacts?"

She nodded. "Actually, it's the library, but it has a lot of artifacts in it."

"And you only brought me one thing to authenticate?" He scratched his dark head, puzzlement evident in his expression. "Pardon me for asking, but if you've got an entire room full of artifacts, why bring me just one?"

Morgan's pleasant expression seemed to tighten. "Excuse me?"

His dark eyes glittered. "You heard me; why bring me just one? What's so special about it?"

She held his gaze for a long moment before looking away, clearing her throat softly. She suddenly seemed ill at ease and Fox watched her, growing more curious and interested by the moment.

"Because," she said quietly. "Because... well, it seems to be one of the nicest pieces and my great-grandfather had a hand-written note attached to it that called it the Lady of Heaven papyrus. I thought maybe it was important and if it is, perhaps you could tell us what we should do with it. Perhaps you could even translate it."

His brow furrowed. "*Translate* it?" he shook his head. "That will take a lot of time. If you want to donate it to the museum, then, of course, we would translate it. But if you want me to translate it right now off the cuff, then I'm sorry to disappoint you. I don't have the time."

"But it's not that big of a scroll," she insisted, gesturing to the document lying flat and exposed in the artwork case. "It shouldn't be too hard for a man of your expertise. I've read about you, Dr. Henredon. You're one of the best. I've read about the awards you've won and the fact that you're a director at a major museum and not even forty years old says a lot. If you could only look at it, maybe you can tell me what it says."

He sat forward, eyes on Morgan as he folded his big hands on the desk top. "Is that really why you came?" he asked her "You want me to translate this?"

Morgan appeared as if she'd been cornered as the truth of her visit began to slip out. She thought she'd been fairly clever at hiding it up until now. "I thought... well, I thought maybe in the course of examining it that you might... you could... just a few words...."

He sighed and shook his head. "Sorry," he said, his tone professional. "I can't translate it for you, at least not today. If that's really what you came here for then I am sorry to have wasted your time. Perhaps you should have been honest when you called and saved us both the time and trouble."

Morgan stared at him. She appeared as if she wanted to say a lot more but thought better of it. After a moment, she lowered her gaze and reached for her enormous purse. As Fox watched, she reached in and pulled forth something that he first thought was a book. Then she turned it in his direction and he could see that it was a very old album, like one would use for photographs. He could see the leather binding and the careful stitching, made in the days when craftsmanship meant something. It was worn and dog-eared and she sat for a moment with it in her lap, looking at it. Fox's curiosity grew as she fingered it carefully before finally daring to look at him.

She opened her mouth to speak but ended up sighing heavily. Then she collected herself and tried again.

"Look," she said, her voice soft. "I wasn't trying to lie when I set up this meeting but I thought if I came out with everything right off the bat that you would never meet with me. And I really need help with this, if not from you then from someone else who knows about Egyptology. I've got a situation on my hands that I just can't figure out. I really need answers."

He lifted a dark eyebrow. "Answers to what?"

She lifted the album, gesturing at it. "This."

She stood up and walked around his desk. Fox watched her as she came to stand next to him, sweet wafts of her perfume assaulting his senses. She smelled as good as she looked and he was thinking of telling her that but he bit his tongue. He didn't think she would take it well if he was complimenting her in one breath and rejecting her in the next. He decided it was best to lay off the charm. His observations were interrupted as she set the album carefully on the desk and opened it.

"This is my great-grandmother's journal," she said softly. "She began keeping one when she and my great-grandfather traveled to Egypt for the first time. She was so young, only eighteen, and this journal starts just after she and my great-grandfather were married. If nothing else, this journal is a remarkable account of early Egypt and how the wealthy British viewed it. She met so many amazing people like Lord Carnarvon and Howard Carter. All of the adventure, her hopes and dreams and feelings, are on these pages."

Fox tore his gaze away from her long enough to glance at the time-worn pages of the journal. There was carefully written script, accompanied by trinkets, luggage stickers, a boat ticket to Cairo, a receipt for a room reservation at the Winter Palace Hotel in Luxor, and other remnants of a bygone era of exploration and travel. In just those first few moments, he was hooked. He hated to admit it, but he was. Mementos like this were rare and, as a historian, he valued them. Without even asking, he carefully turned the pages.

Sketches jumped out at him of the Valley of the Kings before it became commercial. Lady Frances had even sketched the great statues of Memnon, as they were known back then, and there was a sketch of the sphinx decades before the sand would be cleared away from its base. As Fox skimmed the first few pages, he could see that every day was carefully documented, if even only in a few words, but Lady Frances Sherburn had been meticulous in her record keeping. When he flipped a page and a few grains of sand fell into his lap, the significance of the journal weighed more heavily upon him.

Morgan stood back and watched him inspect the book, reading the passages and carefully touching the mementos. The journal had worked the magic she had hoped; she had his interest. But what she still needed was his help.

From what she had read about Dr. Fox Henredon, he was something of a whiz kid. True, she'd brought the papyrus to the Bolton Museum because it was close to Heaven's Gate, but she had also done her research on the person she needed to speak with. The go-to guy had been Henredon and it had been her intention since walking in the door earlier to hook him. The journal had been the key; *come into my web said the spider to the fly*, she thought.

Her gaze moved over the man as he put his reading glasses on to scrutinize a particular passage that was faded by time; as she'd noted before, he was very big and very beautiful, certainly not the bookworm she had expected. Quietly, she moved back to the guest chair and reclaimed it, sitting silent and still as Fox perused the journal, lingering over the faded pages that had seen dust and sandstorms in the days when Egypt was still mysterious and ancient. Morgan's eyes never left his face. When Fox finally looked up at her, it was with wonder.

"Your great-grandmother knew Howard Carter on a first-name basis," he said, stunned. "She was on-hand when he was clearing out Tut's tomb. She writes about visiting the dig when they were removing the artifacts."

Morgan smiled faintly. "I know," she replied. "I read that, too. Pretty amazing."

Fox shook his head, half in agreement, half in wonder. His gaze returned to the journal for a moment longer before finally removing his glasses.

"Amazing, yes," he agreed, looking at her. "But what does this journal have to do with the papyrus?"

The smile faded from Morgan's lush lips and the dimples vanished. She stood up and rounded the desk again, taking hold of the journal and carefully thumbing through it until she came to the last page that had any manner of writing on it. She opened the book, displaying the pages fully; on the right hand page was a massive brown stain with streaks all the way off the page. The page itself was warped as a result. Something wet had been spilled on the page, had run and finally dried, leaving the warped paper.

"See that stain?" she asked.

He glanced at it. "I do."

She could see that he wasn't particularly concerned with it so she decided to throw caution to the wind and tell him everything at this point. She reckoned that she had nothing to lose; she had his interest. Now was the time to spring the rest of it.

"You need to read her entire journal, Dr. Henredon, to see what a truly remarkable woman my great-grandmother was," she said frankly. "She and my great-grandfather were two of the great explorers of early Egyptian studies. They would comb the Cairo bazaar for ancient artifacts and maps, getting to know the locals to find out where the tombs and monuments were located. If you read these pages, then you will see that they would find ancient places to study them; not plunder, but study. They wanted to understand the history of Egypt to enrich their knowledge, not necessarily to amass wealth, although they do have a significant collection. But it seems to me that the collection was their way of preserving something they'd come to love very much; Egypt and its people. They didn't do it to boast about it or to sell it for gain. They did it to save it."

Fox was watching her carefully, the way her lovely mouth moved and the way her nose wrinkled when she spoke. He realized he was becoming more interested in the woman by the moment in spite of everything. He could feel his interest moving from initial attraction to something else. Morgan Sherburn was beautiful, intelligent and well-spoken. He didn't know the first thing about the woman, but what he did know had him quickly captivated.

"I can appreciate that," he said evenly. "It's admirable. But it still doesn't explain why you need me to translate the papyrus."

Morgan took a deep breath, collecting her thoughts. Her gaze moved back to the journal on the table.

"My great-grandparents returned to Britain after spending six months in Egypt on their honeymoon," she said quietly. "They returned because my great-grandmother was pregnant with my grandfather. He was born in 1923 and when he was about six months old, they returned to Egypt because my great-grandmother just couldn't seem to stay away. She had come to love it. When they went back the second time, according to her journal, they reconnected with friends and ended up purchasing a papyrus that was said to have been recovered at a dig in ancient Thebes. My great-grandmother wrote about this papyrus in her journal. She said that an antiquities dealer told her it contained the details of the burial of the Lady of Heaven, the Mistress of the Gods, the Mother of the Lands and The Great Wife. The translation he gave her is even written in the journal. He told her that the papyrus gave clues to the tomb of Isis and my great-grandmother, ever the adventurer, set off in search of it."

By this time, Fox was looking at her as if she had lost her mind. "What did she find?"

Morgan put her finger on the stained journal page. "She didn't," she whispered, her voice rising as she continued. "Dr. Henredon, I'm pretty sure that my great-grandmother disappeared in her attempt to follow the clues on this scroll. I believe she was murdered because of it and I believe this stain on the page confirms it. My great-grandfather and grandfather fled Egypt back to England, where my great-grandfather refused to ever speak of it again. He never remarried, living to the ripe old age of one hundred and six years old until dying this past June. He put the scroll away and never spoke of it again."

Fox's dark eyes glimmered. "Then how do you know about it?"

Morgan sighed and carefully closed the pages of the journal. "Because I came across the story while cleaning out the house." She picked it up and moved back to her purse. "I found the journal in the library, tucked away in the drawer of a desk, and read the entire thing. The papyrus was in a box in my great-grandfather's closet. I felt like I was piecing together a giant puzzle, finding things all over the place, putting them together to make one big picture. We were always told that my great-grandmother died of fever in Egypt, but it's just not true. When you read her journal, you can see that she was verging on something that had her incredibly excited. Never once did she mention illness or fever, and as she's happily writing about this papyrus and the clues she's piecing together, her journal suddenly ends and there's this massive brown stain on the page. I think it's blood and I think she was killed for whatever was contained in that papyrus."

Fox watched her carefully slip the journal into her big purse, lured in spite of his better judgment by her tale. It really *was* a fascinating story.

"It could be coffee," he said softly.

She nodded in reluctant agreement. "Or tea," she conceded. "Or wine, or a hundred other things; I realize that. But I just don't think it is."

He pondered that for a moment. "And you said that the papyrus had been translated by the dealer who sold it to her?" he clarified.

She nodded. "Yes."

"Then why do you need me to do it?"

"Because I want confirmation that the translation she was given is correct."

His gaze was steady on her. After several moments' deliberation, he reached for the case that was open on his desk, pulling it towards him so he could get a look at what it contained. He supposed he could offer her that much but realized he was doing it because he was attracted to her more than because he believed her story. It was dastardly, but true. As he reached for the wax paper that she had used to protect the sheets of the papyrus, his phone rang. Fox hit the speaker button.

"Henredon," he said, peeling back the wax paper.

"Dr. Henredon?" came a female voice. "Dr. Loyes would like to see you if you have a moment, sir."

Fox's fingers paused from where they were lingering on the wax paper. "Now?"

"Yes, please. He has people waiting in his office."

"I'll be right there."

Morgan watched as he carefully replaced the wax paper and hung up the phone. He stood up, facing her somewhat apologetically.

"Sorry," he said. "I need to go."

Morgan's eyes were hopeful. "I can wait if that's okay."

He shook his head. "I'm sorry; I just don't have the time today. Maybe another time."

Morgan waved him off, suddenly feeling foolish and exposed. She had played her hand and figured she had lost, so she couldn't move fast enough in her attempt to get out of his office. She felt like an idiot.

"Don't worry about it," she told him. "I'm sorry to have wasted your time."

She was fumbling with closing the artwork case and he took pity on her, helping her close it and fasten the lock. He picked it up and handed it to her.

"You didn't waste my time," he replied, somewhat gently. He was starting to feel sorry for her. "Thank you for bringing that journal. It's really remarkable. I would like to read the entire thing someday."

"Sure; anytime."

Morgan took the case and her purse and made haste out of his office. Fox was right behind her, watching her rounded buttocks beneath the tight jeans. Before he could say anything further, she swung on him and extended a free hand.

"Thanks again for your time, Dr. Henredon," she said hastily. "I really appreciate it. Sorry to have bothered you."

He shook her hand but she didn't give him a chance to reply. She bolted from the offices, awkwardly clutching her artwork case and purse, hurrying away as if she were fearful that someone might follow her or, worse, comment on her foolish visit.

As Fox watched her disappear down the hallway towards the museum lobby, Mrs. Moberley walked up beside him. The woman peered at the fading figure over the top of her reading glasses.

"What on earth did you do to that woman?" she asked, perplexed.

Fox shook his head. "Nothing," he replied honestly,

scratching casually at his neck. "Not what I wanted to do to her, anyway."

Mrs. Moberley shot him a vicious glare and moved back towards her desk. "Dr. Loyes wants to see you in his office. *Now.*"

Fox glanced at the woman, a lazy smile on his face. "Don't you want to know what...?"

"No," she said flatly, cutting him off. "I don't want to know."

"Sure you do. You always want to know."

"Go," the woman snapped, pointing in the direction of the executive offices. "Go before I lose my temper, you cheeky boy."

Still smiling, Fox did as he was told.

We have traveled into the city to explore. Mr. Arak has taken us to interesting places so far, including an old Turkish bazaar that has been here for centuries. The people are so helpful and friendly. Perhaps we will find treasure here!
    ~ FS

TWO
HEAVEN'S GATE MANOR, LANCASHIRE

THE RAIN HAD STARTED the day before and had grown worse by the hour. Sheets of it pounded mercilessly against the old stone of Heaven's Gate, drenching the ancient gray rocks and the countryside surrounding the expansive home. The land was brilliant, wet green as far as the eye could see. In the distance, the forests of Cumbria lined the horizon, dancing with the lightning that tickled the treetops.

Morgan was walking in the middle of the wet and green wonderland. Since returning from the Bolton Museum a few hours earlier, she had been depressed and moody, unwilling to resume her duties of helping clean out the old manor and wanting very much to be alone for a time. But with her mother around, solitude was difficult; Laura Sherburn was a vivacious woman who doted on her children. There were three of them, Morgan being the oldest girl and, as Laura viewed it, her closest friend. Morgan didn't usually mind her mother's company but that particular moment was an exception.

So she had donned a borrowed pair of Wellington rain boots, a raincoat, told her mother that she was going for a walk, and ventured out into the weather. England had seen unseasonable rains all summer, bleeding over into September, and nearly every day had been a wet barrage. Coming from Southern California, Morgan wasn't used to so much rain but discovered that she liked it a great deal.

So she walked, feeling the heart of the lands that had given birth to her family. She felt a real connection here, unlike her home in Southern California. Here, it was different. Heaven's Gate Manor had been built in 1561, an Elizabethan jewel built during the reign of the great Virgin Queen by Sir Robert Sherburn, Baron Dunscar, a man who was supremely loyal to Lord Burghley, Queen Elizabeth's chief advisor. Up until that time, the Sherburns had resided in Bromley Cross Castle, an enormous Medieval fortress that was two miles east of the present manor. The Sherburns had been a powerful and warring family.

Although it was now mostly ruins, there were still walls and a keep at Bromley Cross. Morgan, having only been to her great-grandparents' home once in her life when she was very small, remembered being frightened by the skeletal remains of the once-great castle. Her brother had told her that it was filled with ghosts and she had been terrified. Now, she found the ruins romantic and impressive. Maybe there were ghosts but she wouldn't bother them if they didn't bother her. As she strolled among the ruins with the rain and lightning bearing down on her, she found peace and comfort in the walls that had stood for almost nine hundred years. She would miss them when she went home.

She found a seat in the gatehouse entry, shielded from the elements by the passageway that led from the entry to the bailey beyond. It was quiet here and she could think. She didn't blame Dr. Henredon for telling her to take a hike. Well, not so much take a hike as accusing her of being less than honest with the purpose of her visit. He had been right, of course, but in her defense, she had been positive the man would have never agreed to meet with her had she told him the true purpose of her visit.

But she had run into a dead-end with Henredon. Morgan shouldn't have been so emotional about it but it was difficult. Her great-grandfather had been a man she'd met four times in her life, a tall man with clear brown eyes and a sharp wit. The last time she had seen him had been during her senior year of high school. The man had come to visit for her graduation, taken one look at her, and got misty-eyed. When pressed, he said it was because Morgan was the spitting image of her great-grandmother. And with that, an odd connection to the woman had formed in Morgan's mind, this woman she mirrored. She wanted to know more about her.

But the story hadn't been a kind one. Frances Sherburn, or Fanny as her great-grandfather called her, had been a beautiful woman of ambition and intelligence. All of that was cut short when she died of a fever in Egypt at nineteen years of age. Morgan remembered asking where the woman was buried but her great-grandfather simply told her that he had left her in Egypt because it was what she would have wanted. He would say no more than that. For fifteen years, Fanny's demise and resting place had been established in Morgan's mind. Or at least she thought.

The journal she discovered in the old desk had changed all of that. Both she and her mother had read it from cover to cover, discovering what a truly brave and unique woman Fanny Sherburn had been. Towards the end of the journal, however, she began to allude to fears for her safety. It was difficult to read between the lines of Fanny's romantic and enthusiastic musings, but Morgan began to suspect that something was troubling Fanny, something strong enough to cause her to write about it. There was even a section of the journal where it looked as if pages had been torn out. It was very odd. But maybe that was just Morgan's suspicious police mind talking.

She was fairly confident she could figure it out; nine years as a cop for the City of Pasadena, California, and two rotations in the detective bureau would be put to good use. Once she was on to something, she didn't easily let it go. It was her job to figure it out. That instinct had come in especially handy when she'd figured out her now ex-husband had been cheating on her.

But it was something she didn't like to think about, the marriage that had only lasted four years. She and Nathan had been very happy for a time, or at least she thought so, but she was still trying to figure out why the man cheated on her with a woman he'd met in a coffee shop. He had told her it was because the woman made him feel like he wasn't competing with her career for attention. Five years later, it still hurt.

The rain was increasing, pelting the ground with pea-sized drops as Morgan pushed thoughts of her ex-husband from her mind. She rose from the cold, hard stone bench and wandered to the great entry, watching the sky as the rain came down. Pulling her hood down over her forehead, she had her head down, fairly blinded by the rain, as she trudged off.

"I've never been up here before. It's really lovely."

The voice came from behind. Morgan whirled around, hands out defensively as if she were about to take someone's head off. Fox Henredon was standing a few feet behind her, his hands suddenly lifting when he saw she was preparing to throw a punch. The smile on his face vanished.

"Easy," he admonished. "Sorry I startled you. I thought you heard me coming."

Heart in her throat, Morgan lowered her hands and exhaled sharply. It took her a moment to recover as she lifted both eyes and a hand to the sky.

"How could I have heard you?" she asked the obvious. "All I can hear is rain."

Fox shoved his hands in his pockets. "Point taken."

Shock faded, now she was irritated at the man for sneaking up on her. "How did you get here?"

He pointed in the general direction of Heaven's Gate. "I walked up the road from the house."

She glanced over at the dirt road that came in from the west side of the castle; it had been behind her so he had literally walked up on her blind side. Her brown gaze returned to him, regarding him carefully.

"Did my mother tell you I was up here?"

He nodded. "She did."

"Why are you here?"

Fox could see that her expression was laced with suspicion. Suddenly, the shoe was on the other foot and he was the unwelcome visitor in her world. In hindsight, he realized he had been rather excited to see her again and was moderately disappointed that she didn't feel the same way. He'd even changed shirts before coming. Why *was* he here? It had seemed like a good idea at the time but gazing into her wary face, he was coming to rethink his strategy. He was coming to feel defensive.

"I came because I had to chase you out of my office so quickly," he said, not really knowing where to start. He gave up trying to give her a pretty explanation and went for the truth. "Look; I'm sorry if I was rude earlier. I shouldn't have called you dishonest about the purpose for your visit. Once you explained everything to me, I saw your logic. I came because I wanted to apologize for being abrupt over something that is obviously important to you. Plus, I was hoping you'd let me take another look at that journal. It's not often we come across records like that and I'd love to see it again."

Morgan watched him carefully, his apologetic body language

and the sincerity of his tone. It took her a moment to realize the man didn't have a raincoat on; he was wearing a turtleneck and a leather jacket but his head was soaked. More than that, it gave her a second look at what a truly stunning male specimen he was; her first impression at the museum hadn't been wrong.

He was easily six and a half feet tall, maybe more, with black eyes and black hair that was neatly cut and combed, and his biceps had to be larger in circumference than her waist. She thought she might have seen him somewhere on the cover of a romance novel because that's clearly where he belonged. But the truth was that she was baffled to see him, handsome or not, and wasn't quite sure what to say.

"You came all the way out here to tell me this?" she clarified. "All you had to do was pick up the phone."

"If I called, I wouldn't have the chance to see the journal."

"You seem more interested in the journal than in the papyrus."

He shrugged his enormous shoulders. "Not really. I'm interested in both."

She eyed him, eventually cocking her head. "You told me you were too busy to translate it."

He drew in a soft breath, shoving his hands deeper into his pockets as he realized this wasn't going to be an easy sell. "I'm not busy now."

A look of disbelief came over her lovely face. "Let me get this straight," she said. "You drove all the way up here to translate a document that, four hours ago, you told me you were too busy to translate? Plus, you called me dishonest for not having told you the entire story about why I was there."

"Well, you *were*."

Her eyebrows flew up. "Is that so?"

"It is."

She scowled. "I told you why, Dr. Henredon. It wasn't being deliberately subversive."

He nodded patiently. "I realize that, which is why I felt bad about how I handled it. So I thought I'd come out here to see what I could accomplish this evening as far as translating the papyrus. I'm offering my professional assistance, Miss Sherburn. I charge most people thousands of dollars for my time but I'll do it for you at no cost if you'll just let me read the rest of that journal."

She cooled somewhat, the lure of having him translate the papyrus dousing her temper. But she wasn't willing to forgive him yet for humiliating her, especially on a subject so close to her heart.

"No need," she told him, watching carefully for his reaction. "I'm going to take it all back with me to Los Angeles and find someone there who will help me. Maybe they won't be too busy."

The warm expression on his face faded. His features turned stone-cold. "Sure," he finally said. "That's your prerogative. Sorry to have bothered you."

He turned to leave without a fight. Morgan began to feel very bad for being such a bitch, folding before the man had taken two steps.

"Wait," she said, watching him pause and turn to her with a passive expression. She took a couple of steps towards him, her brown eyes without the glare they'd held only moments before. "I'm sorry... I shouldn't have been mean about it. Your offer is generous."

"You weren't mean," he replied evenly. "You were honest. I appreciate that. Good luck, Miss Sherburn."

He turned to leave again and she called out to him a second time. She raced to catch up with him but with her shorter legs and his longer strides, by the time he turned around, she smacked right into him.

Fox instinctively grabbed her to steady her, finding himself gazing down into brown eyes that were so clear and pure that he swore there was a hint of red to them, almost like a deep brick brown. They were quite stunning, as was the rest of her.

"Sorry," she rubbed at her nose where she smashed it against his chest. As she looked up at him, she was starting to feel stupid again and her guard went down completely. "The truth is that you and I couldn't have had a rougher introduction if we'd tried. You were blunt at the museum, I got upset, and, well... I'm sure I'm to blame for everything so maybe we could just forget about the past four hours and start over. Okay?"

The warmth was returning to his obsidian eyes, slowly. "Okay."

"Truce?"

"Truce."

She smiled timidly, dimples carving through her cheeks. "Good." She eyed him a moment in increasingly awkward silence before finally raising her eyebrows. "Now what?"

He laughed. "Have any ideas?"

She took a step back so she wasn't so close to the man; his close proximity was causing her cheeks to flush. Even in the cold weather, she was feeling heated, like she wanted to rip all of her clothes off. But she settled for putting a safe distance between them. Then she extended her hand.

"Hi," she said. "I'm Morgan Sherburn. It's nice to meet you."

Fox's dark eyes glittered as a smile spread across his face. He took her hand, enfolding it gently but firmly in his massive palm.

"Hi," he replied. "Fox Henredon. And it is, indeed, a pleasure to meet you."

He continued to hold her hand and her smile brightened hopefully. "Will you please help me with my papyrus?"

His smile broadened and he squeezed her hand. Her sweet dimpled smile absolutely had him hooked. "I'd be happy to."

Now her smile was real. "Thanks," she said, pulling her hand free and turning for the road. "It's back at the house. Can you stay for dinner?"

"I'd love to," he told her, following her as she moved back towards the road. "So you intend to ply me with food and wine in exchange for my services?"

She grinned, an expression he found flirtatious and sweet. "No," she shook her head. "Dinner is an added bonus to make up for our rough start. I'll let you read the journal, too. In fact, maybe you can help me piece this whole thing together."

The rain was coming down in sheets as they moved onto the road that led back to the manor house almost two miles away. In spite of the weather and the fact that he was cold, Fox was feeling giddy and warm in the presence of a beautiful woman. As the rain came down, Morgan settled in beside him with the hood pulled down over her head. Fox felt an odd sense of contentment as they walked together in the pouring rain.

"It's an interesting story, I have to admit," he said. "You must have a very analytical mind to have figured it all out."

Morgan shrugged. "It wasn't difficult," she replied. "You'll see that when you read the journal."

He nodded, alternately watching her lowered head and the road beyond. They walked in silence for a few moments before he spoke.

"At the risk of getting off the subject," he ventured, "what does Morgan Sherburn do back in America? Wait; let me guess. You're a television model."

She peered up at him with a strange look on her face,

although she was grinning. "A television model?" she repeated. "What's that?"

He shrugged his big shoulders. "You know," he made weird box-shapes in the air with a wet hand. "Those beautiful women who work on game shows. Aren't all the game shows made in Los Angeles?"

She giggled, stepping around a large puddle. "I don't know," she replied. "I guess so. But in answer to your question, I am not a television model. I'm a cop."

His eyebrows flew up. "What?" he exclaimed. "You're the dibble?"

She looked at him strangely. "The *what?*"

"It means the police."

"Oh," she laughed softly. "Yes, I am. For nine years."

"Nine years!" he looked stricken. "Good God, I don't believe it. How in the world did you get into that line of work?"

She shrugged. "I've always wanted to help people."

"Oh." There wasn't much he could say to that, although it was clear that he was still surprised. "And your husband let you?"

Morgan should have suspected it was a leading question but she really didn't care. She gave him a sidelong glance. "I'm not married. Even if I was, like he'd have any say in the matter."

Fox lifted his eyebrows. "I can't imagine he would."

"You would be correct, sir."

He snorted and she grinned. "And you, Dr. Henredon?" she asked pleasantly, much more comfortable with the man now than she had been just a few minutes earlier. "What made you become an Egyptologist?"

He watched his feet as they moved along the muddy road. "Because my great-grandparents were like yours," he said frankly. "They traveled to Egypt many times during the early part of the century and amassed quite a collection of artifacts. I grew up around it and it always fascinated me."

Morgan jumped when a bolt of lightning streaked across the sky; the sun was going down and the landscape was becoming shadowed and creepy.

"Where did you grow up?" she asked, eyeing the flickering sky.

"A town in Dorset called Dorchester," he replied. "My parents still live there."

"And your great-grandparents?"

"Passed on," he replied, grinning when she inadvertently jumped against him as another lightning bolt streaked across the sky. "You know, for a bobby, you're rather jumpy."

She looked up at him, giving him her very best sneer. "If I can't shoot it or pepper spray it, then I don't like it."

He laughed. "Is that your answer to everything?"

"Want to find out?"

He boomed with laughter.

NOVEMBER 11, 1922

I am very excited about the treasures we are accumulating so far. I have a lovely necklace with a vulture on it and several small figurines that dear Louis has purchased for me. Louis and Mr. Arak seem not to like one another, which is unfortunate. The trip would be perfect but for that.

~ FS

THREE

HEAVEN'S GATE MANOR was an Elizabethan jewel on the outside, but inside, it hadn't made it past the turn of the century. It was a decaying corpse, forgotten by time.

Everything was extremely outdated, bathrooms and kitchen included. Fox found that out when they returned from Bromley Cross and he used the toilet, because the entire bathroom and its fixtures were something that belonged in a museum. The toilet had a big overhead reservoir and it was flushed with an old-fashion chain pull. The pipes rattled and groaned when the toilet flushed and Fox beat a hasty retreat from the bathroom before the entire room collapsed around him.

Morgan was waiting for him when he emerged. She had removed the Wellies and the raincoat, and was dressed in the clinging gray sweater and jeans he had seen her in earlier. As he approached from the hall, it was a struggle not to stare at her figure; she had magnificent breasts beneath the sweater and a narrow waist, flaring into womanly hips. All in all, she was completely his taste, not a board-flat skinny female, but a woman with curves and a narrow waist. She looked like a goddess and he had to make a conscious effort not to gape at her.

She was fumbling with her shoe when he walked up, grinning her dimpled grin when their eyes met. "So the evil bathroom chased you out, did it?" she asked.

He scratched his head, glancing back in the direction he had come from. "I thought the walls were going to cave in."

She laughed softly. "I should have warned you," she put her foot down and straightened up. "All of the plumbing in this place is from the turn of the century. It's a miracle it still works at all."

He tore his eyes away from her long enough to look around the main foyer, where they were standing. "How big is this place?"

She followed his gaze. "Fifty-nine rooms," she told him. "Eight parlors, two dining rooms, a kitchen, a billiard room, a library, a men's club, a woman's parlor, an east tea room, a west tea room, a hunt room, a steam room, a gymnasium that's nothing like the gym you and I know, plus servants quarters, thirteen bedrooms, eighteen bathrooms, and a basement with a bunch of storage rooms."

By the time she was finished rattling off the stats, he was staring at her. "Seriously?" He lifted his eyebrows, giving the foyer another look as he shoved his hands into his pockets again. "This place is massive."

She nodded. "Massive and expensive," she said as she gestured to a room at their right. He took the hint and followed her into a parlor furnished with furniture that had to date back to the 1920s. "I'd like you to take a look at some of the Egyptian artifacts if you have the time. Do you think the museum might be interested in purchasing some of the pieces?"

He shrugged his shoulders. "Maybe. I'll have to see them first."

She smiled. "I can arrange that," she replied as they passed through the antiquated formal parlor and into another foyer that adjoined an enormous dining room. She indicated the room around them. "I have no idea how Louis ran this place on his limited income. Even though he's titled, I think the family money ran out a long time ago. His bank accounts don't have more than a few hundred dollars in them. His caretaker told me that Louis had him take pieces of jewelry to pawn shops in Manchester to help pay the upkeep. I can't even imagine what priceless pieces he pawned off just to eat and pay the electric bill."

Fox was nodding his head even before she finished her sentence. "That's an old story," he told her. "The deterioration of the British aristocracy is a sad tale. My grandparents and parents have suffered the same thing."

She looked up at him as they passed into the ornate, if not slightly run down, smaller foyer. "You come from British nobility?"

He nodded. "My father is Viscount Winterborne, a title that has been in my family since 1483. It was one of the very few titles bestowed by Richard III during his short reign. It's something of an anomaly and one of the longest continuous titles in England. It's never been out of the family since it was created."

She lifted her eyebrow, impressed. "Wow," she said. "That's pretty cool. Will you inherit it when your father dies?"

Again, he nodded. "I will," he replied. "And my son will inherit it from me."

"How old is your son?"

"I don't have one yet. But when I do, he will."

She grinned. "Pretty confident that you'll have a boy one of these days, aren't you? What does your wife say about that?"

It was a leading question, like the one he had given her, but his reaction was the same. He couldn't have cared less. "I don't have one of those either," he told her. "Do you know where I might be able to find one?"

She laughed heartily. "With your looks and education? I'm sure you don't have any trouble impressing women. In fact, I'd be willing to bet that they follow you around by the truckload."

He smiled, humored by her laughter. "Not exactly truckloads," he admitted, sobering. "But I was almost married, once. It just didn't work out."

She sobered because he was. "Sorry to hear that," she said, somewhat softer. "I was married for about four years. That didn't work out, either."

He made a face as if in complete sympathy. "And we're so perfect, you and I," he snorted. "What's wrong with these people?"

Her smile was back. "I wish I knew."

He cast a long glance at her, returning her smile, feeling something magical spark between them. He made the decision then and there that he was going to milk his visit for everything it was worth, up to and including getting kicked out because he had stayed so long. But they passed into the dining room and his attention was pulled off of Morgan by a woman approaching. Laura Sherburn smiled brightly at them, a mirror image of her daughter's dimples, holding out her hand to Fox.

"Dr. Henredon," she greeted. "I'm so glad you could join us for dinner."

Fox shook the woman's soft hand; she faintly resembled her beauteous daughter, a small and attractive woman.

"Thank you for inviting me," he replied. "It's not often I am lucky enough to have a home-cooked meal."

Laura laughed; she was very social, very gracious. She indicated the far end of the long and elaborate dining table where plates had been set out.

"Dinner is ready so have a seat," she told him. "I will admit that cooking on that ancient stove was something of a challenge. I hope everything turns out all right."

"I'm sure it will be wonderful."

Laura disappeared into the kitchen while Morgan called after her. "Do you need any help, Mom?"

"No," Laura replied, banging around in the kitchen. "You and Dr. Henredon have a seat."

Morgan wriggled her eyebrows at him. "Sit on this side of the table next to me," she told him. "I'll go get the journal and you can read it while you eat."

He looked stricken. "So I can't even enjoy my meal first before you're putting me to work?"

She laughed. "I didn't mean it that way," she said. "I just meant that I'm sure your time is limited so maybe you'll want to get right to work."

He lifted an eyebrow at her, his black eyes glimmering with warmth. "I can spare all of the time you need," he told her. "I have no place else to go."

The statement had a double meaning; she sensed his interest in her as plainly as if he had spelled it out. Truth was, she was growing interested in him, too. She wanted to know more about him.

Laura brought out a lovely roast and the three of them sat down to feast. While Laura and Morgan enjoyed petite portions, Fox was polite with his portion control at first until Laura insisted he have a second helping and then a third. When all was over and the battle damage tallied, Fox had eaten nearly three-quarters of a very good beef roast. He'd also had more than a half bottle of red wine.

The conversation had been witty, light, and Fox had thoroughly enjoyed the company of Morgan and her mother. They were sweet, bright and fun. He felt more comfortable with these ladies in just an hour than he had with anyone, at any time, in his life. It was an oddly settled feeling, one he realized he loathed to lose. He'd always heard that visions of Heaven were only fleeting; now he knew what that meant. He would be sorry to see this vision go.

Dinner eventually ended and as Laura cleared away the dishes, Fox offered to help but was quickly shut down. He even handed her a plate, getting mildly scolded in the process. Grinning, Morgan took Fox out of the dining room before he could get into more trouble and escorted him down a labyrinth of dark, eerie halls until they came to a set of double doors. The doors themselves were works of art, carved and ornate, with lion's head door knobs. As Fox inspected the brass knob, Morgan shoved open the panels.

The smell of smoke and tobacco hit him full-on. It was like one giant *whoosh* of air, filled with untold centuries of men, secrets, books and conversations. A fairly large library opened up before him and Fox stood in the doorway for a moment, drinking in the sight; books and trinkets lined every inch of wall space from floor to ceiling, stuffed to the rafters with treasures.

There was a loft to his right, even more stuffed with clutter and books. A small, iron spiral staircase ran from a small alcove to the loft above. Fox took a few steps into the room, awed by the sight, as Morgan switched on a couple of old light fixtures to brighten the place up.

"Welcome to the heart of the Heaven's Gate," she said, a smile on her face. "Before we get to the journal and the papyrus, I want to show you something that your museum might be interested in."

She went over to the stair alcove, motioning for him to follow. He obeyed, walking on her heels and nearly running her over when she suddenly stopped. He apologized, but he really wasn't sorry; it gave him a chance to touch her and he wasn't sorry about that at all. He just shrugged apologetically and she gave him a quirky smile. But then she turned around and began to pull a table away from some clutter against the wall.

Fox saw what she was doing and he lent his considerable strength, easily pulling the table away as several books fell off its surface. The both bent over to pick up the books, their hands brushing as he handed her the few he had collected. Morgan felt the heat from his flesh, trying not to get too upswept by the fact that she was quite attracted to the man. All through dinner, he had been polite, intelligent and hilarious. It was very endearing and if he had been trying to impress her, it had worked.

Putting the books on the table, she picked her way among several items that were in a muss upon the floor in her quest to reach the wall. There were two massive bookshelves and in between was a pile of clutter, stacked up against the wall, covered with a sheet. At least, Fox thought it was clutter until she removed the sheet. Suddenly, he found himself gazing at an Egyptian sarcophagus, the vision of which could only be described as magnificent.

The coffin was at least six feet in length, a massive wooden thing that was covered in gold foil and semi-precious stones. There were some stones missing and it had a big gash along the left side, but other than that, it was in pristine condition. The design was classic Middle Kingdom, something wonderful and rare, and Fox's jaw dropped at the sight. He very quickly moved up beside her to get a better look it.

"Oh, my God," he breathed, visually inspecting the coffin before daring to put his fingers on the gold and lapis lazuli. "Where in the hell did they get this?"

Morgan could have stepped back to allow him better access to it, but she frankly didn't want to. She was rather enjoying the very close proximity of the man, smelling faint whiffs of after-shave. It was enough to set her heart thumping and she struggled to keep her mind on the subject.

"My great-grandfather kept very meticulous notes," she replied. "According to the records he kept, he purchased this in

1922 on their first trip to Egypt. He got it from a dealer in Cairo who was rumored to have gotten it on the black market. Louis bought it for Fanny but they were so afraid that the Egyptian authorities would catch wind of it that they brought it back to England, put it in the corner and covered it up. And here it has remained."

Fox's black eyes glittered as he inspected the hieroglyphics on the cover. He turned his head slightly, trying to get a better read of what it said. The truth was that he could hardly believe what he was seeing; such a relic was uncommon and precious, especially in this day and age. As Morgan stood so close to him that he could smell her perfume, Fox carefully studied the text on the breast of the coffin.

"Is the mummy still in it?" he asked.

"As far as I know."

Morgan waited patiently as he inspected it but she couldn't tell by his expression what he really thought of the piece. After his initial surprise, he seemed rather stone-faced as he studied. Maybe he wasn't as impressed as she thought. After what seemed like a small eternity, she finally dared to speak.

"Can you read any of the hieroglyphics?" she asked.

Having gradually bent himself over in his quest to read down the sides of the sarcophagus, he straightened out his big frame and nodded his head.

"All of them so far," he told her, touching a portion of the gold foil on the face mask that seemed to be pulling up from the wood beneath. "They're spells from the Book of the Two Ways. Most, if not all, Middle Kingdom sarcophagi will have spells written on them to make the deceased's passage into the Netherworld seamless. In fact, it was a fairly common theme throughout Egyptian history."

"Is there a name for who's inside this thing?"

He nodded slowly, peering at the cartouche at the base of

the neck. "Yes," he scrutinized the symbols for a few moments before speaking. "Hetep-Ankh-Sheri; She who is Beloved, Favored of the Gods, The One who does Right."

Morgan's eyes widened. "That's *so* cool," she declared, looking at the ancient drawings as if she could read them, too. "What else does it say?"

He tilted his head again so he could read down the sides. "Words spoken by him whose name remains hidden; proceed in peace as the Lord of the Limit speaks," he looked at her. "I could go on for hours; there's a whole litany of spells. I've just never seen them so intact before on a sarcophagus."

She nodded, her gaze moving over the sarcophagus before coming to rest on his handsome face again. "Do you think the museum would be interested in buying this?"

He stood up straight, hands on his slender hips. "Hell, yes," he said firmly. "We'd need to get it authenticated and valued, but I'd say this would be a huge score for the museum. It's magnificent."

"How much do you think it's worth?"

He shrugged. "Enough to run Heaven's Gate quite comfortably for a few years. Millions, at least."

Her surprise was evident. "Really?" she gaped. "That's great. At least, it's a start."

He looked at her. "What do you mean?"

She frowned in thought. "Louis left a huge amount of debt along with the legacy. There are so many overdue bills, I don't even know where to start. Hospitals, lawyers; you name it. I'm not even interested in keeping Heaven's Gate at this point; we just want to pay off everyone Louis owed money to."

Fox could see that the idea distressed her. "So you're going to sell the manor?"

She shrugged. "I don't know; maybe. My grandfather is the heir, as Louis and Fanny's only child, and he's in ill health right now. He doesn't want to sell the home where he was born but he can't keep it, either. He can't afford it."

"Where does he live now?"

"Los Angeles, with my mom and dad. They take care of both of my grandparents. When Louis died, we all drew straws to see who was going to come and settle the estate; my mom and I lost, so I took a month off of work to come out here to help take care of things. But we didn't know how bad 'things' were until we got here. Now... I just don't know. I suppose it'll really be up to my dad because he's ultimately the heir to all of this. He needs to make the final decision about what to do because this is all such a huge mess."

Fox drew in a long breath, his gaze moving over the library and spying more pieces that belonged in a museum. He could only imagine what more there was that he hadn't seen yet.

"Well," he finally said. "It looks like your family has quite a collection. Maybe there's enough to settle the bills and keep the estate going when all is said and done."

She looked over the room, too. "Maybe," she shrugged. Then she looked up at him. "Thanks a lot for taking a look at this. I really appreciate it. I've had a lot to deal with over the past few weeks and your assessment of the sarcophagus really helps."

He smiled at her, her sweet little doll-like face and big brown eyes. "Good," he said. "Now, do you want to show me that papyrus that you were so fired up about?"

She flashed her dimples, nodding her head and heading off into the main part of the library. "Sure," she said, glancing over her shoulder to make sure he was following her. "It's right here on the table. I have the journal here, too."

There was a massive table in the center of the library, dusty, with neat stacks of books on it. It was a heavy piece of furniture, dark with age and use, and Fox took a seat next to Morgan at the end of the table. Behind them, an enormous floor-to-ceiling window displayed a view across the yard towards the east wing of the manse. When lightning lit up the sky, it was an eerie view.

The artwork briefcase that Morgan had brought to the museum was on the table in front of them with the journal next to it.

"What do you want to see first?" Morgan asked. "The journal or the papyrus?"

He eyed both items before his gaze inexplicably moved to the sarcophagus across the room. He pondered her question.

"Let me see the papyrus," he finally said. "If it's anything like that sarcophagus, then we may have another stunning discovery on our hands."

"All I care about is if it helps me find out what happened to Fanny."

He smiled at her, the dark eyes glittering, as he opened up the artwork briefcase and went to work.

NOVEMBER 15, 1922

We were able to take a ferry ride down the Nile today. What a big river! I would compare it to the Thames but there is no comparison... the blue of the Nile is like no other shade of blue in the world. There is something mesmerizing and other-worldly about it. Dear Louis does not seem to notice my adoration of the river as my love for Egypt grows.

    ~ FS

FOUR

"ISIS, Lady of Heaven, Favored of the Gods, may she be given eternal life by the Gods who love her. May she find peace within...."

Morgan heard the soft drone of Fox's voice, like a warm and languid dream, before gradually becoming aware that she had been sleeping. Her head suddenly shot up from the table where she had laid it down, just for a moment, to rest as Fox poured over the papyrus. She wanted to remain quiet while he did his work, apparently not realizing how exhausted she was, and promptly passed out. The wine at dinner hadn't helped matters. Wine always made her sleepy.

As soon as her head came up and her eyes popped open, Fox turned to look at her with a grin on his face. He put a big hand on her head.

"Go back to sleep, Sleeping Beauty," he gently pushed her head back down. "I'm not going to be done with this for a while."

She let him push her head back down, but her eyes remained open, looking at him. "I'm so sorry," she said sleepily. "I didn't realize I was so tired."

He continued to grin at her, pulling the reading glasses off his nose and setting them to the table. "My suggestion would be that you go to bed," he said. "I'll still probably be here in the morning."

Her head came up, shaking it vigorously even though she was yawning. "No way," she said firmly. "I'm staying right here until you figure out the great mysteries of life."

He stood up, bent over, and scooped her right up from the chair. Morgan was so petite compared to his enormous size that it had been no effort at all on his part.

"That's not going to happen in the next hour," he told her. "To bed with you. Where is your bedroom?"

Morgan threw her arms around his thick neck for support, realizing almost too late that it was a very intimate position. She was sleepy, a little liquored up, and extremely attracted to the man. It would have been so easy to....

"I'm not going to tell you," she said flatly. "I want to stay here."

"Don't argue with me. Where is your bedroom?"

She lifted her eyebrows at him, enjoying his close proximity and struggling to stay on task.

"Uh-uh," she shook her head. "I'm staying here."

"I told you not to argue."

"Put me down or you'll be sorry."

Fox's grin grew. "Really?" he said. "I'm intrigued. Tell me more."

Morgan giggled at him. Then she arched her neck, peering over his big shoulder. "Put me on the couch over there," she told him. "I'll compromise. I'll lie on the couch if you'll let me stay here."

He swung her around, heading for the couch, and then gently set her down on it. "Now, lay down or I'll sit on you."

She scrunched her nose up at him. "I wouldn't if I were you. I bite."

He cocked an eyebrow, biting his lip to keep from laughing. "If you're trying to scare me, it isn't working. You're only succeeding in enticing me further."

Her brow furrowed, but she was smiling. "*Further?*"

He winked at her and turned back for the table. Morgan almost demanded that he clarify his gentle flirt but she thought better of it. Something heated and thrilling was developing between them and she wanted to keep her head. She was all for a fling, but there was something about Fox that went beyond a casual date or sweet flirt. She wasn't sure what it was yet, but she knew she hadn't felt such emotions in years. It was frightening and exciting at the same time.

She lay down on the couch, rolling onto her side to watch him. Fox sat back down and put his glasses back on.

"I heard you saying something earlier," she said. "What were you saying?"

He cleared his throat as he picked up a pencil and began to jot notes on the pad on the table. He was left-handed and his big hand folded over the paper, writing upside-down.

"I was reading the first line of the papyrus," he told her. "'Isis, Lady of Heaven, Favored of the Gods, may she be given eternal life by the Gods who love her. May she find peace within....' That's as far as I've gotten."

Morgan looked thoughtful. "So Isis is mentioned in the papyrus," she murmured, more to herself. "Fanny's journal says the same thing."

"It's not unusual," he told her, looking back to the ancient scroll in front of him. "Isis is a fairly common theme throughout Egypt, in any setting; life, death, birth, sickness. She's kind of the catch-all goddess to pray to."

Morgan thought on that for a moment. "Oh," she could feel

her eyes droopy again and yawned. "Let me ask you something, Dr. Henredon; do you think that the Egyptian gods were just made-up deities or do you think that, at one time, long ago, they were real people, maybe the first real Egyptians, and just became deified over the centuries?"

He stopped what he was doing and looked at her. "The same question could be asked about Jesus. Was he a figment of overactive imaginations or was he a real person who simply became deified over the centuries?"

"I think he was a real person," Morgan answered. "But I'm not sure if I believe he was the son of God. Maybe he was just a really charismatic rabbi."

He smiled faintly. "It's possible," he said. "But if you said that to my mum, she'd have you boiled in oil."

Morgan grinned. "I would never say that to your mother," she said, then paused. "Or my mother for that matter. She would spank me."

Fox chuckled, turning back to the papyrus. "It's my personal opinion that Osiris and Isis and Seth and all the rest of them are probably made-up deities," he said. "No hard evidence that they were actual people exists. And if evidence did exist, it disappeared long ago."

"Kind of cynical, aren't you?"

He continued to smile as he refocused on the papyrus. "Maybe."

She watched him go back to work, studying the shape of his nose, the square cut of his face. He had amazingly smooth skin, the typical English rose complexion, and even though his black hair was neatly slicked back with gel, the ends of the hair suggested there was a wave to it. All in all, she couldn't see anything about the man that was imperfect. As she continued to watch him, lost in thought, Laura entered the library with two steaming cups in her hand.

"I thought you might like some tea," she went straight for Fox as Morgan sat up from the couch. As she set the cups down, she noticed the papyrus, the journal, pencils and a writing pad, and she frowned. "My daughter isn't forcing you to decipher this now, is she?"

Morgan walked over to the table, collecting her cup. "I am not," she insisted, looking at Fox. "He wanted to. He begged me."

Fox's chuckles returned. "Yes, I did. I begged."

Laura shook her head, eyeing her daughter. "Morgan...."

"Really, Mom," she insisted, putting her arm around Fox's massive shoulders, laying her cheek on the top of his head and smiling like the Cheshire Cat with her massive dimples. "He begged me. He told me he wouldn't leave until I let him."

Fox could have sat there with her arm around his shoulders for the rest of his life. He put a hand up, capturing the hand on his shoulder and squeezing it. "Your daughter is very gracious to allow me to do this, Mrs. Sherburn. It's no trouble at all."

Laura didn't buy it for a moment. "You will call me Laura," she told him flatly, looking at her daughter, who still had her cheek on the top of his head. "And as for you, it's getting late. I'm sure Dr. Henredon has to go to work in the morning."

Morgan wasn't going to budge. "I can't let him leave," she told her mother. "I've chained him to the chair and I don't know where the key is."

As Fox snickered, Laura frowned at her daughter. "Let the man go home, Morgan," she lifted her eyebrows. "You and I have a busy day tomorrow as well. You need to go to bed."

"Actually," Fox spoke up, "I'm off tomorrow. This really is a fascinating piece of work and I'd like to stay and finish it if I can."

Laura appeared dubious. "I don't care if you stay, but don't let Morgan force you."

Fox squeezed Morgan's hand, still in his grip. "She's not; I promise."

Laura still wasn't convinced but didn't argue. "Well," she said slowly, her gaze moving between the two. "If he gets too tired, we've got eleven bedrooms he can take his pick from. Don't let him drive home if he's too sleepy."

The last sentence was directed at Morgan, who merely nodded. "I won't, I promise. He can have the haunted bedroom."

Fox lifted an eyebrow, though he was grinning. "Thanks a bunch," he said dryly.

Laura was back to smiling now that everything was settled and bid them a good night with the admonishment that Morgan not keep the man up all night. Then she disappeared, leaving Morgan still hugging Fox's shoulder with her cheek on his head. When Morgan tried to move, he gripped her hand tightly so she couldn't pull away.

"Where are you going?" he asked quietly.

She grinned. "To go lie back down on the couch."

"Why?"

"Because I can't sit here. I'll be in your way."

"Sitting on my lap might be in my way, but you're not in my way at all."

She was silent a moment. "Do you want me to stay?"

It was another leading question but one that had brought all of their flirting to a head. Finally, the question had been presented and it was up to Fox to respond. He turned to look at her, the grin gone from his face but his black eyes blazing with warmth and attraction.

"Haven't I made that obvious?"

Morgan gazed steadily at him before a smile crossed her lips. "I'd say you've been flirting pretty heavily with me since you showed up this afternoon at Bromley Cross."

"Want me to stop?"

"No."

His grin was back. "That's good," he pulled the hand he was still gripping to his lips and kissed it gently. "Because I won't. I'm a sucker for a woman with dimples."

Morgan's heart began thumping so hard that it nearly burst through her ribs. She couldn't breathe. Gazing into his obsidian-colored eyes, she finally burst into snorts.

"Are you like this with all the girls, Dr. Henredon?" she asked frankly. "Because, quite honestly, you've done nothing but charm the socks off of me since you showed up this afternoon. Is that usual behavior with you or am I reading too much into it?"

His dark eyes glittered. "I'm not like this with all the girls. And my name is Fox."

"So you're saying that you're just like this with me?"

"Only women I find blindingly beautiful, of which you are the only one." He gazed at her, pulling back a little. "If I've overstepped myself, I apologize. Every time I look at you, I just can't help myself."

She smiled faintly. "You're pretty cute yourself."

He returned her smile. "I'm glad you think so," he said, suddenly feeling the urge to be completely forthright. The situation called for it. "Look, I'll be honest; the moment I saw you come into the museum, I thought you were the most beautiful woman I'd ever seen. I came out here today for a lot of reasons; I felt bad about cutting our meeting so short, about not being able to help you, but I also came because I wanted to help you if I could and I just felt drawn to see you again. Now, that may be completely out of line because even though you said you aren't married, surely you have a boyfriend and I'm sorry if I'm crossing boundaries. But I just can't help it."

She was smiling openly at him, touched by his honestly. "I

don't have a boyfriend," she said softly. "But you realize I live six thousand miles away, right?"

"I do."

"So... what's the point of opening up to me like that? You just met me. You know I have to go home."

He nodded. "I'm not sure what my point is," he shook his head. "Just my luck I'd click with a woman who lives half a world away."

He seemed depressed by the thought. Truthfully, so did she. Morgan had no idea why she did what she did in the next few seconds, only that it seemed like a good idea. It might be her one and only chance.

Leaning forward, she slanted her lips over his, delivering a warm, soft and titillating kiss that had Fox audibly groaning within the first few moments. When she tried to pull away, he wrapped his enormous arms around her and pulled her tightly against him.

Morgan didn't resist; she let him hold her tightly, his tongue hotly invading her mouth. She invited him in, suckling his tongue, listening to him groan softly and feeling him pull her closer. She had been kissed many times in her thirty-one years by many men, but never like this. There was something overwhelmingly virile and heated about Fox's embrace and wicked mouth.

For a kiss she had started, he was definitely taking the lead and loving every minute of it. Morgan wrapped her arms around his neck and simply held on while he went to work. He was so big, she didn't have much choice, but she frankly didn't care.

Fox's kisses were hot and delicious and he wasn't shy about sharing them. At one point in the heat of passion he gave her a lovely hickey on her neck just below her left ear. Morgan felt the tingle-pain of it as he gently bit and suckled at the same time, giggling to herself when she realized she was going to have a beautiful love bite when all was said and done. She wondered what her mother was going to say about it. She hadn't had a hickey in eighteen years. She wasn't too sorry about getting this one.

But her warm, delirious thoughts took a jolt when Fox's big hand began to stroke the swell of her left breast. She suddenly put a hand on his fingers to still them, pulling away from his seeking lips. He froze, meeting her gaze with a wide-eyed apologetic look. For a few moments, they just stared at each other; Fox was terrified he had, in his lust, irrevocably offended her. But Morgan simply stared at him before leaning forward to sensually peck him on the lips.

"Maybe I'd better go back to the couch," she murmured, running a finger along his lower lip to wipe off the remnants of her pink lipstick. "You've got a papyrus to translate."

With that, she climbed off his lap and wandered back to the couch, leaving Fox with a pounding heart as he watched her go. He'd never in his life been so swept away with a woman and he was still trying to wrap his mind around it. Morgan Sherburn, in less than a day, had managed to get under his skin more than any other woman he had ever known. Her wit, beauty and pure sexuality had him reeling. He decided, at that moment, that an airplane ride back to Los Angeles was not going to end this. He was not going to let her go.

He smiled at her as she sat back down on the couch and eventually lay down. Morgan returned his smile, neither one of them saying a word. They didn't have to. Silently, Fox picked up his reading glasses and struggled to return his focus to the papyrus. He kept licking his lips, tasting her on them. When he glanced over at her again just a few moments later, she was fast asleep.

He didn't know how long he stared at her before resuming his work.

————

Morgan awoke to a gentle, warm kiss on her cheek.

"Wake up, Beautiful," Fox's voice was soft.

Morgan gradually came lucid, yawning as her eyes rolled up and fixed on Fox's handsome face. He was bent over her, his big hand on her shoulder. He smiled when their eyes met.

"Hi," he said.

She smiled sleepily, stretching. "Hi," she whispered. "What time is it?"

He glanced at his watch. "About five a.m.," he murmured. "Get up; I've got something to show you."

Those few words struck her and she blinked her eyes, forcing herself up from the couch. Fox pulled on her arm to help her sit up.

"Did you find something?" she yawned again, rubbing at her eyelids. "What is it?"

"Come over here."

He carefully pulled her to her feet, helping her over to the table. She was groggy, struggling to wake up, but when she sat down and realized there was a steaming cup of coffee in front of her, her brow furrowed.

"Is my mom up?" she asked.

He sat down next to her. "No," he replied. "I made the coffee."

She looked at him, an incredulous smile on her face. "Do you cook, too?"

He met her smile, aware that he was incredibly glad to be sitting next to her again. He also realized something more; he couldn't imagine anything greater than waking up to her face every morning. He didn't know how or why, but in less than twenty-four hours he had fallen in love with the woman. At least, he had fallen in love with what he knew of her. He was sure he would love the rest he didn't even know about yet.

"I do," he said. "I'll prove it to you tonight when I make dinner for you."

Her smile broadened. "You really are a flirt, you know that?"

He laughed. "I'm not flirting. I mean it."

She yawned again, giggling at him because he was smiling at her so intensely. "Are you asking me out on a date?"

He nodded, tearing his gaze away to put his reading glasses back on. "That's a start," he muttered, listening to her snort. He focused on the copious notes in front of him. "But we'll talk about that later. For now, I thought you might like to hear about this papyrus."

She collected the coffee and took a healthy sip. "Did you translate the entire thing?"

He nodded, feeling her scoot up close to him and torn between loving the sensation of it and the work spread before him. He focused on the yellow legal pad with his scribbled notes.

"I did," he said. "There really wasn't that much text, but what text there was showed great promise. I also went through Fanny's journal from start to finish."

Morgan interrupted him. "You went through both the papyrus and the journal in just one night?" He nodded and she cut him off a second time. "You must be the fastest reader on the planet. How did you do it so fast?"

He shrugged. "To begin with, the papyrus only has six rows of hieroglyphs." He pointed to the papyrus, laid open in the middle of the table. He gestured at the contents with the eraser of the pencil. "There's some writing along the base of the two figures of Isis and Osiris as they face one another that is actually hieratic writing, but for the most part, there really wasn't a tremendous amount of writing to decipher. Secondly, this papyrus is written in a very archaic form of hieroglyphics. In fact, I've never seen such remote writings."

"Remote?" she repeated, trying to see what he was pointing at as he gestured at the faded symbols. "What does that mean?"

"It means old," he told her, trying to figure out how to explain what he suspected. "Your papyrus, material-wise, is archaic enough but the writing on it... well, it just doesn't match the manufacture date of the papyrus or the style in which it's written. It's like...like somebody copied really old text onto this from another source."

"Another source?" Morgan was confused. "Like what?"

He sat back, took his glasses off and looked at her. "The closest thing I can equate it to would be if Egyptians of the Middle Kingdom phase of Egyptian history came across some kind of writing or tablets that were ancient even to them. Maybe these tablets were fading out, or breaking apart because they were so old, so they took the script from the tablets and wrote it down on a papyrus to preserve the message itself. Does that make sense?"

She nodded slowly. "It does," she looked at the fading papyrus in the dim light of the dark, shadowed library. "It must have been an important message for them to do that, don't you think?"

He nodded. "That's just it," he puffed his cheeks out and exhaled slowly. "Maybe I'm punchy from having been up all night, but I think you were right."

"About what?"

"Your great-grandmother was on to something."

Morgan stared at him a long moment. "And what was that?"

He sighed again and sat forward. The glasses went back on

and he began to read. "'*Isis, Lady of Heaven, Favored of the Gods, may she be given eternal life by the Gods who love her. May she find peace within the bosom of the Most High, from the Claw of the Ape, ten days as the sun sets to the Holy City of Ranthor which lies deep to the east in the arms of the Syene, to the Fingers that Reach to the Sky. May she know grace and divine protection, our Holy Mistress, foremost Lady of the West, as she Rests in the Shelter of the Sun.'*"

Morgan digested the words as he pulled off his glasses and looked at her. She looked at him, rather awestruck. "That's almost exactly what it says in the journal."

"I know."

"Then the dealer who translated it did it right."

"Yes, he did."

She blinked, surprised, and sat back in her chair. "It definitely sounds like clues or a map of some sort. Doesn't it? It sounds like directions."

"It does."

"Do any of those places sound familiar to you?"

He lifted his eyebrow, gazing back at the papyrus. Then he held out his hand to her. She looked at the outstretched hand, not knowing what else to do but take it. He gripped her hand warmly and shook it.

"Congratulations," he said quietly. "You have officially made a contribution to the field of Egyptology."

"I have?" she said, still shaking his hand. "What for?"

He smiled at her, kissing her hand and still holding it. "Because Ranthor has only been mentioned once in all known Egyptian writings, in a document known as the Dendera Papyrus, alluding to the city where the Gods lived during pre-dynastic times in a period called the Reign of the Gods. It's literally the founding city of ancient Egypt. I've never heard of it or seen it written about again until now. Your great-grandmother's papyrus will go down in history as The Sherburn Papyrus, a key in the further discovery of pre-dynastic studies."

A timid smile spread across her face and her free hand covered her mouth, emotional. Tears glimmered in her eyes.

"Really?" she breathed.

He nodded, kissing the back of her hand again. "Really?"

Her smiled broadened as she looked to the papyrus, the odd ancient symbols that had meant so much to her great-grand-mother. "Well," she sniffled. "If that's really true, then can you please call it The Frances Sherburn Papyrus? I think my great-grandmother would like that."

He nodded. "Absolutely," he said softly. "She will get all the credit."

He let go of her hand and began to rummage through his notes. She watched him, her gaze moving between the journal, his notes and the papyrus.

"So now what?" she asked.

He shrugged. "I will return to the museum and talk to the Board of Directors to see what we can do about purchasing the papyrus and that old sarcophagus from the Sherburn family. Like I told you last night, your great-grandparents collected enough artifacts that you can keep Heaven's Gate solvent for many years to come."

Morgan looked at him as if he had lost his mind. She pushed the coffee aside. "You can have the papyrus when I'm done with it," she said flatly. "I'm not finished with it."

He looked up at her. "What more do you want to do with it? You said you wanted it translated and I have done that. What more could you want?"

She lifted a well-shaped eyebrow. "You said my great-grand-mother knew what she had," she pointed out. "Don't you remember what I told you? I believe that Fanny was killed because of that papyrus. Now here's where it gets tricky; the dealer who translated it knew what she had, too. The papyrus gives clues, like pieces to a puzzle. In fact, the dealer apparently agreed to help them put the puzzle together. I believe, based on what she wrote in her journal, that she tried to follow those clues and was killed because of it. Maybe it was the dealer who killed her; who knows? I explained this when I went to the museum yesterday."

He was watching her quite calmly. "I know," he said. "And you wanted me to translate the papyrus. I've done that, which has confirmed that it does, indeed, sound like clues to a tomb. So I'll ask you the question again; what more do you want to do?"

Morgan put her hands on her hips. "Now I go to Egypt," she said. "I'm going to follow the same trail that Fanny did and hopefully find what happened to her. Even if I don't, I'm going to follow those clues and find what's at the end of it. If she died for it like I think she did, then I'm going to finish what she started."

He digested her declaration. "I respect and appreciate your passion," he said evenly. "But just how are you going to put these clues together? And what makes you think that you'll survive the trip if Fanny didn't?"

She cocked her head at him. "Don't forget that I'm trained to put clues together," she pointed out. "I'll find people who can help me, like you did. And I'll survive it because I have what Fanny didn't — a gun and various other weapons at my disposal. I'll make it."

He took his glasses off. "Are you serious?"

"As a heart attack."

He held her gaze a moment longer before exhaling sharply and looking to the notes in front of him. He scratched his dark head thoughtfully. "Like I said," he said carefully. "I appreciate your passion. I understand you feel you need to vindicate your great-grandmother somehow. But honestly, Morgan, what do you truly expect to find? Your great-grandmother's grave? Her body? Her killer if there is one? I've heard of cold cases, but this is pretty farfetched."

She was quiet a moment; the sun was just starting to rise and a faint glow was beginning to emit from the edges of the heavy curtain pulled over the enormous library window. Rubbing her arms in the chill of the room, she went over to the window and pulled back the heavy velvet drapes.

The landscape beyond was gray with dawn, surprisingly clear. She stood in the window, rubbing her arms, thinking on Fox's words. As she stood there pondering, he walked up beside her.

"I'm not trying to tell you not to do it," he said, standing very close to her. "I'm simply saying that this is a ninety-year-old case. I'm just curious what your motivation is."

She looked at him. "My motivation is to solve Fanny's murder," she said. "But after hearing the translation from that papyrus, I really feel like I need to finish what she started. Fox, what if she really gave her life for this? What if this trek really killed her? For her sake, I feel like I need to finish it. She loved Egypt so much that I think she would have wanted me to."

"She would have wanted you to risk your life based on clues from a five thousand-year-old papyrus?" he murmured.

Morgan shook her head, rubbing her arms. "No," she said quietly. "But what if there really is something at the end of all those clues? I'm guessing Fanny thought so. You spoke of putting her in the history books as having helped the cause of Egyptology. Imagine what finding the tomb that the papyrus alludes to would do for Egyptology."

He snorted. "We would be calling it Fannyology, instead."

Morgan smiled. "It would mean a lot to Egyptology and the world. But it would mean more to me. I feel like I really have to go and at least do what I can. I'm a trained investigator; maybe... maybe I was meant to use my skills for this. For Fanny."

He stood next to her as she rubbed at her cold arms. He eventually had all he could take and put his big arms around her, pulling her against his warm torso. Petite little Morgan didn't resist. She collapsed against his enormous, warm body, relishing the heat and feeling his closeness with more excitement than she had felt in years. They just stood there for several long moments, watching the sunrise, each lost to their own thoughts.

"I can offer my services," he finally said.

Her head was against his chest, hearing his heart beating loud and strong. "You already have," she replied. "You deciphered the papyrus."

"No," he looked down at her as she looked up at him. "That's not what I mean. I mean that I would volunteer to go with you if you are really planning on going to Egypt. I don't want you going alone. I think you need me."

She gazed up at him, this massive man with the black eyes she found so incredibly handsome. The thought of traveling around Egypt with him did not distress her in the least. In fact, it made the trip that much more alluring in spite of the serious purpose.

"Are you serious?" she asked. "We could be gone weeks."

"I'm an Egyptologist. I can write off the trip and justify the time away from the museum."

She hadn't thought of it that way. Still, she needed to make sure of his intentions. All of this was happening so quickly that she was afraid he was upswept in some fantasy idea. She didn't want him to regret it.

"I have to do this trip," she said. "You don't. Think about what you're saying before you commit yourself."

"I already have. If you're going, I'm going. Are you really going?"

She nodded. "You bet," she replied. "But you're telling me that you're just going to drop everything to run off on a wild goose chase with a woman you just met?"

He grinned. "Hell of a wild goose chase."

"You didn't answer my question."

"Yes, I am going to drop everything to go with you. I don't have a lot going on right now at the museum and other than my parents and my brothers, there isn't anyone to leave behind in Britain. It's not like I have a wife and kids anchoring me here."

"You mentioned that."

"You still haven't told me where I can find a wife."

She laughed. "Maybe in Egypt."

"You'll be in Egypt."

She reached up and put a hand over his mouth. "No more of that talk," she scolded softly, changing the subject away from something they shouldn't even be discussing after knowing each other less than a full day. "The first thing I need to do is figure out what the Claw of the Ape is. It seems to me like that's the starting point. Have you ever heard of it?"

He shook his head. "Can I please speak?" he asked through her hand, grinning when she removed it. "I'm going to have to do a little research and let you know."

She was silent a moment, listening to him yawn and feeling him pull her closer as if he were snuggling down. "I need to go back to Los Angeles in a week," she said. "But I have one hundred and twenty hours more of vacation time coming to me. I'll go back, settle a few things, and fly out for Cairo."

"One hundred and twenty hours?" he repeated, shocked. "Have you never taken a holiday, woman?"

She grinned. "Not in four years. It's all accumulated time."

"Will they let you go?"

"They will. They'll have to; I'm entitled to take it."

He was silent as he pondered the course of what the next few months for him were going to take. "Not to rain on your parade, but a trip like this is going to be expensive."

She nodded. "I realize that," she said. "I have a pretty good sized retirement account I can borrow against. What about you?"

"You mean you're not paying for me?"

She laughed and he gave her a squeeze. "I'll present it to the museum as a necessary expedition. Or maybe I'll present it as a work/study term. In any case, they'll pay my expenses."

"You're going to lie to them?"

"No," he assured her. "But I will make you promise something in writing."

"In writing?" she pulled back to look at him. "What's that?"

"That any significant finds go to the Bolton Museum."

She shrugged. "Sure," she said. "I don't have any use for any significant finds. But I want to add a stipulation to that contract."

"What's that?"

Her eyes grew misty. "That if we do find something at the end of all those clues, it will be attributed to Fanny Sherburn."

He nodded. "Of course."

She smiled her thanks, gazing up at the man and realizing he looked exhausted. "You've been up all night," she said. "Maybe you should get some sleep."

He sighed, his dark gaze moved to the morning beyond the giant window. "I am tired," he admitted. "But I don't want to miss this."

"Miss what?"

He looked back down at her. "Watching the sunrise with you."

She stared at him. Then, the smile broke through. "You're flirting again."

He shook his head. "Untrue," he responded. "Flirting is trivial. I mean every word."

There was something in his expression that made her believe him.

It was difficult for Fox to pull himself away, but for necessity's sake, he really had to. He had a ton of work waiting for him back at the museum and the sunrise was signifying the start of another workday. He wasn't sure how he was going to get through it, but somehow, he didn't seem too terribly tired. He'd just experienced something he'd never known before, spending the night with a woman who was starting to light him up in more ways than he could count. Something that he felt as if he wanted to shout to the world.

Picking up his phone, he dialed a familiar number.

"Phipps," a voice on the other end said.

"You're up early," Fox said.

Archer Phipps recognized the voice. "Why in the hell are you calling me so early?" he demanded. Then, he audibly yawned. "I haven't even been to bed yet."

Fox grinned. "I'm going to tell your mother."

Archer burst out laughing. "You always were a horse's arse, Fox," he said, but he didn't mean it. "If you tell her I've been out all night, I'm going to tell her about the time you took two women back to..."

"Easy," Fox Henredon said loudly, interrupting him. "You tell her that and she'll never let us have a play date again."

Archer was still laughing. "Probably," he said. "How have you been? I feel like I haven't spoken to you in a while."

"You haven't," Fox said. "I've been... busy."

"With two women?"

Fox snorted. "With one," he said. "Would you believe me if I told you that I think I'm in love?"

Archer's laughter turned into something that sounded like gasp. "Seriously?"

"Dead serious."

"Do I know her?"

"No," Fox said. "I didn't even know her until a few days ago. She's American, but she just had a great-grandfather die and she's come to clean out his estate. As it turned out, her great-grandparents did a lot of collecting in Egypt back in the 1920s, so she had some things she wants to sell to the museum. Enter me."

"Astonishing," Archer said. "And that's how you met her?"

"That's how I met her," Fox said. "Morgan is her name. You've never seen such a beautiful woman."

"Actually, I have," Archer said after a moment. "I've found an American of my own, in fact. Met her several days ago, but like you, I think I'm very much in love with her."

"Really?" Fox was interested. "What are the chances, Archer? So many years and so little luck for the both of us. I'm ecstatic for you."

"I'm eager to meet your Morgan sometime."

Fox glanced at the date on his phone. "What are you doing next week?"

"I don't know," Archer said. "But something has come up at work... something bad. I have no idea what's coming, Fox, but if you knew... say a prayer for me, lad."

Fox and Archer had been friends for many years and knew the good, the bad, and the ugly about one another. Fox could tell by the tone of Archer's voice that the man was serious.

"Shit," he muttered. "I hope it's not as bad as you think it is."

"Me, too."

"Call me when you've got some open time?"

"You know I will."

"And you'd better call me if you need me."

"If I do, I will. I promise."

"Good," Fox said. "Speaking of schedules, however, I may be going to Egypt soon, so if I don't hear from you in the next couple of weeks, we'll get together when I get back."

"Fair enough."

"Then I'll see you when I see you," Fox said. "Oh, and don't think you're the only one who's been up all night."

"You?" Archer asked incredulously.

All he could hear was laughing before Fox hung up the phone. The truth was that Fox chuckled all the way back to the museum. Somehow, that sunrise that had signaled the start of a new day had also signaled the start of something good for him.

For the rest of the day, he was walking on clouds.

NOVEMBER 21, 1922

I saw the pyramids of Giza today. Joy of joys! To imagine savage man as he built these monstrous structures seems inconceivable. Surely they had divine help!

    ~ FS

FIVE

TWENTY-FOUR DAYS LATER—CAIRO, EGYPT

THE SWISSAIR FLIGHT had been a two-day affair from Los Angeles to Cairo. There had been a direct flight to Zurich, Switzerland, where Morgan had an eleven-hour layover before continuing on to the four-hour flight to Cairo. She had flown coach and slept almost the entire way, so it hadn't been too terribly bad. But her dreams, and her waking moments, had been filled entirely with thoughts of Fox.

The last week in England had been something out of a romance novel. When she needed to be helping her mother with Heaven's Gate, she had been spending time with Fox. They'd had several cozy dinners and he proved that he was a fantastic cook. He had taken her around Bolton and shown her the sights, and one day he had taken her to see the Tyldesley Rugby team play the Bowden Rugby club.

After the game, they had ended up in the same pub as many of the Tyldesley players. Morgan had found out that Fox had played two years with the club. All of the players knew Fox, who had the pleasure of introducing Morgan to his mates. Immediately, the macho rugby players focused in on her and Fox found himself fending off several amorous friends. But it had been great fun and something that still brought a smile to Morgan's lips when she thought of it.

It had gotten better towards the end of the week. While Fox was at work, Morgan had buckled down to help her mother finish off what they could before they returned for the States, including letting Fox and two assistants come and photograph the sarcophagus of Hetep-Ankh-Sheri. Fox had been very professional while photographing and cataloguing, but at one point when Laura and both assistants had left the library, he pulled Morgan into an amorous kiss that still made her hot to think about it.

They hadn't slept together yet but it wasn't because the sexual pull hadn't been overwhelming. Morgan seemed to back off when it came to that point not wanting to submit to what she knew would be an emotional experience she would never recover from. Morgan already felt such an attraction to Fox that she couldn't imagine what it would be like once she turned herself over to him bodily. She was terrified of losing herself to him and then returning to Los Angeles, alone and in love. She'd met a man who was her soulmate and she didn't want to be parted from him, not ever. But the London/Los Angeles differ-ence was a huge issue. She couldn't think straight, unsure what to do about it.

The last twenty-four hours before her flight home had been the most serious. They had stayed up all night talking in the library, lying on the old leather couch and watching the sunrise. They talked about his background, family, education, and his stint in the rugby club. She had also gotten the impression that he was a bit of a brawler when provoked, which had come in handy playing rugby.

He'd talked about his family, his father who was a marine biologist and his four younger brothers, three of whom were in the Royal Marines. Morgan had talked about her own rather uneventful life, her career as a cop and the few times she had been shot at. But he didn't want to hear that part, so the conversation had moved to other things.

When the sun finally rose, he had helped her finish packing, lugging all of her baggage and her mother's baggage down to the rental car and loading them in. He had even driven them to the Manchester airport for their flight that connected in London before going on to Los Angeles.

Because of security at the airport, he couldn't go past the security checkpoint so they had to say goodbye out in the terminal where all of the check-in counters were located. When the baggage was checked and Laura made herself scarce, Morgan and Fox faced each other in the cavernous, busy terminal.

There were a thousand people all around them, busily going about their lives, but Morgan and Fox had eyes only for each other. Fox stared at her for about five seconds before wrapping his enormous arms around her and pulling her into a crushing embrace that had her feet dangling more than a foot off the ground. He kissed her amorously, whispering his feelings for her in her ear but stopping short of telling her that he loved her.

They both knew they were in love with each other but, somehow, only knowing each other for six days, thirteen hours and forty-seven minutes prevented them from making the declaration, like it would be too rash for them to do it. So Morgan got on the plane without telling Fox that she loved him and without hearing him tell her that he loved her in return. She wondered, as the plane landed at Cairo International Airport, if he was kicking himself as much as she had been kicking herself over that. She wished she'd told him.

As the plane pulled up to the terminal, the pilot thanked everyone for choosing Swissair and mentioned that the weather was a balmy eighty degrees. Morgan waited until almost everyone had left the plane before standing up and getting her carry-on from the overhead compartment. She was dressed in jeans, a lightweight, long-sleeved shirt and a lightweight jacket, and her white tennis shoes. Her long blond hair was pulled back in a ponytail, slightly mussed as a result of the seventeen-hour flight, but she was her usual beautiful self in spite of the exhaustion of travel.

Fox's flight was due to land three hours after hers so Morgan knew she had some waiting to do. She hoped to clean up a little bit and look presentable for him. Disembarking the plane, she trudged up the gangway and into the main terminal where a collection of people were greeting each other. Kids, grandparents, parents and lovers were all hugging each other, glad to be together again.

Shifting her carry-on to the other shoulder and hiking up her purse, Morgan had her head down as she moved through the crowd. She was nearing the corridor that led to the baggage claim area when someone suddenly grabbed her from behind.

She was up in the air before she realized what had happened. Panicked, her police training kicked in and she was preparing to take out her attacker's kneecaps when a warm face suddenly nuzzled her neck.

"I thought you'd never get off that bloody plane," Fox was hugging her passionately. "You look good enough to eat."

Morgan gasped in delight, shifting so he had to put her down and then throwing her arms around his neck.

"Oh, my God," she breathed as he smothered her face with kisses. "I thought your plane got in later this afternoon!"

He couldn't seem to kiss her enough. "I lied," he told her. "I wanted to surprise you."

She laughed. "Well, it worked. I'm surprised."

He stopped grinning long enough to look at her. "Good," he took a moment to drink in her face. "You're more beautiful than

I remembered. I've missed those dimples so much I thought I was going to shrivel away."

She smiled, displaying his beloved dimples full-bore and running her hands over his face, watching him kiss her palms. "I've missed you, too."

He pulled her close and kissed her again. "The past seventeen days have been a nightmare," he whispered. "All I could think of was counting down the days until we'd see each other again."

"I know," she agreed. "But now we have at least six weeks together. I hope you can stand me by the end of it."

His features softened. "Of course I can," he murmured. "In fact, there's something you should know."

"What?"

"I love you very much."

She stared at him, her clear brown eyes soft with adoration. "I love you, too," she whispered. Then her eyes started to water. "But I'm afraid to."

She began to sniffle and he wrapped her up in his big arms, rocking her gently. He was thrilled and concerned at the same time. "Why?" he asked.

Her face was pressed into his chest. "Because what's going to happen when we leave Egypt in six weeks?" she lamented. "You'll go back to England and I'll go back to the United States and then what?"

He gave her a squeeze, kissing her forehead. "I'll get a job in Los Angeles," he told her, wiping the tears off her cheeks and turning her around so they could head to baggage claim. "I've already made up my mind. Where you go, I go."

Morgan wiped at her nose, allowing him to herd her to the escalator. "But that's not fair to you," she told him. "Your job at the Bolton Museum is much more prestigious and important. I can move to England and get a job with a police department. They like cops from the United States."

He took her carry-on from her shoulder before she stepped on the escalator, stepping on behind her. He kissed the top of her head as the escalator moved down.

"Anyone would be lucky to have you," he said. "But we can talk about this later. We don't have to settle everything right now."

She patted his hand as it rested on her shoulder, grasping his fingers as they got off the escalator and made their way towards baggage claim. There were dozens of people standing around the giant carousel and when she pointed out her giant purple suitcase, Fox easily retrieved it and hefted the big bag over his head before setting it down beside her. He grunted as he let it go.

"What do you have in that thing?" he huffed. "Boulders?"

She snorted. "There's a second one."

His eyebrows flew up in mock outrage. "What?"

She grinned and pointed to the matching purple suitcase as it came around. He dutifully went to collect it, commenting that he now had a hernia. Morgan giggled, kissed him, and followed him as he lugged her suitcases, plus his own, out to the curb. Once outside in the balmy Egyptian afternoon, he commandeered a taxi and off they went.

Morgan had booked seven days at the Cairo Marriott Hotel with a Nile view. She'd used her credit card points to book the week, wanting to stay at a nice hotel while she and Fox figured out their plan of attack.

The taxi made its way through the airport traffic and to the streets of Cairo, which were wild beyond belief. Fox, having been to Egypt several times as it related to his profession, was used to the chaos but Morgan white-knuckled the ride until they pulled into a nicer part of town and into the garden-like grounds of the Marriott.

The sun was setting as the bellhops raced out to the taxi and began loading the luggage onto rolling racks. Fox paid the taxi driver and took Morgan's hand as they went into the luxurious lobby.

He felt proud to have her on his arm, like nothing he had experienced before. Morgan checked in as Fox stood next to her and noted that she had only booked one room. He was a little curious, since any attempts he had ever made to take her to bed had been thwarted, so he wondered about the single room. He didn't say a word as they took the elevator to the fifth floor and made their way to room 526. Fox used the key card and opened the door.

It was a suite, very luxurious with mock-ancient Egyptian decor, with a living room, kitchenette, and bedroom with a fluffy king-sized bed. Morgan went straight into the bedroom and began setting her stuff down.

"Baby?" she called. "Bring the suitcases in here, please."

He schlepped in the suitcases, one in each hand and one under each arm. He dutifully set them down and she maneuvered both of her big purple suitcases over to the window, heaving one up on a stand and the other up onto the table. Then she began to throw them open and dig through them.

"I'm dying to take a shower," she muttered, pulling out her overnight bag with all of her shampoos and toiletries. "Seventeen hours on a plane. Yuck."

Fox picked up his big suitcase and put it on the bed, opening it up. "How were your flights?" he asked. "Yours were longer than mine."

She shrugged, pulling out a silky white robe. "Luckily, I slept most of the way on both legs, so I guess they were fine."

He watched her as she moved past him and into the bathroom. As soon as she flipped on the light, he heard her squeal with delight. He went to see what had her so excited.

Morgan was already pulling the rubber band from her hair, moving to run water into the giant Roman tub. The fixtures were elaborate and looked as if they were made of gold, with marble counters and beautiful, mock-ancient, Egyptian artwork covering the walls.

Fox watched as she ran bubbles into the big white tub. "I was thinking we could eat in the room tonight and get to bed early," he said. "Sound like a plan?"

She nodded as she pulled off her shoes. "Sounds great," she said. "I'm a little hungry."

"Me, too."

He went back into the living room and collected the room service menu, returning to the bathroom just in time to see her pull her jeans off. He nearly dropped the menu as she proceeded to remove her bra.

"What do they have for dinner?" she asked, completely unaware of the fact that she was stripping naked in front of him.

But Fox wasn't unaware. He'd never been more aware of anything in his life. In fact, he'd been dreaming of this moment nonstop for almost a month.

"Uh," he cleared his throat, tearing his eyes away from her supple breasts and focusing on the menu. "Steak, chicken, whatever you want. What are you hungry for?"

The bath was running full-bore and the bubbles were up to the rim. Morgan pulled off her bikini underwear and plunged into the water. Fox nearly passed out; he'd stopped breathing, not realizing it until she hit the water and her very luscious, very shapely body disappeared from view. When he finally resumed breathing, he sounded like he was gasping for air. Morgan, above the rush of the water, heard him. She looked up from the bath gel in her hand.

"What's wrong?" she asked.

Fox stared at her with the open room service menu in his hand. "Nothing."

He had a very good poker face but Morgan's brow furrowed. "You sounded like you were choking. What's the matter?"

He slapped the room service menu shut. "Bloody hell, Morgan," he put his hands on his hips. "I'm only human. You can't do... do that bloody stuff in front of me and not expect me to react."

Her brow furrowed further. "What are you talking about?"

"That," he pointed to the bra and panties on the ground, the jeans in a pile. "Do you realize you just stripped off your clothing right in front of me?"

She had no idea what he meant, looking over at her clothes on the floor. "I had to take them off to get in the bath."

He pursed his lips, frustrated. "I realize that," he said pointedly. "But you and I haven't even... and that's another thing; you only reserved one room with a king-sized bed. Were you expecting us to share the bed?"

She was baffled. "Yes," she said hesitantly. "I... what's wrong?"

He cocked his head and looked at her; he could see she genuinely had no idea. So he tossed the menu to the ground and began pulling off his clothes in a huff.

"Nothing's bloody wrong," he said as his shoes hit the ground. "Absolutely nothing. I haven't seen you for seventeen days and I've never missed anyone so much in my entire life. So nothing is wrong. I just want to see my girlfriend."

She watched him as he pulled his shirt off. She'd never seen him with his clothes off, either, and it began to occur to her what he had meant. She was so comfortable with the man and was so glad to see him that the fact that they had never been intimate hadn't crossed her mind. She'd only reserved one hotel room because she didn't want him staying in another room. She wanted him with her. She was coming to see why he was so frustrated. He thought she was teasing him.

"Am I your girlfriend?" she asked.

"Yes," he snapped, unbuttoning his pants. "You are. And you're going to be more than that someday, just so we're clear."

A faint smile crossed her lips as her hungry gaze drifted over his sculpted physique, the bulging muscles and broad, defined chest. His skin was smooth and tan, and he had a big tattoo on his left shoulder that wrapped around his upper arm. When he turned, she could see that it was a beautifully sketched ankh, the Egyptian symbol of life. It was obvious that the man spent a good deal of time in a gym because he was absolutely enormous and absolutely magnificent. Her body began to tingle with excitement.

"Hurry up and get in the tub," she sat back, making room for him. "Don't make me wait."

He froze as he prepared to slide the pants off his big frame. "W-What?"

Her smile broadened. "You heard me. Get your ass in here."

He didn't move. "But you told me... back in England, when we would get close, you told me that you weren't ready for intimacy."

She played with the bubbles, a seductive smile on her face. "I wasn't ready then because I just wasn't sure about you and I was afraid to take such a big step," she said. "I was afraid of getting hurt. But I'm not afraid anymore. I'm ready to let my guard down completely if you are."

He didn't say another word. He pulled off his jeans, his boxer briefs, giving Morgan an unobstructed view of his naked body. She was gazing at him, acquainting herself with his spectacular nude form, when he suddenly got into the tub and the water sloshed over the side. His big hands cupped her face, holding her fast as his mouth slanted hungrily over hers.

"I've loved you from nearly the first moment I met you," he murmured against her lips. "I'm willing to do whatever it takes to make you happy and comfortable. I don't want you to feel like I'm rushing you into something you're not ready for."

She met his feverish kisses. "You're not rushing me," she breathed as she suckled his lower lip. "I love you, Fox."

He kissed her so hard that he drove her teeth into her soft lip, drawing blood. He could taste it when he kissed her. In little time, he had her out of the tub and wrapped in a big, fluffy towel. Carrying her into the bedroom, he laid her on the bed and shoved his suitcase aside, dumping the contents onto the floor. But he couldn't have cared less.

She was warm and damp and supple in his arms, a little firebrand of a woman who met him kiss for kiss. She was such a petite woman that he didn't want to hurt her, but she turned the tables on him and became the aggressor.

Morgan somehow managed to roll him onto his back, her soft body across his thighs as her mouth began to work his enormous erection. Fox groaned as she stroked him with her tongue, suckling the head before plunging her entire mouth down on him. It was heavenly and naughty, and his hands wound into her damp hair, holding tighter and tighter the more she worked him. Far too quickly, he could feel himself building to a release so he gripped her head, effectively stopping her. When she looked up to see what the problem was, he sat up and flipped her onto her back.

Now it was his turn to dominate and he took great pleasure in it. His mouth was on her neck, his big hand moving to her silky, slightly damp breasts. She gasped softly when a big, warm palm closed over a nipple, squirming with delight as he alternately massaged her breast and played with the nipple. When his heated mouth finally closed over the hard little pellet and suckled hard, Morgan moaned her pleasure. Fox managed to wedge himself in between her legs, both hands on her breasts as he nursed from one to the other.

Morgan made it very clear that she wanted to feel him inside of her and although he was trying to draw out the foreplay, he wanted to feel himself inside of her as well. Still, he hadn't gorged himself enough on her flesh and as he suckled her breasts, she tried to sit up and grasp his erection. He was too tall, however, and she couldn't get a hold of him, so as he nursed hungrily on her nipples, her fingers moved to her vagina and she began to pleasure herself as he suckled.

It was nearly too much for the man to take. He groaned when he saw what she was doing and moved to help her. Morgan squirmed beneath him, taking his fingers and using them to manipulate her clitoris. As he was gladly doing that, she plunged her fingers into her body, mimicking intercourse, and Fox couldn't take anymore. He removed her fingers from her body, licking them, tasting her on an intimate level, as he lifted himself up and mounted her.

Fox's thick and powerful manhood slid easily into her wet body. Morgan groaned as he pushed into her, wrapping her arms around his neck and her legs around his hips as he began to move, thrusting deep again and again, building that delicious friction they had both been waiting for.

Morgan was assertive and responsive, her hips moving with his, creating wild sensations that had her climaxing within the first few minutes. Fox felt her tremors, struggling not to join her as he ground his pelvis against hers, feeling her body milk at him. Then he shifted slightly, putting a hand between them, playing with her and feeling her body respond to him with another climax a few moments later.

The more he played with her, the more she climaxed until,

eventually, he could no longer hold back and he withdrew from her swiftly, wrapping her hands around his erection so she could stroke him to his orgasm. But Morgan didn't want any part of it; instead of stroking him, she directed him into her again and she took the aggressor role once more, thrusting her pelvis against him until he was quickly overwhelmed by her body and he thrust into her several times, hard, finally releasing himself deep inside her as she wept with pleasure.

But even after he spent himself, he continued to move inside of her, feeling the hot slickness of what he had put into her and loving it. It was the most erotic and satisfying thing he'd ever experienced. Once he caught his breath, he did the whole thing all over again and it was even better the second time.

It was everything he had hoped for, the power of attraction and emotion overwhelming him like nothing he had ever known. When Morgan finally fell asleep somewhere around midnight, Fox lay awake with her wrapped in his arms, staring into the darkness of the room and knowing his life was changed forever. Morgan had succeeded in branding him in ways she could never comprehend, but in ways he wasn't sorry for in the least. He adored her.

Morning came before he realized it.

NOVEMBER 24, 1922

Today, we took camels across the sands to a local casbah. Riding atop a camel is much like sailing the open sea. It was rough seas! Dear Louis was positively green. It is fortunate he did not see me laughing!

~ FS

SIX

MORGAN AWOKE the next morning to the smell of coffee. She stirred, rolling over in the big bed and noticing she that was quite alone. The door to the bedroom was cracked open and she could hear noises out in the living room.

Running her hand over the bed beside her, she remembered the night before with a smile, feeling warm and giddy when she thought of Fox and his powerful body. It was enough to send her heart fluttering. If she thought herself only merely in love with the man before, she knew now that she was madly in love with him. Last night had sealed it.

Rising from bed, she realized quickly that she was still stark-naked. Scooting into the bathroom, she collected the silky white robe she had left there the night before. Wrapping it around her body, she ran a brush through her hair a couple of times before making her way out into the living room.

Fox was setting out coffee cups when she walked in. He was showered and shaved, his black hair combed and still damp. He heard the door squeak and turned, his gaze falling on Morgan. It was all he could do not to turn into a silly, giddy fool. He smiled warmly at her.

"Good morning, sunshine," he said.

"Good morning," she returned his smile. "Have you been up long?"

"A little while," he replied. "I'm used to waking up early so I went down to the gym so I wouldn't wake you up. How did you sleep?"

Morgan moved over to him and kissing him sweetly. "Like a rock," she murmured, kissing him again. "I don't think I've ever slept so well."

He wrapped his arms around her, hugging her tightly, feeling her supple body beneath the silky robe. It was enough to set his heart racing again and his physical reaction to her was almost instantaneous. He could have very easily have taken her back into the bedroom but he didn't want to make it seem like sex was all he was interested in, so he struggled to focus on something else.

"I ordered breakfast," he said. "I hope you're hungry."

Morgan looked at the spread he had on the dining table. "Starving," she said, gently pulling away from him and going for a chair. "We didn't get to eat dinner last night."

"Sorry?"

She looked up at him; the question had a double meaning and she shook her head. "Of course not," she insisted. "I don't even have the words to describe how amazing it was for me. And you?"

His smile returned, warm and adoring. "It was the best night of my life," he said with soft sincerity. Then he pulled out the chair for her and helped her sit. He began removing the dish covers. "I wasn't sure what you would like so I just ordered a bunch of things in the hope it would entice you."

Oatmeal, omelets, pancakes and the like were revealed. Morgan wriggled her eyebrows. "Wow," she exclaimed. "Did you leave anything in the kitchens for anyone else?"

He snorted as he sat down beside her, waiting until she had her pick of the dishes presented before moving in for her leavings. While Morgan ate oatmeal and fruit, Fox devoured the pancakes and eggs. The sliding door was open and a balmy breeze blew in, the blue ribbon of the Nile filling their view.

"This is so beautiful," Morgan sighed. Then she looked at Fox. "I'm so glad you came. I can't imagine sharing this with anyone but you. Thank God I went to the Bolton Museum on that day; I don't think I would have ever met you otherwise."

He took her free hand and kissed it. "You would have had to meet me, eventually," he told her. "With Heaven's Gate so close to Bolton, we would have eventually met up when you made the decision to liquidate Louis and Fanny's collection."

"Maybe," she shrugged, sitting back with her coffee. She watched Fox as he finished off his toast. "So what's on tap for today?"

He wiped his mouth as he chewed. "I have a friend who works at the Cairo Museum of Antiquities," he said. "I thought we'd go to the museum today."

She nodded. "I brought the papyrus. It's in my suitcase, in the lining. I didn't want to get busted for transporting artifacts if they searched my luggage, even if it is mine, so I hid it."

He nodded. "I'd worry more about getting it out of Egypt rather than bringing it in. They are rather particular about their ancient artifacts."

"I know," she replied with a shrug. "There's not much I can do about it. I had to bring it."

He swallowed the bite in his mouth and finished his orange juice. "I'll call my friend and see if she has some time to see us this morning."

"Okay," she said while sipping her coffee. "Are we bringing the papyrus?"

He shook his head. "No," he said flatly. "If we take it in to the museum, I'm afraid we'd never get it out. They would want to keep it. I'll make copies at the hotel business center and we can bring those."

"What about the journal?"

He shrugged. "Maybe. It's not as valuable to them as the papyrus. Plus, it has a lot of notes in it that might be helpful if we somehow get on the scent of something."

She pondered that as her gaze moved between Fox and the blue Nile beyond. "I've been thinking a lot about how we need to go about this," she said. "It makes sense to find the correlation between the sites listed on the papyrus and the reality that they may have existed. Like, the Claw of the Ape; Fanny's diary mentions that the dealer she purchased the papyrus from might have known what it was but she never elaborates. Do you know what would that be? Are there even any apes in Egypt?"

He sat back in his chair. "In ancient times, they were considered living gods, but there are no indigenous monkeys or apes to Egypt. I've done some research into all sites mentioned on the papyrus and have come up with a few things."

"Really?" she perked up. "Like what?"

He rose, kissed her head, and went into the bedroom, emerging a short time later with a small leather-bound notepad. He resumed his seat next to her as she pushed dishes out of the way so he could use the table.

Fox set the pad down and put on his reading glasses. "Well," he said slowly. "I went through all the material available to see if somewhere, at some time, there was a temple or city or some other kind of landmark known as the Claw of the Ape. However, we do know that back in pre-dynastic times, baboons especially were considered vessels of transformation; that is, a deceased king could pass into the body of a baboon and live again. Baboons were very sacred back in pre-dynastic times and even through the Old Kingdom. There are also small, early dynastic plaques that show the king or priests performing the Opening of the Mouth Ceremony and transfiguration before monkeys. So, clearly, monkeys were very sacred to the ancient Egyptians."

Morgan was listening intently, trying to read his scribbled notes. "What's the Opening of the Mouth Ceremony?"

He looked at her. "It's part of the mummification process," he told her. "It's a ritual by which the deceased symbolically becomes reanimated. The priests would perform this ritual and speak the ancient spell, '*Awake! May you be alert as a living one, rejuvenated every day, healthy in millions of occasions of god sleep, while the gods protect you, protection being around you every day*'."

She nodded, digesting the information. "Didn't you say that my papyrus looks like text that was copied from another, more ancient source?"

"That's my belief."

"Then wouldn't it make sense that the more ancient source, if it's pre-dynastic like you've speculated, would make mention of apes because they were so sacred to them? Perhaps even more than later Egyptians?"

He smiled at her. "You've got a brilliant mind, Miss Sherburn. Your statement makes perfect sense."

She grinned in return. "So maybe pre-dynastic Egypt had a city or monument called Claw of the Ape."

He nodded. "I'm way ahead of you on that. I've even looked into the possibility that there was a festival called Claw of the Ape, but I can't find any reference to it in any of the material I've researched."

"So now what?"

He pulled off his glasses and pecked her on the nose, standing up. "That is why we're going to see my friend at the Cairo Museum. Maybe she knows more."

Morgan lifted an eyebrow at him. "You've mentioned 'she' a few times," she said casually. "Who is 'she'?"

He closed the leather-bound tablet. "Dr. Alia el-Shabheen. She and I did a semester of study together at Oxford." He cocked his head, letting out a faint sigh as the mood shifted. "And I'm not even sure it's appropriate to bring this up, but I'm all for honestly in a relationship so here it is: Alia and I dated for a few months but I broke it off and I don't think she's ever quite forgiven me. Seeing you might bring back old memories, so be aware."

Morgan broke into a smile. "And just how did you plan on introducing me? I could just be a co-worker, you know. I don't have to be anything intimate as far as she knows."

He put his hands on his hips. "That would involve hiding our relationship and I have no intention of doing that. As it is, I want to shout it to the world. Why on earth would I try to hide it?"

She lifted her shoulders, standing up and beginning to put the dirty dishes back on the room service tray. "I didn't mean it that way," she said. "Maybe I shouldn't go at all. She might be more forthcoming with helpful information if I'm not there."

He went over to her and grabbed her by the upper arms, forcing her to face him. "Listen to me so there is no mistake," he rumbled. "I am madly in love with you. At some point in the very near future, I plan to marry you, so there is nothing in the world strong enough to cause me to hide my relationship with you. If Alia, or anyone else, can't accept it, then they can go to hell. I mean it."

Morgan gazed up at him, wide-eyed and stunned by his admission. He'd made a comment about their future association last night as well but she had let it slide. Now, he was speaking plainly and she was both overjoyed and speechless.

"If you plan to marry me, don't you think you'd better ask

my opinion about that first?" she asked, a smile playing on her lips.

He cocked a defiant eyebrow. "No," he said firmly. "Well, maybe. Why? Do you have anything to say about it?"

"Maybe," she reached out and wrapped her arms around his narrow waist, gazing up into his obsidian eyes. "When is this all supposed to take place?"

He was trying to be firm but felt himself melting in the grip of her gaze. "I'm thinking that March would be good," he told her. "My great-grandparents were married on March twenty-fourth and they were married for sixty-seven years. I think that's a lucky date."

She nodded, still suppressing a knowing smile. "I see," she said. "I don't suppose I have anything to say about all of this, right?"

"No."

"Really?"

He faltered. "If you want to," he corrected himself. "What do you have to say about it?"

She reached up and patted his stubbled cheek. "That I love you very much," she murmured. "And I want the biggest diamond you can find."

He pretended to be full of regret when the fact was that he was elated. "Oh, God," he groaned. "I knew it. You're only after me for my money."

"And you're only after me for my Egyptian artifacts."

"That's *not* true," he insisted. "Well, maybe for the sarcophagus of Hetep-Ankh-Sheri, but the rest of it can take second priority behind you."

"Ugh," she rolled her eyes at him and pulled from his grip, moving back towards the bedroom. "You're impossible."

"No, I'm not," he kissed her loudly on each cheek. "But I can't live without those dimples. They drive me mad."

She batted at him, giggling as she went into the bedroom. He grinned as he watched her go.

"Can I at least introduce you from now on as my fiancée?" he called after her.

Her head suddenly appeared in the doorway. "Not until you slap that big diamond on my finger."

He laughed as he followed her into the bedroom. "What if I can't find one?"

"Then you're out of luck, buddy. I'll go find someone who can."

He stepped inside the doorway, looking at her as she dug into her suitcases. "But that's just cruel," he told her. "Does a piece of crystallized carbon mean more to you than I do?"

She threw a pillow and hit him in the face.

NOVEMBER 26, 1922

We explored several ancient tombs today. The ancients communicated with pictures called hieroglyphs. I took a try at writing them. What a marvelous and beautiful way to communicate, as they are both words and art!

∼ FS

SEVEN

THE CAIRO MUSEUM was a massive building built in 1891, housing the world's finest collection of Egyptian antiquities. It was also extremely busy by mid-morning as Fox and Morgan's taxi pulled up to the curb.

The day was bright and warm. Fox climbed out of the taxi first, carrying a photocopy of the papyrus that they had made at the hotel. He extended his hand to Morgan, who stepped out behind him. She was dressed in tight jeans, sandals with a four-inch heel, and a short-sleeved top that, although it didn't show cleavage or too much skin, still clung to every curve of her torso. Only a dead man wouldn't have noticed her fabulous body and Fox was no exception.

He had noticed it from the onset, even going so far as to suggest she might want to wear something a little less flattering, but she had made a face at him and, not wanting a fight on his hands, he backed off. Truth was, he had absolutely no problem with the shirt but knew that conservative Muslims would. When he explained it to her that way, she took him seriously and wrapped a matching scarf around her neck, looking stylish yet still covering up somewhat. Collecting her giant designer purse with Fanny's journal safely inside, she was ready to go. Satisfied and damn proud to have such a gorgeous woman on his arm, Fox took her hand possessively as they made their way towards the museum.

Morgan pulled out her digital camera as they approached the museum, snapping several shots, including a few of Fox, standing in front of the museum. He took her hand again as they went in, entering the old halls that smelled of all things timeless and Egyptian. As Morgan stood in the middle of the lobby and snapped away with her camera, Fox went to the Information kiosk and asked for Dr. el-Shabheen.

As the information clerk got on the phone, he turned to watch Morgan shoot pictures. He found himself inspecting her from head to toe. Everything about her was fluid and lovely. When she finally put the camera away and began walking towards him, he was giddy with delight.

"Can we look around a little while we're here?" she asked. "I'd love to see some of it."

He nodded. "Sure," he replied. "In fact, I'd like to see the collection myself. It's been years since I've been here and they change out pieces from time to time."

She looked at him. "As an Egyptologist, surely you must have spent a lot of time here when you were working for your degree."

He shrugged. "My time was spent on two digs," he told her. "One of them was far south, almost to Aswan, and another was at Saqqara. I didn't spend a lot of time in the museum."

"Do you miss digging out in the field?"

His gaze moved over the heights and architecture of the museum. "I do," he admitted. "It took me six years to get my doctorate and out of those years, I spent three seasons digging in Egypt. After I graduated, I spent four years in various other pursuits, which took me out of digging entirely, and then I found my way to the museum. I've sort of lost touch with the field work."

"But you must have been on digs since then," she persisted.

He nodded. "When I first joined the museum staff, I spent three seasons on a dig that the museum sponsored in Edfu. I was in charge of clearing a temple dedicated to Horus. In fact, I'm directly responsible for several of the artifacts in the Bolton Museum's Egyptian collection from the Edfu dig."

She gazed up at him, her brown eyes soft and bright. "You've lived quite a life," she commented. "I can't say I've done anything quite so exciting."

He put his arm around her, giving her a squeeze. "That is quite possibly about to change."

She nodded in agreement, smiling at him as he returned her smile. She was gently patting his cheek when he suddenly looked over her head and his expression changed.

"Alia," he put his arm around Morgan as she turned around. "It's good to see you."

Morgan's gaze immediately fixed on an elegant-looking Middle Eastern woman with bright green eyes. She was quite exotic looking and lovely. Alia el-Shabheen's gaze was fixed on Fox as if Morgan didn't exist.

"Fox," she said in her thickly accented English. "It's been forever. It's so good to see you again as well."

"Thanks," he smiled as he indicated Morgan. "This is Morgan Sherburn."

Alia's green gaze fixed on Morgan as if seeing her for the first time and there was immediate tension in the air. Perhaps Fox didn't sense it, but Morgan certainly did and her guard went up. She didn't like what she was sensing and she smiled thinly at the woman.

"It's nice to meet you, Dr. el-Shabheen," she said politely. "Your museum is beautiful."

Alia el-Shabheen looked like a goddess with her kohl-lined eyes and dark-lined lips. She was about a head taller than Morgan and scrutinized her very closely before speaking. It was apparent that, at least to Morgan, the woman was sizing her up. Fox had warned her but she hadn't really believed it until this moment. Truthfully, she was a little shocked at the juvenile behavior.

"Of course," was all Dr. el-Shabheen would say. Her gaze moved up and down Morgan's body, scrutinizing her. "Are you a colleague?"

Morgan could see that the line was being drawn, right then and there. She almost laughed but managed to hold herself in check. She shook her head.

"No," she replied evenly. "I'm a...."

Fox interrupted her before she could finish; he didn't pull any punches. "Morgan and I are getting married in the spring."

Alia's green eyes flickered with fury but her features never changed expression. Morgan met the woman's gaze strongly until Alia returned her focus to Fox.

"Congratulations," she told him. "I had no idea you were the marrying kind."

The barbs were flying already. Morgan looked at Fox, who was beginning to see what she was seeing. She could tell by his expression as he faced Alia.

"I'm the marrying kind with the right person," he said evenly and Morgan very nearly broke a grin. "And you? Have you finally married?"

It was a double-whammy and Morgan lowered her head lest Fox, or Alia, see the grin she was desperately trying to fight off. But Alia did nothing more than smile weakly.

"Actually, I did," she replied. "Two years ago to a lovely man of my father's choosing. He breeds racehorses."

"Wonderful," Fox said, hoping the conversation would go a

little better from this point on. "You always did like horse racing."

"I do," Alia agreed, her gaze not as harsh as the situation seemed to settle. "I'm sorry to rush you, but how can I help you? You mentioned in your phone call that you had something you wanted me to take a look at."

Fox reached out and took Morgan by the hand. "I do," he agreed. "Is there somewhere we can go and talk for a few minutes? It shouldn't take long."

Alia nodded, motioning for the two of them to follow. When Morgan finally looked at Fox, he rolled his eyes and shook his head. He was already regretting the woman's behavior. Together, they followed Alia across the lobby and towards the back of the museum where the administrative offices were. As they entered the office complex, a small, brown man with bulging eyes and a leather-worn face rapidly approached Fox.

"Dr. Fox!" he cried gleefully, shaking Fox's hand enthusiastically. "Dr. el-Shabheen said you were coming. I am so happy to see you again."

Fox shook the man's hand as Alia came to a stop and turned around. "I see that you remember my assistant, Beni," she said, somewhat more pleasant than she had been earlier. "Beni, this is Dr. Fox's wife."

Beni, a little man with sun-wrinkled skin, fixed his dark eyes on Morgan and his mouth popped open.

"Mrs. Fox," he exclaimed, awed. "Dr. Fox is very fortunate, madam. It is an honor to meet you."

Morgan smiled her thanks, looking to Fox and wondering when he was going to clarify that they weren't married. But he didn't clarify, instead, urged her along as they continued to follow Alia to her office. Beni brought up the rear.

Alia's office was nothing like Fox's. It was clean and modern, and she indicated for them to take a seat at a small conversation table. Meanwhile, Beni had gone to collect three bottles of chilled water and brought them in, setting them before the guests. Alia took her seat across the table from them and primly folded her hands.

"Now," she began, suddenly all-business. "What did you wish to speak of?"

Fox wasn't sure how much he was going to tell her given the way their meeting had started off. He knew several people at the Cairo Museum but he'd always shared a good friendship with Alia, at least he thought he had until Morgan was introduced into the mix. Now Alia seemed clipped and rushed, and he was frankly disappointed. When Morgan opened up one of the chilled bottles and handed it to him, he took it gratefully as he pondered his next move.

"I've come across some interesting information lately that I need to solicit your advice on," he began. "Have you ever heard of a location or monument called Claw of the Ape? The reference period should be pre-dynastic. I've done some research on the subject but my focus is Middle and New Kingdom, not pre-dynastic. I thought you might know."

Alia looked thoughtful. "Claw of the Ape," she repeated to herself, thinking. She looked over at Beni, who was hovering at the edge of the table. "Have you ever heard of the Claw of the Ape?"

Beni came from a family who had been entrenched in Egyptology for over one hundred years; his grandfather and great-grandfather had pioneered the plundering of ancient gravesites until somewhere in the 1930s, his family joined forces with the museum rather than work against them. Consequently, Beni had grown up knowing more about Egyptology than most Egyptologists and he knew more about the collection in the Cairo Museum than most of the curators. He thought hard on Dr. el-Shabheen's question.

"Do you recall The Mamas Tablet that we have in storage, Dr. el-Shabheen?" he asked her. "The Mamas was brought from the expedition of Dr. Gentry back in the 1950s. As I recall, he was excavating far to the south near Amada just below the second cataract. As I remember, The Mamas Tablet had a mention of an Ape's Hand. Could it be the same?"

Alia blinked her great green eyes as if suddenly remembering. She stood up and Fox with her. "Yes," she murmured, looking at Fox. "I had forgotten about The Mamas Tablet. We have not had it on display in many years but it does make mention of an Ape's Hand."

Fox was riveted to the information. "It has to be the same," he said. "The reference is so remote; I've never heard of anything else described as an ape's claw or hand. What does it refer to?"

Alia shook her head, looking to Beni. "Do you remember?"

Beni shook his head. "I do not."

Alia looked back to Fox. "Then let us go and see." When they began to move away from the table, Alia held out a hand to Morgan. "Only Dr. Henredon. We do not allow civilians in the archives."

Fox opened his mouth to put up a fight but Morgan put her hand on his arm, squeezing gently.

"That's fine," she said evenly. "I wouldn't be any help, anyway. Can I wait here?"

Alia nodded. "Please," she said, looking to Fox with a hint of warmth in her eyes. It was evident that she was pleased to have him to herself. "Shall we go?"

Fox nodded, but not before kissing Morgan very sweetly in front of Alia. His message was clear. He turned back to Alia and motioned towards the door.

"Let's go," he told her.

Some of the warmth was gone from Alia's expression as she

headed out the door. Without benefit of words, she had gotten Fox's message loud and clear. Beni scampered after them as they left the room, leaving Morgan sitting alone in the neat office.

Morgan sat there for about five minutes before she stood up and began pacing the floor. She was nervous and excited to see if they could figure out a piece of the puzzle. She began to wonder how Fanny must have felt, surrounded by Egyptians who more than likely only wanted to be with her for the money she could provide them, offering what service they could and perhaps false interpretations of questions she might have had. Morgan knew that although Egypt around the turn of the twentieth century was undoubtedly an exciting place, it was also a very dangerous place.

Her great-grandfather seemed to have really loved his wife so it was difficult for Morgan to imagine that he would willingly put Fanny is such danger. But, then again, if Fanny was anything like her great-granddaughter, then she was a willful and stubborn woman, and Louis probably didn't have much say in what she did.

Pacing Dr. el-Shabheen's office for a few minutes only made her more bored and edgy so she decided to head out into the museum and take a look around while she was waiting. Emerging into the museum from Dr. el-Shabheen's office, she came to a kiosk directory and found her way to the Old Kingdom artifacts section.

Once inside the avocado-painted walls of the gallery, she settled in to visit display after display; a necklace and earring set from a King's Valley tomb, a statue found at a dig near Saqqara. All things ancient and Egyptian met her gaze and she found herself looking for symbols that matched the symbols on her papyrus. She kept looking for a link. But her thoughts were suddenly interrupted when someone screamed.

Morgan's head came up from the case she had been looking at, straining to catch a glimpse of the source. About fifteen feet away, an elderly Caucasian woman suddenly fell to her knees as a young Middle Eastern man yanked a purse from her arm. The kid took off at a run, smacking the woman's elderly husband as he went. As the old man fell back on something undoubtedly priceless, Morgan kicked off her platform sandals and barreled after the thief.

The young man was fast but without her shoes, Morgan was faster. Moreover, there were patrons in the lobby of the museum that slowed the youth's flight. When he bashed into an elderly Muslim woman and teetered, Morgan launched herself and tackled him.

The young man was taller than she was but he was very thin. Morgan wrapped her elbow around his neck and put him in a chokehold, keeping him on the ground as museum security began descending on them. She squeezed hard enough to cause the young man to pass out just as one of the museum guards hit her on the shoulder with his baton. Furious, she grabbed the baton and turned it on guard, cracking him over the head. The man went down and the entire museum was in an uproar.

Someone pulled her up by the waist and Morgan began shouting that she was a Los Angeles police officer. A couple of the guards spoke English and beat back the other guards who didn't. While the English-speaking guards tried to figure out what happened, the young man on the floor came around and several of the museum guards hauled him to his feet and dragged him off.

There was a great deal of chatter going, now including the elderly couple who had been mugged in the gallery. They were from Florida, shaken but not really hurt, and Morgan went out of her way to comfort and protect the old couple from the harsh Egyptian guards. The Egyptian sense of security and justice was different from what it was in America; it clearly wasn't innocent until proven guilty. The guards were wondering what the Americans did to provoke it.

All in all, it was a chaotic scene, made worse when the man who was evidently Head of Security tried to kick Morgan and the old couple out of the museum. Morgan let the man have it, telling him in no certain terms what an idiot he was. Muslim countries, including Egypt, didn't tolerate outspoken women very well and the Security Chief, an older fat man with bad teeth, had enough of Morgan's anger and slapped her across the face to shut her up. She attacked the man, sending him to the ground, and someone called the Cairo Police.

The situation went from bad to worse.

———

In the archives of the Cairo Museum, Fox had no idea what was transpiring in the lobby. He, Alia and Beni had managed to locate The Mamas Tablet with the help of one of the archivists, who brought the piece out from its storage place, wrapped in protective casing and surrounded by bubble wrap. The archivist set it out on a table for them and very carefully unwrapped it until the entire tablet was exposed to the light.

Fox put on his reading glasses as he moved in to get a good look at it. Alia collected a soft bristle brush from the archivist and brushed gently on the gray stone surface.

"Nice," Fox commented. "I've heard of The Mamas Tablet but I've never seen it. Limestone, isn't it?"

Alia nodded. "Very old limestone," she replied. "This was found near Amada, a Middle Kingdom Fortress near the second cataract. I've asked the archivist for the full translation of the text."

Fox bent over the stone, slowly reading the ancient and

faded symbols, as the archivist came around again and handed the translation to Beni. He handed it to Fox, who immediately began to compare it to what he saw on the table.

"'One will build the Walls-of-the-Ruler, to bar foes from entering Egypt; They shall beg water as supplicants, So as to let their cattle drink. Then Order will return to its seat, While Chaos is driven to the fortress of the Ape's Hand to the west; a valley by which the Brave shall Live Forever.'"

Fox's head shot up, his gaze fixing on Alia. "It's a canyon to the west of Amada," he said quietly. "Since Amada sits on the east side of the Nile, it must be on the bluffs to the west."

Alia watched him carefully. "You know the region?"

He nodded. "Remember that I was on a dig in Edfu for three years. I know it pretty well," he was beginning to get excited. "There are big bluffs on the west of the river there and several small canyons as I recall."

"I know this," Beni suddenly hissed. "I did not think at first... it did not occur to me, but I have heard of this before *Khmsh 'Ṣāb' Mn 'Ābl,* or Five Fingers of the Ape, is an ancient burial ground for the soldiers who manned the fortresses along the upper Nile. It is a canyon with five small offshoots, like fingers. They ancients used to call it Five Fingers of the Ape."

Fox grasped the man's arm. "Where is it?"

Beni began pointing to the south. "Not far from the ancient city of Amada," he told him. "I believe it is to the northwest, on the left bank of the Nile, but I will let you know for sure."

He darted off, winding his way back into the archives and disappearing. Fox turned to Alia curiously and was about to speak when Beni suddenly reemerged, this time with a big leather-bound book in his hand. He was reading and walking at the same time and remarkably not crashing into anything. Fox waited patiently while Beni flipped pages around until he came to what he was looking for.

"Ah," he pointed to the page. "Here it is. Dr. Gentry wrote of the location in 1953 in his book entitled *Egyptian Antiquities* that the Five Fingers of the Ape was located approximately two miles north and west of the city of Amada, away from the Nile in the Upper Nubian badlands."

Fox stared at the man, a faint smile coming over his lips. He shook Beni's hand. "Thank you," he said sincerely. "You've saved me weeks, if not months, of research."

"But what is it all about?" Alia wanted to know. "What does it mean?"

Fox turned to the woman, knowing he wasn't going to divulge his purpose, not after seeing her reaction to Morgan. He'd known Alia a long time and knew she could be petty and underhanded; he'd seen it. So he did the best he could in trying to throw her off the track.

"I'm not sure yet," he said honestly. "I've been researching a project and this was a part of it I was unable to figure out. You and Beni have been a huge help."

Alia smiled. "I am glad," she said. "Is there anything else I can help you with?"

It was a leading question; he could just see it. He turned around and looked at Beni. "You seem to be the man with all the answers," he said. "How would you like to help me with my project?"

Beni absolutely glowed. "It would be an honor, Dr. Fox," he nodded eagerly, looking to Dr. el-Shabheen for approval. "Dr. Alia must give permission, of course."

Fox looked at Alia, who was mildly perturbed that he hadn't asked for her help on the project. "Beni is knowledgeable, no doubt, but I could probably provide more assistance," she insisted. "What kind of project is it?"

Fox cast a glance at Beni. "Would you give us a moment, please?"

Beni, realizing he was being asked to leave so Fox could discuss private matters with Alia, made a mad dash for the archive entry. He skittered past rows of shelves containing priceless artifacts, past the archivist who watched him flee with a queer expression on her face. When Beni had cleared the room and the archivist disappeared into another part of the storage area, Fox let down his guard.

"Alia, I think it would be best if you allow Beni to help me with this," he said frankly. "You know as well as I do that you would be uncomfortable around Morgan and I won't let her be put in that kind of position."

Alia tried to pretend she didn't know what he was talking about. "I'm a professional, Fox. My personal feelings have nothing to do with...."

He cut her off. "They have everything to do with it," he told her. "You and I dated for a few months, had a good time, and that was the end of it. I've tried to maintain a friendship with you over the past few years because I like you and we have a lot in common, but that's where it ends. It will never be anything more than that and I've told you that time and time again. I'd like Beni's help, not yours, because I think it would be extremely disrespectful to Morgan to work with you on this project. You would constantly be viewing her as competition and I won't stand for it. Is this in any way unclear?"

Alia's face was pale by the time he finished. She met his obsidian gaze for a few moments before averting her eyes, looking at anything other than his piercing orbs.

"I'm sorry," she said quietly. "I didn't realize my feelings for you were still that obvious."

He tried to feel sorry for her but couldn't quite bring himself to do it. "You're a married woman," he reminded her. "And I will soon be married as well. It's been over between us for years and the sooner you get that through your head, the happier we'll both be. Grow up, Alia. Please. I need for you to."

Her eyes snapped to him, a flash of fury in the green depths that quickly cooled. After a moment, she sighed heavily and looked away, laboring to compose herself. "If that's how you feel, then I'll do my best," she said. "I don't want to lose your friendship."

"And I don't want to lose yours. But if you keep this up, I'll cut it off without a second thought."

Alia simply nodded, fidgeting around until finally lifting her head and smiling bravely at him. "Of course you can have Beni," she said, more at ease than she had been since he had arrived. It was apparent that his words had impacted her and she was trying to relax. "But if you need my help, my offer stills stands."

He smiled at her. "Thanks for everything."

She patted his arm and they turned away from The Mamas Tablet, heading for the door of the archive area. "Your fiancée is quite lovely," Alia commented. "But I was honest when I said that I didn't believe you were the marrying kind."

He grinned. "I didn't think so, either," he admitted. "But she changed that."

"She's American?"

"Yes," he replied. "From Los Angeles."

Alia lifted her eyebrows. "And just where do you two plan to live? I would say you have a logistical problem."

He laughed. "I told her I'd move to Los Angeles but she said she would move to England," he shrugged. "I'm not sure where we'll end up, but we'll be together and that's all that matters."

Alia put her hand into the crook of his elbow as they quit the storage area. "Ever the romantic, Fox. You were always good with sweet words."

"I'm even better when I actually mean it."

Alia laughed as they entered the dark, cool corridor that led to the main part of the museum. Just as they began their walk back to Alia's office, Beni came running at them from the far end of the corridor.

"Dr. Fox!" he cried. "You must come!"

Fox felt a stab of fear. "What's wrong?"

Beni was waving his arms. "Your wife is in trouble," he told him. "I do not know what trouble, but she is in trouble."

Fox took off at a dead run. "Where is she?" he roared.

"The lobby!" Beni cried.

Alia couldn't keep up with Fox but Beni could. The two of them raced through the corridor, into the rear section of the museum and through the main corridor into the lobby area. There were guards and people everywhere and several Cairo police officers. Fox plowed into the crowd, tossing people aside in his search for Morgan.

As big a man as he was, he was extremely strong and extremely formidable. People started to scatter as he began shouting her name.

"Morgan!" he bellowed. "Mor-!"

A cry went up, cutting him off. He saw a blond head in the sea of dark-haired people and he shoved anyone aside who got in his way until he came to Morgan. He threw his arms around her, noticing almost immediately that she had an angry red welt on her left cheek. He grabbed her face to get a better look.

"What in the bloody hell happened?" he half-demanded, half-pleaded.

Morgan was still furious from all of the hassle going on and struggled to stay calm. "I was in one of the galleries when some-body mugged an old lady," she explained, pointing to the elderly couple a few feet away. "I ran after the guy and caught him, only the museum guards saw it and they thought I was attacking him. I've tried to explain what happened but they want to take me to jail."

Fox's dark eyes were blazing. "Nobody is taking you to jail," he growled. "What happened to your cheek?"

She made a face. "The fat-ass Head of Security slapped me," she told him. "I was trying to tell him that...."

It was all Fox needed to hear. He let her go, turning for the group of police and security guards behind him and, spying a fat man with gold braiding on his uniform, plowed through the group to get at him.

Morgan saw what was happening and she ran after him, putting herself in the very precarious position between Fox and the security chief. Men were jostling, yelling, and somewhere on top of it Beni and Alia were trying to calm everyone down. Still, Morgan's only focus was on Fox.

"No, Fox," she insisted, pressing herself up against his chest in an attempt to stop his charge. "Please; let's just get out of here, okay? If you assault this man, they'll throw us both in jail and we'll never get out."

Fox's teeth were grinding. "He's not going to get away with hitting you."

She put her hands on his face, forcing him to look at her. "Please *don't*," she hissed. "We've only got six weeks together here and I don't want to spend five of them in an Egyptian jail."

Through his haze of fury, he could see her point. He struggled to calm down. "All right," he murmured, taking a deep breath to steady himself. "Don't get upset. We'll get the bloody hell out of here."

Morgan simply nodded, holding on to him tightly because she was afraid he was going to go on the rampage again. As big as he was, she was sure he could plaster pretty much everyone there and not even break a sweat. She didn't want the man to end up on the gallows for murder.

"Come on," she begged. "Let's go."

He nodded his head, herding her away from the shouting guards and aggressive police, moving towards Alia because he hoped she could help defuse the situation. He was almost to Alia when he suddenly noticed that Morgan was shoeless.

"Where are your shoes, love?" he demanded.

She looked at her bare feet. "I kicked them off in the gallery so I could run," she said. "I dropped my purse there, too."

By this time, Alia was listening. "What gallery?" she asked.

Morgan pointed off to her left. "Middle Kingdom, I think. It's the gallery with the green walls."

Alia leaned over and said something to Beni, who went on the run to retrieve the items. Meanwhile, the cops were getting restless and Alia started yelling at them in Arabic, pointing to the main doors vigorously. It was apparent that she was telling them to leave but when they pointed at Morgan, Alia evidently knew the right thing to say to shut them down.

While all of this was going on, Morgan left Fox's side to go over to the elderly American couple who had been assaulted, gently assuring them that everything would be all right. Fox watched her deal with the couple, his heart swelling with love and pride at her sweet, professional manner. Simply watching her lovely lines and deep dimples relaxed him, centered him. He felt whole and calm as he watched her.

But his calm state was rattled when a Cairo policeman approached her and barked something about the "transient couple". Whatever he meant, Morgan's manner turned from soft to rock-hard in a split-second and she got in the man's face about it. It was like watching a beautiful kitten turn into the Tasmanian Devil.

Fox stepped in when things got heated and the policeman couldn't move fast enough in the opposite direction. As Alia continued to struggle to calm everybody down, Beni came racing from the Middle Kingdom gallery with Morgan's shoes in one hand and her big black Dolce & Gabbana purse in the other.

Morgan took the shoes and slipped them on, reaching out to take her purse. But the moment she grabbed it, her eyes widened and she swiftly open the purse up.

"Oh, my God," she hissed.

Fox looked at her. "What's wrong?"

She looked up at him with such shock that it physically rocked him. "The journal," she gasped. "It's not in here."

Fox's face turned shades of red and he suddenly turned to the group of people wrestling and shouting in the lobby. He lifted his big arms to get everyone's attention.

"Nobody is going anywhere!" he bellowed, then looked to Alia with an expression of vengeance she would never forget. "Lock this place down."

She did.

Mr. Arak has explained to us that ancient Egyptian kings were seen as gods, all sons of Mother Isis. He also explained that most kings were brothers and fathers of one another, which I find odd and uncomfortable. Dear Louis believes that the kings of Egypt were great sinners, but even so, I am increasingly enamored with this country!

~ FS

EIGHT

FOX GOT out of the shower to find Morgan huddled up on the couch in their hotel bedroom, sobbing softly as she gazed out over the moonlit Nile.

He sighed faintly, a towel wrapped around his waist as he dried his black hair with another. He paused, watching her sniffle into a tissue as she looked out into the Egyptian night. He wasn't sure what to say to her, knowing her heart was broken. With another sigh, he tossed the hair-drying towel back into the bathroom and went over to her.

There were three bright lights on in the room. He turned off two of them as he made his way over to her, creating a romantic dim atmosphere in the bedroom. He went to his knees beside the couch, wrapping his arms around her and burying his face against her soft shoulder.

"Why don't we go for a moonlit ride along the Nile?" he asked, kissing the exposed skin on her shoulder. "We can find a cozy little romantic restaurant somewhere and have dinner."

She sniffled into the tissue, her eyes running over with tears. "I can't believe someone stole it," she whispered. "Why would they take it? It doesn't mean anything to anyone other than me."

He hugged her gently, kissing the side of her head as she wept. "I don't know, love," he murmured. "Alia and her people searched the museum from top to bottom and it wasn't there. It's possible that someone stole it out of your purse and ran off when you were distracted with the security guards. I just don't know why someone would take a ninety-year-old journal."

She wiped at her eyes as she turned to him. "My wallet was in there, my credit cards, and those weren't taken. Nothing else but the journal."

He nodded. "I know," he wiped at a stray tear on her temple. "The thief probably doesn't even know what he has. He probably just grabbed the first thing he could and ran."

She agreed with him. "This is my profession, you know," she cast him a long glance. "You'd think that I would evaluate this more clinically. I'm sure it was just a theft of convenience and I made it easy for them by dumping my stuff to go run after that mugger."

He lifted an eyebrow. "You can't beat yourself up because you reacted the way you are trained. You saw a crime and you went to help."

She half-shrugged, half-nodded, and wiped her nose with the wadded tissue. "They'll probably try to sell it," she said. "Maybe in the Cairo bazaar or on the black market. Maybe we should check all of the antique stores in the area. It's not like the Cairo police are going to do anything about this since I'm on their shit list now."

He chuckled. "I wouldn't worry about that too much." He kissed her dimpled cheek, wet with tears. "Alia's already put out the word to all of the dealers she knows in the city and she probably has more contacts than the police do. But I'm more concerned right now with getting some food in you and getting a good night's sleep. We can't do anything tonight about it, anyway."

She sniffled sadly, turning back to the view of the moonlit city. She leaned back against him and he pulled her close against his naked chest.

"I'm really glad you're here," she whispered.

He kissed her head, her neck. "I'm glad I'm here, too," he said. "Speaking of which, I didn't have a chance to tell you what we found out about the Claw of the Ape."

As he hoped, it distracted her. He hadn't mentioned it before now because she had been so distraught about losing the journal, but now seemed like the perfect time.

"What did you find out?" she asked, perking up somewhat.

He wriggled his eyebrows and stood up, going to his suitcase to get some clothes. "Very interesting stuff," he told her, digging into the bag. "Did you hear us talking about The Mamas Tablet?"

She nodded. "What about it?"

"Well," he began as he pulled out his boxer briefs and dropped the towel. "There is a place in Upper Egypt called *Khmsh 'Ṣāb' Mn 'Ābl*, or Five Fingers of the Ape."

"Really?" her eyes widened and her tears disappeared. "What is it?"

He pulled on the underwear and went in search of his pants. "It's an ancient burial ground for the soldiers who manned the fortresses along the upper Nile. It's actually a canyon with five small offshoots, like fingers. They ancients used to call it Five Fingers of the Ape, or as I suspect, the Claw of the Ape."

She was awed. "So we have a starting point," she jumped up and ran to find her laptop. "Did you look it up on the map?"

He shook his head as he pulled on a pair of casual jeans. "I haven't had the opportunity yet."

Morgan found her laptop buried in her suitcase and she pulled it out, booting it up. Setting it down on the desk as she pulled up a chair, waiting for the icon screen to come up, she watched Fox as he finished dressing by pulling a stylish shirt on. However, he left it unbuttoned, exposing his magnificent chest, as he went over to the desk and leaned over her, watching the screen come alive. Morgan could feel the heat from his body.

"Uh...," she clicked on the internet icon as he hovered. "We're not going anywhere if you walk around like that."

"Walk around like what?"

"Half-naked. You know what that does to me."

He grinned and began to nuzzle her neck. "Good," he nibbled on her tender flesh. "My mojo is working on you."

She laughed. "Of course it's working on me."

He continued to nuzzle her neck and shoulder, coming to a sudden halt when confronted by an angry bruise on the top of her left shoulder. He sighed heavily.

"What in the bloody hell is this?" he asked.

She had no idea what he meant until she got up and looked in the mirror. Then she shrugged and went to sit back down in front of the computer.

"One of the museum guards belted me with his nightstick," she said. "I took it away from him and hit him over the head with it."

He stared at her. "Are you always so casual about a fight?"

She looked at him, meeting his black-eyed gaze. "I'm a cop," she said matter-of-factly. "It's part of the job."

He sighed, resting his chin on her undamaged shoulder. "I'm going to have to get used to this, aren't I?"

She nodded, eyes glued to the computer screen. "Yes."

"What if I don't like it?"

She grinned. "Like or not, you're going to have to deal with it."

He made a face. "What if I want you to work in a nice, safe little job?"

"Then you're going to be disappointed."

He grunted with some frustration. "But you're such a tiny little thing, love," he didn't want to start a fight with her. "You can't be more than an inch or two over five feet. I'm scared to death that you're going to get hurt."

She was typing furiously. "I'm five feet two inches tall, one hundred and six pounds of tiger meat," she told him frankly. "I can take down a man twice my size, including you. Do you want to find out?"

He laughed at her. "No, I don't," he assured her as he began nuzzling her neck again. "At least, not in the manner you're speaking of."

Chills ran down her spine and she shivered, smiling because he was nuzzling and snickering at the same time. "Smart man," she muttered.

He heard her. "Speaking of smart, didn't you tell me that you had a degree in Law?"

She nodded as she stopped typing and started reading something on the screen. "I got my undergrad in Political Science and my Masters in Law," she replied. "Why?"

"Then why not become a barrister? That's a nice, safe job and you'd still be helping people."

She stopped reading and looked at him. "You're not going to let this rest, are you?"

He kissed her dimpled cheek. "Only because I love you."

She pursed her lips at him. "I love my job, Fox. You're going to have to accept that for now."

He grinned, kissed her on the nose, and shut his mouth. She turned back around and they began reading the computer screen together.

She had produced an earth-mapping website that brought up satellite images of the world. Morgan zeroed in on Egypt and together they mapped their way down the Nile until they reached Edfu, which Fox was very familiar with. Even further south was the Upper Nubian Desert and Fox began to map out the area around Amada. Morgan eventually got up from the chair, giving the computer over to him so he could scrutinize the landscape.

Using the measuring tool on the mapping program, he was able to reduce his search area significantly. Although the topography had changed significantly in four thousand years, he couldn't imagine an entire canyon would be swallowed up by the desert. He studied the screen closely as Morgan went into the bathroom to shower and change. By the time she came out, wrapped up in a big white towel, he was still seated in front of the computer.

Morgan went to her suitcase and began to pull out an outfit. She alternately dug around in the suitcase and watched the back of Fox's head.

"Find it yet?" she finally asked.

He nodded slowly but didn't speak. Curious, Morgan left her clothes laid out on the bed and went to stand next to him, trying to see what he was seeing. It was then that she noticed he had the copies of the papyrus spread out on the desk next to him along with the leather-bound notepad where he kept all of his notes.

"What are you doing?" she asked.

He grunted as if she had broken his train of thought. Then he shifted, looked at her, and wrapped an enormous arm around her waist before looking back to the screen.

"I am trying to piece together these clues using satellite images," he told her, pointing to the computer screen with the pencil. "Here's what I believe to be the Five Fingers of the Ape. See it here?"

She peered closely at the screen; it looked like desert to her, the way the erosion patterns and drainage patterns made feathery lines over the sand. But she could see the area he was speaking of; it did, indeed, look like an oddly—shaped hand with five fingers. She put her finger on the computer screen, right on top of it.

"This?" she asked.

"Right."

She pulled her finger away. "It really does look like a hand," she agreed, then looked at the notes and papyrus copies he had spread out. "Isn't the next step the city of Ranthor?"

He nodded. "Yes," he was evidently swept up in his thoughts. "On a good day at a normal pace, one could cross between twelve and twenty miles of the desert on foot. The papyrus says that it takes ten days as the sun sets to reach the holy city of Ranthor, which puts us somewhere in the middle of the Godforsaken Nubian Desert. Not a rat or a bird lives in that desolate area. There's no oasis or natural springs that I know of. It puts the holy city out in the middle of nowhere, literally."

Morgan gazed at the screen. "What does it mean 'ten days as the sun sets'?"

He shrugged. "I'm presuming it means that you travel east each day due east until the sun sets."

She thought a moment. "I'm no archaeologist so I'm sorry if this is going to come across as stupid speculation, but what if it doesn't mean what you think it means."

He pulled his glasses off. "Explain."

She shrugged, wrapping an arm around his big shoulders as she pondered her answer. "Well," she cocked her head. "What if it means just heading in the direction of the setting sun and not traveling every day, due east, until the sun sets. Would that make a difference?"

He looked at her a moment before putting his glasses back on and focusing on the screen again. As Morgan watched, he used a measuring tool on the mapping program to plot several courses to the northeast.

"The earth was rotated differently four thousand years ago," he told her. "There was much more of a tilt, so the sun would set at a different angle than it does now. More than that, the Sahara was actually sub-tropical for millions of years, pretty much until the end of the last ice age. Up until six thousand years ago, it received monsoonal flow. It's only within the past five or six thousand years that the Sahara has turned into the desert we know today."

Morgan watched him map. "Then maybe in pre-dynastic times, the city of Ranthor wasn't out in the middle of nowhere. Maybe it was in a green valley or oasis."

He nodded. "Absolutely," he said firmly. "I'm not sure why that didn't occur to me until now."

"Maybe because I've been crying over a lost journal and you've been distracted."

He grinned as he continued to map out the eastern Egyptian desert. "I've been distracted with you but it doesn't have anything to do with a lost journal."

Morgan grinned in response, moving away from the computer to go and finish dressing. She went back into the bathroom to pull her long hair into a stylish ponytail and do her makeup, emerging back into the bedroom to put her clothes on.

It was a mild evening outside so she pulled on a soft green sheath dress that hugged her curves and a pair of flashy silver pumps that were about five inches high. Putting on a pair of glittery silver earrings, she was on the hunt for a smaller purse she could carry when Fox suddenly spoke.

"I think I may have something," he stated, still staring at the computer screen. "Ten days travel from Amada to the northeast would put us about ninety miles northeast of Aswan. It's a very rocky area with mountains and canyons but, as I recall, there is a spread out population of Bedouins."

She pulled out a small silver purse from her suitcase and began to put things in it. "Do we go investigate?"

He nodded, eyes glued to the information in front of him. "Absolutely," he confirmed. "But not before I figure out the last part of this papyrus."

"Can we eat dinner before you do?"

He took off his glasses and rubbed his eyes, realizing he had been quite swept up in the task. He pushed himself to relax a little. "Of course," he replied. "Ready for that romantic walk by the Nile?"

She nodded. "I am," she replied, her mind drifting to the journal again. "But I have to tell you, the love of this search has kind of gone out of me without Fanny's journal. That was the most important part and now I just feel kind of empty."

He turned around, rising out of the chair and taking a step when his eyes fell on her and he realized how good she looked. He staggered and put a hand over his chest.

"Bloody hell, woman," he exclaimed, his obsidian eyes drinking her in. "Do you have any idea how beautiful you look right now?"

She cast him a coy glance, grinning with a flash of deep dimples. "Thank you very much."

Fox forced himself to move forward, inspecting every inch of her. "God, you're gorgeous."

She turned to him to display the outfit, turning a slow circle so he could see everything. "You like?"

His eyes were fixed on her fantastic legs and sexy shoes. His heart was literally pounding with excitement.

"You seriously have to ask that question?" he snorted, putting his hands on his hips as he continued to inspect her.

"I've only ever seen you in jeans or coats or sweaters, and you have by far the best legs I have ever seen in my life. Why in the hell do you cover them up? There should be a law against that."

She stopped prancing around and snickered softly. "Thanks," she said sincerely. "I'm glad you think so."

He swooped in on her, going for a lusty kiss but she turned her head and he ended up kissing her cheek. "You'll mess up my lipstick," she told him.

He growled. "I don't give a bloody damn about your lipstick."

He slanted his lips over hers hungrily, tasting the fruity flavor of the lipstick along with her sweet musky taste. The kiss was hot and forceful and in little time, Fox picked her up and laid her on the bed, covering her with his enormous body and ravaging her with his mouth. Morgan very quickly gave up protesting the fact that she would have to redo her makeup and hair, and as his shirt and her dress came off, she gave herself over to his lust completely. With the moonlight streaming in through the window and illuminating their naked bodies, it was a perfect, sensuous night.

They were deep into heated, sweaty sex when there was a knock on the hotel room door. Fox pretended like he didn't hear it until the knock came again, louder this time. He paused in mid-stroke, his head coming up from where it had been buried against Morgan's shoulder, and their eyes met.

"Bloody hell," he hissed a curse. "Are you kidding me right now?"

She didn't know why, but she started to giggle. Maybe it was the completely aggravated look on his face that set her off. "Maybe it's important," she suggested, biting her lip.

The knock came again and he reluctantly pushed himself off of her. "It better be bloody well critical," he growled, looking around for his pants and quickly pulling them on. "It had better be a message from God himself or heads are going to roll."

He was genuinely angry and Morgan pulled the sheet over her body, pressing her hands against her mouth and laughing silently. She could hear him grumbling as he passed through the living room and to the door. When he opened the door with a "what the hell do you want?" greeting, she burst out into soft laughter. She just couldn't help it. But she made sure the giggles died down before he came back into the bedroom.

By this time, she was laying there with the remote in her hand and had turned on the television. She could see Fox in her peripheral vision as he entered the room.

"Well?" she wanted to know. "What did God have to say?"

He didn't say anything, which made her look over at him. When she did, he held up something in his hand. Morgan recognized it as Fanny's journal immediately.

"He said to give you this."

Morgan bolted up, sheet wrapped around her body as she reached for the journal with both hands. Fox handed it to her and together, they set it on the bed between them.

"Who brought it?" she demanded, inspecting the cover to see if there was any damage.

"The night manager," he replied. "He said that someone dropped it off at the front desk and said it was for me."

"Who?" she was fired up. "Who was it?"

He put his hand on her arm. "I don't know, love," he replied steadily. "The night manager said that the man ran in, dumped it on the desk, and took off. No one had ever seen him before."

She was furious and grateful at the same time. "I'm going to get dressed and go down there and find out what I can," she replied as she was already climbing off the bed. "I want to find out who did this."

He grabbed her arm before she could move away. "Why?" he asked.

She froze, looking at him as if he were crazy. "*Why?*" she repeated. "Because stealing is a crime. Moreover, I want to know why they took it."

"Isn't it more important that it's been returned?" he asked. "You have the journal back. That should be all that matters."

She didn't understand why he was so casual about the whole thing. "I want to know why they took it," she insisted. "Maybe there's something more...."

He put both hands on her arms, pulling her between his legs. One giant palm went to her cheek. "Sweetheart," he interrupted patiently. "Listen to me; you're going to waste time chasing after some thief who probably won't tell you anything. Like you speculated, it was probably just a crime of convenience. While you were off rumbling with the Egyptian police, some thief slipped in and stole the journal, thinking it was something of value. When he realized it wasn't anything of worth, he returned it. End of story. Even if you find who it was, you know that the Cairo police aren't going to prosecute them."

She stared at him, realizing he was more than likely right. She had the journal back and whoever stole it was long gone by now. As she started to calm, something more puzzling came to mind.

"You mentioned that the night manager said that whoever dropped the journal off said it belonged to you?" she clarified.

He nodded. "That's what he said."

She cocked her head. "*How* did he know it belonged to you?" When he looked rather blank, she pressed. "If it was stolen out of my purse by a random thief, how did he know to return it to you?"

Fox shook his head, stumped. "I have no idea."

It didn't make any sense to Morgan but she was beginning to agree that interrogating the hotel staff and running off in search of the thief wasn't the best course of action. Her gaze moved to the journal on the bed.

"Something isn't making sense," she murmured, moving to sit on the bed beside Fox. "Something's not right. I don't know what it is yet, but give me time. I'll figure it out."

He stroked her back comfortingly as she opened up the journal and began inspecting it page by page to make sure nothing was missing or out of place. Then he kissed her on the temple, stood up, and went to retrieve his shirt.

"Does it look intact?" he asked.

She nodded slowly as she carefully turned page after page. "It looks like it's been leafed through, but nothing seems to be missing."

"Thank God," he pulled his shirt on. "All things considered, do you at least feel better now?"

Again, she nodded, coming to the last page of the journal and running her fingers over the dark stains on the page. There was sadness in her touch and, perhaps, a silent apology to Fanny for letting her precious journal get stolen. But there was also gratitude for the reunion. Then she looked up, suddenly noticing he was dressing.

"What are you doing?" she asked.

His dark brow furrowed. "What do you mean?" he asked, watching her point to his shirt, his pants. "I'm getting dressed. Let's go eat."

She sat there a moment, looking at him, before setting the journal aside. Then she shifted and the sheet fell off of her chest, exposing her luscious bare breasts. Rising to her feet, she let go of the sheet and walked towards him, the sheet falling to her feet, until she came to stand in front of him. With their height difference, she came to his sternum. Reaching up, she unbuttoned the two buttons he had fastened and pulled open the shirt. Naked, soft and warm, she pressed herself against his torso and began to sensually kiss his flesh.

It was all the enticement Fox needed to drop the shirt and his pants, in that order, pick her up and carry her back over to the bed to finish what he had started.

DECEMBER 5, 1922

Great and sorrowful news today. I have discovered that I am with child and dear Louis insists we return to England right away. Although I must leave Egypt, I have made Louis promise that we shall return very soon. There are tears in my eyes as I think of leaving my beloved pyramids behind.

Farewell, Egypt!

~ FS

NINE

"SO HIS QUESTIONS were based on this... this old book?" Alia was shuffling through page after page of photocopies of Fanny Sherburn's journal. "Why is he asking such questions?"

The door to Alia's office was closed lest anyone see what she was doing. Beni stood over her desk, watching her examine the copies of the pages of the journal he had swiped from Morgan's purse. A few quick copies, a few coins to a homeless boy to return the journal, and no one would be the wiser. At least, he hoped not. He was feeling rather dirty for what he had done. But Alia had insisted.

"If you read the pages closer to the end, you will see that the woman mentions the Claw of the Ape and something else," Beni pointed out. "She mentions a papyrus."

Alia looked up at him. "I read that for myself," she said. "But what papyrus does she mean?"

Beni shook his head. "I don't know," he said honestly. Then he began to shuffle through the pages on her desk. "But there's some kind of translation in the journal that is said to be from a papyrus and Fanny Sherburn keeps mentioning her search for the tomb of the Lady of Heaven."

Alia snorted. "Isis?" she said. "Do you believe he's seriously looking for the tomb of Isis? He knows better than that. I wonder what that woman has been telling him to send him off on a futile chase like that."

Beni merely shook his head, watching Alia sort through the copied pages. He had his own opinions, of course; he had been around years ago when Fox had been working in Edfu and he had worked by the man's side in a joint venture between the Bolton and the Cairo Museum.

He remembered how Alia had been smitten with the man, someone she had dated when they had been in school back in England and someone she had never quite gotten over. Fox was never impolite with Alia but he never encouraged her, either. The appearance of Fox's fiancée yesterday had Alia reeling. Beni could just see the wheels turning in her brain, deeply threatened by the beautiful, blond, American woman.

"He has asked me to assist him in his project," Beni told her. "Perhaps I will know more once I find out what this project is."

Alia thumped the pages on the table. "If what this journal says is true, then he is searching for something that doesn't exist," she insisted. "Being led astray by a woman who has him by the genitals. You saw how he behaved yesterday when she got into trouble. He's obsessed."

"If he is going to marry her then I would suspect he is in love with her," Beni said quietly, watching Alia flame. "Perhaps it is just best to leave well enough alone. I did what you asked yesterday; I went through her purse and brought you the journal. Now you can see for yourself what is happening. Perhaps you should just leave it alone."

Alia's jaw ticked. "I knew he was on to something when he came here yesterday," she muttered. "I knew that woman had something to do with it. Fox Henredon would not have come to

Egypt just to ask random questions if there wasn't something bigger involved."

"But the journal?" Beni began to straighten up the copied sheets. "It belonged to a woman named Fanny Sherburn who toured Egypt ninety years ago. She speaks of searching for the tomb of the Lady of Heaven, referring to a papyrus that she had purchased in Cairo that gave clues where to find it. If Dr. Fox has the journal to guide him on this quest, do… do you suppose that Dr. Fox has the papyrus with him, too?"

Alia looked at him as if the thought hadn't occurred to her. "Do you think?" she repeated, more to herself than to him. "If it even exists, it would be foolish of him to have brought it into this country. If Customs found it, they would never return it to him."

Beni simply shrugged. "Perhaps if I help him with his project, I will have more answers for you," he suggested again.

Alia nodded, looking thoughtful as her focus returned to the copies of the journal. She picked them up, thumbing through them pensively.

"I will make sure these are put in a safe place," she said. "You will work with Fox and see for yourself what this is all about."

"What if he has a papyrus?"

Alia lifted an eyebrow. "Then an anonymous call to the Supreme Council of Antiquities should take care of it. They'll send the police to pick it up and he won't have it for long."

Beni looked dubious. "Is that necessary?" he asked, knowing he was treading on thin ice. "If he brought it into this country, then it obviously belongs to him. It is not as if he stole it."

Alia's expression shifted, a hardness coming to her features as if she were dealing with the most idiotic person in the world. "It would be a shame if the police knew that it was you who stole Fox's journal," she snapped, jabbing a finger at him. "You will do what I say, Beni. Get out of my sight."

Beni opened the door to the office quietly and left before she could use him for more of her dirty work. He wasn't really afraid of her, but she meant what she said. She never threatened unless she intended to follow through.

Torn, somewhat disgusted, Beni did the only thing he could do. He did what he was told.

OCTOBER 18, 1923

Egypt again!

After nineteen days at sea, we have finally docked in Cairo. Mr. Arak was again waiting for us and now he and dear Louis seem to have settled their differences. I am thrilled to be here once again and to introduce my son, William, to this great and mysterious land.

~ FS

TEN

THE NEXT DAY dawned warm and clear and after a light breakfast, Fox took Morgan down to the oldest marketplace in Cairo, the Khan el-Khalili bazaar.

He hadn't deciphered anymore of the clues since last night, particularly the last part, because he wanted the opinion of a man he'd known since his days digging at Edfu. Like many of the antiquity dealers in Cairo, this man came from generations of dealers, the same family in the same business for hundreds of years. Like Beni, he knew more about Egypt and antiquities than many Egyptologists. Since Fox wasn't inclined to solicit Alia's help again, he had decided to search out his old dealer friend.

His friend's family business was in the Khan el-Khalili bazaar, which served a double purpose for him — Fox realized that he and Morgan spent the entire previous day moving from one crisis to the next. He wanted to spend at least one day with her that didn't involve a calamity or a mystery. He'd go see Allahaba and spend money on Morgan at the same time.

Before leaving the hotel, Morgan absolutely refused in no uncertain terms to leave the journal or the papyrus behind.

After what had happened the day before, she was terrified that they would disappear from the hotel room. So she shoved the journal into a big straw bag and Fox took the papyrus with him. They caught a taxi at the hotel and headed over to the great Khan el-Khalili bazaar.

Dressed in a sweet sundress with her hair in a lovely braid and a big straw hat on her head, Morgan looked like a doll. Fox was positive he couldn't be any more in love with her than he already was but he was wrong. Every day, every hour, saw his feelings for her deepen. He was having the time of his life.

The taxi dropped them off curbside in front of the busy marketplace. Fox climbed out first with the papyrus in its case in one hand and extended the other to Morgan. She put her small hand in his and allowed him to help her from the cab. All around them was the dirt and bustle of modern Cairo, very much a third world country but very much alive. It was smelly, polluted and loud. Morgan clutched her purse tightly against her body as Fox took her hand and led her into the mass of stalls, products and people.

"This is the oldest bazaar in the city," he told her as they entered the mouth of the bazaar. "It was built in the fourteenth century by the Turks when the Ottoman Empire ruled the country and Cairo was a major crossroads for trade. Parts of this place are centuries old."

Although it was mostly open air, it had apparently once been enclosed because brick walls that were centuries old surrounded them, creating space that held dozens of merchant stalls. Amidst the dirt and clutter, there were some lovely items and Morgan stopped to look at a locked acrylic case full of gold chains and bracelets. Fox peered over her shoulder.

"See anything you like?" he asked.

She nodded. "All of it. It's beautiful."

Fox turned to the man behind the counter and began chatting to him in Arabic. Morgan abruptly found herself with several different gold chains for inspection, all of them lovely and carefully crafted. The owner's wife pulled out the stops and brought out gold earrings and other precious baubles and when all was said and done, Morgan walked away with a gorgeous necklace and earring set. She packed them carefully away into her straw purse.

"Thank you," she said to Fox. "Where'd you learn to speak Arabic like that?"

He grinned. "Remember that I was in charge of a dig in Edfu for three years," he said. "I can say 'dig faster', 'stand back', 'my camel moves faster than you do' and 'you're fired' and really make it sound like I know what I'm talking about."

She laughed at the comical way he delivered his lines. "Impressive," she said. "But you really didn't have to buy me anything."

He winked at her. "I know," he replied. "But it's been a long time since I've been able to buy anything for the lady in my life. Don't deny me the pleasure."

She grinned. "If you say so."

"I do."

She studied him as he collected her hand and they continued into the dusty bowels of the bazaar. His comment about a lady in his life brought about her curiosity, things they hadn't really talked about during the fantastic week they spent together in Britain.

"It's *that* time, Dr. Henredon," she said as they moved deeper into the bazaar.

"What time?"

"Time for total truth. You said you're all for honesty in a relationship."

He cast her a sidelong glance. "I am," he agreed. "What do you want to know?"

"When was your last girlfriend and how serious was it?"

He thought on the question a moment. "About eighteen months ago," he told her. "And it wasn't too serious, at least not for me. She, however, had us married almost the moment we met."

"Was it a bad breakup?"

He shrugged. "As bad as most I suppose," he looked at her. "What about you? When was your last boyfriend and just how serious was it?"

"Hold your horses, bucko," she threw out a block, watching him grin. "I'm not done with you yet."

He snorted. "All right," he conceded. "Keep going. What else do you want to know?"

She looked thoughtful. "I'm going to go out on a limb and say that you haven't been living the life of a hermit for the past eighteen months."

"No," he said honestly. "But I'll wager that you haven't been, either. So answer my question; when was your last boyfriend and how serious was it?"

Morgan's reply was casual. "Nine months ago," she said. "It wasn't too serious. He was a nice guy but he wanted to party constantly. It was like he never moved out of the Frat house. Every night was a party and at my age, I just wasn't into it."

Fox digested the statement. "I know what you mean," he said. "Sometimes I think I'm the most boring bloke in the world because I work, I go home, I go to the gym on occasion, I sleep and eat, and that's about it. But right now, my career is very important to me."

"But you do date?"

He nodded. "If a worthy candidate comes along, I do," he said. "At least, I did until I met you. But I really hate dating."

She laughed. "Me, too."

He squeezed her hand. "But what you and I are doing... I don't consider it dating. I consider it a relationship."

She smiled at him. "That's because it is."

He kissed her hand and held it possessively against his big chest as they passed beneath a beautiful archway, Moorish in design with lovely turquoise tiles, all part of the original marketplace built by the Turks so long ago. In spite of its age, the arch was beautifully intact. Fox was looking up at the arch as he spoke.

"Is there anything else you want to know?" he asked.

"Yes," she replied without hesitation. "Where did you get your unique first name?"

He smiled, tearing his attention from the archway to look at her. "It was my mother's maiden name," he told her. "All of my brothers have old family names as well; Chase, Marsh, Chat and Lowe."

She lifted an eyebrow. "Very unique," she said. "Are all of them as big and good-looking as you are?"

His grin broadened. "Of course not," he joked. "I'm the Adonis of the group. Now let's talk about you. Where did you get your name? That's not a standard American girl name."

Morgan grinned at him. "You're not going to believe this, but my father is a huge Old West buff. I'm named after Morgan Earp because I was supposed to be a boy. My older brother's name is Wyatt and my younger sister's name is Josie."

Fox looked at her with a big grin on his face. "You're certainly not a boy."

She laughed. "No, I'm not, but until Josie was born, my dad had Wyatt and Morgan in the family. He was thrilled.

Fox chuckled. "Morgan Earp was a lawman, wasn't he?"

"Yes."

"So you take after him not only in name, but in career choices."

She grinned, her dimples deep. "If you know anything about Old American West history, then you know he was murdered by outlaws."

Fox made a horrific face. "God, I can't even think about it," he shuddered, eyeing her as she strolled beside him. "Are you sure I can't talk Officer Sherburn into taking a desk job after we're married?"

She snorted. "First of all, it's Sergeant Sherburn and secondly, my name probably won't be Sherburn unless you're comfortable with your wife keeping her maiden name."

His eyebrows flew up. "You're a sergeant?"

She nodded. "I am," she said, amused. "Why do you look so shocked?"

Fox's jaw was hanging open. "Well... well, *because*," he didn't want to offend her but he had a big opinion to share. "You're such a pretty little thing, love. You should be a movie star or a supermodel, not a constable."

She shook her head, smiling. "Yet I'm not," she lifted her shoulders. "I told you that you would have to get used to it. I am what I am."

"Now you sound like Popeye the Sailor."

Morgan laughed. "Good one," she said as she wriggled her eyebrows. "I'm hip to your American cartoon references."

"Believe it or not, we've seen a few American cartoons in England."

They laughed at each other, Fox eventually falling silent because there really wasn't much more he could say on the subject of her profession without risking offending her. He'd already expressed enough concern about it. So he kept his mouth shut as they moved into a large section of merchant stalls, basically no more than shanties with piles of local and imported merchandise.

This was a more chaotic section, a sort of low-rent district, and Morgan was assaulted by a ten-year-old girl who sold her a giant straw bag for about two American dollars. Fox shook his head at her for being a sucker until the same little girl plied him with merchandise until he ended up buying Morgan a gorgeous sundress made from a gauzy lavender material. He bought her some scarves, too, piling them all in the new giant straw bag. Morgan wondered aloud who was really the sucker between them but had at least stopped fighting him about buying things for her. He seemed very happy about it so she let him.

The large, open market packed with stalls emptied into an old building that was also set up with several ancient and mysterious shops. Fox took a corridor that led to the left, taking her down a narrow, arched walkway, passing a couple of shops, until they came to an arched doorway that looked as if it were hundreds of years old.

The open door was splintered and warped, anchored to the wall with ancient hardware. Fox led her inside the shop but that's as far as they got; Morgan was immediately interested in all of the beautiful merchandise so he left her inspecting the goods as he made his way into the smelly depths of the shop.

Morgan had her hands on a beautiful vase, listening to Fox call for someone. It wasn't long before his calls were answered and suddenly, a handsome, slender man in flowing white robes appeared in the door at the rear of the shop. He saw Fox and his eyes bulged.

"Fox!" the man boomed. He rushed at Fox, grasping the man by the arms and trying to kiss him on both cheeks, but Fox was so tall that he had to bend down to assist. "It's been years, my friend, years. Where have you been keeping yourself?"

The man was chattering nonstop as Fox patted him on the shoulder. "In England, buried in a museum," he said, smiling. "How have you been? You look well."

Allahaba ibn Sula still wasn't finished patting, hugging or

otherwise touching his long-lost friend. He was average in height, in his late forties, with a neatly trimmed beard and mustache, and moved with the agility of a cat. And it was clear that he was very happy to see Fox again.

"Life is good," he informed Fox. "Allah is kind. The children are growing up and I am growing old. And you? How have you been?"

"Great," Fox motioned to Morgan, who put the vase down and made her way to him. "My work with the museum is going great and life has been really good. In fact, I want you to meet someone."

By this time, Morgan appeared at Fox's side, smiling at the dark-skinned merchant. Fox put his arm around her shoulders.

"Al, I'd like you to meet Morgan." He felt a great amount of satisfaction introducing her. "Morgan and I are getting married. Morgan, this is my good friend, Allahaba ibn Sula."

Allahaba, in an uncharacteristic Muslim greeting, shook Morgan's hand gently. His tanned face was alight with surprise and delight.

"Morgan," he repeated the name as if he rather liked it. "It is a pleasure. I am so happy to meet you."

Morgan's dimpled smile grew. "Thank you," she said sincerely.

Allahaba shook her hand a moment longer, as if inspecting her, before releasing her hand and looking to Fox. "She is very beautiful," he said. "You are a fortunate man."

Fox nodded, feeling puffed up with pride. "Believe me, I know."

"When is the happy occasion?"

Fox cast a glance at Morgan. "Well," he began. "I was hoping in the spring, but to be honest, all I've done is bully her about it. I haven't even officially asked her. I don't even have a ring yet but I was...."

Allahaba suddenly threw his hands up, startling Morgan so that she actually flinched. "Wait!" he exclaimed. "I have something for you!"

In a rush, he sprinted to the rear of the shop, leaving Morgan and Fox looking somewhat curiously at each other. Fox simply shrugged his shoulders, listening to Allahaba rummage around in the back. There was some banging going on, something fell to the floor, and somewhere in the chaos was a muttered word that sounded suspiciously like a curse. It was fairly comical and Morgan struggled to suppress her giggles, lowering her head when Allahaba bolted back in their direction so he wouldn't see her smile.

"It's here!" Allahaba held up something neither Fox nor Morgan could see. "I thought perhaps I had moved it, but I had not. It was well-hidden."

They still had no idea what he was talking about as he rubbed the edge of his sleeve over something they couldn't make out. Finally, a small wooden box emerged in his hand and he held it up, mostly to Morgan. When he spoke, it was with less enthusiasm and more intensity. The change in his manner was evident.

"My family has been traders for generations," he told Morgan, his dark eyes glimmering. "My ancestors brought caravans across the desert into Egypt to sell wares and treasures from faraway lands. The treasure in this box is no exception; my grandfather's grandfather purchased it from the last of a great noble Roman family, a treasure that had been in their family for centuries."

Morgan and Fox watched curiously as Allahaba took the lid of the box, revealing the trinket inside. It was a magnificent gold ring with a massive diamond crowning it. Morgan gasped with delight as Allahaba pulled it out of the box and carefully set it in the palm of her outstretched hand.

"The ring is at least two thousand years old," he told her, watching the thrill in her expression. "When my grandfather's grandfather purchased it, it was without the stone so he set a great diamond within it and hoped to sell it, but alas, he did not. This is a Roman wedding ring, something that has survived the centuries as a symbol of strength and everlasting love. I want you to have this, Fox. It is my gift to you for your wedding. It will bring you luck."

Fox was stunned. He took the ring out of Morgan's hand to inspect it; the band was about six millimeters thick, with exquisite vines and tiny grapes, all of it embracing the brilliant diamond on the crest. There were even tiny horseheads and a miniature banquet scene etched along the band. The detail work was astonishing on the dark and very yellow gold. All in all, it was an absolutely exquisite piece. He looked at Allahaba.

"This is a magnificent artifact," he said. "It belongs in a museum."

Allahaba shook his head. "It belongs on your wife's hand. You are an archaeologist, Fox. You understand the meaning of all things old and timeless."

Fox wasn't sure what to say. He looked at the ring again, at Morgan's face as she inspected it, and felt a little overwhelmed. "Of course I do," he groped for words. "As a scientist, if I had the means to buy any ring at all for my wife, it would be something like this. I look at it and all I can see is immortality. That's what every marriage should be; immortal."

"Then you will take it. I insist."

"It's priceless, Al."

"Give it to her."

Fox scratched the back of his neck, almost nervously. "I told you; I haven't even officially asked her yet," he said "I'm not sure this is...."

Allahaba threw his arms up again, causing Morgan to flinch

for a second time as he went tearing back through the shop and out the back entrance. He left Morgan standing there, confused, with the ring still in her hand and Fox wondering how on earth he was going to accept such a priceless artifact as a wedding gift.

Truthfully, the ring was perfect. Fox couldn't have selected something better had he traveled the entire world looking for it. He wasn't exactly sure he could turn Allahaba down, however, the man was insistent and, in fact, the artifact did belong to him. He could do with it as he pleased. As Fox internally debated the situation, Morgan stirred beside him.

"What do we do?" she whispered.

Fox shook his head. "I have no idea."

"Where did he go?"

"Beats the bloody hell out of me."

She was trying not to giggle again. "Has he always been that flighty?"

Fox nodded, making a bit of a bewildered expression. "Always," he said quietly. "But he is one of the most honest, generous people you'll ever meet."

"I believe it," she whispered, looking at the ring again. "Have you ever seen anything like this in your life?"

He shook his head slowly. "Not outside of a museum." He studied her expression as she looked at the ring. "Do you like it?"

She couldn't take her eyes off it. "It's the most beautiful thing I've ever seen."

Suddenly, voices arose from the rear of the shop. They could hear Allahaba chattering in Arabic and a woman's voice chiming in. The voices began to rise in tone and a few things were slammed around, causing Morgan and Fox to look at each other in concern. But Morgan couldn't help the giggling when a woman began yelling in Arabic and there was a loud slapping sound. She almost lost her composure, gripping Fox's forearm for support as giggles overwhelmed her. Fox, too, fought off a grin as Allahaba appeared in the rear of the shop with a short woman in tow.

The woman wore the traditional *burqa*, covering everything but her face. Allahaba had her firmly by the arm, dragging her with him until they reached Fox and Morgan. The woman fussed and slapped at him until they came to a stop, at which time she looked rather chagrined when she realized she had an audience. Allahaba indicated the woman at his side.

"Dr. Fox, you remember my wife, Ziva?" he asked.

Fox nodded. "*Salaam*," he greeted the woman.

She smiled shyly at Fox, nodding her head slightly at Morgan as if very embarrassed by the behavior these people undoubtedly heard. Allahaba shifted his grip on the woman, putting his arm around her shoulders as his brown eyes twinkled.

"My wife and I are honored to witness your proposal," he said. "Now that you have a ring, there is no longer any reason to delay."

Fox looked at Morgan, surprised, as Morgan gazed back at him with wide eyes. But there was humor in her expression and Fox broke into a weak smile.

"I'm not sure I wanted spectators when I did this," he whispered.

She fought off a grin. "Feeling rushed?"

He scowled gently. "God, no."

She just looked at him, expectantly, and he knew it was because he had been intimating or otherwise suggesting marriage since practically the moment they met. Now, with the spotlight on him, he was hesitant and she found it very funny. Maybe she even thought he would back off.

He was about to disappoint her.

OCTOBER 23, 1923

Today, Mr. Arak took us to a friend of his at the Khan el-Khalili bazaar. We were introduced to Mr. Sula, a man whose family has been in the antiquities business for three hundred years. Imagine that! Mr. Sula presented us with a papyrus that is said to describe the tomb of the goddess Isis. Dare I believe him? I must convince Louis to purchase it for me!

~ FS

ELEVEN

SILENTLY, Fox reached out and plucked the magnificent antique ring from the palm of Morgan's hand. He inspected it closely, all the while thinking what he was going to say to her. Even though he'd been engaged once, he hadn't actually proposed; *she* had. Therefore, this was virgin territory. He wanted to do it right.

"I don't even know where to start," his eyes came up from the ring, focusing on Morgan's beautiful face. "All I can tell you is that the moment you walked into the museum twenty-nine days ago, it was like I was reborn. I can't even remember when you haven't occupied every thought of every moment of every waking day. You've made me experience joy and contentment like I never knew existed and it's occurred to me that, for the first time in my life, I actually know what it's like to be in love. I've never really known that feeling until now. I can't think of a greater honor than becoming your husband, Morgan. I really hope you'll give me that privilege."

By this time, the humor was gone from Morgan's face and she was watching him with great crocodile tears in her eyes. She blinked and they spattered onto her cheeks.

"That is the sweetest thing I've ever heard," she whispered. "Are you sure?"

"Never more sure of anything in my life."

"You're not just saying all of this because you've got a million dollar ring and an audience?"

The corner of his mouth twitched. "I'd say it without either of those things. I'm saying it because I feel it in my heart."

She wiped at her wet cheeks. "I feel it, too," she murmured. "Of course I'll marry you."

Fox grinned, full on, and swept her into his big arms, holding her off the floor. Morgan wrapped her arms around his neck, hugging him tightly, listening to Allahaba translate Fox's proposal and Ziva bursting into happy tears.

Both Morgan and Fox laughed as the woman wept, eventually losing themselves in a kiss that was powerful and passionate, full of emotion and feeling. Fox kissed her cheeks, her forehead, finally setting her gently to her feet and slipping the ring onto her left hand. It was a snug fit but not uncomfortable. Morgan watched him kiss the ring after he slipped it on her finger, giving her a confident wink for good measure.

"There," he turned to Allahaba and his wife with a mixture of irritation and joy. "Satisfied?"

Allahaba clapped Fox on the arm in congratulations while his wife wiped at her cheeks. She said something to her husband in Arabic and rushed off to the rear of the shop, disappearing through the back door. Allahaba began to pull Fox and Morgan with him.

"Come," he told them. "Let us celebrate this wonderful day. My wife will bring us refreshment."

Fox couldn't refuse so he took Morgan by the hand as Allahaba led them into the rear of the shop where a big, cluttered table and a few ratty chairs await. A fat, gray cat sat upon a stack of old books, dozing, and Morgan stroked the cat as she took a seat.

Morgan kept looking at her ring as Fox chatted with Allahaba, thinking the whole situation felt surreal. She was so happy that she literally felt as if she were walking on clouds; there was a tremendous lightness in her heart. It was all happening so fast but she knew that it was right. It had been right from the beginning. All joy aside, however, she reminded herself that she and Fox were here for a very serious reason. She struggled not to lose sight of it and hoped Fox wouldn't lose sight, too.

Morgan continued to sit silently as Fox and Allahaba caught up on the past few years. Every so often, Fox would wink at her or squeeze her hand, letting her know she was not forgotten. As the sun hit its peak in the smoggy Cairo sky, Ziva and two young girls brought out trays of food and drink. Ziva produced a very dark, sweet tea and boiled fruit juice while the young girls offered Morgan a selection of something called *Halva*, which was a combination of nuts and rose water in a paste, plus *Knafe*, which was phyllo dough, sweet ricotta cheese and pistachios, and other delectable items.

Morgan took a little of everything and sipped at the dark, sweet tea as Fox began to turn the conversation with Allahaba towards Morgan's great-grandparents. It was clever the way he did it, subtle yet with purpose. With her mouth full of baklava, Morgan suddenly found herself the center of the conversation.

"So your great-grandparents were devotees to Egyptian history?" Allahaba asked her. "When did they visit Egypt?"

Morgan discreetly swallowed the bite in her mouth. "In 1922," she told him, wondering just how much she should reveal. "They visited right after they were married."

Allahaba nodded with interest. "Back in those days, the wealthy Europeans would spend their winters in Egypt and, sorry to say, buy or steal every artifact they could come across.

Belzoni and the others made sure of that," he shrugged his shoulders carelessly. "My family made a fortune off of the Europeans, especially the British. I cannot fathom the items my grandfather and great-grandfather sold to the rich, pieces of our history that should have stayed in Egypt."

Fox toyed with his teacup, knowing that Allahaba mostly meant the British. "Too bad that your family didn't keep records of what they sold," he said. "We might have an idea of what kinds of priceless pieces they had."

Allahaba lifted an eyebrow. "But they did keep records," he insisted. "Going back three hundred years, everything my family has sold is written down. I have an entire chest full of old sales records. I, too, will write down the ring I have given you and note it as a gift to a friend. That way, my children and their children will know what I have done and they will learn to be generous as well. We are blessed and, in turn, we are generous. Allah favors the generous."

Fox nodded faintly. "I'd love to see the sales records someday, especially around the turn of the century. It would be very interesting to see what kinds of items your family has sold over the years." He took a generous bite of the *Knafe*. "You were commissioned with some of the artifacts from the Edfu find, weren't you?"

Allahaba nodded. "I was," he nodded. "The Supreme Council of Antiquities allowed that I should represent a few of the pieces for them that were, in turn, sold through auction to fine collectors. Of course, it helps that I have a brother-in-law that works for the SCA."

He winked at Morgan as he said it and she chuckled. But he seemed rather bitter about the wealthy Europeans who had basically raped Egypt for artifacts around the turn of the century so she wasn't about to tell him what a massive collection her great-grandparents had accumulated. She looked to Fox, waiting for him to take the lead in the conversation. Fox caught her glance and took the hint.

"Actually, I wanted to pick your brain on something," he said to Allahaba. "I'm working on a project and it's been a bit of a puzzle."

"Puzzle?" Allahaba's eyes lit up. "I love puzzles. What do you wish to know?"

Fox didn't hesitate. "What do you know about the mythical city of Ranthor?"

Allahaba's eyebrows rose. "Ranthor?" he repeated. "It is the City of the Gods, my friend. What about it?"

"Do you believe it existed?"

"I do."

"Why?"

Allahaba lifted his hands as if grasping for reasons. "Because the Dendera Papyrus speaks of it," he said. "It is considered to be an authentic description of the City of the Gods from a reliable source, the scribe, Hepti, who served the pharaoh, Ka. Most scholars agree on this account."

"Ka?" Morgan repeated. "When did he rule?"

Fox turned to her. "He's pre-dynastic," he told her. "He preceded King Narmer, the first king of the first Egyptian dynasty. Narmer is also known as King Catfish."

"Why?"

"Because his name is written as a chisel above a catfish; hence, King Catfish."

As Morgan nodded in understanding, Allahaba continued with his knowledge of Ranthor.

"It is said that during the reign of the Gods that Egypt was very green, like an oasis, and there was plenty of water and grass," he went on. "Ranthor is said to have been in the valley of the Syene, which is rumored to be located in the Red Hills that stretch across Eastern Egypt to the Red Sea."

Morgan couldn't help it; he'd just repeated, nearly verbatim, what her great-grandmother's papyrus said and her shock was evident. She asked the obvious question before Fox could stop her.

"How do you know that it's in the Syene?" she asked. "Where did you hear that?"

Allahaba smiled at her. "My father would tell me stories about Ranthor and the Valley of the Syene," he told her, sipping on his tea. "To tell you the truth, my father heard the story from his father, who at one time was in possession of a papyrus that told a very great story. But my grandfather was a very foolish man. He fell in love with a British woman who talked him into selling her the papyrus that described the resting place of the gods."

Morgan didn't dare look at Fox; she was stunned. She sat like stone as Fox, quite calmly, sipped at his tea. If he was surprised, he didn't show it. The man had an impeccable poker face.

"Do you believe such a papyrus really existed?" Fox asked casually. "Think about it; if something like that really existed, it would advance Egyptology to unfathomable heights. It would be mind-blowing to say the least."

Allahaba shrugged. "My grandfather said that he translated the papyrus for this woman," he replied. "It spoke of the sacred Valley of Apes, of Ranthor, and of the final resting place of the most high. He called it the Lady of Heaven papyrus. In all of your studies, have you ever heard of such an artifact?"

Morgan choked on her tea, throwing a napkin over her mouth and assuring Fox and Allahaba that she was fine when they looked to her with concern. As she struggled to recover, Fox continued to remain as cool as ice.

"What did you mean by saying the final resting place of the

most high?" he asked, hoping Allahaba wouldn't notice that he didn't answer his question. "Who is the most high?"

Allahaba's dark eyes took on a distant cast. "The greatest lady of all," he assured him. "The mighty Isis."

Fox's eyebrows lifted. "Isis' tomb?"

Allahaba nodded faintly. "It is possible."

Fox pursed his lips thoughtfully but Morgan's hand on his arm stopped him from continuing the conversation. She was still coughing from having choked on her tea and he turned to her, concerned.

"Are you all right, love?" he asked.

"No," she shook her head, sputtering. "I really don't feel well. I know you haven't seen Allahaba in years and I'm sorry to cut this short, but I would really like to return to the hotel."

Fox was already on his feet before she finished speaking. "Sure," he helped her stand up, making sure to collect her giant straw purse with all of their bazaar booty in it. "We can come back and visit with Allahaba another time; let's get you back to the hotel."

Fox had all of her stuff so Morgan kept the napkin to her mouth as she continued to cough. "I'm really sorry," she turned to Allahaba. "I was hoping to get to know you a little better so I'm really sorry that I'm not feeling all that well right now."

Allahaba was following them to the door. "Not to worry," he assured her. "There will be plenty of time for us to know each other."

Morgan smiled weakly, so anxious to leave that she couldn't even describe it. She kept moving for the door with Fox and Allahaba behind her.

"Thank you," she said sincerely. "And thank you so much for the ring. It's the best wedding gift we could ever hope for. It'll be a treasure that Fox and I will keep for our children as well. Maybe we can give it another two thousand years of use in the same family."

Allahaba laughed. "You are welcome, Mrs. Fox. May God go with you."

They were at the ancient door of the shop, the warped panel that had seen better days. Morgan waved at Allahaba as Fox closed in behind her, holding her in one hand and clutching her big straw bag with the other. She continued to hold the napkin to her mouth as they wound their way out of the bazaar, fending off the children selling candy and purses as they retraced their steps beneath the big Moorish arch.

"Is there anything I can get for you?" Fox asked her gently. "Do we need to stop by a chemist on our way back to the hotel?"

She shook her head vigorously and the napkin came away from her mouth. "Did you hear what he said?" she finally burst.

He was unruffled. "I did."

She looked at him. "How can you be so calm about this?" she demanded. "He said that his grandfather sold my great-grandmother the Lady of Heaven papyrus; worse yet, he said his grandfather was in love with her!"

Fox sighed faintly as they approached the taxi stand from a distance. He put his arm around her shoulders as they walked.

"I know what he said," he replied steadily. "Let's not talk about this until we get back to the hotel, okay? We don't want anyone else catching wind of this. In spite of the size of the city, word can get around and we really need to think this through."

"But...!"

"Please, love; not a word. Not here."

She coughed, grumbled, but did as he asked. By the time they got in the taxi, she was weeping softly. He held her hand, glancing over at her now and again as the taxi sped through the Cairo streets, watching her wipe tears off her cheeks. He wasn't sure what to say to comfort her because the truth was that he was still processing everything himself. It was shocking to say the least.

The afternoon was warm and smoggy as they pulled up to the Marriott, climbed out of the taxi and went straight into the hotel. By the time they hit the modern, spacious lobby, Fox heard someone call his name.

"Dr. Fox!"

Fox and Morgan came to a halt, turning to the sound of the voice. Beni was running at them from the area of the lobby that looked like a doctor's waiting room. He appeared thrilled and excited to see them.

"Dr. Fox!" he rushed upon them, bowing respectfully to Morgan as he focused on Fox. "Dr. Alia has sent me to help you with your project. I have been waiting for you to return."

Fox eyed the man a moment. He was growing increasingly uncertain about letting Beni in on what they were doing. Anything he told Beni would undoubtedly get back to Alia. But at the moment, he wasn't sure how he wanted to proceed given the conversation with Allahaba. He needed to talk to Morgan and decide a course of action based on what she wanted to do. The situation was becoming odd and complex and, at the moment, Beni's appearance was unwelcome. He had to treat it carefully. But as he looked at the man, something even more concerning came to mind.

"Beni," he greeted evenly. "How did you know where we were staying?"

Beni's face fell somewhat as he appeared to grope for words. "Dr. Alia... she called the big hotels in Cairo until she found you. She has sent me here to help you."

Fox didn't like that answer at all. Alia calling every hotel in the city looking for him was not a good sign.

"Oh," he said, belying the irritation and concern he felt. "Well, I wish you would have just called and left a message. It would have saved you the trouble from coming to the hotel. I'm not working on the project today."

Beni's hopeful expression fell. "Oh," he suddenly looked uncomfortable and apologetic. "I am sorry to have disturbed you. Perhaps tomorrow?"

Fox nodded. "Probably," he replied. "I'll call you at the museum."

Beni nodded eagerly, his gaze moving between Morgan and Fox. "Are you shopping today?"

Fox nodded. "We are," he replied. "We just came from the Khan el-Khalili bazaar."

Beni was back to being hopeful. "Would you like for me to take you around and show you the good shopping places?"

Fox shook his head. "Morgan isn't feeling well," he told him. "I think we're going to stay here the rest of the day."

Beni looked stricken. "I see," he said, suddenly backing away from them as if he had taken too much of their time. "I will see you tomorrow, Dr. Fox."

Fox just waved a hand at him and began heading back to the elevators with Morgan in tow. The elevator door opened and they stepped in, listening to the doors shut swiftly behind them.

"That was kind of weird," Morgan said.

He looked at her. "Why do you say that?"

She shrugged. "I'm not sure," she said. "Tracking down our hotel for one. And he just seemed like he wanted to hang out with us."

Fox squeezed her hand, leaning back against the elevator and looking up at the floor numbers as they advanced.

"I thought it was strange, too," he said. "But the last thing we need is Beni hanging around right now. Although I've known him for a few years and respect his knowledge, anything I say to him will undoubtedly get back to Alia and I'm not sure I want her to know what I'm doing."

Morgan was watching him closely. "Why not?"

He didn't look at her as the elevator doors opened onto their floor. "You saw her back at the museum," he said, letting go of her hand so he could reach into his pocket for the key card. "She's still... well, anyway, she's obviously jealous of you and I don't trust her. I don't want her around you in any way, shape or form."

Morgan's eyebrows lifted. "You don't *trust* her?" she repeated. "Then why did we go to the museum and ask her for help in the first place?"

He unlocked the hotel room door and held it open for her. "Because I really thought after all of these years, she'd be over the fact that I didn't want to do anything more than date her," he said. "Obviously, she's not. She can be ruthless and bitchy, and I don't want you exposed to it."

Morgan pulled off her straw hat, setting it on the kitchenette counter. She looked up at him with her clear brown eyes. "I can't say I'd get over it, either, if all you wanted to do was date me," she said with a twinkle in her eye. "I can't fault the woman her good taste."

He smiled, setting the giant straw bag down on the couch and taking her in his arms. He just held her a moment, his forehead on the top of her head, feeling her supple body against him. The mere act of feeling her warmth and life against him settled his spirit, brought him peace, more than anything he had ever known. It was a feeling he'd searched for his entire life.

"And I probably would have hung myself if you had sent me away when I showed up at Heaven's Gate the day we met, begging to translate the papyrus," he murmured. "I think that was the best day of my life until today. It just keeps getting better and better with you."

She wrapped her arms around his neck as he nuzzled her. With their height difference, Morgan found herself staring up at the ceiling as he bent over her, swamping her with his massive presence, feeling his gentle kisses on her neck. The tranquil moment between them, however, was a cover for her rapidly-moving thoughts. Even as she stared at the painted ceiling from the envelope of his enormous arms, her mind was working furiously.

"So I'm calmer now," she said as he nibbled her ear. "What do we do about the fact that Allahaba's grandfather apparently sold Fanny the papyrus?"

He stopped nibbling and she felt him sigh. He pulled back to look at her. "Of all the wild coincidences," he muttered. "I still can't believe it. To tell you the truth, I'm not sure what we should do. Do we tell him? Do we not? I just don't know."

Morgan pulled away from him and leaned against the couch to remove her shoes. "In her journal, Fanny referred to the dealer she purchased the papyrus from as Mr. Sula. What is Allahaba's last name?"

Fox cocked an eyebrow. "Sula," he said frankly. "But to be fair, it's a fairly common Arabic name. It's like Smith or Jones."

"Still, I feel stupid for not having made the connection."

"I wouldn't worry about it. We certainly know now, don't we?"

She pulled off the other shoe. "That's for sure," she cocked her head thoughtfully. "He seemed bitter about it."

"I'd say so," he moved over to a second couch and plopped his big body down. "Given his reaction, we need to tread very carefully with this. I don't want to risk offending Allahaba. The man was invaluable to me when I was on the Edfu dig and his friendship means a great deal."

Morgan pondered his statement. With her shoes in her hand, she sat down on the couch opposite him, lost in thought.

"I don't like what he said about Fanny," she whispered. "He

implied that she coerced his grandfather into selling her the papyrus."

Fox's black eyes were soft on her. "I know, love," he agreed. "I'm sure he's speaking from his family's point of view and you know they'd be bitter about it."

"I guess so," she regarded him a moment. "What do you think we should do?"

He pursed his lips thoughtfully, looking off into the room as he thought on her question. "If it were my papyrus and my family involved, I would want to know everything Allahaba knows from his perspective," he told her. "He may have clues as to what really happened to Fanny. That's what this is all about anyway, right?"

She nodded faintly. "It's about that... and finding the end of the rainbow as far as the papyrus is concerned," she said. "I told you that for Fanny's sake, I wanted to see where the trail ended. I still want to do that."

He sighed, lacing his fingers behind his head and leaning back. "I'll tell you what I think, then."

"Please do."

"I think we should tell Allahaba we have the papyrus and what our true purpose is," he told her. "Honestly, I think finding him was a gold mine for us. He brings another perspective to the situation and more information than we could ever dream of finding. I think we need to tell him everything and ask for his help."

"Do you trust him?"

"With my life."

Morgan absorbed his advice, thinking it made some sense. The truth was that she wanted to know what Allahaba knew about Fanny regardless of the circumstances involving his grandfather. She wanted the truth, no matter what it was. She had to reconcile herself to the fact that the truth may not be as pleasant as she had hoped.

"Then why don't you call him and see if he'll come to the hotel for dinner?" she offered, rising from the couch and collecting her bag of goodies. "We can have dinner in the room and tell him everything."

Fox watched her go. "He may want the papyrus back."

She stopped at the doorway, turning to look at him. "Fanny purchased it. It belongs to my family."

Fox shrugged and lowered his big arms, standing wearily. "I'm just saying that he might want it returned," he said. "Are you prepared to do that?"

Instead of becoming angry about it, she just hung her head and looked at the shoes in her hand. Then she walked into the bedroom with Fox on her heels.

"What would you do?" she asked.

He lifted his big shoulders. "Do you really need it?"

She looked at him as she put her shoes on the floor. "What do you mean?"

"Just that — do you really need it? If so, why?"

"Because it belonged to Fanny."

"But you have her journal, which includes the translation in it. Plus, I've translated it for you and we have a photocopy of it. Why do you need the actual papyrus?"

She saw what he was driving at and knew he was right. With an irritable sigh, she plopped down on the bed and lay flat on her back, gazing up at the ceiling.

"I guess I don't," she said. "If it means that much to him, I'll give it back."

He smiled as he went over to her, staring down at her as she looked up at him. Her blond hair was spread out over the comforter like angel's wings.

"*We'll* give it back to him and tell him that it's called the Frances Sherburn Papyrus and he needs to donate it or sell it to a museum," he told her. "Don't worry; I've got your back on this one. One way or another, Fanny's memory will be honored."

She smiled up at him, though it was with less enthusiasm than usual. He knew she didn't want to give up the papyrus and was touched that she was willing to take his advice on something that meant a great deal to her. He lay down next to her, lying on his side as he threw a big arm across her torso. Morgan put her hands on his big arm, gazing out of the window and into the blue Egyptian sky, pondering the course of events. It was just too fantastic to believe and she was still trying to wrap her mind around it.

As they lay silently, eventually, Morgan began to hear Fox's soft snoring in her ear. She looked over at him, seeing that he had fallen asleep. It looked like a good idea because she really didn't want to think about the papyrus, the journal, or the odd relationship they'd just discovered with Allahaba anymore. She just wanted to shut off for a while.

Snuggling against him, she fell asleep in the warm, languid Egyptian afternoon.

OCTOBER 31, 1923

I returned to Mr. Sula today to purchase the papyrus. Mr. Arak came with me because dear Louis did not want to go. Mr. Sula offered Mr. Arak and me strong Egyptian tea and produced a translation of the papyrus. It is called the "Lady of Heaven" papyrus and is said to describe the greatest tomb of all — the tomb of the goddess, Isis. Can this be true? Something deep inside me is yearning to find out!

*   ~ FS*

TWELVE

ALLAHABA ARRIVED at the Marriott promptly at eight o'clock. Fox was waiting for him in the grand lobby and escorted him up to the hotel room.

There were candles everywhere, purchased in the gift shop earlier in the day, creating a lovely atmosphere. Morgan was in the kitchenette, setting out the last of the hors d'oeuvres they had ordered from the exclusive Saraya restaurant downstairs. Allahaba was thrilled to see them both so soon, following Fox out onto the balcony where they had a beautiful table set. Candles burned, fine china glistened, and in the velvet sky above, a big silver moon gleamed. Fox indicated Allahaba's chair and the man took it happily. As they sat, Morgan brought out the appetizers.

As Morgan moved around the table, Fox was having a difficult time focusing on Allahaba. Morgan was dressed in a form-fitting silver dress with spaghetti straps and a short hemline. On her feet were the silver sassy shoes she had worn the night before that had made her legs look so great. Fox had left to get Allahaba before she'd gotten completely dressed, so the slinky cocktail dress was a sexy surprise for him.

He'd never been so hot for a woman in his life, right now as he was entertaining an old friend, of all places. When she bent over to put the tray of asparagus with spinach and beef on the table, he deliberately ran his hand up the back of her calf; her skin was like silk. She cast him a glance, knowing what he was up to, but he did nothing more than wink at her.

"Can I help you with anything, love?" he asked innocently.

Morgan shook her head, her blond ponytail dusting her back. "No, thank you," she replied, smiling at him as he licked his lips when Allahaba wasn't looking. "You and Allahaba enjoy yourselves."

Fox watched her walk back to the kitchenette, her great butt beneath the dress, picking up his wine glass as he did so. Suddenly, the glass tipped and red wine dribbled onto his shirt.

"Christ," he hissed, setting the glass down and backing away from the table. "Sorry, Al. I'll be right back."

Allahaba waved him off; he was stuffing himself on the asparagus. Fox left the table and crossed through the living room on his way to the bedroom. Morgan, behind the counter in the kitchen, saw the mess on his white dress shirt.

"What happened?" she wanted to know.

He crooked a finger at her as he headed into the bedroom. "Can you come and help me, please?"

Morgan dropped what she was doing and followed him into the bedroom. As soon as she entered the room, he shut the door softly behind her. When she turned to help him with the shirt, he grabbed her with one arm and began ripping off his shirt with the other.

"How dare you wear something so bloody sexy when we have a guest," he growled, his mouth slanting over hers. "I'll never be able to sit still through dinner with you wearing this thing."

Morgan was giggling, trying to fend off his onslaught. "Not right now," she hissed at him. "Later; I promise."

"No," he managed to unbutton his shirt with one hand and yanked it halfway off. "Not later; *now*."

She was full-blown laughing by this time, trying to push him away. "Did you spill that wine just so you could get me in here to help you change?"

"What do you think?"

He let go of her for a split-second to pull the rest of his shirt off and she made a break for the door. He was on her in an instant, swinging her up in his arms and carrying her, giggling and all, into the bathroom.

The door shut loudly behind them and Fox set her on the bathroom counter, his mouth slanting hungrily over hers. Morgan finally gave up resisting him and gave in to his lust, her arms around his neck, holding him tightly. His hands were roaming everywhere until they snaked up her short skirt with the intention of pulling her panties off. But he suddenly came to a halt and his eyes flew open wide, looking at her with such astonishment that she started giggling again.

"You're not wearing any panties," he breathed, half-accusing and half-thrilled.

She gave him a devilish grin. "Nope."

His eyebrows flew up with mock fury. "And you were going to tease me with that all night?"

"You better believe it."

Fox cast a glance to the heavens, the most sincere look of reverence on his face. "Thank you, God," he prayed. And then the hands went back to work.

Nearly ten minutes later, Fox emerged from the bedroom with a new shirt, looking completely calm and collected. He returned to the balcony just as Morgan emerged from the bedroom, looking unruffled. She went straight into the kitchen and resumed where she left off as if nothing out of the ordinary had occurred.

Truth was, her legs felt like spaghetti thanks to two orgasms in the past ten minutes, but she put it all aside to focus on the meal. Collecting a big tray with three plates of lamb and rice on it, she carried it out to the patio.

Fox stood up again when he saw her coming, taking the tray from her. She smiled her thanks, with perhaps a little extra warmth, as she set a plate before Allahaba, Fox, and then herself. Fox set the tray aside and held her seat out for her.

"This looks delicious," Allahaba told her. "I am so glad you are feeling better."

Morgan nodded as she picked up her fork. "Much better, thank you," she replied. "Thanks for coming to dinner on such short notice."

Allahaba waved her off. "This is a delight. My wife cooks nothing but Kufta. Have you ever had it?"

Morgan shook her head. "What is it?"

"Chopped beef with cinnamon," he told her with some disgust. "It is all she knows how to make."

Morgan grinned as they delved into the lamb and rice. She ate silently as Fox and Allahaba discussed the days on the Edfu dig, the poor conditions, the food and flies. Fox and Morgan had a bottle of good red wine, sharing it between them, while Allahaba abstained due to his Muslim practice. Fox had about three quarters of the bottle while Morgan only had one glass, but the more Fox drank, the more animated he became. She remembered that from the first night they'd had dinner together at Heaven's Gate. While wine made her sleepy, wine made him happy.

Eventually, the conversation came around to their current visit to Egypt. Allahaba wanted to know what they planned to see on their holiday, at which time Morgan looked at Fox to see if he was about to bring about the true purpose of their visit. Fox caught her expression, knowing she was thinking the same thing as he was; no better time than the present to work the truth into the conversation.

"Truthfully, there's something we think you should know," he said to Allahaba. "I met Morgan in England because she came to me with an artifact her great-grandparents had purchased in Egypt."

Allahaba looked at Morgan. "Is that so?" he asked, interested. "What was the artifact?"

Morgan looked at Fox beseechingly, who answered for her. "It was a papyrus," he said quietly. "Al, there's really no simple way to explain this, so I'll just come out with it. You and I have been friends long enough that I know you'll appreciate that I'm being truthful with you. Today, you asked me if I'd ever heard of the Lady of Heaven papyrus. The answer is that I have."

Allahaba grew more interested. "Where did you hear of it?"

"From me," Morgan spoke, watching Allahaba's dark eyes turn in her direction. "My great-grandfather recently passed away and my mother and I were cleaning out his home in England. When we visited you earlier today, Fox mentioned to you that my great-grandparents spent a great deal of time in Egypt and had collected many wonderful artifacts. One of these artifacts was a papyrus and the label on it said 'Lady of Heaven'."

Allahaba stared at her. "The... the Lady of Heaven papyrus?"

Morgan nodded, feeling less intimidated to speak on the subject. "I was told that my great-grandmother had purchased the papyrus from a dealer. I was further told that this dealer translated the hieroglyphics for her and the story they told were clues to what is believed to be Isis' tomb. My great-grandmother set off in search of the tomb but she never made it. My great-grandfather told me that she died of a fever in Egypt." She sat forward in her chair, her brown eyes intense. "I have my great-grandmother's journal which records her visits to Egypt. In it, she writes of her quest to follow the clues on the papyrus but the journal abruptly ends and I believe it was because she was murdered in her search to find the truth. Fox has been helping me decipher the text of the papyrus and that is why we came to visit you today. Fox thought you could help us but when you spoke of the Lady of Heaven papyrus, we weren't sure if we should ask. That's why we left early. And that's why we invited you to dinner; so we could tell you the truth."

Allahaba was staring at her as if she had grown two heads. His stunned gaze moved back and forth between Fox and Morgan, clearly trying to reconcile everything he had just been told. After several long and tense moments, he finally shook his head. Then he reached for Fox's half-full wine glass and tossed back the contents like a shot of whiskey. He set the glass down, hard, and looked at Morgan.

"*You* have the papyrus?" he nearly demanded.

She nodded. "I have it." She watched his body language, trying to read his thoughts. "You mentioned that your grandfather had fallen in love with my great-grandmother. Can you tell me more about that?"

Allahaba was struggling to compose himself; while Fox and Morgan had had an entire afternoon to reconcile themselves to the news, Allahaba had not. It was clear he was reeling and struggling very hard not to show it. He reached for his water glass with shaking hands and drained it before speaking.

"What is your great-grandmother's name?" He avoided her question to ask one of his own.

Morgan didn't hesitate. "Frances," she told him. "But everyone called her Fanny. Did your grandfather ever mention her?"

"And you were told she was murdered?"

Morgan realized he hadn't answered any of her questions but she was trying to be polite about it.

"No," Morgan clarified. "I was told that she died of fever in Egypt. It's my belief, based on her journal, that I wasn't told the truth. I believe she was murdered."

Allahaba stared at her a moment before looking at Fox. "May I speak with you in private?"

Fox's black eyes glittered. "There's nothing you can say to me in private that you can't say in front of Morgan."

Morgan put a hand on his arm and was already rising from her chair. "It's okay," she said, hoping that Allahaba would tell Fox more about the situation if she weren't there. "I'll take care of the dishes while you two talk."

She was collecting plates and glasses. Fox stood up to help her but she shooed him away, telling him to sit. In her slinky silver dress, she went back to the kitchen and set the dishes down. Fox watched her, noting when she disappeared into the bedroom and shut the door. He could hear the television go on with the volume loud.

He returned his attention to Allahaba. "I don't appreciate you being rude to her," he said quietly.

Allahaba didn't back down and he didn't apologize. "You would appreciate it a lot less if I said to her what I am going to say to you."

"What's that?"

Allahaba threw up his hands in frustration and stood up, moving to the edge of the balcony and gazing out over the dark blue Nile. His manner was agitated.

"My grandfather was married when he met Fanny Sherburn," he told him, watching Fox's eyebrows lift. "That is correct; he was married. For whatever reason, the British woman captivated him. In little time, he left my grandmother for Fanny and you must remember that in those days, divorce was a horrible scandal. It simply wasn't done."

Fox remained cool. "You can't fault a man because he falls in love. And you can't blame Fanny because he left your grandmother."

Allahaba shook his head. "I do not blame her," he insisted. "My grandfather was a handsome man with flowing dark hair and dark eyes. He loved women and they loved him in return. Fanny, by all accounts, was a beautiful woman and very charming, much like your fiancée. When they came together, it was a terrible disgrace. My father was very young at the time but he remembered the pain the family went through because of it. In fact, I do believe that there were some attempts on Fanny's life because of it. My grandfather's wife came from a powerful family and they did not take the betrayal well at all."

Fox toyed with his empty wine glass. "So what happened?"

Allahaba turned away from the Nile to look at him. "Fanny Sherburn did not die of a fever, Fox," he said frankly. "What your Morgan was told was not true. Fanny's husband must have returned to England to tell everyone that Fanny died of a fever in Egypt because of the shame of his wife leaving him for another man. To tell others she died in Egypt is much better than saying she is living in sin with a heathen."

For the first time in the conversation, Fox showed emotion. He sat forward, his eyes wide. "It makes perfect sense," he hissed. "But he took the papyrus back to England with him. I wonder why?"

Allahaba shrugged. "What better revenge than to keep what meant a great deal to his wife and to her heathen lover?"

Fox couldn't help his surprise as he pondered the twists of the story. But there was something far more important he needed to know. "If Fanny didn't die of a fever, what happened to her?"

Allahaba moved away from the balcony and plopped into the seat next to Fox. Putting his hand on the man's arm, he looked him in the eye.

"Fanny Sherburn, my grandfather's wife, is alive and living in my home," he lifted his eyebrows at the irony of it all. "The entire time you were at my shop, she was directly above your head."

I have met with Mr. Sula regularly over the translation of the Lady of Heaven papyrus. He is helping me with the clues presented. Mr. Sula believes the papyrus is true and is willing to help guide our search. Dear Louis, however, does not believe in the clues but I am still determined to go. I feel that I must. More and more, this country is becoming a part of me

~ FS

THIRTEEN

"DR. FOX MET tonight with a man I did not recognize," Beni said. "I remained at the hotel all day, as you instructed, to see if Dr. Fox left during the day but he did not. He met a man in the lobby around dinnertime and the two of them went up to his room."

It was late, but not too late that Alia didn't want to know what Fox was up to. In the living room at her lovely home in the northern Cairo suburbs, she was in her robe as Beni huddled at her front door with the news. Exhausted, perturbed, she yanked Beni inside and slammed the door.

"This man he met with," she snapped. "How long was he with Fox?"

Beni shrugged. "A couple of hours, at least."

Alia exhaled sharply. "If you did not recognize the man, did you at least follow him when he left to see where he lived? It might give us a clue as to who he is."

Beni nodded eagerly. "I did, indeed, follow him," he assured her. "He took a taxi to the Khan el-Khalili bazaar and went to one of the shops there."

"Did you follow him into the shop?"

"I did not," he said. "I wanted to come and tell you what had happened. I know where his shop is and we can go there tomorrow if you wish. Perhaps we can ask the man a few questions and find out what Dr. Fox is up to."

Alia thought on that, growing more confused and obsessed by the moment. "You said that Fox refused your help when you offered?"

Beni bobbed his head. "He told me he was not working on his project today. He said he would call me tomorrow."

Alia eyed Beni, thinking many things at that moment; Fox, his project, the blond American whore who was with him. None of it made her happy. After several moments of deliberation, she shrugged and turned away.

"Perhaps it is nothing at all," she mused, looking up to the lovely walls of her home with the colored glass tiles. "Perhaps Fox was simply meeting with an old friend. He has many here, you know."

"An old friend who works at an antiquities shop?" Beni asked pointedly, watching her turn around and look at him. "The man I followed went into an antiquities shop called the Azraq Nahr."

Alia blinked as she recognized the name. "Azraq Nahr?" she repeated, surprised. "Blue River Antiquities has been around for hundreds of years. The Cairo Museum has done business with them."

Beni looked eager. "Do you know the man I speak of?"

A light came to Alia's eyes. It was evident that her obsession was taking dimension. "Perhaps," she said slowly, thoughtfully. "I will let you know tomorrow."

"May I go home now?"

"Yes." Alia went to her front door and threw it open. "Get out. Be at work early tomorrow."

She slammed the door in Beni's face as he was replying.

Then she went into the kitchen, poured herself a glass of beer, and plotted her next move because she knew, without a doubt, that Fox was plotting his.

———

When Fox entered the bedroom around eleven o'clock, he found Morgan asleep in her slinky silver dress with the television blasting. He smiled at her, shook his head at the irony of sleeping through such loud noise, and quietly began to remove his clothes.

The shirt and shoes came off, followed by the pants. In his boxer briefs, he quietly went to the bed and very carefully removed one of her shoes. When he went to remove the other, Morgan suddenly woke.

Her brown eyes were sleepy as she gazed up at him. He smiled at her and pulled off her other shoe, tossing it to the floor.

"How can you sleep with the television so loud?" he asked.

She yawned. "I don't know," she rolled onto her side and hugged a pillow. "I just can."

He saw that she was going back to sleep. "No, no," he grabbed her gently around the waist and pulled her up. "Let's get the dress off and get under the covers."

She grumbled as he lifted her arms and pulled the sexy cocktail dress over her head. She was completely nude beneath it and he tossed the covers back, picking her up and depositing her against the sheets. Covering her up, he pulled off his briefs, turned off the light, and slid into bed beside her.

The television went off as Fox pulled her warm, soft body against him, snuggling down against the feathery mattress. She squirmed a little, finally settling down with a sigh of contentment. Fox wrapped his big arms around her, his chin against the top of her head.

But he wasn't tired nor could he sleep after his conversation with Allahaba. He stared off into the darkness of the room, wondering how he was going to tell Morgan about her great-grandmother. It was a shocking revelation even to him and Fanny Sherburn wasn't even a blood relative. But because the situation was so important to Morgan, he felt it as deeply as she did. He was concerned how she would take the news.

"What's the matter?" she asked, muffled against his chest.

He did nothing more than caress her hip with a free hand. "Nothing, love," he murmured. "Go back to sleep."

"You keep sighing," she mumbled. "What's wrong?"

He kissed her head. "Nothing is wrong. Go back to sleep."

She was still for a few moments and he thought she had drifted off again. But her head came up and she gazed sleepily at him. "What did Allahaba have to say about Fanny?"

Fox looked at her in the darkness, knowing he couldn't defer the subject to the morning. She was asking a direct question and he suspected that if he dodged it, even to spare her feelings, that it would damage the trust they were building between them. He sighed as he gazed into her groggy face.

"Are you sure you want to hear this right now?" he asked.

She nodded, becoming more alert. "Of course I do," she said. "What did he say?"

He reached up, smoothing wisps of blond hair from her eyes, all the while thinking of how he was going to carefully couch the bombshell he was about to deliver. He decided that being straightforward would be the best tactic to take with her. Morgan wasn't a beat-around-the-bush kind of girl.

"He said a lot of very interesting things," he told her honestly. "Apparently, the romance between Fanny and his grandfather caused quite the uproar because his grandfather was married to another woman at the time."

Morgan's eyebrows rose and she sat up, propping herself up

on an elbow. "Really?" she responded, shocked. "But Fanny was married, too, to Louis. So did she really have an affair with Allahaba's grandfather?"

"It was more than that, evidently," he went on. "Do you remember in Fanny's journal where she writes about bad tidings, and we thought they were associated with the papyrus?"

Morgan nodded firmly. "Yes, I do."

"I think she was alluding to the affair." Fox shifted, putting an enormous arm behind his head and lying back on the pillow. "The papyrus is what brought Fanny and Allahaba's grandfather together, so perhaps the 'bad tidings' she mentioned in relation to the papyrus had to do with his family's reaction to what was going on. It was apparently very scandalous, to the point where the grandfather's wife's family made a few attempts on Fanny's life."

Morgan's eyebrows flew up. "I knew it!" she hissed. "She *was* murdered, but not because of the papyrus; it was because of the affair. I knew she was murdered!"

"Hold on," Fox reached out, running a massive hand down the side of her blond hair to calm her. "Apparently, Louis, shamed by Fanny's affair with the Egyptian, fled back to England, taking the papyrus and Fanny's journal with him. He didn't want anyone to know that his wife left him for a heathen so he told everyone that she had died in Egypt. Doesn't that make sense with what he always told you? Didn't you say he dodged the subject if asked a direct question?"

Morgan was stunned, enthralled, and feeling an odd sense of contentment, as if she were finally learning the truth. It was a truly fulfilling moment.

"He never gave me a straight answer to any of my questions," she agreed, pondering the great revelations. "Now it makes perfect sense. I just can't believe it."

His hand was still on her head, stroking the mussed blond

hair. "It gets better," he said. "Fanny and Allahaba's grandfather were married. His ex-wife's family never did murder her."

Morgan's eyebrows lifted. "So she *wasn't* murdered?"

He shook his head, his fingers gentle on her skull as he caressed. "No, love" he murmured. "She wasn't killed, in spite of the attempts on her life. She and Allahaba's grandfather got married and had a long life together; so long, in fact, that Fanny outlived him. She is still alive."

Morgan stared at him a moment as if not comprehending what he'd told her. When his statement finally registered, she bolted to her knees with her hands over her mouth.

"Oh, my God!" she gasped. "She's still alive?"

Fox sat up, his big hands on her arms to keep her from jumping off the bed. "According to Allahaba, she is," he kept his tone calm. "If she was nineteen years old in 1924, then she is one hundred and five years old today. That's remarkable."

Tears began pouring from Morgan's eyes. "My God," she wept. "She's really still alive?"

He smiled gently, nodding. "She is."

"Are you sure?"

"Allahaba said so. He has no reason to lie."

Morgan was furiously wiping the cascades of tears that poured down her cheeks. "Where... where is she?"

"Living with Allahaba and his family," his gaze lingered on her a moment. "When we were at his shop earlier today, she was apparently right above our heads in the apartment on the second floor."

Morgan shrieked and leapt off the bed before Fox could stop her. "I want to go see her," she demanded. "I want to go now!"

Fox threw the covers off and swung his big legs over the side of the bed. "Love, it's late," he explained steadily. "I'm sure Allahaba and his family are asleep by now, including Fanny, so it would be much better if we go first thing in the morning. All right?"

She was standing naked in the middle of the bedroom, hands to her mouth and tears on her face. But through her haze of shock and excitement, she understood what he was telling her. After a moment, she nodded unsteadily.

"O-okay," she sniffled, wiping at her face as she wandered back over to the bed. "Promise?"

He reached out, taking her by the wrists and pulling her back onto the bed. "Of course I promise," he kissed her head as he settled her down. "Lay down, now. Go back to sleep and we'll go first thing in the morning."

Sniffling, shaken, Morgan lay back down as Fox pulled the covers over her. He hovered against her, kissing her temple, gently rubbing her shoulders. She was shocked, worn out and thrilled beyond measure, which translated into a very exhausted sleep when she finally drifted off. She twitched and snored, keeping Fox up most of the night, but he wasn't sorry about it. He was just glad he could be with her to solve one of the important mysteries of her life.

NOVEMBER 6, 1923

Louis has agreed to bring William and we will all travel south to Luxor, where Mr. Sula believes the start of our search for Isis will begin. I am hoping we can find the Ape's Claw mentioned on the papyrus as our first landmark. Mr. Sula is a very nice man and feels strongly that he knows where it is. May the Gods and Luck go with us!

~ FS

FOURTEEN

THE DOOR to the Blue River shop wasn't even open when Fox and Morgan arrived early the next morning. Chains and an old lock held the warped door shut and Fox knocked heavily on it a couple of times before he began to hear someone stirring.

He looked at Morgan beside him, winking at her when their eyes met. He took a moment to inspect her as he heard someone coming for the door; he'd already inspected her about a hundred times since they woke up but the truth was that he couldn't keep his eyes off her. She was dressed in a pair of slender jeans and a gathered, pink-colored shirt that, although it didn't cling like most shirts she had, still accentuated her beautiful shape. Her blond hair was long down her back, the stylish cut with long bangs that draped down over one eye, and she wore one of the scarves that Fox had bought her the day before. It was multi-colored, matching the pink shirt perfectly.

She smiled wanly at Fox as someone on the other side of the door began fumbling with the locks. He touched her cheek affectionately, shifting the artwork case containing the papyrus on one massive shoulder as he stepped back so the door could open. Morgan stepped back also, clutching her big purse with Fanny's journal shoved deep inside. They had come prepared.

The door lurched open and Allahaba's smiling face greeted them. "Good morning, my friends," he greeted pleasantly. "It is a beautiful day today."

Fox put his hand on Morgan's back and entered the shop behind her. "Yes, it is," he replied. "Sorry we've come so early, but Morgan was hoping for a word with Fanny if she's awake."

Allahaba already knew why they were here. He and Fox had discussed it long and hard last night. They both knew that Morgan would want to see her great-grandmother, so he was prepared. When he spoke, he was fixed on Morgan.

"Mrs. Fox," he said softly. "I realize the story you have been told is surprising and I understand your need to see your great-grandmother, but there are a few things you should know about her."

Morgan glanced nervously at Fox as she spoke. "What's that?"

Allahaba began to lead them towards the rear of the shop. "First of all, she is very old. Very, very old. And she is completely blind. But her mind is mostly sharp." He looked at Morgan. "I have not told her you were coming. The time in her life when she met my grandfather is a time in which she still lives; although my grandfather has been dead for twenty-five years, she still speaks of him daily and speaks as if he is still living with us. That has not changed for her. I am not sure how she will react being introduced to her great-granddaughter from her first husband so we must proceed carefully."

Morgan eyed him as they moved around the displays, trying not to bump into anything. "You speak as if you care about her," she said. "Given her history with the family, I'm honestly surprised to hear that you're taking care of her."

Allahaba shrugged. "She is my grandfather's wife," he said

simply. "She is family. And if you must know the truth, I have become fond of her over the years."

Morgan paused as they came to the rear entrance to the shop. There was a courtyard beyond and stairs leading to a second level. She looked at Allahaba.

"Then I hope you know that I don't want to upset her," she said, her arms folded across her chest; to Fox, she seemed ill at ease. "If there's a chance she's going to get upset, I'll pass on the meeting. But if she is completely blind, I... I just want to see her. She won't even know I'm there."

Allahaba nodded, urging her forward towards the courtyard and the stairs. Fox put his arm around her shoulders and all but pushed her through the doorway.

"I have been thinking to simply introduce you and Fox as my old friends," Allahaba said. "Perhaps it will be easier on her that way. She does not need to know who you truly are and if we feel after a time she can accept the truth, then we shall tell her."

"Whatever you think is best," Morgan replied.

As they ascended the stairs, Morgan was wrought with indecision. She was excited to meet her great-grandmother but fearful the intrusion would upset the woman. Last night, she had thought only of herself when demanding to meet Fanny but upon reflection, she should have been more sensitive. In fact, she should have been more sensitive to everyone. She had plowed through this entire endeavor as if her feelings and needs were the only ones that mattered and was coming to feel some uncertainty and remorse.

As they reached the top of the stairs, the double-wide doors to the apartment were open and she could see people beyond. The walls of the apartment were whitewashed, lumpy and uneven with age, and the floor had terracotta tile that had to be decades old. But in spite of the age and leaning floor, it was very clean and airy. Morgan stopped before they could proceed any further, turning to Allahaba and Fox.

"Look," she said quietly. "I just want you both to know how extremely grateful I am for this opportunity. Allahaba, you've been utterly gracious and kind since I've known you, even when we figured out how you and I were related, and I want to thank you. Please know this means the world to me and I won't ever forget your kindness."

Allahaba smiled. "You are always welcome in my home," he told her. "Now you have made me related to one of my dearest friends, Dr. Fox. You are the tie that binds us."

She half-grinned, glancing at Fox's smiling face. "Let me see," she said thoughtfully. "Your grandfather married my great-grandmother, which makes us third or fourth cousins, I think."

Allahaba laughed. "My family will be thrilled to have an American movie star in the family."

Morgan snorted. "I'm not a movie star."

Allahaba waved her off. "All Americans are movie stars," he motioned for Morgan and Fox to continue following him to the apartments. "My children will think you are an angel because all angels have golden hair."

Morgan grinned at Fox, who bent down to kiss her on the head as they continued into the apartments. Inside, it smelled strongly of bread and coffee as the morning meal was underway. Allahaba led them into the living room space and immediately began shouting at his children, who were rushing around like mad. He started grabbing them as they ran by, forcing them to stand and face Fox and Morgan, who smiled somewhat hesitantly at the growing collection of children. When all was said and done, seven girls stood in a row and Allahaba indicated his daughters.

"My children," he said proudly, indicating the girls in order. "Abia, Aisha, Amala, Hala, Fadila, Lina and Kalila."

Morgan waved at the girls, who gazed back at her with mostly open curiosity. The two older ones looked particularly interested while the youngest girl waved back. But that all ended when Allahaba snapped at them and they scattered, running for dishes, hair brushes, and anything else they needed. Morgan grabbed on to Fox as the girls rushed past and disappeared into various rooms like mice into a hole.

"I feel like I'm caught in a tornado," she quipped, listening to him laugh.

Allahaba noted their amused expressions as his daughters disbursed. "They are good girls," he said. "Foolish, but good."

"They're all beautiful," Morgan told him.

Allahaba smiled proudly and motioned for them to follow. He led them down a corridor that paralleled the balcony outside; a couple of orange-painted French doors were open, letting air into the apartments. At the end of the hall was a door, slightly ajar, and Allahaba slowly pushed it open.

The room was bright from the early morning sun and it smelled strongly of bleach. Morgan followed Allahaba into the room, noting it was sparsely furnished with a bed, a dresser, a chair and little more. There were white curtains on a set of windows that were cracked open, letting a small amount of air inside, and the floor was clean-swept terracotta tile. Morgan spied the bed almost immediately after entering the room and stopped, staying by the open door as Fox stood beside her. Allahaba continued on to the wooden-framed bed.

"*Jadda*," he said softly. "Are you awake?"

The tiny lump on the bed stirred, moving beneath the white bedspread. Allahaba stood next to the bed, peering down at the figure. When he touched the bedspread, a thin hand suddenly appeared from underneath the covers and smacked him.

"I'm awake," the voice was thin and faint, but most decidedly British. "How can I not be awake with your herd of animals running through the house?"

Oh, but the voice was sharp and so was the mind behind it. Morgan's wide eyes tried to catch a glimpse of the woman on the bed, struggling to sit up as Allahaba bellowed for his wife. As a Muslim, he would not touch another woman other than his wife and therefore did not reach out to assist. But rather than wait for Ziva, Morgan rushed forward and grabbed hold of the elderly woman as she struggled to sit up in the bed.

"There," Morgan had hold of her wrist while she shoved a fat pillow behind the woman's back. "How's that?"

The elderly woman's sightless eyes moved in Morgan's direction. "It's very well, thank you," she said. "And you are not Ziva."

Morgan gazed into the small face that was faintly similar to her own and the tears started to come. Even the eyes were the same color, perhaps had once been the same shape. Morgan looked into the old woman's wrinkled face and saw the beauty from long ago, mesmerized by her first look at something she had only known as a family memory.

"No, I'm not," she said quietly, struggling not to sound like she was about to burst into tears. "My name is Morgan."

"Morgan?" the woman repeated. "Lovely. Who are you?"

Allahaba, a little startled that Morgan had jumped in to assist with Fanny, recovered quickly. "*Jadda,* I would like to introduce you to my friends, Dr. Fox Henredon and his wife, Morgan. Fox and I met each other in Edfu years ago. He and his wife have come to Egypt to... visit."

The elderly woman smoothed at her wild white hair, like cotton, pushing it away from her face. Then she tugged at the top of her nightgown as if to make sure she was all covered up and ready to receive visitors.

"I'm sorry you're not catching me at my best," she said in her thin but firm voice, then hissed at Allahaba. "You didn't have to bring them to my room, you know."

Morgan could see in those few gestures that Fanny was, indeed, the woman that had been described to her. There was so much bittersweet emotion in her chest that she was nearly bursting with it.

"It's my fault," she insisted. "We were shopping early and stopped by to visit. Allahaba has told me so much about you and I... I felt compelled to meet you."

The sightless brown eyes moved in her direction; Fanny's movements were sharp and bird-like. "I'm honored," she said in her clipped British accent. "Where are you from, Mrs...?"

"Morgan," she said quickly, not wanting to reveal her last name for obvious reasons. "My name is Morgan. I'm from Los Angeles."

"Ah!" Fanny's face came alive. "A beautiful place, I've been told. I never made it to America but I've seen many pictures of it. I always wanted to meet Gary Cooper. Do you know who he is?"

Morgan couldn't help the tears that were coursing down her cheeks. She could feel Fox's strong hand on her shoulder, comforting her.

"I know who he is," she whispered, struggling not to make crying noises that would alert Fanny. "He was quite a stud."

Fanny giggled like a girl. "Yes, he was, wasn't he?" her sightless eyes shifted somewhat. "Am I to understand you've brought your husband with you?"

Morgan looked at Fox, who reached up to silently wipe away the tears on her cheek. "Well, he's not my husband just yet," she said. "We're planning on getting married in the spring."

Fanny held out a thin hand with tissue-paper skin covering the bones. "Frances," she introduced herself.

Fox took the hand, so tiny and warm, and shook it gently.

He was afraid he was going crush it. "Fox Henredon," he said. "It's very nice to meet you."

Fanny suddenly cocked her head at the sound of his voice. "British?" she said, almost gleefully. "I am catching wind of a Manchester accent."

Fox wriggled his eyebrows at the sharp old lady. "A little," he admitted. "I work in Bolton but I was born in Dorchester."

Fanny closed her eyes as if envisioning his birthplace. After a moment, the sightless eyes opened. "I was born in Manchester," she told him. "When I married my husband, I never saw England again. It is the one thing I miss the most. I would have loved to have seen the green fields of Cumbria just once more before I died."

Morgan couldn't take it; she covered her mouth and turned away, struggling not to sob. Fox, saddened by her distress, took charge of the conversation.

"I used to play for a rugby club in Manchester," he told her, "but most of my time is spent at the Bolton Museum. Did you ever visit when you lived there?"

Fanny nodded. "Certainly," she assured him. "I have been there several times. My very dear friend, Annie Barlow, was one of the great patronesses of the museum and spent a good deal of time in Egypt collecting artifacts. It was visiting those artifacts at the Bolton Museum that first stirred my interest in Egypt."

Fox was watching her expression, seeing something of Morgan in the delicate features. "Do you still have family in Manchester?" he asked a calculating question.

Fanny shook her head, waving him off with a bird-like hand. "Not any longer," she told him. "Before I married my husband, I was married to another man at a very young age. I don't suppose my ex-husband or our son is still alive."

She spoke of it without particular distress, not as if she was attempting to hide it, and Fox took the lead.

"So you were married before?" he said casually.

Fanny nodded. "Long ago," she didn't seem willing to elaborate even if she wasn't concerned about hiding it. "It's been a very long time."

"And you've not had any contact with your family since then?"

Fanny shook her head. "No."

"Surely you must wonder what became of them?"

Fanny didn't reply for a moment; the sightless eyes turned in Fox's direction. "You're a nosy young man."

Fox chuckled. "Not really," he replied. "I'm just making conversation."

Morgan, who had been standing on the other side of the room as she struggled to compose herself, turned to Fox beseechingly, silently asking him not to let this line of conversation die. It would, perhaps, be her only chance to bring up the reason of her visit, something she very badly wanted to do. She didn't want to throw herself at Fanny and upset the old woman but she knew, at that moment, that she couldn't leave the room without having revealed herself. It was selfish but she didn't care. Fanny had to know.

Fox seemed to be the only one who wasn't too deeply emotional about the entire situation. Silently, Morgan pleaded for his calm and deliberate help. He read her message loud and clear.

"It has been a very long time but families live on and people don't forget those they have missed," he told the old woman. "Your name, a long time ago, used to be Fanny Sherburn."

Fanny perked up, the sightless eyes accusing. "How would you know that?"

Fox looked at Morgan, silently asking her to explain. It was time, no matter how emotional the subject, and Morgan understood that. She was up to bat. Morgan wiped at her cheeks, squared her shoulders, and approached the bed.

"Because my name is Morgan Sherburn," she said softly. "William Sherburn is my grandfather and Louis Sherburn was my great-grandfather. All my life, I had been told that my great-grandmother, Fanny Sherburn, had died in Egypt so I came to Egypt to find out what really happened to her. But instead, I found you. It was by pure coincidence, believe me. A trail of clues and an old acquaintance led us to you. I haven't come to bring you home or condemn you for leaving Louis; all I wanted to know is what happened to you. Now I know and I'm just incredibly grateful to have met you."

Fanny's thin face was a mask of shock. The sightless eyes were on Morgan, whether or not she could see her. Morgan gazed back at the woman, waiting for her reaction, feeling her stomach churn with nerves and praying that Fanny didn't kick her out on the streets. It was such a deeply personal and pivotal moment, the culmination of a ninety-year-old family mystery coming to fruition.

After several long seconds of tense silence, of bated breath, Fanny finally extended a frail hand in Morgan's direction.

"Your name is Morgan Sherburn?" she whispered.

"Yes, ma'am."

"Come here."

Morgan obeyed, moving to within reach of the woman, somewhat hesitantly, hoping she wasn't going to slap her or otherwise physically demonstrate her shock. Instead, Fanny gently grasped Morgan by the wrist and tugged.

"Sit," she commanded.

Morgan did. With wide eyes, she watched Fanny as the woman put frail hands on her shoulders. Morgan held her breath as Fanny's sightless eyes seemed to grow distant, then warm, and then the fragile hands moved from Morgan's shoulders to her face.

"I want to see you," Fanny whispered. "I didn't know I had a great-granddaughter, you know. I barely remember my son. I just want to see if you are as beautiful as you sound."

That was it for Morgan. She burst into soft tears as Fanny ran her fingers over her face, as delicate as a butterfly's kiss, feeling her round cheeks, her dimples, her nose and finally the shape of her eyes. Morgan sobbed as the woman touched her hair, seeing her with sightless eyes and imagining a young woman with beauty beyond compare. It was a deeply tender and personal journey, something the sightless old woman could never have dreamed of. And when she was finished seeing Morgan for the first time, she felt down her arms until she came to her hands and gripped them tightly.

"Tell me of my son, Morgan," she asked quietly. "The last time I saw him, he was six months old. What kind of man did he grow to be?"

Morgan was sobbing so hard she could barely speak. Tears dripped off her chin as Fox took the tissue handed to him by Allahaba and dried them off. When Morgan looked up to whisper her thanks, she wasn't surprised to see that he was teary-eyed, too. It would have been difficult to watch the reunion and not be deeply touched by it.

"He... he grew up to be a barrister," she told her. "He married my grandmother, Lucy, and they had four children, one of them being my father whose name is also William. Your son is also a painter and he does beautiful watercolors. He's a wonderful man and I love him very much."

Frances's sightless eyes glistened with unshed tears and she smiled bravely, her hands moving back to Morgan's face.

"And Louis?" she whispered, touching her cheeks. "When did he pass away?"

"In June," Morgan told her. "He was one hundred and six years old and he never remarried."

Fanny closed her eyes tightly at the news but she held herself together. She was a strong, strong woman in the best tradition of the British. Her hands moved from Morgan's face back to her hands, holding them tightly.

"Louis was a kind man," she whispered. "We were promised to each other as children and I never knew another lover before I married him. But it was expected that we marry, so I did, but it was almost as if I'd married my brother. I loved him, but not as a husband. When we traveled to Egypt and I met Kadin, it was as if my heart had wings. I didn't mean it to happen; it just did. I was sorry for the fact that I left Louis, but it was something I had to do. Had I remained with Louis, I would have been miserable for the rest of my life."

Morgan squeezed her hands gently. "I'm not here to judge you, Fanny," she said. "I know what it's like to love someone so much that you'd do anything to be with them. I can't blame you for following your heart."

Fanny smiled. "I can hear in your voice that you do understand."

Morgan caressed the paper-thin flesh, feeling the mood of the room lighten with understanding and warmth. Her tears were fading as she gazed into the old, tired face.

"I do," she said quietly. "Fox is the man who made me understand what it's like to love someone so powerfully."

Fanny turned her sightless eyes in Fox's direction. "And you, nosy young man?" she addressed him. "I would assume you feel the same way for Morgan."

Fox went over to the bed, taking a knee beside the ladies because he was far too big to sit on the bed. He put his arm around Morgan, kissing her cheek as his enormous hand covered Fanny and Morgan's intertwined hands.

"I loved her first," he joked. "I had to stalk her before she succumbed to my charms."

Fanny laughed, her teeth old and yellow but the smile still was bright. She let go of Morgan's hand and began feeling Fox's wrist. She moved up his arm, eyes widening when she realized how big he was.

"Sweet Heaven," she exclaimed. "He's a big one."

Morgan snorted. "He's huge. I didn't know the British bred them so big."

Fanny's hands were still moving up Fox's arm. "How big are you, darling?"

Fox suppressed a grin as Fanny felt up his arm. "Six feet seven inches and around twenty stone," he told her. "I'm bigger than you are, love, but not nearly as beautiful."

Fanny stopped poking at him. "Cheeky devil," she sniffed, but they could tell she wasn't serious. "A pity I can't see you. I think I'd like to."

So she was a flirt, too, even at her age. Morgan laughed as Fox winked at her, grinning, and stood up. Morgan watched him walk over and stand near Allahaba.

"I think you've scared him, Fanny," she teased. "His cheeks are red."

"I would hope so," she said. "If he's going to flirt with me, he's going to pay the price."

Morgan laughed joyously. The writings in Fanny's journal mirrored the sparkling personality of the elderly woman and Morgan was deeply in love her. There was so much life and spirit still left in the old veins and Morgan thought, at that moment, that she was the luckiest woman on the face of the earth. She got a second chance to know Fanny Sherburn.

"I'm so glad I found you," she said, squeezing the frail old hands. "I feel like this is a dream. Never in my life did I imagine I'd be sitting here, talking to you."

Fanny grinned. "You are a beautiful soul, Morgan," she squeezed her hands in return. "I am so glad I had the chance to meet you as well."

Morgan grinned up at Fox, who was smiling sweetly at the two of them. He looked at Morgan and swore he'd never seen a happier person, not ever. She was nearly bursting. He mouthed "journal" to her and Morgan nodded quickly in agreement. She returned her focus to Fanny.

"I brought something of yours with me to Egypt," she said, fumbling with the purse still strung over her shoulder. "I think you'll recognize it."

Fanny folded her hands patiently as Morgan brought forth the journal that was so old and precious. Morgan put it carefully in Fanny's lap and placed the old woman's hand on it, watching the woman's expression as she did so. Fanny ran her hands over the journal for only a few moments before her sightless eyes widened.

"This?" she hissed. "Is it… is it true?"

Morgan watched the thrill, the disbelief, in the woman's expression. "It's your journal from your trips to Egypt," she confirmed. "After Louis died, my mother and I were going through his possessions and we came across your journal."

Fanny was upswept in the journal, opening the old pages and running her fingers over them as if remembering every word, every scrap. The pages were faded and the cover worn, but to her sightless eyes, it was still as new and beautiful as it had been the last time she saw it. It was a deeply poignant moment, one not lost on Morgan or Fox. When the old woman finally spoke, it was clear she was holding back tears.

"Louis took this back with him when he returned to England," she whispered. "He took all of my possessions, in fact. He left me with only the clothes on my back. I suppose it was easier to tell people that I'd died in Egypt if he returned with all of my possessions. It was his way of saving his pride. I didn't really mind too much since I started my life with Kadin anew, but I... I've missed this."

Morgan was back to being weepy at the sight of Fanny with her journal. She knelt beside the bed, watching Fanny's expression as she caressed the pages of the old journal. It was an amazing moment as history and reality came together.

"We found something else, too," Morgan murmured. "The Lady of Heaven papyrus."

Fanny's head snapped to her, the sightless eyes glazed with shock. "You found it?"

"Yes."

"Intact?"

"Yes," Morgan replied. "Why do you ask?"

Fanny shrugged her frail shoulders. "Because... because Louis hated that papyrus," she said. "It was what brought Kadin and me together. I was sure that when he took it with him, he would destroy it purely out of spite. He hated everything it represented. Kadin had translated it for me but when Louis left, he took both the journal and the papyrus so we would not have the translations. He took everything."

Morgan glanced at Fox as she spoke. "I gathered from reading your journal that you were following the clues on the papyrus."

Fanny nodded. "I was." The brown eyes glistened with long ago memories, things she hadn't thought of in years. It had been the best time of her life. "Kadin and I began following them, positive we would make an astounding discovery. But when the scandal broke, Louis left with everything and Kadin and I decided it would be best to get on with our lives and not worry about the clues on the papyrus. There would be time later to resume where we left off, but that time never came."

"How far did you get?" Fox was standing behind Morgan,

his massive arms folded across his chest, listening to every word. "The papyrus has several major clues."

Fanny lifted her face in his general direction. "Not far," she admitted. "Kadin knew where the Ape's Claw was located, or at least he thought he did, but we went no further. I wish we had. Kadin wanted to, but he ended up having to protect me from his first wife's family, instead. It took most of his time. It was... messy, so we simply put our quest aside and forgot about it."

Morgan gazed at the old woman, digesting her words, reading between the lines. After reading Fanny's journal and with all of the pieces she had put together from the past, she understood everything perfectly. It all made sense.

"What you did for love... it's something that people write stories about," she murmured, clasping a frail old hand. "It's quite a tale."

Fanny smiled faintly; she was beginning to feel very fatigued but trying not to show it. The excitement of the past several moments had her wondering if she was dreaming. If she was, she didn't want to awaken. She could live in this dream forever.

"It was a romantic adventure," she agreed.

Morgan squeezed her hand. "It's not over yet."

"What do you mean?"

"The end of your story hasn't been written yet," Morgan insisted. "I'm going to finish it for you."

Fanny cocked her head, not understanding. "How, darling?"

Morgan smiled at the old woman even though she couldn't see her, feeling hope and joy and ambition. Everything Fanny had come to Egypt with those years ago, Morgan felt now. She was going to finish Fanny's romantic adventure with a bang.

"Fox and I are going to follow the clues of the papyrus to the end," she told her. "Fox is an Egyptologist and a very good one. If anyone can figure it out, he can. For you, for Kadin, even for

Louis and William, we're going to find what's at the end of this trail and write the ending to your story."

Fanny understood. She was both surprised and humbled. But most of her was thrilled. She took both of Morgan's hands within her thin, cold ones and brought them to her lips. She kissed Morgan's hands sweetly.

"Something *is* there, darling," she whispered. "I've always felt it."

"If it's there, we'll find it."

Fox made the declaration over Morgan's shoulder, gazing down at the petite pair. He didn't know why, but in watching the two of them, he suddenly felt more driven to follow the clues of the papyrus than even Morgan did. Morgan was right; Fanny's story needed to have an ending. As he spoke, both Fanny and Morgan looked up at him.

"I believe you will," Fanny replied, finally letting go of Morgan's hands and sinking back against the pillows. She was worn out. "I will apologize that I'm feeling my age right now. Perhaps we can continue this conversation another time."

Morgan stood up. "Of course," she said, regarding the old woman a moment. "I can't tell you what this has meant to me today, Fanny. Thank you so much."

Fanny reached up a thin hand, which Morgan clutched tightly. "And you have made me very happy," she said. "I feel... I feel as if I have come full circle somehow. May I make one request?"

"Of course."

The journal was still in her lap and she laid her hands upon it, reverently. "May...," she began again. "May I hold this for a while?"

Morgan could feel the tears again, stronger than before. "Absolutely," she whispered. "Keep it. It's yours, anyway."

Fanny smiled, sighed, and closed her eyes. "I will hold it and dream of the days when I was young and attractive, and this land was still mysterious and beautiful," she murmured. "I will see Kadin in my dreams, the tall, beautiful man with the flowing black hair. And I will see you there, my beautiful great-granddaughter with the pure soul. Will you meet me in my dreams, Morgan?"

Tears poured down Morgan's cheeks, so much emotion churning within her that she couldn't describe it. "I'll be there," she whispered.

Fanny sighed with contentment, drifting off to meet those dreams. "And bring Fox," she murmured. "I think I would like to see him, too."

"I will."

She drifted off to sleep, still holding Morgan's hand. Struggling not to let loose with gut-busting sobs, Morgan set the old woman's hand down gently on top of the journal and quietly left the room with Fox and Allahaba in tow. Allahaba shut the door softly behind them.

Once outside in the hallway, Fox stood there and held her as she sobbed deeply into his chest.

NOVEMBER 8, 1923

The journey down the Nile to Luxor has been one of the most wonderful journeys of my life. Louis and William stayed to the room but I was able to speak with many fascinating travelers as they headed south. There was even a couple from Russia! Mr. Sula has been very gracious in explaining Egyptian customs and history. Tomorrow Luxor!

~ FS

FIFTEEN

THE BLUE RIVER antiquities shop was open but no one seemed to be around. Beni stood in the front of the shop, calling for the merchant but, after several minutes of no results, moved into the back of the shop where he found a bell and started ringing. That seemed to bring a response.

A man with a manicured beard and flowing white robes came in from the rear of the shop, his dark eyes focused intently on Beni.

"*Salaam*," Allahaba greeted.

Beni bowed. "*Salaam*," he replied.

Having just come from a very emotional scene upstairs with Fanny and Morgan, Allahaba's patience wasn't at its best. He was still swept up in the family reunion ninety years in the making. He focused on the thin, older man.

"What may I help you with?" he asked tolerantly.

Beni sensed that the man was rushed, or impatient, or both, and he didn't want their meeting to start out on the wrong foot. Alia would punish him greatly if he didn't return with some information about the man and why Fox Henredon met with him. Alia had even concocted a story for Beni to relay to see what the man's reaction would be, a cover story that would sound somewhat plausible coming from a museum representative. So Beni took a stab at it.

"My name is Kasim and I work for the Cairo Museum," he said. "We suspect that a very valuable artifact is being marketed around to local dealers and we wanted to inform you so that you may be on the lookout."

Allahaba's brow furrowed. "What kind of artifact?"

Beni shook his head. "We're not sure, but we have reason to believe it's very valuable." His gaze lingered on the man, watching for a reaction. "We believe that it has something to do with *Khmsh 'Ṣāb' Mn 'Ābl*, or Five Fingers of the Ape, which is an ancient burial ground for early Middle Kingdom soldiers near the second cataract. We have information that alludes to treasure hunters or vandals who have illegally excavated in this protected area and perhaps might be attempting to sell the artifacts to reputable dealers."

Allahaba shook his head, waving him off even before he finished his sentence. "My sources are licensed through the Supreme Council for Antiquities," he said shortly. "I would not jeopardize my business so."

Beni nodded in agreement. "I understand completely," he said. "Still, there are rumors about. One of the vandals is alleged to be British, so be vigilant. You haven't met with any British treasure hunters over the past few weeks, have you? Has someone tried to sell you something?"

It was a leading, transparent question and not very well couched. Allahaba began to suspect there was more behind this man's appearance than merely to warn of suspected thieves. The mention of a British citizen was suspect, considering Fox Henredon had been in town for a couple of days. The questions were too coincidental to be merely chance and his manner stiffened.

"No, I have not," he said, clipped. "I am very busy. You will leave now."

Beni respectfully moved for the door, shooed into a faster pace by Allahaba on his heels. "Will you notify the museum if someone tries to sell you any artifacts at all?" he almost tripped over his own feet in his haste. "It is very important that we follow the trail of these suspects."

"Get out," Allahaba practically shoved Beni out of the door. "Go away."

Beni stood on the dusty walkway outside of Allahaba's shop. "Sir, you must understand this is very important."

"I understand completely," Allahaba snapped. "I will not see your face here again. If I have something I think the museum should know, then I will tell them."

With that, he turned on his heel and disappeared back into the bowels of the shop. Beni watched the man disappear through the back door, lingering in the walkway a moment before finally leaving. But he didn't go completely.

Beni found a cool corner in which to sit, watching Allahaba's door to see if Fox Henredon would make an appearance.

———

The strong, sweet tea had calmed Morgan's nerves and the delicious honey pastries had filled her belly. Seated at a clean-scrubbed table in Allahaba and Ziva's apartment, Fox sat next to her with a cup of coffee, listening to Allahaba's oldest daughters practice their English as Ziva bustled about in the kitchen. The oldest daughter couldn't quite pronounce the words "thoroughly" or "cloth", as she was having trouble with the "th" sound. It sounded like a "d" when she said it. Fox guided the girl through her English lesson as Morgan sat quietly and calmed down.

Allahaba had disappeared into the shop when a customer arrived. He made a sudden reappearance, snapping at the girls so that they fled the table. When Ziva scolded him, he snapped at her, too, and she fled the kitchen. Alone with Fox and Morgan, he took a seat opposite the pair.

"I just had a very strange visitor," he lowered his voice as he focused on Fox. "A man who said he was from the Cairo Museum came to warn me about vandals or treasure hunters selling illegally obtained artifacts."

Fox sipped his strong, black, Arabic coffee. "Why is that strange?"

Allahaba lifted his eyebrows. "Because he asked me if any British treasure hunters had been to see me, coincidentally, during a time in which you have been to Cairo. He mentioned something about *Khmsh 'Ṣāb' Mn 'Ābl* as the source of the illegally obtained treasure. Does this mean anything to you?"

The cup froze halfway to Fox's lips. He stared at Allahaba with his intense black eyes as he lowered the cup to the table.

"Five Fingers of the Ape," he muttered. Then his face screwed up in a scowl. "What in the f...?"

He trailed off, looking at Allahaba as if the man had gone nuts. Allahaba merely lifted his shoulders. "What did he mean?"

Fox was growing increasingly troubled. "Who was this bloke?" he demanded. "What did he say his name was?"

"He said his name was Kasim," Allahaba told him. "I have never seen him before. He seemed nervous, odd. But I chased him away. What does it all mean, Fox?"

Fox looked at Morgan, who was gazing back at him with wide eyes. After a moment, he sighed and returned his focus to Allahaba.

"Oh, bugger," he exhaled as he sat back in his chair and raked his hand through his dark hair. He snorted with irony and some bafflement. "This just keeps getting better and better."

Allahaba had no idea what he meant. "Fox?" he pressed. "What is it?"

Fox had a pensive, curious expression on his face, staring off to the ceiling as he collected his thoughts. "I'm not sure," he said. "But the phrase you mentioned comes directly from the Lady of Heaven papyrus and the only person I mentioned that to, other than Morgan, is a colleague at the Cairo Museum."

Allahaba's eyebrows rose. "Does the museum believe you have stolen something?"

Fox exhaled sharply and shook his head. "No," he said flatly. "But I made a big mistake when I first arrived in Cairo yesterday. I went to see a colleague at the museum that I once dated. She helped me figure out the first part of the papyrus, which refers to the Ape's Claw or, as we figured out, the Five Fingers of the Ape. But this woman still apparently has feelings for me, which makes her wildly jealous of Morgan and apparently wildly curious as to my purpose here in Egypt. Whoever came to your shop, I have no doubt she sent him, which means she's been watching Morgan and me for the past two days. She knows where we've been and who we've talked to. That's why he came to you; my guess is that he was going to try and find out what you knew about me."

Allahaba shook his head in disapproval. "She will get nothing out of me, my friend," he said. "But... the papyrus. I never did know the full translation other than what my grandfather told me. Did you translate all of it?"

"I did," Fox nodded his head, "but it's full of clues, like a puzzle, and I was hoping you could help. That's really why I came to see you yesterday before we were sidetracked with the beautiful ring you gave us. Do you remember when I asked you about the mythical city of Ranthor?"

"I do."

"Clues in the papyrus may lead to it. Would you be willing to help us follow the clues?"

Allahaba smiled. "As Fanny and my grandfather did?" he bobbed his head. "I would go to the ends of the earth, Fox. Moreover, I feel as if I should help you since you are marrying my cousin. We must keep this in the family."

Fox grinned, winking at Morgan as she sat quietly and sipped her tea. The case containing the papyrus was leaning against the wall and he collected it, putting it on the tabletop and releasing the fastens. When he finally peeled back the cover and removed a piece of soft cotton cloth that was covering the papyrus, the beauty of the amazing artifact suddenly came to light.

Allahaba stared at it, his dark eyes glittering as he beheld the papyrus that broke up his grandfather's marriage. He'd only heard of it until this point and as he gazed at the still-vibrant artwork, he was, indeed, entranced.

"Now," Fox stood over it with his hands on his hips; he hadn't brought his reading glasses so he squinted as he inspected the papyrus. "I've already translated it and it says *'Isis, Lady of Heaven, Favored of the Gods, may she be given eternal life by the Gods who love her. May she find peace within the bosom of the Most High, from the Claw of the Ape, ten days as the sun sets to the Holy City of Ranthor which lies deep to the east in the arms of the Syene, to the Fingers that Reach to the Sky. May she know grace and divine protection, our Holy Mistress, foremost Lady of the West, as she Rests in the Shelter of the Sun'.*"

Allahaba stared at it a moment longer before collecting his seat, most closely scrutinizing the lettering, the materials. He shook his head in wonder.

"This is a magnificent artifact," he breathed. "I've seen many papyruses but never like this one. It's truly beautiful."

Fox nodded in agreement, his black eyes riveted to the papyrus. "Since you can translate hieroglyphics better than I can, you can confirm my translation."

In Allahaba's business, the advanced knowledge of Egyptian history, hieroglyphics and hieratic was imperative. The truth was that he was much faster at deciphering hieroglyphics because he'd learned at a very young age from his grandfather. It was, literally, his second language and as Fox and Morgan watched in silence, Allahaba began to read.

"*Isis, Lady of Heaven, Favored of the Gods, may she be given eternal life by the Gods who love her,*" he read softly. "*May she find peace within the bosom of the Most High, from the Claw of the Ape....*" His head came up and he focused on Fox. "And you said you have already figured out where this is located?"

Fox nodded. "Near the ancient border fortress of Amada."

"That's south of Lake Aswan, south of Abu Simbel."

"Right," Fox picked up his coffee cup again, making sure it was well away from the papyrus. "As I told you, *Khmsh 'Şāb' Mn 'Ābl*, or Five Fingers of the Ape, is an ancient burial ground for the soldiers who manned the fortresses along the upper Nile. It's a canyon with five small offshoots, like fingers. They ancients used to call it Five Fingers of the Ape which, in my professional opinion, can also translate to 'Ape's Claw'. So we've figured out the first part of the text."

"I agree," Allahaba said, looking back to the text to continue reading. "*Ten days as the sun sets to the Holy City of Ranthor which lies deep to the east in the arms of the Syene.*"

Fox interrupted. "That's where we are at present," he said. "I've mapped out ten days travel from the Five Fingers of the Ape, using the angle of the sun around 2000 B.C., basically around the reign of Mentuhotep II, and figuring about twenty miles per day takes us about ninety miles northwest of Aswan."

"How did you figure the angle of the sun?" Allahaba wanted to know.

Fox shrugged. "Because we know that the tilt of the earth's axis was more severe at that time. Right now, the earth sits at about a 23.4° axial tilt. Four thousand years ago, the list was variable at about 28.26°, which caused it to rise at a more severe northeasterly direction in ancient times, or at about a 75° angle on the eastern horizon. Using that guideline, I plotted a two hundred mile course from Amada and ended up in the Arabian Desert; specifically, in the Manjam Hamsh Wilderness Area. That's the closest I can come."

Allahaba thought on that information a moment, his gaze moving back over the ancient papyrus. He fixated on the last row of hieroglyphs. "Syene," he murmured. "*Syene*. Does that not ring a bell, Fox?"

Fox's brow furrowed. "It does, but I can't place it. I've heard it before but I can't find it in any of the reference material I have. Why? Have you heard it before?"

Allahaba nodded, closing his eyes as he struggled to recollect where he had heard the term before. "When I was young, we had a woman that worked for my mother who was Bedouin. I seem to recall...," he suddenly slapped the table, startling Morgan into almost spilling her tea. He smiled apologetically at her as he returned his eager focus to Fox. "There is an ancient caravan trail in the Arabian Desert used by the Romans to transport precious stones from their mines near the Red Sea. Fox, do you not recall this? It runs from Edfu all the way to the Red Sea."

Fox's face suddenly lit up. "Yes, I do," his dark eyes were wide as recollection dawned. "The road was old even in ancient times. When we were in Edfu, we were focused on the Temple of Horus so I really didn't have the time to do any research on the ancient road but I do remember that from what I'd read, it was several thousand years old even before the Roman's used it. They used to call that road the...."

"Synethium," Allahaba interrupted him, excited. "It is a Romanized name for the existing name of the road and the region, but the Bedouin who still live there call it the Syene. They have for thousands of years."

"Bloody Hell," Fox suddenly stood up, energized, running his fingers through his black hair. His wide eyes came to rest on Allahaba. "I feel like the biggest idiot in the world. I worked near that road for three years. The Manjam Hamsh Wilderness is just to the south of the road, inland by about eighty miles. I've been using Aswan as a major landmark when I damn well should have been using Edfu."

Allahaba was perhaps more excited than Fox. "It would make sense that a caravan road thousands of years old would cross near the Wilderness," he said enthusiastically. "If Ranthor was in the Manjam Hamsh Wilderness, then perhaps the Syene is even older than we've ever believed. It could be one of the oldest trade routes in existence."

Fox and Allahaba just stared at each other as if something so monumental had occurred that they could hardly process it. Morgan, having sat silent as the men conversed, watched the two faces for a moment before setting her teacup down.

"So you think Ranthor is in that Wilderness?" she asked either one of them.

They both turned to her, Fox speaking first. "It makes sense," he told her.

"Are we going there?"

Fox looked at Allahaba. "I believe so," he replied. "It's smack in the middle of nowhere, but I believe we should check it out and see if we can find any signs of civilization."

Morgan cocked her head. "Correct me if I'm wrong, but

haven't most, if not all, archaeological sites been pretty much picked over in Egypt?"

Fox shook his head. "Not even close, love. There are sites and rumors of sites all over the place. I've never heard of anyone doing any excavating in Manjam Hamsh. Have you, Al?"

Allahaba shook his head. "There are Roman ruins along the trade route between Edfu and the Red Sea and there is some commerce and civilization still there, but I do not believe anyone has excavated Manjam Hamsh. There is no reason to."

"Until now," Fox lifted a black eyebrow at him.

Allahaba looked at him, nodding his head. "Until now," he agreed.

"Are we excavating, then?" Morgan wanted to know.

Fox sat down next to her, rubbing his eyes wearily. His eyes always got tired when he read without his glasses. "Maybe a little, just to see what we can see," he told her, putting a big hand on her knee affectionately. "But presuming that Ranthor is in the area, there's still the last part of the puzzle."

Allahaba looked back to the papyrus. "*...to the Fingers that Reach to the Sky. May she know grace and divine protection, our Holy Mistress, foremost Lady of the West, as she Rests in the Shelter of the Sun.*"

Fox leaned back in his chair and gazed up at the ceiling in thought. "Any ideas on that?" he asked Allahaba.

The man gazed at the papyrus as if it would give him just one more clue that would solve the mystery. "I will have to think."

Fox laced his fingers behind his dark head as he continued to gaze up at the white-painted ceiling, deep in thought. "Have you ever heard of anything referring to fingers that reach to the sky?"

Allahaba shook his head. "No."

"Not a monument, tomb or town?"

Again, Allahaba shook his head. "I have not," he replied. "But it sounds to me as if it might be a mountain of some kind, something that would reach to touch the sky. Or perhaps a pyramid, an artificial mountain, that is no longer standing?"

Fox suddenly sat forward in his chair, his expression wrought with concentration. "Back in the days of the pre-dynastic reign of the Gods, there were no pyramids," he said, reasoning out his thoughts. "Those didn't come until a thousand years later. But there were mountains, natural ones. That would have been the highest point in Egypt at that time and there are plenty of mountains in the Red Sea hills where the Manjam Hamsh Wilderness is. In fact, when you look at them, they do look like fingers that are reaching for the sky. So what... what if the papyrus is talking about a mountain?"

Allahaba nodded eagerly, following his train of thought. "It would make sense," he agreed. "The tallest mountain in the region is Mt. Nuqrus where the Romans used to mine gold. In fact, the area surrounding the mountain still has a small population. Back in ancient times, it used to be one of the resting places along the trade route. The ancients used to call it...."

He suddenly trailed off, looking as if he was about to choke. His eyes bugged and he looked at Fox with such shock that Fox instinctively grew concerned.

"What's wrong?" he demanded. "What did it used to be called?"

Allahaba took a deep breath; he had to. He was stunned with something he should have thought of before. He couldn't believe it had just occurred to him now.

"It was a resting place, a small oasis, for caravans along the Syene trade route," his eyes reached out imploringly. "The ancients used to call Mt. Nuqrus the Shelter Mountain."

"Oh, my God!" Morgan suddenly burst, hands to her mouth. "The Shelter of the Sun!"

Fox snapped his head to her, the dark eyes intense with realization. They just stared at each other a moment until Morgan suddenly bolted from her chair and threw her arms around Fox's neck. He held her tightly, listening to Allahaba's low laughter.

"If Isis' resting place is there, it would make complete and utter sense," Allahaba said. "It would be the highest point around, a sacred mountain with sacred gold and a small oasis. Where better to spend eternity than at Shelter Mountain?"

"Fingers that touch the sky," Fox murmured. "The Shelter of the Sun."

"Exactly."

By this time, Morgan had stopped hugging Fox and was now sitting on his lap with his big arms wrapped around her.

"I can't believe it," she said excitedly, kissing Fox's cheek. "You and Allahaba are the smartest men alive. The way you read the clues make so much sense; it just has to be true."

Fox looked at her, studying her magnificent face, feeling happier and more content than he ever had in his life. So much of his life had come together and now, a potential of something that would make Howard Carter's discovery pale by comparison. He struggled to think calmly about it and not jump in a car that very moment to rush off to the Arabian Desert.

"We're going to check it out, that's for sure," he told her. "I think our next step is to return to the hotel and make arrangements to travel to Mt. Nuqrus to see what we can see."

Allahaba entered the conversation. "I have a cousin who runs tours out of Thebes," he said. "He can take us to the mountain."

Fox looked him. "I'd like to check out Manjam Hamsh also. I've an itch to do some excavating."

Allahaba grinned. "It has been a long time since I have

worked with Dr. Fox in the field," he said. "This is an exciting prospect."

Fox wriggled his eyebrows. "Exciting but secretive," he told him. "What we discuss can't go beyond the three of us for obvious reasons. Too much is at stake."

Allahaba nodded vigorously. "Absolutely," he agreed. "I will not even tell my wife. But we are going to need supplies and a plan."

Fox nodded. "Let's make them now so Morgan and I can return to the hotel and prepare. I think we've got a big trip ahead of us."

Allahaba's brown eyes glittered, suddenly serious, suddenly intense. "You have a trip of a lifetime ahead of you."

Morgan looked at Fox and they grinned; neither one of them could disagree. This is what they had come for, what had brought them together in the first place. But it was more than that; now, it was writing the final chapters of the story.

"For Fanny," Morgan said with emotion.

Allahaba nodded his head, with understanding. "For Fanny."

NOVEMBER 12, 1923

We saw the most wonderful and magical statues today. Some call them the statues of Memnon but some call them Tammy and Shammy. They are two enormous statues of a man seated, though you cannot make out his face. They are very ancient. Mr. Sula says they are images of a god but Mr. Sula likes to tease me. I am not sure if they are statues of a god, but they are quite fascinating!
~ FS

SIXTEEN

"LOVE, come and take a look at this," Fox called.

It was dusk on their third day in Egypt. After a busy day making plans with Allahaba, Fox and Morgan had retreated back to the hotel to make preparations. Part of those preparations involved Fox mapping out their destinations down to the last inch. He was at the desk in their bedroom with the computer on while Morgan was in the bathroom getting ready for dinner. But she was just out of the shower, putting lotion on her legs and not inclined to go running out into the bedroom at the moment.

"What is it?" she called. "Can it wait a moment? I'm almost done."

"Sure."

Fox's eyes were glued to the computer screen, the LCD display reflecting off his glasses. He was on the satellite earth mapping program again, now fixated on the Manjam Hamsh Wilderness. With the detailed satellite images, he was getting a feel for the lay of the land. It took him back to his days at Edfu, the desolation of the desert yet the undeniable primordial beauty of it. He was very much looking forward to it.

"God, I love modern technology," he snorted as he jotted down some notes and printed off a page on the inkjet printer they had purchased on their way back to the hotel. "These satellite images are amazing."

"What did you say?" Morgan called from the bathroom.

He grinned. "Nothing," he told her. "I'm just talking to myself."

As he continued to jot notes, she suddenly came out of the bathroom with a towel wrapped around her body.

"You know what they say about people who talk to themselves," she warned him.

He snorted as he wrote. "Want to see something cool?"

She was digging in her suitcase but stopped and went over to him, leaning against one massive shoulder and peering at the computer screen.

"What?" she asked.

He took the eraser end of the pencil and pointed to the screen. "See this?"

"Yes."

"It's the Manjam Hamsh Wilderness," he told her. "See what looks like a crazy road right over here?"

"Yep."

"That's a fossil river," he told her. "If you track it, you can see that it ran all the way back to the Nile at one time."

She stared at the screen. "What does that mean?"

He puffed out his cheeks as he thought on her question. "It means that thousands of years ago, there was a subsidiary of the Nile that ran in this direction," he told her. "It runs right through the Manjam Hamsh area."

Morgan knew that was significant. "A big enough river to support an ancient city?"

"More than enough."

"Why didn't anyone see this before?"

"Because no one knew what to look for; there are hundreds of fossil rivers all over Egypt. Only this one, because of the clues from the papyrus, is just a little more significant."

He turned to look at her, catching her dimpled smile before she kissed the end of his nose and went back to getting dressed. Fox watched her a moment before turning back to his maps and notes.

Morgan pulled out a lightweight black dress with a silver chain belt from the suitcase, laying it on the bed. It was stylish and clingy. But as she pulled out undergarments and shoes, her mind began to move from the Manjam Hamsh Wilderness to other things.

"I've been thinking," she said.

He was focused on his printed map. "What about?"

She looked down at the finger with the beautiful ring on it. "Well," she began. "Now that you've officially proposed, it looks like we have some logistics to work out. Like, where we're going to live, for instance."

He didn't miss a beat. "I already told you," he said. "I'll move to Los Angeles and get a job there."

She shook her head. "And I told you that it's silly for you to do that," she countered. "Your job at the Bolton Museum is much more important and prestigious than mine is with the Pasadena Police. I'll quit my job and we'll live in England."

He stopped looking at his maps and pulled off his glasses. He turned to her, the black eyes glittering. "Are you sure about that?" he asked. "It will be a major change for you and I don't want you resenting me at some point for taking you away from your family and friends."

"The same can be said for you."

"I know myself well enough to know I'd never resent you. It's my choice and I've made it."

"Well, *un*-make it because I think we should live in

England," she said, sitting on the bed and facing him. "I'll do some research into police departments in the Manchester area and see if any are hiring. Anyway, I think it makes more sense for me to move to England than for you to move to Los Angeles. You even said yourself that at this point in your life, your career is very important to you."

He nodded. "It is," he replied. "But you're more important even than that."

She smiled widely, the dimples deep. "I've been thinking something else," she ventured. "Do you own your home or do you lease?"

"I own it," he replied.

"Would you have a problem selling it or at least leasing it out?"

He shook his head. "No," he cocked his head. "Why?"

She flipped over so that she was stretched out on her belly, chin resting on her hands. The clear brown eyes glimmered with ideas.

"Because," she began. "I've been thinking that maybe we should live at Heaven's Gate. But I have a plan. I've been thinking that we could use the house as a bed and breakfast and also open it up to tours and weddings; you know, like an event venue. Many stately homes and castles all over the world rent out their grounds or have tours to help with the upkeep. Heaven's Gate is such a unique property and with all of those arti-facts my great-grandparents collected, it would be a really cool place to tour. All I'm saying is that maybe we should open up the house and make it pay for itself."

He pondered that a moment, a light of warmth coming to his eyes. "I'd love to live at Heaven's Gate," he said. "But Fanny is alive and the place belongs to her. Maybe she has other ideas."

Morgan cocked an eyebrow. "The place doesn't belong to her because she and my great-grandfather divorced," she shrugged. "Even if that weren't the case, she's one hundred and five years old. I doubt she cares about it. Her life has been in Egypt for the past ninety years. England's just a memory; you heard what she said. She knows she's never going home again so I would think that as long as Heaven's Gate thrives, she should be in full support."

He thought about it, shrugged, and then nodded. "True," he replied. "But back to the bed and breakfast idea, I'll live anywhere you want, to be truthful. If you wanted to live in a cardboard box in an alley, I'd live there with you. It really doesn't matter where, as long as you're there."

She smiled. "You're so sweet," she murmured. "But do you think it's a good idea?"

He nodded. "I think it's a brilliant idea."

"You wouldn't have a problem opening our home to tours and strangers?"

He shook his head. "No," he assured her. "In fact, I'll even give the tours."

She laughed in delight. "That's great," she exclaimed, sitting up again and returning to her clothes. "My tall, gorgeous husband giving tours. Well, at least I know we'd draw every woman in Britain to the place at some point."

He laughed at her. "And that's another thing."

"What is?"

His humor sobered. "You mentioned your husband," he said, his voice softening to a warm rumble. He stood up and moved towards her. "I'd like to set a date before we leave Egypt. I don't want to return home with an open-ended agreement. I just don't think I could take it."

She watched him approach, caving in to the enormous arms that embraced her. He was warm, powerful and comforting, and Morgan knew she felt the very same way as he did. She couldn't take an open-ended arrangement, either. She never wanted to be without the man, not even for a day, ever again. The more time she spent with him, the more attached she became. She held him close, running her fingers up the back of his dark head.

"Then why not get married before we return?" she suggested.

His eyes widened and he suddenly held her out at arm's length, looking her in the eye. "Are you serious?"

"Of course," she replied. "I don't need a big wedding. I just need you. Why can't we just get married here? I'm sure the hotel is set up for weddings."

"Seriously? Get married at the hotel?"

"Yes. Tomorrow before we leave for Upper Egypt."

He just stared at her as if trying to determine just how serious she was. Then, the black eyes began to dance with excitement.

"That's the best idea I've ever heard," he told her with genuine sincerity. "But are you sure your parents won't mind? I'm going to have to do some serious explaining to my mum so she doesn't get offended. The woman had five boys and you'll be her first daughter. She's dying to meet you."

"I'm dying to meet her, too," she replied, then shrugged. "If you think it's a problem, we can set a proper date so everyone can attend."

"No, no," he said quickly. "We can get married tomorrow and then maybe have another ceremony when we get home so the families can attend. That way, everyone will be happy. Especially me."

As Morgan gazed up at him, it suddenly dawned on her that he was agreeing with her. They were getting married right away. She started to giggle and he joined in her laughter, picking her up and swinging her around joyfully until she squealed to be put down. Even then, he stopped spinning but continued to hold her, kissing her sweetly.

"I'm going to get married tomorrow," he whispered against her mouth.

Morgan continued to giggle with him, so incredibly happy. She never knew she could be so happy. "Me, too," she murmured. "I need to contact the hotel's event coordinator. We should probably let them in on this, too, since we want to use their hotel."

"I love you so much," he whispered.

"I love you, too."

He kissed her furiously before finally setting her to her feet. Morgan, still wrapped in the fluffy white towel, padded over to the phone and called the front desk.

Within thirty minutes, the time and place was set. Morgan's next call was to her mother.

NOVEMBER 15, 1923

Luxor is a fascinating city with many ancient monuments. As much as I like it, I am anxious to continue on our hunt for the tomb of Isis. However, before we continue, we must make a stop at the Valley of the Kings and also at the mysterious island of Philae. I am very eager to continue although Louis is increasingly sullen. I have spent much time with Mr. Sula as a result.

    ~ FS

SEVENTEEN

MORGAN HADN'T SEEN Fox since that morning. Allahaba had him somewhere, like some impromptu bachelor party that didn't involve alcohol or women, so that Morgan could prepare for their wedding.

Laura Sherburn had been thrilled at the news; disappointed she wouldn't be attending her oldest daughter's wedding, but thrilled nonetheless. She told Morgan that she had been expecting it, just not so soon. Bill Sherburn, Morgan's father, got on the phone and grilled his daughter for a solid half hour about Fox Henredon and what kind of man he was. Morgan assured her father that he was a keeper. Not that Bill had any say in the matter, but as her father, he had to do his due diligence.

On Laura's glowing recommendation, Bill finally gave his daughter his blessing with the stipulation that the Sherburns would host a grand reception once the Egyptian trip was over. Morgan was overjoyed to agree.

During the phone call, Morgan had refrained from telling them about Fanny simply because she felt that her wedding and Fanny's appearance would have been too much for her parents to take at one time. It was difficult to hold back the truth but, in the end, she felt it was the right decision. There would be time enough later to devote an entire conversation to something as important as Fanny Sherburn and she knew it wouldn't end there. The revelation that Fanny was still alive would bring all sorts of plans for bringing her home and visits. It would occupy the Sherburn family for months to come. Morgan was being selfish that she wanted at least one day that centered around her and Fox.

Oblivious to her daughter's dilemma and the bombshell she was withholding, Laura Sherburn had plans. After hanging up with Morgan, she had called the hotel's concierge and arranged for a spa day for her daughter, hair and nails done, makeup, and everything else the hotel had to offer. She'd spoken with one of the wedding coordinators and explained the situation to the woman, so early in the morning on the following day, two swanky bridal shops sent up several dresses for Morgan to try on. Fox had started to go through them but Morgan had chased him out of the bedroom and into Allahaba's waiting arms. With Fox occupied, Morgan focused on what would arguably be the most important day of her life.

They would be getting married at sunset in the hotel gardens, an extremely lush and exotic location with blooming plants, an antique fountain, and beautiful lawns. The wedding coordinator, a woman named Saba, was young and hip and looked at the short notice of the wedding as a personal challenge. Fortunately, the hotel didn't have any weddings booked for the day so she was able to turn the entire wedding staff on to the task of the Henredon/Sherburn wedding. The marriage license was number one on the list.

The second biggest challenge was to find a wedding band for the groom, as the bride was tied up with spas and hair and makeup. There was a jewelry store in the hotel's casino and in between beauty sessions, Morgan was able to select an 8 millimeter titanium band that reflected Fox's strength and masculinity perfectly. Not knowing his size, she guessed, but the jewelry store assured her they could size it.

After a morning at the spa getting pampered, Morgan returned to their rooms to find that Saba had lunch set out for her. As she was finishing with the delicious lunch, Ziva and her seven daughters showed up to help. Morgan was touched but didn't see the need for the eight women in her room. However, Ziva felt very compelled to attend her since Morgan didn't have any relatives in Egypt. Since Allahaba had told his wife of their relation to Morgan, Ziva was technically family and therefore determined to fill the role.

Morgan found the gesture very sweet but wished that instead of the seven daughters, Ziva had brought Fanny with her. She was her true family. Yet, Morgan understood that the transport of a one hundred and five-year-old woman was a logistical impossibility. She didn't even ask for the old woman but wished with all her heart that she could have made the trip.

All of the daughters spoke English to varying degrees thanks to American cartoons and movies. The older two daughters, Abia and Aisha, were particularly well spoken and they translated between their mother and Morgan. When Morgan tried on the wedding dresses, the ladies all gave their opinions. But they were all western style dresses and Morgan realized after trying on every one that they weren't exactly what she was looking for. Her fiancé was an Egyptologist, after all. She wanted to do something to honor that and to honor him, and to honor the country that had meant so much to Fanny. After explaining her wants to Abia and Aisha, they discussed it with their mother and the three of them fled to parts, and stores, unknown.

Sunset came and the gardens of the Marriott were lit with a thousand candles. Blue spotlights with star-shaped gels cast a spectacular galaxy of stars across the plants and trees, and silver spotlights pointed down from several palm trees, illuminating the area near the antique fountain where Fox and Morgan would say their vows. With the candles and spotlights, Saba and her crew had created one of the most romantic venues ever seen. Myrrh incense burned in silver bowls, lending a heady and timeless scent to the ceremony. With nine white-satin chairs set out for Allahaba and his family, the scene was set.

Morgan was up in her room with Saba for the final touches. She hadn't seen the ceremony sight yet, nor had she seen Fox and Allahaba arrive. She didn't see Fox pushing Fanny in a brand new wheelchair borrowed from the hotel, placing her in prime position so that she would hear everything. Dressed in a beautiful blue *burqa* with a lovely white scarf on her head, Fanny didn't look her age. She looked happy, timeless and serene. It had taken Fox and Allahaba a good portion of the day to move her out of her room, into a taxi and to the hotel, but they had done it for Morgan. She hadn't asked him to, but Fox knew what it would mean to her. It meant a lot to him, too.

Dressed in a crisp black suit, white shirt and white satin tie, Fox was giddy with excitement as the taped classical music began to play through hidden speakers in the plants. Not wanting to get married in jeans, his first stop that morning after leaving Morgan had been to a suit broker, but he was such an enormous man that the tailor had to take one of the largest suits he had and alter it to fit. It had taken a few hours and about four hundred American dollars, but when all was said and done, it was a beautiful suit that fit him very well.

As the appointed ceremony time arrived, Fox stood nervously next to the antique fountain, waiting for Morgan to make her grand entrance. The official stood next to him, a brown man in a white suit, a Christian minister that had been secured by the hotel.

As the music continued to play and Morgan finally appeared, Fox could hardly believe his eyes. She was dressed in a sheer, flowing white gown of gossamer chiffon that looked like an elegant Egyptian garment that a queen would have worn in days gone by. It had a one-shoulder neckline with a crystal-encrusted sash encircling her waist, and her blond hair was piled high on top of her head, embraced by a magnificent Egyptian-style tiara. A massive bouquet of lilies and lotus blooms lodged in hands that were covered with full-length white gloves.

She looked absolutely exquisite, like a goddess, and Fox took her gloved hand when she drew near and kissed it reverently. He just stared at her.

"Oh, my God," he breathed as she stood before him. "You are the most beautiful creature I have ever seen in my life."

Morgan smiled broadly, her dimples deep. She started to compliment him as well, because he looked unbelievably handsome, when she caught sight of something out of the corner of her eye. It took her a moment to realize that Fanny was in attendance, a tiny woman in a wheelchair, but when realization hit the tears began to come. That set off Ziva and the older daughters and before the ceremony even began, the sounds of women weeping filled the air.

Morgan went to Fanny, kneeling beside her in a rush of sheer white fabric and mounds of lilies. She clasped the old woman's hand.

"You came," she whispered, wiping the tears on her cheeks. "I didn't think you would be able to. I didn't dare to hope."

Fanny squeezed her hand. "And miss my great-granddaughter's wedding?" she smiled. "I would not have missed this for the world, even if I had to walk. But Fox made sure I didn't have to walk, so he is the man to thank."

Morgan squeezed her hand and stood up, kissing the old woman's cheek. "I'm so glad you're here," she murmured.

Fanny's sightless eyes twinkled. "So am I."

Morgan gave her a lily from her bouquet before reclaiming Fox's arm and approached the minister. She gazed lovingly up at Fox, feeling like the most fortunate woman in the world.

"I can't thank you enough for what you did," she whispered as they came to stand in front of the official. "I'm so lucky to have you. Thank you so much."

Fox winked at her, refraining from answering as the minister began the ceremony. Her hand was tucked in the crook of his left elbow and his right hand held her fingers tightly against him as if afraid she was going to try and pull away. Never in his life had he felt so much joy or contentment. It was like everything was finally coming together for him and he had the woman of his dreams to spend the rest of his life with. Truth was, everything could fall apart around him and as long as he had Morgan, he would be content and deliriously happy. He couldn't even verbalize how much she meant to him.

The ceremony was fairly short as far as weddings went. With the hotel photographer clicking away, they repeated their vows. When it came to exchanging rings, Fox put the antique Roman ring back on Morgan's hand with the added addition of a gold eternity band that matched it almost perfectly. He had purchased it while waiting for his suit to be finished. Morgan was surprised at the eternity band but she loved it, and Fox was equally surprised when she slipped the titanium band on his left hand. He hadn't even really thought about a ring for himself until this very moment and had to admit he liked it very much. It made him feel complete, married, linked to Morgan in a way he couldn't describe. And with the final kiss to seal the deal, they became Dr. and Mrs. Fox Henredon.

Congratulations went all around, from Allahaba and Ziva to the minister to Saba and her staff. Everyone seemed overjoyed but it was nothing compared to what Fox and Morgan were feeling. They couldn't move two feet away from each other without one or both of them reaching out a hand to reel the other one in. They were of one mind now, one heart, and it was evident that two happier people had never existed. After the congratulations went around, the group moved off to the American-style steakhouse in the hotel for the reception dinner with Fox wheeling Fanny inside.

Lingering near the pool with a perfect view of the activity in the gardens stood Beni. He had been loitering at the hotel all day, watching Fox come and go and finally witnessing the wedding between Fox and his fiancée. He knew how Alia was going to react about the entire thing and he didn't relish telling her. But the deed was done, an added element to Fox Henredon's visit to Egypt, but Beni knew that the wedding had nothing to do with the project Fox was working on. That was still a great mystery. Even if Beni wanted to back out of spying on Fox, Alia wouldn't let him. She was determined to know and Beni knew there was no dissuading her. He suspected that now, with the event of the wedding, her obsession was only going to grow worse.

When he reported back to her later that evening on Fox's wedding, Alia reacted so violently that Beni came away with a black eye and orders to continue following Fox if he valued his job at the museum. By now, Alia had Beni completely terrified with the threat of losing his job, so much so that he agreed to do whatever she wished, anything to find out what Fox Henredon was up to.

Beni knew, as he returned to the Marriott later that night, that it wasn't so much what Fox was up to more than it was to report on Fox and his new wife. Beni suspected that whatever Alia had planned, it involved the new Mrs. Fox more than anything.

He wondered what more she would ultimately ask of him. He further wondered if he would be strong enough to refuse it.

———

TWO DAYS LATER

The EgyptAir flight from Cairo to Luxor set down around late morning, pulling into the terminal at the Luxor Airport. Fox commented on how much the airport had grown since he'd last been there about five years before. There were coffee shops and duty-free shops by the truckload, and Morgan purchased three bottles of expensive French perfume and a tall latte before they even left the terminal.

With his wife looking stylish in her tight jeans, massive designer bag and coffee in hand, Fox, as usual, ended up hauling their luggage out to the taxi stand. Allahaba brought up the rear with his own luggage, plus a few other bags.

It was a windy day in Luxor, the warm desert breezes caressing the ancient town with the enormous archaic temples. Morgan stood on the curb, passing a few dollars to the man in charge of the cab stand as he flagged down a taxi. When a battered white vehicle pulled up to the curb, Fox and Allahaba began tossing the luggage into the trunk.

Their destination was the Hilton Luxor, a five star hotel that was along the banks of the Nile. Morgan's parents had sprung for it as a honeymoon gift and Fox and Morgan checked into the Honeymoon suite. Allahaba went on to stay with his cousin on the outskirts of town to finalize the arrangements with the understanding that they would pick Fox and Morgan up at the hotel in the morning to begin their quest.

The afternoon was spent trying to teach Morgan how to pack

for the trip. Fox had been on digs before and understood the concept of packing light. Morgan understood the concept, but she resisted adhering to it. Twice, Fox had to lay down the law to her about what she could and could not take. Twice, she had stuck her tongue out at him. Twice, he had tried to spank her but ended up making love to her, instead. Now, as the afternoon grew late, he tried again to teach his wife how to pack without it ending up in a battle because time was growing short. They had to get organized.

They had gone to the local bazaar early in the afternoon and picked up four big waterproof duffle bags and two canvas backpacks that were fairly well-made. Allahaba had charge of food and shelter, so all they had to worry about was what they were bringing with them.

Fox had the duffle bags laid out in the living room of their suite while Morgan was in the bedroom, still trying to sort the clothing she wanted to bring. Fox had managed to pack very concisely, including a portable excavation kit he had put together from various pieces he had purchased in the bazaar when they bought the bags. He had brushes, magnifying glasses, a portable Abney survey tool, a trowel, and a few other things he had shoved into the second of his duffle bags. He also had a digital camera, batteries, a tape recorder, and several other gadgets that would aid in excavation. He was a professional at this and knew exactly what he needed.

Morgan, however, had both of her giant suitcases pulled apart in her attempt to figure out what was critical and what wasn't. Fox, finished with his packing, joined her in the bedroom and lent his guidance. The first thing she did was shove three pairs of jeans into the bag, to which he approved. Then a couple of pairs of shorts went in. He was fine with that. But when she tried to put a robe in the bag, the battle began again.

"But why can't I take it?" she wanted to know. "I just want something comfortable to wear when we're done for the day."

Fox put his hands over his face in exasperation. "Honeylove, you just don't seem to get it," he pulled his hands from his face. "You're going to be in the middle of the desert. You're going to be dirty all of the time and pretty much sleeping and living in the clothes on your back. We're not going to a resort. Think of no baths and no showers for a couple of weeks, because that's what it's going to be like."

She stuck her lower lip out in a pout. "You said I could use some of our drinking water to clean up with."

He nodded impatiently and began rummaging through her neat piles on the bed, pulling out things he thought were serviceable and handing them to her.

"You can, if there is enough," he told her. "But you really need to buckle down, love."

"I am," she insisted, bordering on a whine. "And that's another thing; what are we going to do with our luggage when we go? Will the hotel store it?"

Fox nodded his head, handing her some shirts. "I have to pay for space rental, but they've agreed to lock it up while we're gone."

"Are we leaving the papyrus here?"

"Absolutely. I'm not bringing that with us and chance it getting damaged."

"Okay" she said reluctantly, packing the shirts in the duffle bag. "But I'd really hate for anything to happen to our stuff."

"Nothing is going to happen to it," he assured her. "But I'm more concerned with packing only your necessities right now into these duffle bags. This isn't going to be a pleasure trip, you know."

She took another load of shirts from him with a frown. "I know that."

He shook his head as he began tossing her balls of socks. "No, you don't," he told her. "You need to stop thinking like a woman who likes spas, fine dining and a bath every night and start thinking like a Bedouin. Do you know that those people are lucky if they take a bath once a year?"

She was really frowning by now, shoving the socks into her bag. "Now you're just being mean."

"I'm being realistic." He stood stoically when she hit him in the head with a balled sock. "You need to be, too. How in the hell did you get through police training? That's hard core. Didn't they make you rough it?"

She puckered her lips irritably. "I wasn't in Boot Camp, for Christ's Sake," she pointed out. "The police academy was tough but we weren't camping out in the desert every night, living off the land. I went home every night and slept in my own comfortable bed."

He just shook his head. "Not this time, love," he scolded gently. "This will be like nothing you've ever experienced."

Morgan sighed heavily as she finished shoving socks into her bag and moved on to the sweatshirts. Fox couldn't help noticed she didn't argue with him after that; she was packing the way he told her to. He watched her zip up her first bag and then start piling sweatpants, a straw hat and toiletries into the second. He began to feel bad, as if he'd been too harsh with her, so he leaned over to kiss her on the head.

"Do you want to go to the temple of Karnak when you're done?" he asked, rubbing her arms affectionately. "It doesn't close until sundown."

She shrugged. "Maybe," she replied, but she still wasn't off the subject of packing. "Can I at least bring my makeup or are you going to get mad at me for bringing that, too?"

He fought off a grin. "You don't need any makeup."

She glared at him. "If I don't need any makeup, then you don't need a razor or shaving cream."

He shrugged carelessly. "Okay; I don't. It won't bother me."

She scowled again. "Well, it will bother me," she declared. "I'm bringing makeup whether or not you like it."

He laughed. "I'm kidding with you," he said. "If you want to bring it, that's fine. Just know that I think you're beautiful without it."

She shook her head at him reproachfully but the corners of her mouth twitched. "You have to say that now. You don't have a choice."

He snorted and took her in his arms, kissing her sweetly before pulling back to look at her. "I do, indeed, have a choice, Mrs. Henredon," he murmured. "I say it because it's the truth."

She softened, patting his cheek before pulling away to finish zipping up her bag. "What time is Allahaba coming to get us?" she asked.

He glanced at his watch. "Before dawn. Why?"

She turned to him, batting her eyelashes obviously. "Because if I'm going to be spending the next six weeks of my life out in the desert without even basic comforts, I want to spend the rest of the day going to the spa and getting a massage."

He stared at her a moment before shaking his head and breaking down into soft laughter. "I should have known," he slapped a hand helplessly against his leg. "Well, go ahead. Get it out of your system before we go. Can I at least expect you for dinner?"

She gave him a rather impish look as she swooped by the desk, picked up a piece of paper, and went over to him. She held it up so he could see it.

"Not just me, big boy," she watched him try to focus on what she was showing him without his glasses. "You, too. My parents sprang for a sunset spa package — a couples' massage, a couples' lavender-infused bath, and dinner on our own private patio overlooking the pool. How does that sound?"

He finally focused on what she was showing him; it was a pre-paid receipt for the hotel's special Honeymoon Spa Package. He also saw the price and his eyebrows flew up.

"Bloody hell!" he hissed. "Your parents could have bought us our own country for what they paid for that package."

Morgan giggled as he gasped. "It's not that much," she said. "Besides, it makes them feel like they're a part of this."

"Hmm," he grunted, handing her back the paper. "Your father must own a mint."

She shrugged. "Dad owns his own business," she told him. "He's in construction. You know, highways and state contracts and all that. My parents are fairly well off."

His jesting mood settled somewhat. "You didn't tell me I married a bank."

"You didn't ask."

He scratched his head, looking somewhat uncomfortable. "I don't make a huge salary, you know. I hope you're not expecting...."

She cut him off, throwing her arms around his neck and pulling him down for a sweet kiss. "I don't care what you make," she murmured as she kissed him. "I married you, not your bank account. Besides, I make a fairly good salary. We'll do fine."

He returned her kisses, holding her fast in his enormous arms. "I hope so," he whispered. "I'll spring for spas every once in a while, but I'd go broke on a weekly basis."

She smiled at him. "Do you seriously feel the need to tell me that?" she wanted to know. "Am I coming across as too high maintenance?"

He shook his head. "No," he replied. "Not at all. You're a perfectly normal woman who likes to spend money perfectly normally. But you should know that I live rather, well, *normally.*"

"So do I," she said. "But you've discovered my vice and it's spas and shopping. Sorry, I can't help it. My sister is even worse. Josie's husband has a meltdown on a weekly basis."

He laughed, kissing her on the nose before releasing her. "I'm hiding the checkbook."

"I have credit cards."

"Not if I steal them out of your purse while you're sleeping."

She laughed at him, going in search of her shoes and glancing at the clock as she did so. She whooped when she saw the time.

"Hurry up," she rushed him. "We'll be late."

Fox made a face, like a kid who was about to be forced into taking medicine he clearly didn't want to take. "Love, I appreciate that your parents wanted to give us this luxurious gift, but I'm really not a spa kind of bloke. If I'm going to get a massage, it's going to be from you. I don't like unfamiliar hands touching me like that. It's nobody's privilege but yours."

She understood, sort of. But it didn't calm her haste. "I'm sure we can find something else for you, like a facial or something. Come on; let's go."

He sighed hesitantly, like she wasn't getting the message. "But...."

"Don't you want to sit in a bathtub with me that has lavender and rose petals floating in it while sipping champagne on ice?"

He thought of her gorgeous, naked body in a warm tub with him right next to her and his resistance fled. "I think I could enjoy that."

"Force yourself."

He laughed, following her out the door. "No force at all, believe me."

NOVEMBER 18, 1923

Today we are visiting the Valley of the Kings. The gentleman we met in Cairo, Howard Carter, discovered the tomb of the ancient king Tutankhamun and we have been invited to view his discovery. I am terribly excited and hope to have my own great discovery someday like Howard Carter!

~ FS

EIGHTEEN

BENI HAD FOLLOWED them all the way to Luxor.

He had followed Fox and his new wife to the airport and, upon discovering their destination, booked a seat on a flight that departed on another airline fifteen minutes ahead of theirs. He therefore arrived before Fox and Morgan at the Luxor Airport and was able to spot them when they departed the EgyptAir flight.

They had company with them, too. The man who Beni had contacted at the Blue River Antiquities shop was close by Fox's side. It occurred to Beni that perhaps this man was helping Fox with his project, which offended Beni. Apparently Fox thought more of the man's skills than he did of Beni's. All insult aside, Beni thought himself rather fortunate that he had managed to keep them within his sight from one city to the next. Failure, for Alia, was not an option, and Beni was determined not to fail. The black eye she gave him would likely turn into a broken neck.

He called Alia while Fox and Morgan were at Baggage Claim, letting her know where he was. Like an eager dog, he was anxious to please a woman who was, thus far, unwilling to be pleased. The more Fox and Morgan progressed with whatever they were doing, the more unstable she seemed to become.

"*Salaam?*" Alia sounded rushed.

"Dr. Alia," Beni could see Fox and Morgan through the crowd of people, waiting in Baggage Claim. "We are in Baggage Claim at the Luxor airport. I am not sure where our destination is, but once I arrive, I will call you and let you know."

Alia's voice was cold. "He hasn't seen you?"

"No," Beni replied. "He has been too focused on other things."

Alia was silent a moment. "You mean his wife."

"And other things."

Alia grunted, falling silent for a time as she gathered her thoughts. For every move Fox made, she must make two. It was imperative she stay ahead of the man if she could. She saw this entire undertaking as a game that she was going to win. Alia always got what she wanted, except in the case of Fox Henredon. But she was determined to change that.

"When you contact me next, I may have some information for you," she told Beni.

He was curious. "What kind of information?"

"There is a man I know who lives in Zeiniyat," she said, her voice low. "He and my father are very good friends. He has a business dealing in arms and other items that have made him very wealthy. I do believe I shall ask a favor of him. He owes my father."

"Favor?" Beni was confused. "What kind of favor?"

"That is not your concern," Alia snapped. "Trust me when I tell you that once I tell him of Fox and his invasive presence in Egypt, he will agree that something must be done."

Beni was not only confused, he was increasingly troubled. "Done about what?" He wasn't trying to pry but he was very bewildered. "Dr. Fox has done nothing."

"Not yet," Alia corrected him. "But if he is on a project, then it stands to reason that, at some point, he will do something that many Egyptians would find offensive. My father's friend can do what you cannot; he can make it so the man will have to return to me for assistance."

Beni wasn't even sure what to say. Alia's instability was growing by the moment, where Fox was concerned, and he didn't want to set her off.

"How would he do that?" he wanted to know. "I am following Dr. Fox and will tell you all that I can. I thought you simply wanted to know where he was going and what he was doing."

Alia sighed; he could hear her. He could also feel the evil that the woman was breeding, the twisted thoughts of a woman scorned long ago.

"Fox and that woman are searching for the Lady of Heaven," she finally said. "The papyrus that the old journal spoke of is involved and it has been my belief from the beginning that she is pushing him to do this. She has turned an otherwise sane man into a treasure-seeker. That is not the Fox Henredon I know. If she was to turn up missing somehow, then perhaps Fox would be forced to return to me for help. He knows that, with my connections, I would be able to find her. Perhaps I would, perhaps I wouldn't. In any case, the woman is the key. She is the one causing all of the trouble."

Beni could see now where she was leading and it sickened him. But he had no choice other than to follow. The woman controlled too much in his world for him to refuse.

"It is not so much what he is seeking as who he is seeking it with," he said.

Alia readily agreed. "There is no tomb of Isis," she said flatly. "Whatever papyrus was mentioned in that journal, I do not believe it. It was probably a forgery. There were so many of them back in the days when the Europeans wintered in Egypt. Some clever dealer probably made the papyrus himself so stupid Americans like Fox's wife would follow it. If I eliminate her, then Fox will have a chance to regain his senses."

Beni remained silent, pondering her threatening words. It wasn't something he agreed with; he had seen Fox's wedding. He had seen how much love there was between them.

"You should not harm her," he finally murmured. "There is no need."

Alia barked at him. "Call me when you reach your destination," she growled. "I will have my father's friend contact you. You will do as he instructs. Is that clear?"

Beni nodded, watching as Fox and Morgan moved from Baggage Claim to curbside. "It is," he told her. "I must go. They are leaving."

"Make sure you...!"

He hung up on her before she could finish, feeling dirty and apprehensive. His directive to follow Fox and his new wife was gaining in intensity in a manner he didn't like at all. He hoped he was strong enough to endure it.

Beni called Alia when they reached the Hilton Luxor and was subsequently contacted by a local drug lord named Alezer bin Akil who ran arms and narcotics out of Luxor to Saudi Arabia and Iran. Alezer had the money and the resources to accomplish what Alia wished; he owed her father a favor, after all. All Beni had to do was keep tabs on Fox and relay his whereabouts back to the drug lord. Beni didn't want to be a part of it any longer but he had no choice.

When Fox and his wife moved south, Beni followed and the drug lord received the information. Fox, having no idea he was being followed, made it very easy for Beni to trail him. Somewhere near Edfu, the drug lord's men picked up Beni and drew him out into the desert with them. Now the drug lord himself was watching Fox. Beni was just along for the ride.

Fox had made it extremely easy for them to set the trap.

———

November in Egypt was the preferred month. The temperatures were warm and mild, and the climate was dry. Not a raindrop or a snowflake in sight. Wealthy Europeans had been wintering in Egypt for one hundred and fifty years. As the Jeep sped south from Luxor towards Edfu, Morgan could see why the snowbirds thought Egypt was such a lovely place for winter. It was eighty-six degrees and crystal clear blue skies overhead.

Allahaba and his cousin, Jabeel ibn Ahmed ibn Sula, were at the hotel promptly at five in the morning. Fox had been up for a couple of hours but Morgan had remained fast asleep. He finally woke her up about an hour before Allahaba and Jabeel arrived so she could take a last hot shower and get dressed, but Fox was coming to discover something about his wife that he found very comical.

In the first place, not only could she fall asleep with the television blaring, but she wasn't easy to wake up. He had to shake her a few times before she finally made a half-hearted attempt at sitting up, but then she fell back down again and he had to physically pick her up and carry her to the bathroom.

Once inside the bathroom, he put her on unsteady feet and turned on the shower for her. She managed to get into the shower under her own power, but he swore she fell asleep again as the hot water beat down on her and he found himself washing her hair as she half-heartedly washed her body. Not that he minded bathing her, but he struggled not to laugh the entire time. She was like a zombie.

She shaved herself, a little more awake by this time, but then she slumped against the shower wall and closed her eyes again, dozing as the hot water washed over her. Fox had stepped out of the bathroom momentarily to open the door for their early-morning room service breakfast, coming back into the bathroom to find her pretty much sleeping standing up. He couldn't help it; he started laughing. He'd never seen anything like it.

Going back to the living room where their breakfast sat untouched and cooling, he put jam on a piece of toast and took it back into the bathroom with him. As Morgan virtually snored leaning against the shower wall, he stuck the toast in her mouth, turned off the water, and wrapped her up in a towel. She sleepily chewed her toast as he pulled her out of the stall and proceeded to vigorously dry her off.

By the time he rubbed the towel over her blond head, she was more awake and grumpy because he was drying her so roughly. He snorted as she batted at him and insisted she was awake enough to take care of herself. When he wondered aloud how she had managed all these years to get herself out of bed and to work, she threw a hairbrush at him. He roared with laughter but wisely cleared the bathroom.

All grogginess aside, she was ready to go when Allahaba arrived. Fox had all of the duffle bags while Morgan carried the two backpacks. Jabeel was a younger man, nice looking and dressed in Levi jeans, and apparently very industrious with his modified twenty-five-year-old Land Rover. Hand-painted signs were fastened to the vehicle announcing "Eye of Horus Tours". There was no air conditioning but the two rows of seats were roomy. He had also removed the windows and made some body modifications so it was much like a tram-car, open air for the most part, to allow for a wider field of vision.

Morgan eyed the car, walking around it with her practiced police-eye and wondering aloud if it was street legal. Jabeel just smiled at her and told her that the car was like a tank, a statement of which she had no doubt. Jumping in when Jabeel revved the engine, they were off.

Jabeel and Allahaba sat in the front seats while Morgan and Fox sat in the second row bench seat. Morgan leaned against Fox, her legs across the seat and her designer sunglasses perched on her nose as they took Highway 2 south. The highway paralleled the Nile and Morgan was enjoying the warm temperatures and stunning view immensely. There was something so timeless and raw about the beauty of the land. Fox had his left arm around her, enjoying his own view off to the west. It didn't get any better than this — Egypt and Morgan were the two things he loved best.

It was a sixty mile drive to Edfu, bumping over the open highway with the wind and dust whipping around. Jabeel had a portable CD player which he plugged into a cigarette lighter that looked like he had jimmied it into the dashboard. When he popped in REO Speedwagon, Morgan gave him the thumbs down. When he popped in Van Halen, she threw up her hands like she was at a rock concert. Fox just grinned and shook his head. With "Dance the Night Away" blasting, the old Land Rover tore down the highway.

This far south, the majority of the agriculture was on the west side of the Nile. Morgan settled back for the ride, using Fox as a seat back, her head on his enormous shoulder as the trip progressed. Allahaba and Jabeel had brought cases upon cases of bottled water and Fox procured a couple of bottles as the drive progressed. By nine o'clock in the morning, they had reached Edfu. Jabeel pulled into a gas station to gas up the Jeep and fill up some gas cans.

Morgan and Fox climbed out of the car to stretch their legs, looking around the area. Shielding her eyes from the bright sun, Morgan peered off in the direction of the Nile.

"Where was your dig?" she asked Fox.

He was standing a few feet away from her, gazing off toward the southwest. "The city is actually on the west side of the Nile," he pointed. "See that bridge about a half-kilometer down the river? If we cross that, it will take us into the city proper. The temple is on the other side of the city, about three kilometers from here."

She peered in the direction he was pointing. "It's a big city. I didn't realize it was so big."

He pulled off his sunglasses and cleaned them with the edge of his shirt. "By Egyptian standards, it's rather new. It was founded during the Ptolemaic reign so the Temple of Horus was technically built by the Greeks."

She looked over at him, smiling. "Very cool," she said. "Too bad we don't have time to see it. I'd love to see where you spent three years of your life."

He winked at her. "As important as the dig was, I have to admit I was glad to get back home. Looking around at this area now makes my skin itch; the dry air, the heat, the sand storms... oh, yes, I was glad to get home."

She sauntered over to him. "Meet any luscious local women?"

He grinned. "A few."

She laughed and poked him in the arm. "Do tell."

He put his glasses back on and shook his head. "Not on your life," he looked around, making an attempt to shift the conversation. "There's a market over there. Do you want to buy some fruit to take with us?"

She bumped him playfully with a slender hip. "Don't change the subject," she said. "Tell me about your harem."

He put his hands on his hips and faced her. "Is that really what you want to talk about on our honeymoon?"

She shrugged. "Probably not. But it's fun watching you squirm."

"I'm not squirming."

"Yes, you are."

Thankfully for Fox, Allahaba caught their attention and waved them back over to the car. But Morgan decided to take Fox's suggestion and she scooted across the street to the open-air market that had a variety of produce on display. She was a little wary about the fresh produce but was assured by the shopkeeper that his produce was irrigated with clean water. The last thing she wanted was to be in the middle of the desert with no facilities and a bad case of the runs. So she selected some oranges and grapes, eventually joined by Fox, who selected a few mangos. With their booty, they were ready to proceed into the desolate wilderness to the east.

The Edfu-Marsa Alam Road was the main drag east that went all the way to the Red Sea. It passed through the Red Sea Hills, skirted the Manjam Hamsh Wilderness to the north, and then circled the north side of Mt. Nuqrus. The agricultural topography stretched for several miles east from the Nile until, eventually, the desert took over and consumed everything. The temperature remained warm as the Land Rover began to bump and grind over the less cared for section of road. Hills of desolate gold stretched as far as the eye could see.

"How far are we traveling today?" Morgan asked as the wind whipped her blond hair around.

"About a hundred and twenty kilometers," he told her. "I have mapped out where I think we need to begin our search, so we'll start there."

Morgan nodded in understanding, so incredibly relieved he was taking charge of the expedition. "I'm so glad you're here," she told him. "I couldn't have gotten this far without you."

He caressed her shoulder. "You could have; you're a police

detective and, I would imagine, have pieced things together more complex than this."

She shook her head. "I mostly work Vice or Narcotics," she said. "Following the clues on the papyrus is more than detective work. You need to have an intricate knowledge of ancient Egyptian history, which I don't have. Maybe I could have worked it out eventually, but I really have to give you all the credit. You've been amazing."

"Vice or Narcotics?" he repeated, fixated on the early part of her statement. "You work hookers and dope?"

She giggled; it sounded so dirty the way he said it with his Manchester accent. "I'm perfect for it," she told him. "I can dress like a hooker and catch pimps or they can put me in a high school as a new student and I can pass for a teenager."

He groaned, wiping his free hand over his face in a weary gesture. "Bloody hell," he grunted. "My wife works whores and pot. How am I going to tell my mum?"

Morgan's laughter grew. "I would advise that you don't. My grandparents still don't know the extent of what I do. They think I sit behind a desk."

"I would vote for that as well," he agreed eagerly.

"Sorry, dude. I'm not the desk type."

He grunted and huffed, not at all pleased with the extent of her job. "Will you at least wear some of your hooker outfits for me?" he wanted to know. "I should at least be able to get some pleasure out of this if I'm going to be so bloody unhappy about it."

She snorted. "I'll see what I can do."

He hugged her as the Land Rover continued along the two-lane road, boxed in on the north and the south by gently rolling sandy hills. Jabeel had switched out the CD from Van Halen to Aerosmith and "Sweet Emotion" echoed off the desert land-scape. Jabeel and Allahaba were chatting in Arabic in the front seat while Fox and Morgan lounged contentedly in the back. Eventually, with the drone of the engine and the boredom, Morgan predictably drifted off to sleep in the comfort of her husband's big arms.

Morgan had no idea how much time had passed when she realized the car had come to a halt. She could hear Jabeel and Allahaba, and a voice she didn't recognize. Peeping an eye open, she saw that they had come to a halt and a man swathed in dirty robes was speaking to Jabeel at the driver's side window.

She didn't see anyone else from her angle, just the man, but the conversation was growing increasingly heated. Fox eventually shifted her, very carefully, so she was lying across the bench seat. She had no idea where he had gone but she suspected he had gotten out of the car. When he left, she felt rather panicked but kept her cool.

So she lay on the seat bench, listening to the voices grow louder and more unhappy. She had no way of seeing that there were more men, now holding guns on Allahaba and Fox as they began to rummage around the back of the car. She heard Fox's stern, frightening tone, speaking in Arabic so she couldn't understand what was being said. But one thing was for certain; whatever was happening couldn't be good. She could hear the tension in their voices. Peeping an eye open to make sure she wasn't being watched, her left hand moved discreetly for her backpack.

She found the pack as the voices grew angrier. Quietly, with great stealth, she unzipped the bag and fumbled around. Wrapped in a scarf and buried deep, she found her service weapon, a Beretta 9mm handgun. It had been with her the entire time she'd been in Egypt, only she'd never told Fox about it. She wasn't sure how he would take it given how much he seemed to not like her job. But as a sworn officer, the gun was a part of her as much as a purse or shoes. It was necessary equipment. Carefully pulling it out, she held it close against her chest and waited for the moment to use it. She didn't have long to wait.

Someone roughly grabbed her and she could hear Fox bellow. But before the man could pull her out of the seat, she coolly pointed the gun at the center of his forehead.

"Get your hands off me," she snarled.

The man had no idea what she said but he knew it was a threat. Allahaba snapped something at him and the man put his hands up as if to show he was surrendering. Morgan kicked the man in the face, sending him out of the car and into the dirt as she sat up, as steady as a rock, the gun still trained on the man who was now picking himself up from the road.

She climbed out of the car, the gun never wavering. A quick glimpse showed several cases of their water and other items on the road next to the car. There were also at least five more bandits that she could count. When she spoke, her voice was low and commanding.

"Who are these guys, Allahaba?" she demanded. "What do they want?"

Allahaba, his eyes wide with surprise at Morgan's firearm, stammered. "They want our water and anything else of value," he told her. "They are robbers, Mrs. Fox."

Morgan could hear guns being unlocked all around her, magazines being loaded, so she took her weapon in both hands, aimed at the man in her sights, and braced her legs as if preparing to fire. Her intended victim threw his hands up in the air and yelled fearfully.

"Tell them to stand down their weapons or I'll blow this guy's head off," she bellowed. "Tell them now!"

Jabeel and Allahaba relayed her orders, receiving a barrage of angry replies in return. It was evident that they were reluctant to cooperate. As the chaos of shouting went on, Morgan unexpectedly fired her weapon, catching her captive in the center of one of his upraised hands. As he screamed and grabbed his hand, she rushed forward and shoved his *hajib* back, grabbing him by the hair. She put the gun barrel against his temple and pressed hard.

"Tell them to go back where they came from or I'll drop a round right into this guy's brain," she hollered. "I'm not bluffing. *Do it!*"

Both Jabeel and Allahaba began rattling off her command. The bandits, dressed in dirty flowing robes and riding in old vehicles, the manufacturers of which were unknown, began to shout to each other angrily. But they were backing away. They weren't moving fast enough for Morgan, however, so she threw her wounded hostage to the ground. When he fell, she put a boot on his neck and leaned down, putting the gun barrel right between the eyes.

"If they're not out of here by the time I count to ten, I'll put more holes in this man," she snapped. "Tell them to get in their cars and get the hell out of here. If they come back, I'll kill them all."

Again, Allahaba and Jabeel began shouting to the others. The bandits, seemingly not willing to take the chance that the woman might actually follow through, scattered back to their sand vehicles. Shouting, waving guns and knives, they began to tear off into the hills. Morgan dared to take her eyes off her captive for a moment to watch them leave but when she did so, the man beneath her twitched. Without hesitation, Morgan pistol-whipped him on the side of the head and knocked him out cold. Furious, not to mention shaken, she immediately looked around for her husband.

Fox had been standing near the hood of the car. He had been watching everything, his heart in his throat as he watched his wife hold a gun on a man probably twice her weight. The shot through his hand had been dead-aim and truly shocking. He would never have guessed his spa-loving wife to be capable of it. When she used the gun to knock him out, Fox rushed at her.

"Bloody hell," he grabbed her by both arms. "Are you all right?"

She nodded, visually inspecting him to reassure herself that he was in one piece. "I'm fine," she assured him. "Are you all right?"

"Never better."

"What in the hell happened?"

"Robbers," Allahaba said as he picked up one of their cases of water from the road. "They blocked the road and when we stopped, they demanded our supplies. But then they saw you and I heard some of them say that they wanted to take you."

Morgan's gaze moved between the distant dust cloud of retreating cars and the bloody man on the ground. As she flipped the safety on the gun and lowered it, Fox noticed that her hands were shaking.

"Oh, my God," she breathed, running a shocked hand over her face. "That was insane."

Fox was watching her, seeing the women through new eyes. She was clearly nothing to be trifled with, unafraid to defend herself or protect others. He found the quality deeply attractive, deeply admirable and a little frightening. The tiny little spitfire of a woman he had married was taking on quality and dimension before his very eyes.

"That's putting it mildly," he joked as he put his arms around her and kissed her forehead. "Are you sure you're all right?"

She nodded, putting her arms around his narrow waist and squeezing tightly. "I'm fine," she assured him.

"Swear it?"

"I swear."

As Fox embraced his wife closely, Allahaba and Jabeel were running around, collecting cases of water and bags of food off the ground and tossing them into the back of the car.

"We had better leave quickly," Allahaba encouraged them, eyeing the unconscious man on the ground. "They will be back to get their friend."

Fox didn't budge; he just wanted to hold his wife, not wanting to admit how utterly terrified he had been for her. But Morgan patted him on the back, gently urging him to release her.

"Come on," she told him. "He's right; we need to get out of here."

Fox reluctantly agreed. He let go of Morgan long enough to pick up the remaining cases of water and deposit them in the back of the Jeep. Morgan collected a box containing crackers and other consumables, handed it over to Fox, and jumped back into the car as Fox put the box of food in with the water. He climbed into the Jeep after his wife, Jabeel floored it, and off they went in a rooster tail of dust.

As the car raced down the highway, putting distance between them and the still-unconscious man on the side of the road, Morgan opened up her backpack and wrapped her gun back up. She tucked it deep inside, zipping up the pack only to notice that Fox was watching her. She smiled weakly at his calm, yet warm, expression.

"I didn't tell you about the gun because I know how you hate the idea of what I do, so I didn't want to upset you," she explained to his silent question. "As a law officer, I'm required to carry it when I'm off duty in the States. I didn't want to come to Egypt without protection."

He didn't say a word; he just grasped her hand and held it tightly as he turned his gaze to the window. Morgan watched him, sensing what she thought was his disapproval, and it ate at her like nothing she had ever experienced.

She pulled her hand from his grip and turned to her own window, pretending she was adjusting her sunglasses when what she was really doing was struggling not to cry. But she couldn't stop the tears; the more she would dab and wipe, the more they would come. As the Land Rover moved through the dusty, heated landscape, she finally gave up the fight altogether and let them fall.

Fox was watching the scenery, lost in his own thoughts, when he caught sight of Morgan wiping at her eyes. He knew she was crying silent tears that she was struggling against, but he had no idea why. Perhaps the confrontation shook her up more than she had let on. He watched her a moment before speaking.

"What's wrong?" he asked gently.

She shook her head, but the simple fact that he noticed her tears made her composure crumble more. She sniffled, wiping at her nose.

"It wasn't like I was hiding it from you," she whispered.

"Hiding what?"

"My gun," she snapped, facing him. "I always carry it. I'm a cop; I'm supposed to."

"I know."

She just turned away from him, softly weeping. Confused, he reached out to stroke her blond head. "What's eating you, love?"

She was wiping furiously at her cheeks. "I can just see the disapproval in your eyes," she wept. "What was I supposed to do? Let them assault me and not fight back?"

He'd had enough; he pulled her against him to comfort her. Morgan resisted for a split second before relenting, allowing him to hold her tightly. He kissed her head repeatedly, his soft voice in her ear.

"I'm sorry," he murmured. "It wasn't what you think. I guess I was just a little stunned that my sweet, beautiful wife shot a man with dead-eye accuracy in his hand before she roughed him up. I've just never seen that side of you before and when I stopped to think about it, it really blew me away. *You* blew me away."

She had stopped sobbing openly, feeling comforted by his words but still confused. "Is that a bad thing?"

"God, no," he comforted, kissing her ear. "I'm just seeing a new dimension to you. You're sweet and beautiful like a delicate little kitten but when cornered, you turn into a lioness. It's the most amazing thing I've ever seen. But you have to give me credit; my first instinct was to run over there and beat that guy to a pulp. But I saw you were in control and that you didn't need my help. I was smart enough, and I trusted you enough, to stay out of it."

Her cheek was against his chest, listening to his heartbeat steady and strong. He was warm, his muscular chest creating a gentle cushion for her head. She snuggled against him, calming with his gentle manner.

"I appreciate that," she said. "I know it must have been hard for you."

"Hard, yes. Terrifying, hell yes."

She smiled in spite of herself, listening to the tone of his voice. She had learned that he could get loud, and his accent heavier, when emotional.

"It's my job, Fox," she muttered hoarsely. "I can't be less than what I am. I can't do less than what my training and instincts tell me or we might all be in trouble."

He held her head against his chest, caressing her silky hair. "I know," he whispered. "It scares me to death and makes me overwhelmingly proud of you at the same time. As you've said many times, I'm just going to have to get used to it."

She pulled her head from his chest, gazing up at him with the wide brown eyes. "Still love me?"

He smiled, kissing her tenderly. "Madly and deeply."

Morgan settled in against him again, her head on his chest, listening to the steady beat of his heart and thinking about the attempted robbery. She watched the road go by, realizing that the rumor of dangers in third world countries was well-founded. She'd heard of gunman and terrorists, of course, but to experience it herself brought it to another level. She suddenly sat up, putting herself between the two front seats.

"Are there a lot of outlaws in this area?" she asked. "Or was that an isolated incident?"

Jabeel spoke. "It is not like it used to be," he told her. "I take tourists out here all of the time and I have hardly had any problems. If there are too many problems, then tourists will not come to Egypt and spend their money, so the government is strict with those who rob and steal."

Morgan watched the road in the distance, the landscape as it shifted from dunes to sand and jagged rocks. Jabeel and Allahaba didn't seem too worried about it, so she settled back once more against Fox, feeling his arm go around her and experiencing the sense of safety and contentment that it brought. Even so, she hoped that Jabeel was right. She didn't want to run into anymore "robbers".

Next time, they might not be so lucky.

NOVEMBER 28, 1923

*Louis is not feeling well so we have remained in Luxor for the
time being. Mr. Sula has explained so many fascinating aspects
of Egyptian life — some things haven't changed from century to
century. For example, they still use the old ways to irrigate farm
fields from the Nile with an odd contraption called a "shadoof".
Mr. Sula is wonderful conversationalist. I do wish that Louis was
feeling better.*

    ~ FS

NINETEEN

BY MID-AFTERNOON, they had pulled off the main road and onto a dirt path that led off to the south. Fox had pulled out his satellite images and he and Allahaba poured over them, looking for landmarks and counting the miles. The road was horribly bumpy and Morgan held on tightly so she wouldn't be bounced right out of the car as the landscape evolved into something eerie and otherworldly. Stark hills and vast sand plains surrounded them. It was as if they had pulled off the main road and driven straight onto Mars.

Fox knew where they were going and directed Jabeel off to the southwest. He not only had satellite imagery, but he also had geological images from a NASA website that imaged the landscape in density. It was from these geological images that his best guess, and most interest, stemmed from.

At one point, they stopped the car so Jabeel could pour a quart of oil into the engine and Morgan had her first taste of raw desert camping; she needed to relieve herself very badly after too much Diet Coke, but there was very little by way of private spot. The area they had stopped in was at least a five-mile stretch of sand with rocky hills on all sides, like a valley, and there were probably two puny bushes in all that space. Realizing this, Morgan put her hands on her hips as she faced her husband.

"All right, bright boy," she cocked a well-shaped eyebrow. "Where am I supposed to do the deed?"

He fought off a grin, looking around. "Anywhere. Just hurry up."

She lost her humor. "Anywhere?" she repeated, outraged. "Seriously? *Anywhere?*"

He could see she was growing agitated but it didn't help his case of giggles. He took her by the shoulders and turned her around towards the rear of the car.

"Find a spot over there somewhere and we'll stay at the front of the car with our backs turned," he told her. "Hurry up; we need to go."

Frustrated, Morgan shrugged her shoulders and dug in the back of the car for the toilet paper. Finding a very scratchy roll, she scooted off to the rear of the car while Fox, still snorting, moved to the front of the car and told Allahaba and Jabeel to face away from the car. They did so, properly, waiting a few minutes while Morgan finished her business. When she was done, she jumped back into the car, the three men climbed back in, and they sped away.

As they cleared the valley, they descended into a vast, open plain that stretched almost as far as the eye could see. There were colors of gold and brown in the sands and rocks, but mostly, it was complete desolation of a non-descript color. The warm wind blew as Fox called a halt just on the rise overlooking the valley depression.

He had his images out, looking between a pair of them. Finally, he looked up and studied the landscape. Then he went back to his notes and read them carefully.

"All right," he looked up again and pointed to the southwest.

"Over there exactly four kilometers to where those small foothills rise from the valley floor. See them?"

Jabeel nodded, threw the old rig into gear, and drove carefully down the sloping hill into the vast valley below. The wind was kicking up, blowing rocks and sand into their faces as they finally hit the valley floor and began heading in the direction Fox had indicated. He was reading his images, looking around to orient himself, as Morgan sat in the back seat and cracked another can of diet cola.

"You may want to ration that," he told her, not looking up from his images. "We've no way of knowing how long we'll be out here and if you run out, I'm not driving all the way back into Edfu to buy you more."

Frowning, and feeling singled out, Morgan flopped back against the seat rest and sipped at her precious cola.

"Don't bring your robe, Morgan," she mocked angrily, more to herself than to him. "Don't drink your diet soda. Go pee on the sand. Don't do this, don't do that. Get with the program, missy."

"I never said that," Fox said steadily, still looking at his images. "Well, not all of that, anyway."

Morgan crossed her arms angrily but kept her mouth shut, watching the desert landscape go by. Fox finally lifted his head, directing Jabeel to a very small range of hills about two kilometers off, before turning to his wife.

"I'm sorry if you think I'm riding you," he told her. "I don't mean to. Would you rather me just not say anything at all and when you run out of your soda tomorrow, realize it's not a simple thing to restock?"

She wasn't sure how she felt. He was right but she didn't like feeling that he was picking on her. So she stuck her tongue out at him and resumed watching the landscape go by. Fighting off a grin, Fox faced forward now that the area he was interested in was coming closer.

Jabeel covered the two kilometers across the valley floor, leaving clouds of dust in his wake. It was a truly dry and desolate wasteland, much like the vast Mojave Desert in Southern California, where miles and miles of rocks and sand covered the earth. This land, the Manjam Hamsh Wilderness of the Arabian Desert, was as bleak and dry as anywhere on earth.

The old Land Rover came to a halt less than fifty yards from the gently sloping group of foothills. Fox climbed out with his images in his hand and began to walk around. He headed towards the west, pointing towards a series of rocky hills.

"The river ran through those hills there," he said. "You can see on the images that a fossil river clearly ran from the Nile, coming through those hills and into this valley. You can see where the water carved away the sides of the hills and eroded a waterway. Also, about seven or eight miles to the west is the ancient Roman fortress of Samut. Maybe the river was still flowing at the time the fort was built; maybe it was just a trickle at that point. Either way, there's a spring there that supported the fort."

Morgan, having forgotten her pout, walked up behind him, trying very hard to see what he was describing. The wind whipped her blond ponytail around as she tried to imagine it.

"So...," she turned around and looked at the valley. "Where did the river go?"

He turned around also. "Through here, right where we're standing," he told her. "Although the imagery isn't clear on where the river ended, I can only guess that it must have gone all the way to the Red Sea and dumped out."

"And you think Ranthor was here?"

His handsome face was intense, the black eyes distant as he pictured what the valley might have looked like five thousand years before. He just stared, his eyes drinking in their surroundings, trying to put his thoughts into words. Morgan looked at him when the silence grew excessive, his enormous presence outlined against the brilliant blue sky.

"Dr. Henredon?" she prompted.

He looked at her when she addressed him formally, smiling at her lovely face. He reached out, pulling her against him and kissing her on the top of the head. Morgan wrapped her arms around his waist and took in the landscape with him.

"I see a river running through this valley," he began to verbalize his ideas. "I see it cutting to the south because that's what the imagery indicates. And this...."

He let go of Morgan and held up one of the images in his hand, looking at the small group of foothills to his right. "... this looks like hills but the geologic imagery suggests otherwise. There are stone formations that I don't see being natural here."

"Really?" Morgan looked around, at the ground, at the hills. "What do you see?"

He held out a picture to her and pointed at it. "This; see it? At the base of the hills? Rocks don't normally run in a perfect line like this."

She saw what he was pointing at on the image, in which different types of geological formations had different colors. "Even though I'm not an archaeologist, I don't think I need to be in order to see that those rocks are forming a straight line," she looked up at him, the brown eyes twinkling. "Maybe a wall that somebody built?"

"Or something," he grinned at her. "We're going to find out."

———

Morgan had never been on anything even remotely resembling an archaeological dig, so watching Fox in his element was truly something to behold. He was concise, driven, and knew exactly what he was doing.

With a couple of hours of daylight left by the time they reached the spot where Fox wanted to dig, he jumped right in to the process. The first thing he did was unpack the portable Abney surveying tool and begin surveying about a quarter square mile area at the northeast base of the small foothills. He had Morgan stand at periodic distances as a sight level for relative measurement and used her to map off his area.

Morgan stood in her straw hat and sunglasses, making faces at him at a distance until he started laughing. Then she would dance like an Egyptian while Fox would just stand there and shake his head at her antics. When she got bored of that, she would stand impatiently and sing the Violent Femme's song "Blister in the Sun". The surveying took longer than it should have as a result, but he'd never had so much fun doing it.

As dusk painted colors of pink and purple across the sky, Fox called a halt to their surveying because he could no longer see well in the dwindling light. Plus, Morgan was about to go nuts standing around. He collected his wife and took her over to where Jabeel and Allahaba had set up a base camp. Neither Morgan nor Fox had paid much attention to the pair as they unloaded supplies and set up tents, so by the time they got there, they were in for a surprise.

Jabeel did this for a living, taking tourists to remote spots, so he had quite a bit of equipment. There were two tents set up, older Coleman models that he told Fox he had purchased on eBay. The canvas was heavy and he had driven the stakes deep into the ground to withstand the winds. He also had old but clean rugs that he used to cover the bottom of the tents to make them more like home, something Morgan found wonderful.

There were four sleeping bags, two that were old and to be used by Jabeel and Allahaba, and two brand new ones that Jabeel had purchased in Luxor. He gave the new ones to Fox and Morgan.

But it was his sanitary facilities that had Morgan laughing at Jabeel's ingenuity; although the Manjam Hamsh Wilderness was desolate and bleak, there were rock formations dotting the landscape. Jabeel and Allahaba had built their encampment near a cluster of rocks, using a small alcove in the natural rock formation for the restroom.

Jabeel had dug a big hole for the outhouse and put a chair with the center cut out of it over it. The chair was pushed down deep into the dirt so it wouldn't tip. Around that, he hammered four five-foot PVC pipes into the ground and hooked up a wire around the top of the pipes. Onto that, he strung two cheap shower curtains for privacy. Morgan almost commented that one good gust of wind would blow the shower curtains open but she refrained. Jabeel had gone to great lengths to provide for a lady's privacy. She wasn't going to laugh at his efforts. She appreciated them.

But the best was yet to come. Thinking himself quite the inventor, Jabeel had built a makeshift shower. The men knew, as did Morgan, that it was purely for her, but she deeply appreciated the effort. He had used the same basic structure he'd used for the toilet, with PVC pipe and shower curtains, but instead of a hole where the toilet was, he'd laid down two cheap and heavy bathmats to keep the bather's feet well off the sand. The shower was tucked back behind the toilet so any water runoff would end up in the toilet hole.

Night eventually fell and there was a full moon out, casting the entire valley in an eerie silver glow. Allahaba had built a roaring blaze, a small spot of light in a thousand square miles of dark and bleak surroundings. Jabeel brought forth something that looked like a portable grill pan, put it on the fire, and began making fresh flat bread on it. He used coarse salt in the flour and on the flat bread, handing Morgan the first disc right off the grill.

Morgan tore into it, hungry, offering half of it to Fox. Jabeel then proceeded to cook rice and a mixture of ground beef, lamb, onions and parsley that he kept sealed up in something that looked like Tupperware. Whatever it was, it was salty and delicious, and Morgan ate until she could eat no more.

The day had been long and exhausting. As Fox, Allahaba and Jabeel talked about British football, Morgan forced herself up from her seated position by the fire and staggered over to the tent that held her and Fox's belongings. Fox, distracted from his conversation, turned to see what she was doing, but the question died on his lips when she emerged from the tent holding one of the brand new sleeping bags.

The three men watched curiously as Morgan trudged over to the fire, laid out the sleeping bag, and then promptly fell on top of it. Fox watched, a smirk on his lips, as she immediately fell asleep with the fire blazing about a foot away from her.

"Oh, bugger," he shook his head, sipping at his very sweet Arabic coffee. "There she goes. Out like a light."

Allahaba shushed him. "Quiet," he whispered. "You will wake her."

Fox laughed. "Are you joking?" he held his cup out when Jabeel offered him more coffee. "She would sleep through a nuclear explosion. I've never seen someone so able to sleep anytime, anyplace. It's too bad, too; she's going to miss dessert."

Morgan's head shot up, blond hair hanging in her face. Fox looked at her and started laughing, realizing her eyes were still closed.

"What dessert?" she asked.

He continued to snort. "Don't worry, love," he told her. "You wouldn't like it anyway. Go back to sleep."

She flopped back down, eyes still closed. "If you eat my

dessert, Fox Henredon, you'll rue the day you were born," she muttered.

He laughed deeply, hands over his mouth so he wouldn't boom. "I promise, I won't."

Morgan yawned. "What dessert?"

She wasn't going to let it go. Fox looked over at Jabeel. "You'd better tell her what you have or she might tear this camp apart looking for it," he told the young man.

Jabeel could see he was joking but moved swiftly to pull out another airtight Tupperware container. "I have cinnamon date cake," he informed them. "I also have chocolate-covered dates."

Morgan's head shot up again; this time, one hand was outstretched. "Chocolate covered dates, please."

Jabeel handed the container to Fox, who stood up and dutifully went over to his wife. He held the container down to her and she picked out a plump, chocolate-covered date. Shoving it into her mouth, she lay back down. Fox stood over her, watching her chew with the enormous date in her mouth.

"You're going to choke if you lie down and try to swallow that," he told her.

She couldn't even reply because her mouth was so full. But she managed to wave him off. With a shake of his head, one of resignation, Fox selected his own date and gave the container back to Jabeel. Reclaiming his seat, he kicked out his enormous legs and gazed up at the brilliant diamond sky above. His dark eyes reflected the night sky as he swallowed his date in one bite.

"It's a time like this that I feel closest to the people of this land," he said. "If I sit here long enough, I swear I can hear ancient Egyptians all around us. Looking up at the sky, you wouldn't know if it was two thousand and ten or two thousand and ten B.C."

Allahaba gazed up into the sky as well. "I understand what

you mean," he agreed, looking away from the beautiful sky to gaze at Fox. "What are your plans for tomorrow, Fox?"

Fox laced his fingers behind his head, leaning back as he continued to gaze skyward.

"I surveyed off the area that I want to do some test digs in tomorrow," he said. "I really should have a permit, but this is such a small scale thing in such a remote area that I'm not going to worry about it. There's about a one hundred foot long, perfectly straight geological formation right over in that area that I marked off. I'm not sure how far down we're going to have to dig to get to it, so that will be our target for the day."

"And if we find something?" Allahaba wanted to know.

Fox looked over at him. "I'll have Morgan take photos and shoot with the video camera. We'll have a record of it. If we do find something, then we've just set the entire field of Egyptology on its ear."

Jabeel, listening to the conversation with interest, cocked his head. "What does that mean?" he asked.

Fox glanced at the man before sitting forward and stretching out the kinks in his back. "It means that this will undoubtedly be a major excavation site and I'm going to fight tooth and nail to claim it for the Bolton Museum. If we have really found Ranthor, then it's my find and I intend to keep it."

Over on the sleeping bag, Morgan suddenly rolled on to her back. "You never said anything about staying in Egypt," she yawned.

He looked at her, mulling over her statement. "I didn't say I would do the excavating," he told her. "But if we really have discovered Ranthor, you can't even imagine what an important find that would be. The impact to the field of Egyptology would be immeasurable."

Morgan didn't say anything; she just lay there with her arms over her face. Five seconds hadn't passed before they heard her snoring softly. Fox sighed heavily and set down his coffee cup.

"Mrs. Henredon is finished for the day," he announced, standing to his considerable height. "In fact, I think we're both finished. I'll see you in the morning."

He went over to Morgan and tried to rouse her so she would get up and he could collect the sleeping bag she was laying on. But she wouldn't awaken and he ended up scooping her up into his arms while Allahaba picked up the sleeping bag. Allahaba went to their tent, opened up the other sleeping bag, and ended up zipping the two of them up together to create one giant sleeping bag. Fox entered the tent with Morgan sleeping against him, thanking Allahaba as the man backed out of the tent and closed the flap.

Fox lay Morgan down upon the open sleeping bag, turning around so he could zip the tent flap close. There was no way with his height that he could stand, so he sat back on the edge of the sleeping bag and pulled Morgan's shoes off. As he went to remove his own shoes, he suddenly felt soft, warm hands grasp the bottom of his shirt.

"Arms up," Morgan said quietly.

He instinctively obeyed, turning to catch a glimpse of her as she pulled his shirt over his head. "What are you doing?" he asked.

She looked sleepy but alert. A seductive smile spread across her lips as she tossed the shirt aside. "Undressing you," she whispered.

He grinned with delight. "Really?" he reached out to pull her against him. "I thought you were too sleepy."

"It was the only way to get you alone. I knew, sooner or later, you would carry me off to bed."

"Clever girl," he nuzzled her, sending chills up her spine.

Morgan gave herself over to him completely, making love to her husband in the dark tent, lit only by the snippets of the brilliant moon outside. Jackals chippered in the distance, lending their eerie song to the timeless quality of the moment. It was sensual, erotic, infused with the deep love they felt for one another. When she finally fell asleep for good, it was wrapped in Fox's enormous arms, as warm and safe as she could possibly feel.

———

On the same road that Fox, Morgan, Allahaba and Jabeel had used to enter the Manjam Hamsh Valley, several pairs of eyes watched the encampment from a distance. The Henredon group hadn't been hard to find, laying down the invitation with tire tracks and the beacon of a distant campfire. The moon was bright and the night still, and it would have been very easy to roust the camp.

But Alezer bin Akil wasn't particularly interested in rousting them at the moment. He knew the American woman was packing a gun and she had every intention of using it. It had been something completely unexpected to a man who had been expecting easy quarry.

Still, he had promised Alia that he would kidnap the woman and hold her. He hadn't been given any reasons for the deed and he hadn't asked; all that mattered to him was that he had a long-standing debt to pay to the el-Shabheen family. Alia's father was a criminal defense attorney in Cairo who had helped Alezer through some government charges against him. Alezer had been on the government's radar for quite some time now and, frankly, he was not inclined to make more trouble for himself, even if it was in repayment of a debt.

So he decided to settle back, watch the Henredon group, and bide his time. He was sure, at some point, the opportunity to abduct the gun-toting American woman would present itself. He would have to be sharp enough to take it.

DECEMBER 5, 1923

Louis is still not feeling well. He stays with William constantly although William is thriving in the wonderful Egyptian climate. Mr. Sula escorted me to a marvelous bazaar in Luxor today. We ate Egyptian delicacies and sipped strong, sweet, Egyptian tea. Mr. Sula has a great love for this country, as do I. He has asked me to call him Kadin, of which I am honored. We have become great friends.

~ FS

TWENTY

THE FOLLOWING day dawned windy and warm. Fox was up as dawn broke, trying to pull Morgan up with him but she refused to budge. So he dressed alone and emerged from the tent to find Jabeel and Allahaba already at the fire, cooking breakfast. The smell of fresh bread and coffee filled the cool dawn air.

Yawning, Fox stood by the fire as Allahaba handed him a cup of strong Arabic coffee. He took a couple of sips, surveying the valley at dawn. It was shades of gray and blue as the sun peeked over the eastern horizon. He felt at peace, content, and back in his element. He'd missed communing with ancient Egypt.

"Too bad that Morgan is still asleep," he said loudly. "She's going to miss a fantastic breakfast."

If Fox had learned one thing about his wife, it was that she had selective hearing. She could sleep through a hurricane and then he'd say the smallest thing and she'd wake up. He continued to sip at his coffee, smelling fresh bread, increasingly eager to get on with the day. Glancing over his shoulder, he didn't see any activity in his tent.

"The coffee is good," he told Allahaba loudly, glancing over his shoulder again. "And the bread smells wonderful. I'm starving."

The flap to his tent suddenly jerked back and Morgan stumbled through, gathering her hair back into a ponytail and winding a rubber band around it. She marched up on the men, unhappy and sleepy.

"I heard you the first time," she grumbled. "I was awake."

Fox bit his lip so she wouldn't see him grin. "I just wanted to make sure."

"Stop nagging."

He did grin, then. "Nagging, am I?" he wrapped a big arm around her and pulled her close. He must have pulled too hard because she grunted when he slammed her against his torso. He kissed her on the cheek. "Good morning to you, too, sunshine of my life. Did you sleep well?"

"Fine." In spite of her grumpy mood, she returned his kiss and turned to Allahaba. "Coffee, please?" she asked.

Allahaba handed her a cup, very sweet, and she took a first contented sip. With Fox's arm still around her, she gazed out over the Manjam Hamsh Wilderness. It was a beautiful, desolate sight.

"What did you want me to do this morning?" she asked Fox.

He was gazing out over his dig site. "Take pictures."

"I'd rather dig."

He looked at her. "It's a lot of work, especially in this soil," he told her. "The ground will be hard."

"I'd still like to try."

He shrugged, nodding reluctantly, secretly suspecting that she'd dig for about an hour and be exhausted. He was completely surprised when she proved him wrong.

After a breakfast of fresh bread, dried fruit and much cinnamon date cake, Morgan followed Fox out to the area he had surveyed. Fox wanted to do at least three test holes so he put Morgan on one of them. She took a pick and shovel that Jabeel had brought in the back of his beat-up Land Rover and began to dig. Fox went over to his own test area but the truth was that he was watching Morgan to see how long it would be before she gave up. Much to his astonishment, she didn't.

She hacked and shoveled well into the morning. Her hole wasn't nearly as deep as Fox's or Allahaba's, but it was neat and methodical. Jabeel brought everyone water when he wasn't helping. Allahaba and Morgan made sure to drink regularly. Fox watched her from the corner of his eye, deeply impressed with her fortitude. Every day he saw something new in her that he loved. As the morning progressed towards noon, she was still digging steadily and Fox paused to pull off his shirt because he was sweating so profusely. Once he did that, she immediately ground to a halt.

"That's *not* fair, Henredon," she pointed a gloved finger at him. "You're doing that to distract me. I'm trying to do a job here."

Fighting off a smirk, he began to flex and pose like a body-builder, displaying his fantastic physique. The man was mouth-watering and he knew it, posing specifically so the beautifully artistic tattoo on his left arm received maximum attention. The ankh symbol was particularly appropriate at the moment. She watched him for a few moments before rolling her eyes and turning away.

"You'd better cut that out," she went back to digging with her back to him.

"Why?" he flexed an enormous bicep, kissing it as if completely self-absorbed. "Don't you like what you see?"

She fought off the giggles. "You big jerk," she muttered.

He heard her laughter in her reply. With a grin, he picked up his shovel and resumed working, his skin turning bronze under the Egyptian winter sun. Morgan was aware that he had left his shirt off and tried to catch a glimpse of him now and then, but Fox must have had radar; every time she looked, he would catch her and flex like a self-centered body builder in the midst of a competition. She would start giggling and pretend like she didn't care.

Noon rolled around and they were all still digging with dedication. Fox's hole was about four feet deep and he hadn't come across anything he could categorize as a ruin. He was coming to think that perhaps he needed to start another hole somewhere else. While he stood and pondered the layers of earth inside his hole, Morgan was on to something.

She had only managed to dig about half of Fox's depth, but her hole was wider than his was. Consequently, she had more underlying earth to work with. As they dug, Fox had them all dump their dirt into a bucket which was, in turn, dumped into a mesh screen that would sift out anything caught in the pile. Jabeel had been working the sifter in between handing out water. Morgan hauled her bucket over to the sifter and poured it in; Jabeel was over with Allahaba so she sifted the dirt herself.

She was expecting all of the dirt to slide through without incident, but this particular batch was different. As she shook the sifter, she noticed small pieces that she first thought were rocks. When she picked one of them up, she realized that it wasn't a rock; it was too round to be a rock in addition to being a dark shade of blue when brushed off. Morgan turned it over in her hand, realizing there was a hole through the center of it. Her eyebrows flew up as she picked it up to more closely inspect it.

"Oh, my God," she breathed. "It looks like a... bead. It's a bead!"

She whirled to Fox; he was about thirty feet away, on his knees as he peered down into his test hole. She started jumping up and down.

"Fox!" she cried excitedly. "A bead! I found a bead!"

Fox's head snapped up to her, registering what she was saying, before bolting to his feet and racing in her direction. He rushed up to her as she practically put his eye out holding up the small relic.

"Let me see," he said calmly.

He took it from her gently, inspecting it carefully and closely in the palm of his hand. By this time, Allahaba and Jabeel had joined Morgan and the three of them watched Fox very carefully inspect the item.

"Well?" Morgan said eagerly.

Fox wasn't so quick to react. He looked at her. "Did you find any more like this?"

She nodded, racing back over to the mesh sifter and picking out the six remaining bits of blue rock. Fox had followed her and she placed them carefully in his hand. He continued to study them, silently, as Morgan, Allahaba and Jabeel wait anxiously. Finally, Fox spoke.

"Show me where you found these," he told Morgan.

She took him back to her hole, pointing down into it. "They came from the very bottom of the hole," she told him. "I was scraping around, trying to widen it, at the bottom."

Fox knelt down beside the hole and just stared at it. Morgan watched him, realizing he was studying all of the layers of the hole itself. Pulling a small, soft paint brush from his back pocket, he began to carefully brush the edges of the hole.

Time marched on and Fox continued brushing. At one point, he had Morgan go over to his test hole and collect a small trowel had been using. Morgan brought it back over to him and he alternately brushed and picked at the sides of her test hole. He found more interest near the bottom of the hole and concentrated his efforts there. Morgan continued to stand over him while Jabeel finally left the group to start lunch.

Morgan didn't want to bother him but the suspense was killing her. When the boredom began to set in, she took to pacing around, but never very far from Fox as he continued to very carefully brush away centuries of earth. He was swept up in what he was doing and, as the day progressed, his bronzed shoulders began to turn red from the sun. Jabeel brought lunch over to them, sandwiches made from cucumber and hummus, but Fox didn't stop to eat. He was busy. So Morgan sat down a few feet away from him with her sandwich, watching him as he worked.

Lunch came and went. Just as Morgan was contemplating a nap, Fox suddenly sat up from the hole with something in his hand. Morgan jumped up from where she had been sitting on the ground a few feet away and went to him.

"What did you find?" she asked.

He was still looking at whatever it was, putting it in the palm of his right hand while he examined it with his left. After a moment, he sighed and shook his head.

"Well," he said slowly. "There's something there; that's for certain. I'm seeing a stratum that looks like some kind of flooring or tile. It's clear as day."

Morgan looked at him, absorbing his words. She noticed that he was still holding a small piece of something in his hand. "What do you have?"

He held it up to her. It was a fragment of pottery that had faint swipes of color on it. "A potsherd," he told her frankly, turning it over in his big fingers. "I can make out a glyph on it, I think."

"Really?" Morgan was very interested. "What does it say?"

He gazed down at the fragment for a moment before speaking. "Egyptian writing is fairly phonetic in nature, meaning that, for example, a drawing of an eye means eye but it also means 'I', as in a first person pronoun. It's also an Abjad alphabet, meaning there are no vowels." He sighed as he looked at the small piece of pottery, the same color as the desert sand. "I'm well-versed in all known forms of Egyptian hieroglyphs, hieratic and demotic. I've made a specialty out of reading any written form of the Egyptian language."

"I know," Morgan interrupted him before he could finish his thoughts. Her brown eyes twinkled at him. "I did my homework on you before I came to see you at the Bolton Museum. You're considered one of the world's foremost experts on written Egyptian language, which is why I came to you with the papyrus. I knew if anyone could decipher it, you could."

He smiled at her, reaching out to gently touch her arm; he didn't want to touch anything else because his hands were so dirty. "Lucky for me," he winked at her before continuing on his train of thought. "Anyway, I've looked at this glyph now for a better part of a half hour and it's the most archaic form of writing I've ever seen. It resembles something I've seen on Gerzean pottery, but even that didn't look quite like this."

Morgan wasn't quite following him. "What's Gerzean?"

"The simplified answer is that it's pre-dynastic Egyptian writing, although there's more to it than that."

"Okay," she lifted her eyebrows expectantly when he didn't elaborate. "So what does it all mean?"

He shook his head. "It means that whatever is here is truly ancient," he looked up at her, the obsidian eyes intense. "There were ancient Egyptian tribes that roamed these deserts prior to the first dynasties, so I wouldn't be surprised if whatever we have here is part of those ancient Egyptian tribes. However, the city of Ranthor is allegedly even more ancient than the pre-dynastic tribes. It's possible that those tribes built their own city on the ruins of Ranthor."

Morgan thought he sounded like he was rambling, trying to

filter out all of the possibilities before forming any kind of opinion. "So what is the symbol on that piece of pottery?"

He looked back at the potsherd. "The glyph is, I'm fairly certain, the symbol for Nut, the goddess of the sky," he replied. "But what's weird about this is that according to the Dendera Papyrus, which is the only recorded reference to the physical city of Ranthor, it refers to Nut as the patron goddess of Ranthor. In later texts throughout the middle and late kingdoms, the term 'ranthor' was used as a pronoun to describe the kingdom of the sky or city of the sky because of the city's close association with Nut."

Morgan stared at him, digesting his explanation. "Then let me ask you this," she asked. "Based on the limited evidence you've been able to glean from this site, what's your professional opinion?"

He sighed, scratching his neck as he looked up at the early afternoon sky. There were vultures high on the drafts; he could see them. He thought on his answer for a moment as he watched the birds cruise.

"It's too soon to form an opinion," he said honestly. "All I have are seven blue beads and a small potsherd. Based on that evidence alone, I would say without a doubt that there is something underneath us. Whether it is the mythical city of Ranthor will have to be determined by massive excavations."

"Are you going to tell somebody about this?"

He nodded, standing on stiff legs. "I have several contacts in the Supreme Council for Antiquities," he replied. "Have no doubt that one way or another, an archaeological excavation will be established here."

"But you're not ready to say it's Ranthor yet?"

"Not yet."

"Are we going to dig here a little more to see if we come up with anything else?"

He shrugged. "I'm not really sure that's necessary," he said. "The papyrus refers to the city of Ranthor being ten days as the sun sets from Amada. With all of the data we could come up with, that puts us right in this spot. And as a result of our test holes today, we've established that there is definitely something here. So I'm satisfied that a city of some kind was here at some point, built along a tributary of the Nile some five or six thousand years ago. Maybe it was Ranthor, maybe it wasn't. But according to you, we're not really out to find the city of Ranthor, are we?"

Morgan gazed up into his dark eyes, slowly shaking her head. "No," she said quietly. "We're looking for Isis' tomb at Mt. Nuqrus."

"And that's about forty kilometers to the east as the crow flies," he told her. "But we'll need to head back up to the main road and cut across, so it will be about sixty kilometers total. We'll get an early start in the morning."

"So you've seen everything you want to see here?"

"I think so."

Morgan wasn't too disappointed about that given that she was off the hook for any more digging, at least for the day. But she was very excited to see what they found at Mr. Nuqrus. She began to collect her shovel and empty water bottles from the sand around her test hole as Fox continued to study the potsherd. She eyed him as she policed her trash.

"How far is Mt. Nuqrus from the Red Sea?" she asked.

He didn't look up from the shard. "About fifteen miles."

"Isn't there a town at the end of the road?"

He nodded. "Marsa Alam."

She walked up next to him, lugging her gear. "There's a resort in that town."

He looked at her. "How would you know that?"

"Because I looked it up on the Internet," she told him. "It's called the Wadi Lahmy Azure Resort. It really looks beautiful."

He lifted an eyebrow, his eyes narrowing suspiciously. "You're trying to tell me something, aren't you?"

She giggled, the dimples deep. "Well, I'm trying to, anyway."

He shook his head. "You've only spent one night on the desert in a tent and already you're talking about a resort?"

She shrugged. "We don't have to sleep in tents every night if the hotel is only fifteen miles away," she pointed out. "That's an easy drive."

He rolled his eyes. "I can see where this is going," he said, already resigned. "I gather you'd rather stay in town tomorrow night?"

She smiled hugely, her baby-doll dimples big. "Thank you for asking, baby. Of course I'd love to stay in a hotel with a real bed and a real bathtub and toilet. You're so sweet to ask."

He snorted, put his arm around her shoulders, and pulled her to him. "You're a character; you know that?"

"That's what you get for knowing me such a short time before you married me."

"I wouldn't have done it any other way."

She hugged him as they turned for the encampment, the mood light. "I wonder if the resort has a spa?" she pondered aloud, knowing that would taunt him.

He squeezed her. "Don't worry about that," he told her. "I'll be your masseuse."

"Do I have to tip you?"

"You better believe it. And not with money, either."

She giggled all the way back to their tent.

DECEMBER 15, 1923

Louis is demanding we return to England, of which I am extremely unhappy. He never developed the love for Egypt that I did. I am still determined to seek the tomb of the goddess Isis and Kadin has sworn to help me. My feelings are torn between my great love for Egypt and my husband and child. It is selfish, I know, but I think I will die if I am not able to see out the final resting place of Isis.

~ FS

TWENTY-ONE

MORGAN AWOKE the next morning with arms and back so sore that she could barely move. She wasn't used to digging and her arms felt like they were about to fall off. Fox was already up and dressed, helping Allahaba and Jabeel load up the Land Rover for departure, and Morgan could hear their voices outside the tent.

Groaning, she struggled to get dressed, managing her jeans and a t-shirt, socks and shoes. She cleaned her face off with a facial-cleansing towelette and even managed to put a little makeup on, at least enough so that she didn't feel like a complete slob. But when it came to doing her hair, she couldn't keep her arms lifted long enough to brush it. Tired, in pain, she called for her husband.

Fox heard her on the third call. He stuck his head inside the tent, smiling at her, but she gave him the big pout and sad face, and held out her hair brush.

"My arms are so sore that I can't lift them up to brush my hair," she told him. "Can you please help me?"

He chuckled and came into the tent, taking the hair brush from her and sitting down on the sleeping bag next to her.

Morgan faced away from him so he could get at her considerable mane of blond hair.

"Just so you know, I've never done this before," he told her, "so I apologize in advance if I mess this up."

"You can't mess it up," she told him. "Just brush it out and then pull it back into a ponytail. You've seen me do it a few times."

"But I won't do it as good as you will."

"Sure you will," she told him. "Besides; I don't have a choice. My arms are killing me."

He grinned, carefully stroking her long hair. It was soft and luscious and he kept running his fingers through it, feeling the sensual texture, remembering how her hair felt when it was splayed on him. But that brought instant arousal so he struggled not to think of how her hair felt against his body as he brushed.

Her hair was fine and straight but she had a lot of it, and it tumbled to her mid-back. He brushed and brushed, finally managing to get a grip on a ponytail at the back of her head but the rubber band wouldn't cooperate, so it took him a few tries. Finally, he was able to put her hair into a respectable ponytail. Morgan inspected it in a mirror, satisfied, and packed the mirror away.

She turned around, kissing him on the lips. "Thank you," she said. "You did a great job. If you every wash out as an Egyptologist, then you can become a hairdresser."

"Not bloody likely," he grunted, standing to a hunched-over position and pulling her to her feet. Morgan groaned with pain.

"Oh, my God," she gasped. "My arms feel like they're going to fall off."

Fox knew what she meant; even though he lifted weights on a regular basis, his arms were still a little sore from the marathon digging they had done the previous day.

"There's some naproxen in my backpack," he told her. "Go take a couple."

Grumbling and groaning, she did what he told her. She washed the naproxen down with a bottle of water as she ate bread, dried fruit and more of the cinnamon date bread while Fox and the others broke down her tent and finished cleaning up the campsite.

As Morgan chewed, she alternately watched the men clean up and the wilderness around her. It was semi-cool on this day; the sand beneath her was cool to the touch and the soft wind that blew had a cool note to it. The sun was struggling to rise, sending out warming rays that hadn't yet reached her. As she looked around, she noticed that the test holes they had dug were filled up. When Fox came to collect the chair she was sitting in, she pointed at the test holes.

"When did you fill those in?" she asked.

He glanced over at the holes. "This morning before you awoke. I didn't want there to be any evidence of digging for treasure hunters or thieves that might cross over this area." He nodded his head in the direction of their dig. "If they catch wind of any kind of undisturbed archaeological dig, they'll tear it apart looking for relics."

Morgan shook her head at the horror of that thought. Fox folded up her chair, took her hand, and led her over to the waiting Land Rover. Piling the chair in the back, he jumped in as Jabeel threw it into gear. In a cloud of dust, they headed back the twenty miles to the main road to start their eastern trek to Mt. Nuqrus.

———

For a day that had started off cool, the temperature rose in a hurry once the sun began to rise. Seated in the third row seat with her legs stretched out across the bench, Morgan was reading a book on Egypt that she had brought along with her from home. With all of the traveling she'd been doing, she hadn't had a chance to sit still for any length of time to read, so as the car sped down the highway and the wind whipped her ponytail around, Morgan read about the Ptolemaic period in Egyptian history.

Fox sat in the bench seat in front of her, stretched out as well, a massive arm over the seat back as he alternately watched Morgan and the passing landscape. He had seen her pull the book out but she was holding it in her lap so he couldn't see the cover. He watched her as she turned the pages.

"What are you reading?" he finally asked.

She didn't look up from the book. "A book on Egypt."

"I wrote one about five years ago, right after the Edfu dig," he told her without a hint of boastfulness. "It centered around...."

She suddenly held the book up from her lap so he could see the book cover. "I know," she pointed to his name across the bottom of the cover. "My mother found this in a bookstore and bought it for me before I left for Egypt. *The Facts of Greek Egypt* by the great Dr. Fox Henredon."

He grinned. "It really does say 'the great' Dr. Henredon, doesn't it?"

She had to laugh at him. "It will on my copy as soon as I find a pen."

He watched her a moment, the gentle pout of her lips, the way her dimples sank deep into her cheeks. She was such an alluring creature. "So... what do you think of it?" he asked hopefully.

She refocused on the book. "I think that you are as intelligent as you are handsome," she said, looking up and winking at him. "Good thing I married you before someone else got to you."

He laughed. "I'll second that," he said. "Want me to auto-graph the book for you?"

She scooted forward on the seat so she was leaning against his arm on the seatback. "Will you write something sexy?" she teased, keeping her voice down so Allahaba and Jabeel couldn't hear her.

He lifted a dark eyebrow, his face looming very close to hers. "I'll write whatever you want," he muttered. "I've got a few ideas. Suggestions for the future, shall we say."

She giggled, kissed his enormous bicep, and sat back against her seat. But he didn't like her back there and patted the seat beside him.

"Come sit with me, love," he said. "I won't bite. Hard."

She laughed. "You stole that line from a movie."

He shrugged. "Maybe," he held out a hand to help her over the seat. "But in your case, it happens to be true."

The car hit a bump and Morgan ended up flipping over the back of the seat and into Fox's lap. She whooped as he grabbed her, holding her tightly so she wouldn't fall off. She put her arms around his big neck as the car lurched over rough road.

"So tell me about Mt. Nuqrus," she said. "You mentioned that it was a gold mine."

He pondered her question. "How technical do you want me to get?"

"As much as you feel the need for," she replied. "But remember that science is not my strong suit. You may see me dozing off if you get too technical."

He snorted. "Okay, let's see," he thought a moment. "To begin with, this entire area is largely underlain by late Precambrian meta-sediments, meta-volcanics and ultramafic rocks intruded by younger to older granitic plutons. The Precambrian sequences are overlain by Cretaceous Nubian sandstone...."

He was cut off when Morgan slapped a hand over his

mouth. "Oh, dear God," she groaned. "Are you serious? I lied. You can't get as technical as you want. Give it to me in simple terms."

He grinned, her hand still over his mouth. "Basically," he said as she removed her hand. "It just means that this was a hotbed for mining from the Pharaonic through Roman times. The Romans had a couple of forts out here to protect the gold mines; one was at Samut, which I mentioned yesterday, and another is at Mt. Nuqrus."

"Are there still Roman ruins there?" she asked.

He nodded. "There are but, more importantly, there have been modern mining operations there in the past few decades. I'm not sure what's there now, so we'll need to be prepared if there is."

"What does that mean?"

"It means we can't jump their mining claim. We can't dig there if there's already another operation."

Morgan didn't like that thought at all; they'd come so far and it made her sick to think that they wouldn't be able to see their quest through to completion. But she remained silent on the matter as Fox shifted her down to the seat beside him and kept a big arm around her.

"The eastern desert is actually very rich in history," he went on, not entirely oblivious to her sudden melancholy. "There are several rock paintings out here from the Old Kingdom. It's also heavy in Roman history because of the gold mines and because of the trade routes from the Red Sea."

"Did you get a chance to travel out here when you were digging at Edfu?" she asked, trying to divert her thoughts from the possibility of not being able to dig around at Mt. Nuqrus.

He gave her a squeeze. "Not really," he said. "I was focused on Edfu and didn't take the time to sightsee. I probably should have, though."

The car continued along the desolate dirt road on its trip north to the main Mars Alam highway. Morgan eventually fell silent, watching the scenery as the twenty kilometers passed before she realized it. Soon, they were at the main highway and Jabeel took a left turn, heading east.

The road was smoother and paved, and much more comfortable. Pushing thoughts of not being able to explore Mt. Nuqrus aside, Morgan settled down against Fox and eventually dozed off in the mid-morning warmth.

Fox felt her go limp against him and he put both arms around her, supporting her so she wouldn't slide off. He knew she was worried about Mt. Nuqrus now and the possibility that there were mining operations going on there. He wasn't concerned, however. He suspected they would be able to walk around and explore the area and if they happened to sink a hole here and there looking for anything that might indicate a tunnel or tomb, then so be it. He was willing to take the heat.

After taking a road off the main highway that took them southeast to Mt. Nuqrus, the mountain range itself appeared around noon. Fox had his maps and images out and was able to pinpoint the mountain easily, so the old Land Rover drew close to the ancient mountain as the desert winds began to kick up.

Morgan stuck her head from the car, peering up at the mountains that supposedly housed Isis' tomb. Coming from Southern California, she was used to big mountains and this one looked more like a foothill to her than a real mountain. But she climbed out of the car, stretching her stiff body and wriggling her sore arms around as Fox, with a big satellite photo in his hands, began to walk around the area to get his bearings. Tired, and feeling carsick to boot, Morgan trailed after him, kicking up rocks and dust as she went.

They walked for several hundred feet until Fox suddenly came to a halt. Morgan walked up beside him, shielding her eyes from the bright noon sun.

"What is it?" she asked.

He pointed off to his left. "The Roman settlement ruins," he said. "See them?"

Morgan was suddenly more interested in her surroundings and less carsick as she walked towards the ancient ruins. The ground was rocky and uneven as she came upon the piles of stone that constituted an ancient Roman camp. She could see what looked like a puzzle, little squares of rocks adjoining bigger squares of rocks. It looked like a giant had walked through and kicked down most of the walls with the way stones were scattered around. There were hundreds of adjoining squares, all of which Morgan found it quite fascinating.

"So what are all of these buildings?" she turned a full circle, looking at all of the piles. "It looks like there were a lot of people here."

Fox wiped the sweat off his brow as he followed her gaze. "Hundreds at the very least," he told her. "Roman mining camps not only contained prisoners for the slave labor, but also soldiers, quartermasters, cooks, commanders; you name it. Over to the west, right over there, looks like it was a big building. Probably either a temple or the commander's quarters. Maybe even a storehouse."

Morgan put a hand up, blocking out the sun as she turned full circle again. "Cool," she commented. "So where was the oasis where travelers would rest?"

Fox pointed toward the south. "There is a cluster of trees to the south end of this range," he said. "It was down there."

"Is there a spring?"

"There was. I don't know if it's still active."

Thoughts lingering on the oasis, Morgan's attention returned once again to the ruins across the dirt road so she went over to inspect them. The wind kicked up, whipping her ponytail around as she stepped inside the ruinous walls. She held on to her hair as she looked around.

"This is really cool," she said, eventually turning so that she faced the southeast. Her brown eyes were fixed on something in the distance. When Fox eventually joined her inside the ruins, she pointed.

"See that down there?" she asked.

He turned casually, looking to what she was pointing at. "I saw it," he said evenly. "It's the mining operations."

"It looks like a big operation."

He nodded before turning to look at her. "Look, love, I know you're worried about that, but I don't think we need to do any digging down where they are."

"Why?"

"Because," he looked back at the image in his hand. "I've been thinking about this and it seems to me that, if I were an ancient Egyptian burying my dead, the last place I would bury it was in the middle of a gold mine. The Egyptians liked to do things secretly, not where people were going to be digging all of the time."

Morgan nodded. "That makes sense," she agreed. "So where would you bury your dead?"

Fox looked up at the hills to the west of the ruins; they were dark and jagged. He pointed to them. "Look at those," he told her. "What do they remind you of?"

Morgan looked up at the dark, ragged hills, and cocked her head thoughtfully. "Like a bunch of knife blades, pointing upwards."

"Or fingers that reach to the sky?"

Her eyes widened and she looked at him. "Yes," she hissed in agreement. "That's exactly what they look like. What did the papyrus say about that again?"

He drew in a long, thoughtful breath as he recalled. "*...which lies deep to the east in the arms of the Syene, to the Fingers that Reach to the Sky. May she know grace and divine protection, our Holy Mistress, foremost Lady of the West, as she Rests in the Shelter of the Sun.*"

Morgan looked around, pondering the passage. "It uses the Fingers that Reach to the Sky like a landmark," she reasoned. "And it says as she rests *in* the Shelter of the Sun, not on it or beneath it. Is that significant?"

Fox shrugged. "It could be," he said. "In could either mean literally inside of it or maybe in view of it."

"So if she's not buried in the gold mine of Mt. Nuqrus, wouldn't it stand to reason that she'd be buried in view of it?"

"It would."

For some reason, Morgan turned to look at the small hill that the Roman ruins were built around. They were spread out all around the small hill but not up the slope or on top of it. She wasn't sure why that hill stuck out to her, but it did. It was equidistance between the dark, jagged hills and the gold mine of Mt. Nuqrus, sitting alone in the wilderness. A thought suddenly occurred to her and she turned to Fox.

"Look at that hill," she pointed at it. "It's got a great view of not only the gold mine but also of the Fingers that Reach to the Sky. See how it's shaped? Almost like a pyramid with a flat top. You said that pyramids weren't built until thousands of years after Ranthor was supposed to have existed. But what if...?"

He was following her with interest. "What if what?"

Morgan shook her head, turning to the hill again. "I don't know," she was out of her element but somehow, what she was thinking made sense. "I'm not an archaeologist, but aren't some of the really old monuments and temples all worn down from thousands of years of erosion and sand?"

He nodded. "Sure."

She was growing more excited about her thoughts. "I've seen pictures of them, looking like lumps and hills," she pointed at the distant hill. "Looking like that. What if... what if, five thousand years ago, that was a temple or a tomb that was built by ancient people? Wouldn't it look like just another hill or lump of sand after all of that time exposed to the elements?"

He looked at the hill and cocked his head. "That's reasonable," he said. "But tombs weren't built like that back then, love. They were...."

"How do you know?" she pressed, cutting him off. "You said yourself that pre-dynastic Egyptians were kind of a mystery. Since it was so long ago and there's so much mystery about how they did things, who says they didn't build a tomb way back then that now looks like a hill? Look at the location of that hill and tell me if it doesn't look out of place to you, a lone hill in the middle of a flat-bottomed sand bed."

He studied it, the shape and size. "It does. Slightly. But that doesn't mean it was a tomb or a temple."

She looked over at it, surrounding by Roman ruins at the base. Another thought occurred to her. "Then tell me this," she said slowly. "Why didn't the Roman's build on it? Is it possible that, two thousand years ago, it looked more like a temple or tomb than it does now? Maybe they could see that. Maybe that's why they didn't build on it. They built all around it, but not *on* it. Why?"

He just looked at her. After a moment, a grin creased his lips. "For someone who's not an archaeologist, that was pretty good. And I'm almost on board with you except for one thing."

"What's that?"

He pointed to the hill. "If the Romans knew that was a temple or a tomb, they would have plundered the hell out of it."

She wouldn't back down. "Who says they didn't?" she countered. "We won't know until we find out if there's anything underneath all that sand and rock."

He thought on that, shrugging his big shoulders after a moment. "Good point."

She watched him as he stared off toward the hill, thinking maybe she was being too pushy about it. She really didn't know anything about the ancient Egyptians, certainly not like Fox knew. She began to feel foolish and backed down a little.

"Did you have another place in mind to start digging?" she asked. "You've been looking over those satellite image photos for days. Maybe you've already figured it out."

He shifted on his big legs, resting his fists on his hips. "I had a few places in mind but nothing as convincing as what you just pointed out," he winked at her. "We can do a few test holes on that hill tomorrow morning and see if we come up with anything. It's as good a place to start as any."

"Hopefully my arms will have recovered a little."

He handed her the images. When she took them, he began massaging her arms. Morgan groaned and grunted with the pleasure-pain of it. Buffeted around in his powerful grip, she ended up off balance and falling into his arms. She laughed when he caught her, scooped her up, and carried her out of the ruins.

Allahaba and Jabeel met them as they crossed the dirt road and Fox set Morgan to her feet. They were discussing where to set up camp when robe-swathed figures approached them from the south, from the direction of the mining camp. It took Fox all of a minute to realize the men were toting guns. He turned his wife for the car.

"Get in the car, love," he told her.

Morgan saw the guns, too. Without a word, she returned to the car but not to stay there; she pulled her service weapon out of her backpack and returned to her husband. Instead of standing next to him, however, she kept walking. Before Fox could stop her, she fired her weapon into the air and watched the robed figures flinch. They came to an instant halt.

"Tell them to stay right there and state their business," she called back to Fox. "If they take another step, I'll take out their legs."

Fox was a little taken-aback by her bold move but in hindsight, he shouldn't have been surprised. Allahaba called to the men, repeating Morgan's command. The men chattered in return, all four of them at the same time, their tone between fear and suspicion.

"They say that we must leave," Allahaba said. "They say this is private property."

Morgan watched the men in the distance. "Tell them we're not leaving," she said. "Tell them we're scientists here to study the Roman ruins. We won't bother their operations."

Allahaba repeated her words. The man who appeared to be in charge took a few angry steps forward, waving his gun around. Morgan assumed a defensive stance, her gun aimed at the guy. As the guy moved closer and began screaming at them, Morgan fired a round into the ground about a foot in front of the man. The concussion was loud and the sand exploded. Startled, the man wisely came to a halt but continued screaming.

"He says that we cannot stay," Allahaba repeated, then shouted something to the man, listening to the response. He shook his head. "He says they will kill us if we stay."

"Not if I kill them first," Morgan said, growing increasingly angry. "You tell them that we're staying. If they stay away from us, we'll stay away from them. But if they try to hurt us, I'll kill every last one of them."

Allahaba cast Fox a concerned expression before relaying the message. The men in the distance began shouting again but they were retracing their steps, turning around to leave. Morgan watched them go, lowering her weapon when they were well out of range. She turned to the men behind her.

"Do you think they'll be back?" she asked.

Allahaba shrugged. "Probably not since they know we have a weapon," he said. "But they will be watching us. We must be vigilant."

"Do they think we want to rob the mine?" Morgan wondered.

"Absolutely," Allahaba nodded. "Remember that we ran into robbers yesterday. They are all over these hills. One can never be too careful."

Allahaba and Jabeel turned back for the car but Fox remained, his gaze lingering on his wife. She walked up to him as she switched the safety on the gun.

"I'm really glad I brought this," she said as she reached him. "It's come in handy twice."

Fox didn't reply so she looked up at him, noting his expression. He looked rather queer and her eyebrows lifted. "What's wrong? Why do you look like that?"

He grunted, scratching his head as he thought on how to tactfully say what he was thinking. Knowing her as he did, however, it was better to be forthright.

"You really should have consulted with me before charging off with a gun like that," he told her. "You immediately put those people on their guard. Of course, they thought we have come to rob them. We have a gun, don't we? They were probably just coming over to talk but you started firing off that gun and I don't blame them for being wary of us."

She gazed up at him, confusion across her lovely face. "But

they had guns," she reminded them. "How did we know they weren't coming over here to shoot us?"

"We didn't," he said. "Which is why I told you to get in the car. I would have rather settled this peacefully if possible without bringing out all of the artillery. You should have, at least, let me talk to them before you started shooting."

Her confusion was leaving her, being replaced by a sense of self-defense. "I saw it as a preemptive measure," she said. "Why are you so willing to trust men you don't even know, men who happen to be carrying guns no less?"

He didn't want to get in a big battle with her but it was clear they had two different approaches to violence; with Morgan, it was what she was trained for. For Fox, he'd never picked up a gun in his life. Any fighting he had done had been purely with his fists. Finally, he just threw up his hands.

"Look," he said pointedly. "I don't want to argue about this but next time, tell me what you're going to do before you do it. You're not John Wayne fending off an Indian attack. Cowboy tactics aren't going to win you any friends out here. You may get somebody killed."

"Cowboy tactics?" she repeated, insulted. "In no way are my tactics outrageous. I was defending us."

"You think so but some might call your actions reckless," he pointed out. "You went off half-cocked before words were even exchanged."

Morgan just stared at him. He could feel the weight of those brown eyes. Rather than spar with him, she simply turned and walked away. He watched her go back to the car, climbing in to pack the gun away. As he watched, she lay down on the bench seat of the car and disappeared from sight.

With a heavy sigh, he went to find Allahaba to see about setting up their camp.

DECEMBER 23, 1923

Christmas is approaching but in Egypt, it is much different. Islam does not celebrate Christmas as we know it. Louis is still determined to return home but I do not want to leave this lovely land. Kadin has been vital in figuring out the clues of the papyrus and I feel compelled to remain in Egypt. I must find what the papyrus alludes to. I only wish Louis understood.

~ FS

TWENTY-TWO

SINCE THEY WERE ALREADY on the radar of the mining company, Fox thought it would be best to put their camp as out of the way as possible. There was a small canyon to the east of the Roman ruins, so Jabeel pulled the car into it and the three men began unloading the supplies and camping equipment.

Fox couldn't concentrate on what he was doing, knowing Morgan was still in the car licking her wounds from the scolding he had given her. But in his opinion, he hadn't been out of line. She had gone off half-cocked at the first sign of trouble and could have gotten herself killed. If he thought about it, that's what he was really upset about; the thought of Morgan with a bullet in her. In a little over a month, the woman had become his entire world. He couldn't imagine living without her.

He knew she was a cop, but somehow, out here in the wilds of Egypt, it was easier to pretend she didn't risk her life on a daily basis. He was secretly glad she wanted to move to England, because it would take her out of her dangerous detective work for a while. Maybe in the time she was job-hunting, he could talk her into a nice desk job somewhere. He'd joked about it before but he was growing increasingly serious about it. He didn't want his wife wearing a badge for a living but maybe that was something he should have thought about before he so swiftly married her. She told him he would have to get used to the idea. He didn't want to get used to it. He hated it.

So he took out his frustrations as he pitched their tent, thinking of the erotic lovemaking that had taken place inside of it the night before. It made him miss her horribly, deeply sorry they had quarreled. Although he didn't think he'd been out of line, he was willing to apologize and forget the whole thing anyway. He would cave in if only to make things well between them again. He wasn't a fighter by nature when it came to women. He was much more the pushover type. As he made his way back over to the car, it occurred to him that this was the first real argument they'd ever had. He hated the feeling.

He arrived at the car, peering into the backseat to see if Morgan was asleep. Mildly surprised to find her gone, he looked around for her. He'd had his back to the car as he'd pitched their tent; moreover, the car was parked in the middle of the small canyon while the men had been pitching their camp back in one of the canyon's many inlets. As Fox looked around, he realized she was nowhere within his line of sight.

"Morgan?" he called.

Only the desert silence answered. Puzzled, he turned to Allahaba and Jabeel as they struggled to erect the makeshift toilet several feet away.

"Al?" he called. "Did you see Morgan walk away?"

Allahaba was driving the PVC pipe into the ground. His head popped up and he came away from the toilet project, hammer still in hand, as he approached Fox.

"She was in the car the last time I saw her," he said, looking around just as Fox was. "She is not there?"

Fox shook his head, growing increasingly concerned. "Maybe she went to find a secluded corner to use as a loo," he said as he started walking towards the north end of the canyon. "Morgan?" he called loudly.

More silence greeted him. In little time, Fox was running, shouting her name as he raced out of the canyon and into an adjoining sandy plain. It was about a half mile in circumference, with a sloping western side that led up to the main dirt road. That road then led to the paved road, about five miles to the north. Fox looked around in a panic, realizing after a moment that he was seeing footprints in the dust. He peered closely at them; they looked like a tennis shoe. Morgan had been wearing tennis shoes. The prints led up to the road.

"Damn," he hissed.

Racing back to the gully where Allahaba and Jabeel were still looking for Morgan, he shouted at Jabeel.

"Give me the keys," he snapped. "She's run off to the road."

Jabeel didn't ask questions; he tossed the man the car keys. Fox jumped in, revved the engine, and tore off.

It didn't take him long to find her. She was about a mile and half up the road, marching purposefully with her backpack slung over her shoulder. Fox pulled the car in front of her, cutting her off, as he bailed from the driver's side. When he came around the side of the car, his obsidian eyes were blazing.

"Where in the hell are you going?" he boomed.

Morgan was sweaty and tired. She stepped back from him as he advanced on her. "Don't you dare yell at me," she hissed. "I'm going to walk to that town near the Red Sea and I'm going to check myself in to a hotel room, and I'm going to stay there alone where I'm not being judged or yelled at or made to feel like I'm the biggest idiot on the face of this earth."

Fox watched her eyes fill with tears, spilling over onto her dusty cheeks, and it undid him. He almost felt like crying himself.

"Is that what you think?" he asked hoarsely. "Do I really judge you and make you feel like the biggest idiot in the world?"

She nodded, breaking into soft sobs. She wiped at her cheeks, smearing mud across her skin. "You hate my job; I get it," she wept. "But you don't have any right to criticize me. You don't have any right to call me names when I react the way I'm trained to react."

He sighed heavily. "I never called you names."

"You called me a cowboy," she countered. "You called me reckless and that's just not fair. Just because I don't think like you do doesn't mean I'm irresponsible. I'm actually very good at what I do, believe it or not."

"I believe it, love," he whispered.

"Then stop acting like you're ashamed of me!" she shouted.

He let her vent; he deserved it. "I'm sorry, Morgan," he murmured. "I'm so sorry. I didn't mean to make you feel foolish. But you scared me today. You rushed out to confront those men without even knowing their business. You started firing off your gun and issuing threats. I worked in Egypt for three years and never did anything close to what you did and I've run into some troublemakers in my time. It's just my policy to talk it out rather than fight it out."

She continued to wipe at the tears streaming down her cheeks. "So you're telling me you're completely non-violent, even if you have to defend yourself?"

He hung his head a moment, listening to her sniffle. He felt like the biggest jerk in the world. But it was also clear that it was time for a confession of sorts. It was important.

"No," he said quietly, lifting his head to look at her. "See this nose? It's been broken a few times. Want to know why? Because I was the ultra-heavyweight champion bare knuckle boxer in the United Kingdom for four years in a row. I used the prize money to pay off my school bills. When I got bored of boxing, I played rugby which, as you know, is another gentle sport. So in answer to your question, I am not completely non-violent. I can knock a man out in one punch and my hands are lethal weapons."

Morgan stared at him, startled by his admission. In all of the deep conversations they'd had over the past month, he'd never mentioned his life as a bare knuckle boxer. Her tears began to dry up as she contemplated his confession.

"Then why do you judge me so harshly?" she wanted to know. "In all of the time I've known you, you've never once told me you were proud of what I did or proud that I have succeeded in a difficult profession. All you've ever tried to do is talk me out of something I really love. Is that really fair, Fox? I've never once tried to talk you out of being an Egyptologist so you could be a lawyer or a doctor. All I've ever done is tell you how wonderful you are at what you do. I would just like the same courtesy."

His jaw ticked faintly as he digested her words, knowing she was right but fighting with the last scraps of reason to defend himself.

"I just don't want to see you get hurt," he offered weakly. "It would just destroy me, Morgan. You have no idea how much it would destroy me."

"So you want to put me in a glass bubble?" she shook her head at him. "I can get killed driving down the street or walking on the sidewalk. It can happen anywhere. What is it you want from me, Fox? A pretty wife who stays home like a good girl, lives in a box and raises children? Because if that's really what you want, then this marriage needs to be annulled."

That was it for Fox; he fixed on her intently, his enormous hands open and pleading. "God, don't even suggest annulment," he whispered. "You're right; you're absolutely right. I'm so sorry I've come across like a chauvinist. I didn't mean to but that's exactly what it looks like. I'm so busy loving this perfect relationship that I want to create a perfect world to go along with it and that means you're not carrying a gun and a badge. It means you're safe always and I have complete control of the situation. But I'm starting to realize that there are some things I can't control. I just have to accept and deal with them and your profession is one of those things."

He looked so sad that Morgan felt herself relenting. "You've been saying that since I met you," she said. "I haven't seen any progress."

He put his hands up in surrender. "I know, I know," he agreed swiftly. "But I will try; I really will try. And just so you know, you have deeply impressed me with your bravery and skills. I think you're extremely good at what you do. But it also scares me to death and I'm having a hard time reconciling that."

Morgan was staring at the ground as he spoke. When he was finished, she just stood there and stared at the sand. Fox watched her, praying she was going to forgive him, feeling more desperate and sad than he ever had in his life. As he watched, Morgan turned and, without a word, climbed into the Jeep.

Fox climbed into the driver's side but he didn't start the rig. He just sat there with her, feeling the silence like a huge weight on his chest. He couldn't breathe. Everything about him hurt.

"Please, love," he whispered, closing his eyes tightly. "Don't hate me. Please don't do that."

Morgan didn't say anything for a moment. "I don't hate you," she finally whispered. "I love you so much that it hurts. Fox, maybe I'm the one being selfish in all of this. If it means that much to you that I'm not a cop, then I guess the bottom line is that you're more important than a job. My ex-husband tried to tell me that once but I just didn't get it. But I get it now; if I had to pick between my career and you, then I would pick you every time."

He turned to her, staring at her beautiful profile, feeling anguish and regret and deep, abiding love. As she continued to stare at her lap, he leaned over, very slowly and very gently, putting an enormous hand on her cheek. Very gently, he pulled her face to his lips, planting the most loving and delicate of kisses on her left cheek. The moment he did it, Morgan burst into tears again, crumbling against him. Fox wrapped his enormous arms around her and held her close.

"We'll go into town tonight and get a room," he whispered. "I won't make you stay out here, I promise."

She couldn't even answer him, all of the hurt and emotion she was feeling finding a release. Fox held her tightly, his enormous hand holding her head against his chest, listening to her sob and feeling about as bad as he possibly could.

"Please don't cry," he whispered, kissing the top of her head. "I love you so much. Just try to remember that everything I say or do stems from the fact that I love you more than I have ever loved anything in my life. I couldn't go on if anything ever happened to you."

She sobbed against his warm, powerful body, eventually quieting to the point of just laying wearily against him, sniffling now and again. She could hear his heart beating steadily in her right ear and feel his hand on her head, stroking her hair gently. She closed her eyes, his beating heart and gentle manner succeeding in calming her.

"Were you really a bare knuckle fighter?" she asked, her nose stuffy from crying.

He grinned. "I was. My ring name was Goliath Jones."

She pulled away from him, looking up at him as she wiped at her nose. "That's fitting," she commented. Then she lifted one of his hands, looking at the knuckles. "I never noticed all the scars you have on your hands."

He watched her as she inspected his flesh. "I've got a few," he agreed. "I had my nose broken four times."

She dropped his hands and inspected his nose. It was long and slightly off center, with a bit of a bump in the middle. She grinned at him. "It doesn't take away from your stunning good looks, you sexy devil," she patted his cheek, watching his impish grin spread. "Bare knuckle boxing is basically street fighting. It's fight club stuff."

"It is."

"It's not legal."

He fought off a grin. "Are you going to arrest me?"

She smirked. "No," she said. "But it's a brutal sport. You just get the crap beat out of you."

"Yes, you do," he agreed. "But, fortunately, I was the one beating the crap out of somebody else most of the time."

Her eyebrows rose. "And you had the nerve to call my profession dangerous?"

His smile faded. "Do we have to get into that again? I said I was sorry. I meant it."

She shook her head, putting her fingers over his lips. "I know," she said. "I wasn't getting back into it. I was just expressing shock because boxing is such a dangerous sport."

He cocked an eyebrow. "No more dangerous than going to Egypt with you," he teased gently.

She scowled at him, pretending to be mad, and he scooped her up against him, nuzzling her neck and shoulders. He couldn't describe the relief he was feeling now that things were well between them again.

"Let's go back to camp and get Allahaba and Jabeel," he said, his mouth muffled against her warm flesh. "We'll bring them into town with us. I don't want to leave them out here alone."

She was quiet a moment. "We really don't have to go into town," she said. "We can stay out here. I'm fine with that. I've done nothing but complain and bitch the entire time we've been out here and I'm sort of embarrassed about it. I guess I was more high maintenance than I thought."

He pulled his face out of her shoulder to look at her, a smile playing on his lips. "I don't think you've been complaining the entire time," he said. "And if you weren't a little high maintenance, I'd worry."

She looked at him, the impish grin on his face, and chuckled. Putting her hands on his cheeks, she kissed him soundly on the lips.

"I love you," she murmured, kissing him again. "Thank you for putting up with my crap."

His enormous arms tightened and he pulled her against him, returning her kisses far more lustily. "Thank you for putting up with mine," he whispered.

Fortunately, the road was deserted and free from prying eyes. The clothes began to come off and the back seat of the car served well for their lovemaking purposes.

———

In the tent in the dark little canyon near the Roman ruins, Morgan dreamt of guns and violence that night. But the morning dawned and she was glad it had only been dreams, rising when Fox did, surprisingly, and using some of the baby wipes she brought to wash up a little before dressing.

As Fox kissed her and left the tent to go about his tasks, Morgan swabbed down with the baby-scented wipes, washing her entire body with them including her feet. Finished and smelling like a baby, she put on clean jeans, t-shirt and socks. The shoes went on, the hair went up, and with sunglasses in hand she bolted from the tent.

She found Fox and Allahaba surveying the hill. Jabeel gave her that morning's breakfast of the last of the cinnamon date cake and a hot cup of coffee. Morgan ate her breakfast as Allahaba and Fox climbed all over the lone hill.

Morgan watched them for a while until she grew bored and began to walk among the ruins of the Roman settlement. She stood inside the stone squares, imagining what the rooms would have looked like and who would have lived there. She'd seen the Gladiator and Roman movies so she knew, at least from a Hollywood standpoint, how the Romans treated their slaves. She walked the ruins, wondering how many men had died there.

Sometime around noon, Fox finished what he was doing and saw her sitting in the ruins of the great house. Handing the Abney surveyor over to Allahaba, he made his way down the hill and crossed the dirt road. He came up behind Morgan as she sat on her bottom, apparently looking at something on the ground. He crouched behind her, his big hands on her arms.

"What are you looking at?" he asked, kissing her on the top of the head.

Morgan pointed to a stone on the ground. "That," she said. "It looks like someone carved something on it."

Fox peered at the stone. It was about a foot wide, maybe eight inches in height, of the same type of rock that littered the area. The Romans had used them for building material and there were tens of thousands of them scattered all over the place. But this stone was different; he could see carvings on it and he reached over her shoulder and picked it up, studying it closely.

"I'll be damned," he moved the stone around to see if he could view more of the carving from another angle. "It looks like Latin."

"Latin?" she repeated, looking around to see if there were more carvings on the ground that she had missed. "Did the Romans do it?"

He nodded. "More than likely," he replied. "It's fairly faded, but I can make out a few letters."

"Can you read Latin?"

He grinned, not taking his eyes off the stone. "You didn't read very much of my book, did you?"

She was guilty. "Well," she said reluctantly. "Not too much. I got distracted. But it was a really good book so far."

He laughed. "Don't sweat it," he told her. "Towards the end of the book, I translate several phrases from hieroglyphs to Latin so in answer to your question, yes, I can read Latin."

"Then what does it say?"

He wished he had his reading glasses as he studied the carving. "A-e-m-i-l-l-i-u-s."

"Really?" she was surprised, rising to her knees and knocking him off balance in the process. As he rocked over onto his bum, she took the stone from him. "Aemillius? Is that a person?"

He nodded. "It must be somebody's name."

"And he carved it on a stone? Wasn't it rare for slaves to read and write?"

He pushed himself up off the dirt, brushing off his jeans when he stood up. "It wasn't just slaves who were used for forced labor," he told her. "It was political prisoners, or prisoners of war. It could have been a senator's son for all I know. This bloke was obviously educated or at least exposed to education if he's carving his name in walls."

Morgan looked at him, looked at the stone, and grinned. The she held the stone up like a trophy. "I'm an archaeologist," she announced. "I discovered two thousand year old graffiti!"

She whooped and danced around and he shook his head at her, grinning, as he turned and headed back towards the surveyed hill.

"Come along, doctor," he told her. "You've got some digging to do."

She stopped mid-whoop. "Really? Cool." She skipped after him with her precious artifact. "Let's dig."

She caught up to him, almost tripping because she was still looking at her stone. He laughed, shaking his head at her antics. As always, she was a humorous joy to be around. "How are your arms?" he asked.

She shrugged. "They're still sore but I think I can dig. I'm going to give it a shot, anyway."

He put his dinner plate-sized hand on her head affectionately as they approached the hill. Allahaba and Jabeel were already there with the shovels, picks, brushes and buckets. Jabeel was putting together the mesh sifter for the spoils. Morgan ran all the way back to the car to put her precious stone into her backpack before returning, collecting a shovel, and going to the area where Fox was indicating. He had her section off a twelve inch square area and got to work.

Morgan was right on the top of the hill, on the cusp of the edge, as she began to dig. Her arms were sore but she refused to give in to the pain, instead, working through it even to the point of groaning every time she pushed the shovel into the dirt. This dirt was fairly loose and rocky as compared to the dirt they were digging in over at Ranthor, so the first several inches came off easily. After that, however, it turned into something just this side of cement. After the first few hacking tries with the shovel, Morgan broke out the pick and began to chip away.

Fox was down the slope, watching her throw her entire body into her swings and knowing how sore she was going to be by the evening. But she didn't back down and his admiration for her was renewed as he watch her pound away at the hole. He finally left his own hole to go offer to help her, but she refused his aid. Fox tried to insist but she just smiled and pushed him away. So he left her to her pick and shovel, returning to his own dig hole, watching his wife in between shovelfuls of earth. Mostly, he just didn't want her to hurt herself but he also liked watching her breasts jiggle every time she moved. He had lied to her; he really *was* a chauvinist.

Morgan, Fox and Allahaba continued digging into the late afternoon. Twice, they had seen armed guards from the gold mine to the south watching them but the men came no closer. Morgan saw them, too, but after what happened between her and Fox yesterday, she was less inclined to go running for her gun. So she kept an eye on the men in the distance, watching them fade in and out of view as the day progressed.

Morgan didn't realize how much of her focus had been on the gun-toting men from the gold mine. Even though she had been looking at the hole in the ground, her mind had been reaching out towards the south. By the time she really took a good, hard look at what she was doing, she realized she had chipped away a fairly deep hole. Her shoulders and triceps were killing her, but she didn't want to stop. She had to keep digging.

Jabeel kept running up the hill and taking her buckets of spoils, running them through the mesh sifter and then bringing the empty buckets up to her. As dusk began to turn the sky colors of orange and pink, Fox finally ceased digging on his own test hole. He turned the shovels and brushes back over to Jabeel before turning to his wife, still up on the crest of the hill.

Morgan was about forty feet from the floor of the valley, still plugging away with her pick and shovel. Fox stood there a moment, watching her, shaking his head when he realized he'd be rubbing her arms and shoulders all night after her strenuous day. The woman was digging like a coal miner. He climbed up the hill, making sure to stay in her line of sight so she wouldn't nail him with the shovel.

Morgan saw him coming and she came to a halt, panting

with exertion. But she managed to smile at him as he came upon her.

"Whew," she breathed. "I'm exhausted."

"Ready to quit for the day?"

She looked around, down the slope at the two other test holes that had been dug. "I don't know," she said. "Did you guys come across anything?"

He shook his head. "Nothing at all. The stone you found is the only artifact we've found all day."

She sighed heavily, looking down at her hole, which was now about three and a half feet deep by about five feet in diameter. She knelt down, pointing at it.

"Only the top eight inches of soil were sandy and loose," she said. "After that, it was almost like cement. It's been a bitch to chip away at."

He nodded, inspecting her hole. "I had about two feet of loose soil before it turned into this hard stuff," he told her. "It's probably the location, up here on the rise. This area would get more of the winds and erosion. Some winds blow loose soil away and some deposit it. It's kind of a never-ending circle."

Morgan sat down on her bum, coming to realize that she was extremely tired. "Well, the packed dirt underneath is certainly hard," she picked up her water bottle and drank the last of her water. "How long before we should know something?"

His gaze was in the hole. "I would think that by tomorrow if we keep digging and find nothing, we can pretty much assume there's nothing here and move on to another area."

Morgan didn't like that thought. "Don't you usually keep digging for a few days just to be sure?"

He shrugged. "It depends," he replied. "At Edfu, there was stuff on the surface so it was just a matter of clearing away the soil and debris. Howard Carter dug for years before he found

Tutankhamun's tomb, and even then, it was kind of a stroke of blind luck."

Morgan looked at her hole thoughtfully, growing increasingly depressed that he was willing to give up digging after only a couple of days.

"It's possible that we'll dig around here for weeks and never find anything," she murmured.

He watched her, noting the gloomy expression on her face. "It's not only possible, it's probable," he said, somewhat gently. "Love, I know you want to finish this quest for Fanny's sake and I do, too, but surely you didn't come here expecting to actually find something the first time out."

She shrugged, her gaze moving from the hole to the stars that were starting to appear in the sky. "The papyrus said we would."

He sighed faintly. "Honey-love, you know as well as I do that all of the clues we pieced together from the papyrus are guesses. There are no guarantees. We could be hundreds of miles off base. Or the papyrus could simply be pretty poetry and nothing more. But as much as I know that, even I'm hoping for a miracle."

"Me, too," she said, somewhat depressed. "But I'm realistic; I don't really expect it. I just really, really wanted to finish Fanny's story. I wanted to give her a happy ending."

He smiled at her, the dark eyes glimmering. "You just don't get it, do you?"

"Get what?"

He reached out to touch her hand. "Fanny already *has* a happy ending," he pointed out. "Married to the love of her life for seventy-five years is a hell of a happy ending. Plus, she got to meet you. Don't you see that by finding her, however accidental, you've already written the end to the woman's story? You brought her life full circle. You already gave her that happy ending and you don't even realize it."

Morgan was looking at him with tears in her eyes. "You say the sweetest things," she breathed.

His smile broadened. "It's true," he murmured. "So why don't we shut this down for the night and start fresh tomorrow. Okay?"

She sniffled and blinked away the tears, struggling to rise on weary legs. "Okay," she said, but she picked up the pick again anyway and took another few hits.

Fox stood up and watched her, hands on his hips. "Morgan, my love," he said gently, as if to encourage her to stop. "Let's go get some dinner. I'm starving."

Morgan sighed heavily and made one more chop at the hard, hard earth. "Just a few more minutes and I'll stop, I promise."

He shook his head and reached out for the pick. "No," he told her as kindly as he could. "Stop now. We'll start first thing in the morning. You need to eat and get some sleep."

She pulled the pick out of his reach, losing her grip on it in the process. The thing sailed into the hole, smacking the bottom of the hard-packed earth with a thud. But instead of simply laying there, the pick disappeared. Morgan and Fox watched, shocked, as a hole opened up at the bottom of the pit and the pick fell through. They could hear it hitting something hard down in the hole, clanging and banging as it seemed to fall further and further away from them.

"Oh, my God," Morgan gasped, falling to her knees. "A... a hole!"

Fox was right beside her, trying to peer down into the eight inch in diameter hole at the bottom of the test pit. He didn't miss a beat; he pushed himself up and yelled.

"Al!" he boomed. "Bring a flashlight!"

Morgan was starting to move into the pit but he grabbed her. "No," he commanded. "Stay where you are. We have no way of knowing what's under that hole."

Morgan was electrified. She was practically jumping up and down as he held her. "A hole," she repeated over and over. "There's something here; I told you there was!"

He had her around the waist, tightly, so she couldn't get away from him as he gazed at the black hole three feet down in the pit. Truth was, he wasn't quite sure what to think. He was struggling not to let the excitement get the better of him, so his professional, clinical persona took over.

"This area has been mined for gold for centuries," he said calmly. "It could be a mine shaft."

"Or it could be a tomb!"

He wouldn't give in to her enthusiasm, not just yet. He struggled to stay on an even keel as Morgan squirmed excitedly in his arms. Fox swore that if he didn't have a good grip on her, she would have jumped head-first into that hole and disappeared just like the pick. As he held on to his wriggling wife, Allahaba and Jabeel appeared at his side.

Both men were huffing and puffing from their run up the rocky hill. Allahaba had two big flashlights, handing one to Fox. Fox flipped the switch and directed the light into the jagged, black hole.

Unfortunately, they couldn't see anything from their vantage point three feet above on the rim of the depression. The fact that the sun was setting only made visibility worse. Fox lay on his stomach and shimmied down the side of the pit, trying to catch a better glimpse, but it wasn't enough. He pulled himself back out of the pit and looked at Allahaba.

"We need to get a better look but I'm afraid I'm too heavy to do it," he said to the man. "Get on your belly and slide down there. I'll hold your feet."

Allahaba shook his head. "This is your find, Fox. You must do it."

Fox waved him off. "I'm too heavy for you to hold." He began to push the man down onto his belly. "Slide down there. I'll hold your feet."

Allahaba did as he was told. With Fox holding his ankles and Morgan all but crawling out of her skin with excitement, Allahaba slid down the side of the pit, flashlight blaring in his hand. He reached the bottom of the cavity, picking away at the existing hole as he poked the flashlight down inside. He struggled to make heads or tails out of what he could see, laboring to get a good vantage point without chipping away more of the hole. He had no way of knowing if a bigger section would collapse and dump him down into the unknown depths.

Morgan was on her knees next to Fox, so excited she couldn't stand it. Her hands were folded in front of her mouth as if praying and Fox could hear excited grunts now and again. But he kept cool, as smooth as silk and as right as rain while Allahaba finally gained a peek at what was beyond in the darkness of the hole.

After several long moments of waiting, Fox finally asked the fateful question. He had to.

"Well?" he asked. "What do you see?"

Allahaba didn't say anything for a moment. Then, he rolled onto his side, craning his neck back so he could look at Fox.

"Fox," he said in a low, calm voice. "You had better see this."

Fox's calm demeanor was slipping. "Why? What is it?"

Allahaba sighed faintly, his dark eyes glimmering in the fading sunlight. "Stairs," he replied faintly. "Sixteen of them leading down to a doorway."

Because of Louis and William, we have remained in Luxor. Kadin has told me many tales of ancient Egypt and the goddess we are searching for, Isis. He told me the tale of Isis and Osiris, and of the evil brother, Seth, who cut Osiris into pieces. Isis loved Osiris so much that she found his body parts and sewed him together again. I am coming to understand what love she must have felt for him.

    ~ FS

TWENTY-THREE

"HE HAS MOVED," Beni was getting spotty reception on his cell phone even though he was near Edfu and the cell towers built there to look like palm trees. "We followed him to the Manjam Hamsh Wilderness and now he's at the old Roman gold mines near Marsa Alam."

Alia, in her office in Cairo, rose from her seat to close the office door before replying. "Marsa Alam?" she repeated. "What in the world is he doing there? There's nothing there but old ruins and desert."

Beni was trying not to make eye contact with any of the drug lord's men around him, hard and bitter men who would kill with the wrong look or wrong word. The past few days with them, following Dr. Henredon through the desert, had been a nightmare. He sincerely wished there was some way to get out of all of this. With the drug lord on one side and Alia on the other, he was in hell.

"I am not sure," Beni replied. "He was digging as of two days ago in the Manjam Hamsh Wilderness."

"Did you see what it was?"

Beni shook his head. "No," he replied. "You gave these men

orders to follow Dr. Fox and that is what they are doing. We are following him. We did not stop to see what he had been digging."

Alia fell silent, contemplating the strange actions of Fox. He was obviously following some pre-planned path; Fox Henredon was methodical if nothing else. She knew that much about him to know he had something in mind. She began to think about the ancient journal and the papyrus translation contained therein. Maybe it wasn't such a worthless venture as she thought it was because Fox was still pursuing something that had him fascinated. Maybe he had actually found something in spite of Alia's prediction that he wouldn't.

"What about his wife?" she asked. "Do you have her yet?"

Beni cleared his throat; she wasn't going to like the answer. "We made an attempt," he said. "Mrs. Fox carries a gun and she is very good with it. Alezer is not so inclined to abduct her because she shot one of his men."

On the other end of the line, Alia growled. "I cannot believe this," she hissed. "She is one small woman. Alezer has many men. It cannot be difficult to take the gun from her."

"You would think not, but it is," Beni replied steadily. "Alezer will not try to take her again for fear he will lose more men in the process. So he follows Dr. Fox as you asked him to. What more do you want us to do?"

Alia was furious. She stomped around her office, knocking things angrily off her desk, throwing pencils to the floor. In her warped mind, this was turning into more and more of a game, a competition, and it was one she intended to win. Fox and his stupid American wife would not outsmart her.

"Idiots!" she fumed. "You're all idiots!"

"Is that what you wish for me to tell Alezer?"

Alia froze, hearing something of a taunt in Beni's voice. She didn't like it one bit. "Listen to me and listen well," she hissed.

"Since you cannot seem to do what has been asked of you, I am coming down to Edfu. I will take care of this myself."

Beni didn't like the sound of that. "Take care of what?" he asked sincerely. "Dr. Alia, there is nothing you can do. Dr. Fox has done nothing wrong, nor has his wife. What is it you want from him? I do not understand."

Alia wasn't going to explain herself but she made a mental note to slap Beni silly for his insubordination. And then she would fire him.

"I will be down there tomorrow," she snapped. "There is a flight that runs from Cairo to Luxor around seven thirty in the evening. I have taken it before. You will pick me up at the airport and take me to Fox. I will handle this myself; is that clear?"

Beni didn't say a word. Chilled, full of regret and torn by the knowledge of what Alia was capable of, he hung up the phone. He just couldn't take it anymore, fear or no fear.

He turned the phone off.

———

Morgan had been wide awake for hours. Fox thought he had put her to sleep sometime around midnight, when he had massaged her sore shoulders and back until his hands hurt. She had been still and unmoving so he had fallen asleep beside her, only to awaken a couple of hours later to find her sitting up next to him. He sighed heavily, glanced at his watch, and put his hand on her back again.

"Love, please lie down and get some sleep," he was lying on his side, gazing up at her. "Morning is a few hours off yet."

She looked down at him, her blond hair mussed and circles under her lovely eyes. "I know," she whispered. "I'm trying to sleep but I just can't. Fox, how can you be so calm when the discovery of the century is right outside of this tent?"

He tugged on her, pulling her down against him. He swallowed her up in his big arms, his chin on the top of her head.

"There's absolutely nothing I can do about it right now," he murmured. "We didn't come prepared for night excavations, so until the sun comes up, we're just going to have to wait."

"I don't know if I can."

"What's your alterative? Running up that hill in complete darkness and breaking your neck because you can't see anything?"

"Maybe."

He grinned and began rubbing her back again, hoping to relax her enough so she would fall asleep. "You know," he said, "this is something I've never faced with you before. I've never seen anyone fall asleep at the drop of a hat like you do. Now you can't fall asleep no matter what I do. Maybe I should blast some music. Or maybe we should have wild, passionate sex."

She smiled in spite of herself, her eyelids becoming droopy as she lay against his warmth. "What do you think is underneath that hole?"

He sighed, closing his eyes. "I told you earlier," he said quietly. "I'm not going to speculate until we open it up and I can see what Allahaba saw. I'm not going to even guess."

Morgan was growing increasingly sleepy; something about his heat and deep, soothing voice lulled her. "If it is a tomb, are you going to excavate it?"

"Don't get ahead of yourself."

"But if you had a choice, would you excavate Ranthor or Isis' tomb?"

"Will you go to sleep if I give you an answer?"

"Yes."

"The tomb. Good night."

"You'll go into the history books." She wouldn't shut up. "You'll be bigger than Howard Carter. The greatest archaeologist who's ever lived."

He rolled his eyes. "Good night, Morgan."

She fell silent but it was all a ruse. Her mind was still working.

"Think of our kids," she murmured. "If you're going to excavate the tomb, then I'm staying with you. Our kids will be born in Egypt. I don't think I like that; I don't want them raised out here in the sticks."

He sighed heavily. "Love, we don't have to decide that tonight."

"Why not?" she mumbled. "And just so you know, I'm not naming our kids any odd family names, okay? I don't know where your parents came up with Chase, Marsh, Chat and Lowe, but I'm not naming my kid Rudell."

Half-asleep, his eyes suddenly lolled open in the darkness. "Rudell? What's that?"

"My mother's maiden name."

He started laughing. "Bloody hell, Morgan, go to sleep. I mean it."

She giggled. "And don't think I'm naming our daughter Foxy."

He shook with laughter, joining hers, and together they finally laughed themselves to sleep. It was all the noise that Morgan needed to be lulled into a deep, dreamless slumber.

The next morning, Fox was up before dawn. Morgan was still asleep and he knew she'd kill him if he started without her, so he quietly dressed, got his coffee, and then went back to the tent to wake her up. He thought he'd have to dress her himself, but to his surprise, she struggled through her extreme grogginess and managed to dress herself. She wasn't going to miss this moment no matter what.

Jabeel had brewed very strong Arabic coffee, very sweet, and Morgan swallowed an entire cup before they even made it to the top of the hill. The morning was cool, with very high scattered clouds across the pale blue expanse of sky. They had covered up the hole the night before with a tarp held down by heavy rocks, so Fox and Allahaba went about removing the rocks and peeling back the blue plastic tarp.

The five foot wide by three and half foot deep pit looked the same as it did the night before. There was an eight inch in diameter open, black hole yawning at the bottom of the cavity. Fox and Allahaba had brought ropes, picks, shovels and the flashlights with them and Morgan had the implements all organized neatly by the time the men pulled off the tarp. Fox neatly folded up the massive tarp and set it down beside his wife.

She was gazing up at him expectantly and when he looked at her, she smiled brightly with her big, baby doll dimples. He couldn't help but smile back as he picked up a rope and began to tie it around his waist.

"I don't think I've ever seen you quite so happy in the morning," he teased her. "I always thought waking up to me would be reason enough to be happy every morning but I guess I was wrong."

She gave him an intolerant expression. "Stop feeling sorry for yourself, Henredon," she shook her head. "I wake up every morning, look at your face, and still think I'm dreaming. I have to pinch myself even now. How did I get so lucky to rate such an amazing guy?"

He fought off a smile. "So you're not just in this for the fact I'm willing to go down into a deep, dark hole for you?"

"Of course not," her smile faded. "I'm going with you."

He lost his smile as well. "Not right now. You're going to stay here until I secure whatever this is. I don't want you getting hurt."

They were gearing up for a disagreement in the most unexpected of places; Morgan could feel it and she tried to stay cool. "I appreciate that, baby," she said. "But I can take care of myself. I have for thirty-one years. I promise I won't do anything stupid. Let's see what's down there together, okay?"

He didn't look happy at all. She could see his jaw ticking faintly, which was rare for him. Given his boxing and rugby background and tremendous size, he was one of the calmest people she had ever met. Other than the incident at the Cairo Museum, she'd never seen him truly angry since she'd known him.

"Love, I really wish you would let me scope this out first," he said patiently. "If something happened to you down there, I'd never forgive myself."

Morgan didn't want to fight with him, not on this day of all days. She stood up from where she had been seated next to the shovels and went to him, wrapping her arms around his narrow waist and laying her head against his sternum.

"I just really want to be a part of this," she said. "I don't want to sit on the sidelines while you do all of the dirty work. This means so much to me, you know? It's the entire reason we met, the entire reason why we're here."

He just closed his eyes, his arms around her, knowing he was about to cave in like a fool. He hugged her gently.

"I know," he said quietly. "And I don't have any intention of doing all of the dirty work by myself. But you need to at least let me make sure it's safe. I'd do that with anything like this under normal circumstances, regardless of if you were involved or not. It just needs to be done. As soon as I make sure it's safe, I'll let you take a look; I promise."

She craned her neck back to gaze up at him; the baby doll dimples were back. "Good enough."

He leaned down and kissed her before letting her go to

finish tying off the rope around his waist. He handed Morgan the rest of the rope as he reached down to collect a pick. Then the two of them moved over to the pit where Allahaba and Jabeel were standing.

"Well," he said decisively as he looked between his helpers and the hole, "I'm going to see what I can do about chipping away at the hole and try not to fall through in the process. I figure with the three of you holding on to the rope, I have a better chance of not crashing to the bottom of whatever this is. Three of you outweigh me, but not by much. Al, when you looked through yesterday, how far would you say it was from that opening to the stairs below?"

Allahaba appeared thoughtful. "Not far," he said. "The first step can't be more than a meter down, but then the steps descend at a steep rate. I could see the doorway at the bottom."

"About how far down was that?"

"Perhaps four or five meters."

Fox thought on that. But rather than try to picture what Allahaba was describing, he wanted to see for himself.

"Very well," he pointed at Allahaba and Jabeel. "You two anchor the rope at the front and the back. Morgan, you get in between them. Be prepared to dig in if this hole starts to go and I start to go with it."

Everyone shifted around and took position. Morgan had a pair of work gloves on that were too big for her hands but she didn't let that stop her; she held tight and braced her legs. When everyone was situated, Fox took a few steps into the pit and began to swing at the hole in the bottom.

Even though the ground was hard, it began to give way quickly. In little time, the hole was about two feet in diameter and Fox could see at least three of the stone-cut steps. He stopped swinging for a moment and shifted position to get a better look.

Morgan saw what he was doing and she was wildly curious. "Baby?" she called. "What does it look like?"

He was still staring. "Well," he said after a moment. "The stairs don't look like they're cut into the mountain. They look like stone."

"What does that mean?"

"That means my theory that this might be a mine shaft just got shot to hell. These stairs look as if they were built rather than carved out of the hillside."

Morgan's excitement blossomed. "Can you see the doorway down below?"

He shook his head. "Not yet," he said. "It's still too dark down there. I need to widen this hole a little more."

With that, he began swinging the pick again. With his power, he was able to knock out several more inches of dirt fairly quickly. As he moved to the westerly section of the hole, the pick hit what felt like cement. It wouldn't move any further as he tried to chip it away. But it was too hard so he began to scrape with the pick, trying to move through whatever it was. The more he scraped, however, the more he appeared to reveal what looked like a flat, hard surface. Curious, he dropped to a knee to take a look.

Morgan dropped the rope and scooted to the edge of the pit. "What is it?" she demanded. "What did you find?"

Fox didn't know how to answer her. He was brushing away at the flat surface with his gloved hands. The more he brushed, the more surface was cleared until finally, he began to see what it was. He let out a snort of surprise.

"I'll be bloody damned," he shook his head, both stunned and deeply pleased. "It's like a landing or a floor of some kind. I can see the contact points where the stones come together. The stairs descend off this landing."

Morgan was at the edge of the pit, beginning to squirm with excitement. "Can I come down, please? Please, please, please?"

She sounded like a little kid. He held out a hand to her and she took it, carefully making her way down the side of the pit with his powerful assistance. She stood next to him, holding on to him as if he would save her from sliding down into the gaping stairs. It was a little scary, but incredibly fascinating. She looked all around her feet.

"Do you know what this looks like to me?" she gripped his arm with two hands. "I'm obviously no expert, but it looks to me like the way the stones fit together on the pyramids. You know how precise they are on the interior? Like, you can't even get a piece of paper in between them? That's what it looks like to me."

Fox was staring at whatever it was they were standing on. He could see at least six stones, all fit together with striking precision, and then the stairs adjoined them, disappearing down into darkness.

Of all the things he thought he might be thinking or feeling at this moment, unadulterated shock wasn't one of them. He thought he would have been quite clinical and professional about everything. But he just wasn't. All he felt was astonishment. He lifted his head and began to survey their surroundings, watching the desert change color as the sun rose.

"The Romans built their settlement around this," he muttered, his gaze moving over to the great house off to the west. "Over there are the bath house and the commander's quarters, but the encampment was built around this. It was built around a... temple."

Morgan was gazing up at him, her brown eyes wide with curiosity. "Remember what I said about that?" she put in. "I noticed they didn't build on the hill but all around it. I thought it looked strange."

Fox could hardly believe it. He looked down at his wife, a myriad of emotions on his face. "I can't even explain what I'm feeling right now because I don't know," he said. "All I know is that this is astonishing, all of it."

She smiled at him. "Can we go down the stairs and see what's at the bottom?"

He slapped a hand against his leg in a gesture of consent. "Why not?" he replied. "Let's do this."

Morgan was grinning so broadly that it nearly split her face in half. Fox winked at her as he turned to Allahaba and Jabeel. "Jabeel, clear away what you can from this surface. I want to see how far it extends and what, exactly, it's a part of. Al, you're going to monitor Morgan and me as we descend the stairs."

Jabeel took Fox's pick eagerly while Allahaba collected the end of the rope. But Fox waved him off, instead removing the rope from around his waist. He didn't see any need for it, at least not at the moment.

"I go first, all right?" he looked Morgan pointedly in the eye.

She nodded innocently. "Of course."

"No running ahead."

"I won't; I promise."

He lifted an eyebrow like he wouldn't be surprised if she lied to him just to keep him happy, to which she simply smiled. The dimples always cooled him off, caved him in, and bent him to her will. For Fox Henredon, those dimples could move mountains. Fox took the flashlight from Allahaba and positioned her behind him.

"Stay behind me, please," he told her. "Hold on to me so you don't slip and fall down the stairs. They're dusty and slippery."

Morgan did as she was told and began to follow him down the steps. With Allahaba watching vigilantly at the top of the stairs, Fox and Morgan proceeded carefully down the steps. Fox would take a step and pause, taken another one and pause again.

Morgan stayed right behind him, holding his torso as if they were on a motorcycle ride together. Any move he made, she made.

Fox inspected the walls and stairs as they descended; they were made of limestone, cut and fitted together with astonishing precision. Rather than a terracotta or sand color, they were very pale, nearly white. Fox ran his hands along the stones, wondering where they had been quarried and suspecting that little search alone would take several years. The fact that they were quarried and carted out into the middle of nowhere by people who didn't even use wheels had him baffled. Greater minds than his were going to have to figure it out.

About halfway down the stairs he switched on the flashlight and shined it down the steps so they could see where they were going. Dust floated up in the yellow beam as they reached the bottom steps and Morgan finally came out from behind him, wanting to see what was on the other side of the doorway. Until Fox flashed the light through the archway, it was pitch black. But when the light finally shone through the ancient doorway, through the dust and flotsam floating in the air, it was as if they had stepped into another time.

Fox stood in the doorway, the flashlight shining on a pillar that was approximately ten feet in front of them. He just stood there, staring, the Maglite beam falling upon scenes that hadn't seen the light of day in thousands of years. Morgan gasped as her astonished gaze beheld a limestone column that had been carved with lotus blooms and fish, delicately winding their way up the stone as if to swim in an imaginary river. Carvings of people, like nothing she had ever seen before, adored the columns in neat rows and up towards the ceiling, a line of fierce limestone cobras bordered the top of each pillar. There was no color, only carvings, and Morgan was astounded.

"Oh, my God," she breathed. "Look at all of the art work. It's beautiful!"

Fox was speechless. His wide-eyed gaze drank in the most magnificent carvings he had ever seen, like a man walking into an art gallery of undiscovered masterpieces. He forced himself to move forward, his flashlight falling on a limestone column of such magnificence that he could hardly believe it was real.

There were rows and rows of carvings in front of him; he could see Nut, the goddess of the sky, as she held up the night for her loving subjects. There was a row below it with a throne scene where Isis and Osiris sat atop their thrones, being adored by their subjects. He just stood there and stared at it, unaware that his wife was now wandering.

Morgan wasn't wandering to disobey him; she was wandering because she was so fascinated. The stairs descended into the far end of a small hypostyle hall, eight large limestone columns rising from floor to ceiling.

All of the columns, from what Morgan could see, were delicately carved with lotus flowers and fish. The hall wasn't very big, exactly the size of the hill that encased it, but it was tall and rectangular shaped. When she looked at her feet, the floor itself was mosaic, like something one would find in an ancient Roman villa. It was covered with dust and dirt, but as far as she could see, the entire floor was mosaic pattern made from little chunks of colored materials. She could make out more fish and flowers.

Just as she opened her mouth to call her husband, something caught her attention and she turned to her left, seeing something ghostly and box-shaped looming in the darkness. Wildly curious, she made her way over to whatever it was, barely illuminated by the sunlight that was filtering down through the stairwell.

Morgan approached, realizing it was a rectangular box on some kind of raised pedestal. She could see lotus petals carved around the base. The floor around her was dusty and uneven and the mosaics seemed to have disappeared as she circled the box, reaching out to touch it. It was coated with dust but the moment she stroked her fingers across it, some kind of white-veined material became evident.

She brushed away at the surface, blowing off the dust, realizing that the structure was polished white stone with black veins running through it. She could see little flecks of something in the white, realizing when the light caught it that they were gold glints. Thrilled, she was moving around the side of the pedestal, moving in the dark as she headed for her husband, when the floor suddenly gave out.

Morgan screamed and Fox bolted. As the floor opened up and began to swallow her, Fox raced across the floor and slid to his knees, like a baseball player sliding into second base, grabbing for his wife before she could fall away completely. He grabbed her by her arms, the sheer force of his strength keeping her from going any further. She was up to her armpits, the rest of her body hanging down into a void.

Fox rose to his knees and easily pulled her out of the hole. Morgan threw her arms around his neck, shaken but unharmed. She held him tightly as if afraid the hole was going to suck her back in again.

"What in the hell happened?" Fox demanded.

Morgan shook her head, turning to look at the black hole that had nearly swallowed her up. "I don't know," she breathed, struggling to catch her breath. "I was walking and suddenly the floor collapsed."

Fox began to back away from the hole with her in his arms, fearful that more of the floor might collapse under his weight. But in doing so, the flashlight beam fell on the big rectangular block in front of him and his fascination, for the moment, outweighed his sense of caution.

"Bloody hell," he breathed. "What *is* this?"

Morgan was still clinging to him as he stood up. "It's made out of something with gold in it," she said. "You can see the gold flecks in the material. It's really beautiful."

Fox gave the hole a wide berth as he went to inspect the massive, dusty block. He ran his gloved hands over it, brushing off the centuries of dust, peering closely at it. After several long moments of scrutiny, he finally shook his head.

"It looks like a sarcophagus," he said.

"Is that what it really is?"

He shrugged. "I'd wager it is, although I've never seen one made out of quartz like this."

Morgan looked at the giant, heavy coffin. "Is that what this is made of?"

He nodded, running his fingers over it again. "The gold around here is quarried in veins of quartz," he told her. "White quartz, just like this. The material they built this from was local."

"Is it Egyptian?"

"It looks like it."

Morgan didn't say anything further as Fox continued to study the coffin. She was suddenly more interested in the hole that had opened up beneath her. She took the flashlight from Fox and, preoccupied, he didn't ask what she wanted with it. Lying on her stomach near the hole that had nearly consumed her, she scooted forward, bit by bit, making sure the floor didn't collapse further until she could peer inside.

The yellow light beam fell on a chamber in some disarray. The floor was about eight feet below and she could see debris all over the floor. The flashlight beam moved across the floor, noting remnants of what looked like leaves. But that didn't make any sense. Shaking her head, baffled, she followed the flashlight beam as it trailed across the floor as far as she could go, hit what looked like part of the wall, before finally coming to rest on something she couldn't quite make out. It looked like a dark box of sorts but she could only see the corner of it. By this time, Fox had joined her.

He lay on his belly beside her. "What are you looking at?"

She handed him the flashlight. "It looks like there was a mad party down there," she told him. "There's debris everywhere."

Fox was silent as he shined his flashlight into the hole. Although Morgan followed what he was looking at, she couldn't make heads or tails out of it. But the chamber below was cluttered, as if homeless people had been congregating down there. In silence, she lay beside Fox, watching him inspect the ancient trash below. It was strange to know that they were the first people in several centuries to survey the scene. After several long minutes of inspection, Fox finally sighed.

"Well," he began, grunting when he shifted his weight on the floor. "I'll tell you what I think this is."

"What?" she was eager to know.

He flashed the beam directly below them. "See all of that down there?"

She looked at the leaves. "Yes?"

"Those are wrappings," he said. "I don't even have to get close to know they're mummy wrappings. And all of the debris down there looks like pieces of wood or even charcoal."

Morgan had no idea what he was saying. "What does that mean?"

He sighed heavily. "It means that I would hazard to guess that back when the Romans built their encampment here, there was enough of this temple uncovered that they could tell what it was. It was ancient even to the Romans at that point and so, being Romans, they did what Romans do best; they trashed it. All of that stuff down there leads me to believe that some of them might have even lived down there, totally desecrating the holy Egyptian temple. I'd really like to go down there and take a look but I'm concerned I wouldn't be able to get back out again if I did."

Morgan looked at the clutter below. "I can go down there and take some pictures," she said helpfully. "You can lower me with a rope. I'm much lighter to pull up than you are."

He nodded faintly. "That's an idea," he said as the beam moved to the pile of leaves. "I'm shuddering to think of which mummy those wrappings belonged to. The Romans must have unwrapped it looking for jewels."

Morgan suddenly stood up and went to the stairs leading up to the daylight. Allahaba was on the top stair, looking down at her eagerly, and she called to him.

"Bring the rope down here, please," she told him, shielding her eyes from the blinding sunlight. "And bring the camera and more flashlights."

Allahaba scrambled and Morgan went back to Fox, who was now picking himself up off the ground. She put her hands on her hips, looking around the dimly lit chamber.

"So that's what you think?" she asked. "Was this was an Egyptian temple and the Roman's trashed it?"

He nodded. "It makes complete sense." He pointed to the stairs. "That stairway right there; it's not the entrance. It's leading to the roof. We came down from the roof access, which I am totally surprised is still intact. Look at the columns on the periphery of the chamber; see how they look as if they're just part of the walls? These walls aren't really walls; they're centuries of sand and dirt, built up to fill in the space between the columns. This was all open air at one point, thousands of years ago. The desert has simply reclaimed it."

Morgan looked around the room, wide eyed. "My God," she breathed. "I didn't even notice. It never occurred to me; I thought it was just another pyramid."

"No," he shook his head. "This thing was wide open, like Karnak."

Morgan continued to survey the room with awe. "You're so amazing," she murmured. "You see this as it was. I can't even picture that."

He looked at Allahaba as the man emerged from the stairwell, noting the expression of awe on his friend's face. In the dim light of the ancient temple, Allahaba was toting ropes and flashlights and other gear, nearly tripping because he wasn't paying attention to where he was walking. He was more interested in his surroundings.

"I may see it as it was, but you were the one who saw it in the first place," Fox kissed his wife on the head as he made his way to Allahaba. "Had we not followed up on your hunch, we'd be digging somewhere else and maybe never have found this. I'm just sorry the Romans got to it before we did."

Morgan contemplated that statement as Fox showed Allahaba around the chamber briefly before moving to the hole in the floor. Explaining to the man what they intended to do, Fox then brought his wife over and tied the rope around her waist, between her legs, and then secured it all in a big knot near her navel. Allahaba handed her the digital camera and away she went.

Morgan had repelled before during police training so it wasn't a big deal for them to lower her into the chamber below. She held on securely, snapping pictures rapidly until she reached the bottom. Once her feet hit the floor, she tried hard to avoid the leaves, which weren't so much leaves as they were old linen bindings. She didn't want to step on anything and damage it more than it already was, making her footing very timid.

"Morgan," Fox called down to her. "I'm going to commit a cardinal sin here, but I want you to pick up some of those bindings and bring them back up."

"Why is it a cardinal sin?"

"Because you're moving archaeological evidence; more than that, you don't have any protective gloves on. Just pick up a small amount of it and bring it back up with you."

She nodded, reaching down to gingerly pick up a strip of linen that felt more like paper. As she looked around for more stuff to bring up to Fox, she began to feel very creepy. The smell of the chamber was old and musty, the ancient air that hadn't been breathed in centuries, and she began to see clearly what some of the debris was.

"Fox?" she called up to him.

"What?"

She peered closely at something on ground. "It... it looks like a cup or something," she told him. "It looks like it's made of silver. It's really dented and tarnished."

"Get it."

Obediently, she picked up the vessel. Walking deeper into the chamber, she moved towards the black box she had spied earlier, noting at closer range that it looked like another sarcophagus. As the beam of light fell on it, illuminating the dark and mysterious box, she could see that there was no top or lid to it. As she drew closer, the beam fell on the area to the left of the sarcophagus and shock filled her veins. She yelped, startled, as her eyes beheld something both shocking and ghastly.

Fox heard her cry and he hung his head down through the hole, trying to see her. "Morgan?" he said urgently. "What's wrong? Are you okay?"

Morgan nodded even though he couldn't see her, her eyes fixed on the subject of her horror. "I'm fine," she said. "But... there are zombies in here!"

"Zombies?" Fox repeated.

She made a face of disgust as she moved closer to the corpse that was now coming to light in the weak flash of the beam.

"Yes," she called back. "Zombies. Mummies. There's a mummy down here."

"Pictures!" he commanded. "Take a few shots and throw me the camera so I can take a look."

Morgan did as she was told. About ten frames later, she scooted over to the hole and tossed the camera up to him. She couldn't really see his face but she could hear him hiss as he clicked through the photos on the viewer.

"Bloody hell," he muttered after several long moments. "The left arm is bent over the chest. That's the telltale sign of Egyptian royalty. I really need to get down there to see it."

As Fox and Allahaba discussed how they could lower Fox down and not break everyone's backs, Morgan returned her attention to the mummy in the corner.

It looked as if it had been tossed haphazardly as it leaned casually against the wall. The skin was well preserved and very dark, the color of beef jerky, and the facial features were twisted with time and decay. Not all of the bindings were off; most of the bindings around the head and legs were gone but the torso, oddly enough, seemed to be somewhat intact. The mummy was very tiny and as she peered more closely at it, she could see long dark hair in hundreds of braids upon its head. The left arm was bent up across the chest and she could see that there was something clutched in the mummy's withered left hand.

Morgan moved towards the mummy as Fox and Allahaba collaborated, hearing their faint conversation as she knelt beside the mummy to study it closer. Now that she was next to it, she could see broken pieces of a wooden sarcophagus but a fully intact facial mask that wasn't like anything she had ever seen before. The features were broad and flat. Looking closer at the face, she could see that one semi-precious eye was missing from the mask but the other one was intact. Overall, it was apparent that the mummy and its coffin had been seriously vandalized. She sighed heavily, looking back to the mummy.

"I'm so sorry," she whispered to the corpse. "Damn Romans."

The mummy didn't reply. She didn't expect it to. Her gaze was, once again, drawn to whatever it was the mummy held in its left hand and she touched it just to see how secure it was. It seemed to be a roll of something, perhaps papyrus or linen, and she gave a couple of gentle tugs on it before it slipped free with relative ease.

She inspected it carefully and closely, realizing it was a scroll of some kind. Without even unrolling it, she could see hints of glyphs, faded black markings made by someone thousands of years ago. It was an amazing concept. She picked her way back among the debris to where her husband and Allahaba were still figuring out how to lower him into the pit.

"Fox?" she called up to him.

He looked down at her. "What, love?"

She held up the scroll. "This was in the mummy's left hand."

He stared at her a moment. "You took it out?"

She nodded. "It came out pretty easily," she said, not sensing that she probably should not have done that. She pointed to the mess behind her. "There's a black box like the white one upstairs which I'm guessing is a sarcophagus. You can see where someone smashed it open and pulled out the wooden sarcophagus, which they then busted up to get at the mummy. But there's a really beautiful face mask that seems to have survived almost intact."

By this time, Fox was leaning down into the hole with a big arm outstretched. "Give me the scroll."

"Can I come out now? It's kind of creepy down here."

"Sure."

He retracted his arm and took the rope that was still tied

around her. Swiftly pulling her up, he took the time to untie the rope from her waist before taking the piece from her hand. Allahaba was still scrolling through the photographs from the chamber as Fox very carefully unrolled the scroll.

"Bloody hell," he hissed, getting his first good look at what the scroll contained. "I should be fired for handling artifacts like this. Bare-handed, without a proper clean area, without proper study or excavation… any reputable archaeologist would never do something like this. When this is all over, I may fire myself."

"I could put it back."

He grunted. "Not on your life. I want to see what this is."

Morgan grinned as he glanced up and winked at her, returning his attention to the object in his hands. His dark eyes glittered as he began to read through the symbols.

"What does it say?" Morgan wanted to know almost immediately.

Fox was reading carefully. The missive was written on linen, not papyrus, and was surprisingly flexible for its advanced age. He began to describe what he was seeing and feeling to Morgan.

"To begin with, this is linen," he told her. "The fibers are broad and rough, not smooth and smaller as they were in later periods, indicating that this was made in an earlier phase of Egypt's history. Generally, looms that early were just stakes in the ground and women would weave the thick fiber linen on them. Vertical looms weren't used until much later, during the New Kingdom."

Morgan absorbed her history lesson. "So this is old?"

He nodded. "Very, very old," he replied, holding out his hand for the other relic she had in her hand; a strip of linen she had picked off the floor. He examined the two pieces closely. "The weave and fiber resemble each other."

By this time, Allahaba had finished with the photos and was

standing next to Fox, reading the symbols on the linen. As Fox scrutinized the symbols without his reading glasses, and in dim light to boot, Allahaba had a much faster grasp of what he was reading.

"*'Worship of Her, Who is Pure Being, Consciousness, Bliss,*" he said softly, slowly. "*Lady of Heaven, Who Exists in all Forms of Time, And All That is Therein, Who is the Divine Illumina-trix in All Beings, Mother Isis, as she sails to Her final Rest, May her Story be Told in Sanctuary, and Know she is One with the Heavens'.*"

For several long moments, no one moved. Fox stared at the linen, confirming Allahaba's translation, hardly believing what he was hearing. Morgan watched the two men as they studied something older than she could possibly imagine; clues to something so magical, so divine, that it was difficult to comprehend. All she knew was that a spell had been cast over all of them as Allahaba had read the contents of the linen. Something holy and enlightening was settling, and Morgan wasn't sure what it was, but she knew something of significance had been realized.

Fox looked up from the linen, his black eyes on the columns of the chamber around them. He could see the carvings, row upon row of figures and symbols. It began to occur to him that perhaps the message was referring to this chamber as the Sanctuary; he wasn't sure what else it could mean. And there was a story on the columns, something he had seen when he had first entered but something that held much more significance to him now. He lowered the linen and moved towards the pillars, his gaze never leaving them.

"Morgan," he said steadily. "Do me a favor, love, and find my notepad. It should be in my backpack. Please bring it to me with some pens. I think I have some translating to do."

JANUARY 5, 1924

Kadin took Louis and me to Karnak today. It was a truly amazing spectacle of the power of ancient Egypt. Kadin and I have discussed when we shall continue to pursue the clues in the papyrus because Louis refused to go any farther. He has already booked passage back to England and I fear I am in great turmoil over this. Still, my love for this country, and its people, grows. In Egypt, love is, indeed, eternal.

~ FS

TWENTY-FOUR

IT WAS noon and Fox had made Morgan leave the stuffy, dusty temple to fetch him something to eat. Truth was, he just wanted her out of the stale air because she kept sneezing as she sat patiently on the last step, while he methodically translated one of the twenty-four columns he had counted. Fox knew that the translation would take years but he wanted to at least translate as much as he could before they left. It might help determine what, exactly, this place was, but the fact remained that he was determined to return at some point very soon with an army of help.

So he sent Morgan to their encampment with Jabeel to help the man with the noon meal. Jabeel had brought couscous and bulgur wheat, and he cooked the grains in hot water, mixing the mash with salt, chopped garlic and onions. It was hot and delicious, and Morgan had several spoonfuls before the grain was even fully cooked. Add to that hummus from canned chickpeas, garlic and sesame paste, fresh bread hot off the makeshift grill pan, and she was in heaven. She ate a good portion of the hummus and bread before she even thought about taking a plate to her husband.

But she piled one paper plate with bread, hummus and cucumber and a second plate with the bulgur and couscous, preparing to take it to Fox. Just as she balanced both plates in one hand and took a bottle of water with the other, she noticed a figure approaching from the north. She couldn't tell who it was at a distance but given that they were still seeing the robed security men from the gold mine lurking about, she wasn't going to take any chances. Setting the food down, she ran to her tent for her weapon.

By the time she emerged from the tent, she could see the figure wobbling towards them. The man was dressed in dirty white robes, no *hajib*, and looked absolutely exhausted. He was literally staggering. Curious, Morgan joined Jabeel and the two of them watched the man weave unsteadily towards them. When he was within twenty yards, he finally collapsed face-first into the ground.

Morgan and Jabeel ran to the man, falling to their knees beside him. Morgan took the man by the shoulders and carefully rolled him onto his back. When his face, caked with sand, came into view, her eyes widened.

"Beni!" she hissed. Then she looked at Jabeel. "Bring some water; hurry!"

Jabeel dashed off as Morgan felt Beni's pulse, his breathing, and brushed the sand off his face. He was semi-conscious.

"Beni?" Morgan shook him gently. "Beni, can you hear me?"

Jabeel returned with the water, pouring it over Beni's face and watching the man revive somewhat. When Beni realized it was water, he opened his mouth, like a hungry bird, and Jabeel poured water into his mouth as it splashed onto his shaking lips.

"Beni?" Morgan said again. "What are you doing here? What happened to you?"

Beni was gasping for breath; he grabbed Morgan's arm. "Dr... Dr. Fox," he gasped. "I must speak to Dr. Fox."

Morgan looked at Jabeel, who took off in a hurry. When he was gone, Morgan brushed more sand off Beni's face and tried to shield his face from the bright noon sun.

"What's wrong?" she asked, urgently. "Why do you need to speak to him?"

Beni's dark eyes were open, looking up at her. He struggled to speak. "You," he whispered, swallowing hard, and Morgan gave him more water. He settled down to speak again. "Dr. Alia wants you."

Morgan looked surprised. "She wants *me*? Why?"

Beni wasn't sure how to continue; his mind wasn't working very well as it was. He simply shook his head and closed his eyes, exhausted and dehydrated, so Morgan didn't push him. She sat there on the dirt with his head in her lap, shielding his face from the sun, until Fox arrived.

And he arrived swiftly. Fox ran like a wide receiver, with long, powerful strides and arms pumping. He came upon his wife sitting on the ground with Beni stretched out beside her and kicked up some dirt as he came to a swift stop. He went down on one knee, his handsome features wrought with curiosity and dread. He fixed on Beni.

"Beni?" he said, his hand on the man's shoulder. "What's happened to you?"

Beni opened his dark eyes, the pleasure of seeing Fox evident on his features. "I... came to warn you, Dr. Fox. Dr. Alia has gone mad; she wanted me to follow you. She wants to know what you are doing. She wants to abduct your wife."

Fox's eyes widened. "What?" He struggled not to roar at the weak man. "What are you talking about?"

Beni nodded faintly, clutching at Fox with weary hands. "She made me do it," he rasped. "She made me steal the journal in your wife's bag. She wanted to know why you were in Egypt."

Morgan nearly exploded. "*You* took the journal?" she exclaimed. "Why in the hell would you do that? You didn't even know what it was!"

Beni coughed wearily. "No, I did not," his voice was scratchy with fatigue. "But Dr. Alia wanted to know why Dr. Fox was asking questions. I took the journal because it was the only thing I could grab before returning your bag to you. But the journal told of the Five Fingers of the Ape, so Dr. Alia began to understand that you were following clues from an ancient papyrus. The journal said so."

Fox was struggling to stay cool. "So... she sent you to see what I'm doing?"

"More than that," Beni insisted weakly. "She made me follow you everywhere to report back to her. At first, it was because she wanted to know if you were truly following the clues that the papyrus spoke of. But then it became something else; somehow, it became more about you and your wife and less about what you were doing in Egypt. When you came to the desert, she called an old friend of her father's, a warlord, and told the man to steal your wife. We have been tracking you through the desert for days, watching you."

Fox stared at him, processing the situation, feeling more fury and dread than he had ever known. "Are you serious?" he shook the man's shoulder gently. "She told someone to abduct Morgan? Why?"

Beni swallowed hard and Morgan poured more water down his throat. "Because," he breathed. "She believed that if your wife was taken, you would turn to her for help in finding her. She is obsessed with you, Dr. Fox. She still wants you even after all of these years."

Fox looked at Morgan then, the two of them exchanging wide-eyed, startled expressions. Fox finally put his hand on her head, dropping his chin to his chest and shaking his head with deep, deep regret. The insanity of Alia was overwhelming and he was ashamed, shocked and furious at the same time. But most importantly, he was concerned with Morgan's safety. He sighed heavily as he looked to Beni again.

"So she has an army of thugs out here to kidnap my wife?" he asked, his anger getting the better of him. "Where are they? And where do you come into all of this?"

Beni seemed to calm somewhat. "I know my guilt," he muttered. "Dr. Alia forced me to follow you and report back to her. But now she is coming to Edfu to follow you herself and I am fearful of what she might do. I had to warn you, Dr. Fox. You must take your wife to safety. These men that Dr. Alia knows... they will kill her if Dr. Alia tells them to."

Fox looked at Morgan, his eyes wide. He was so enraged that he could hardly think straight but above that, his first reaction was to get the hell out of there.

"If what he says is true," he said, "then we need to leave. Now."

Morgan shook her head. "I'm not afraid of that bitch," she said. "We've found something pretty spectacular here and I'm not running off because some crazy whore can't get it through her head that you're not interested in her."

Fox struggled to stay calm. "Love, I understand how you feel," he said steadily. "But you're more valuable to me than any archaeological find. This will be here when we come back. I just want to get you out of here. Please don't fight me on this."

Morgan could see how worried he was. It just made her angrier. She looked at Beni. "Were you a part of that group that tried to rob us a few days ago?" she asked.

Beni nodded. "I was there," he said. "They wanted to take you then but you shot one of them."

By this time, Allahaba jumped in to the conversation. "I

remember!" he hissed, looking at Fox. "They said they wanted to take your wife. Do you recall? But when they tried, she shot them."

Fox nodded in remembrance, recalling that day and what had been said. He looked at Morgan. "It won't stop there," he said. "Those people aren't like normal criminals. If there's money or family honor behind this, they'll push until they get you."

Morgan was torn between agreeing with him and wanting to fight back, to protect herself. "But this find...."

He cut her off. "It'll still be here next week, next month, next year," he insisted. "But it doesn't mean a thing if you're somehow sacrificed in the process. Please, love; please don't fight me on this. I need to get you out of here."

She was growing increasingly inclined to agree with him, simply because he was genuinely frightened for her. But she gave it one last kick.

"But I need to finish this," she whispered. "For Fanny, we need to find out if this is really what she had been searching for. If Isis is *really* here."

He reached out, putting a giant palm on her cheek. "As far as I'm concerned, it is finished," he murmured. "You thought that papyrus finished Fanny, but it didn't. Now it may finish you and I can't live with that. When the madness is over, we'll be back, I promise."

Morgan gave in without another word. As Fox hauled Beni to his feet, Allahaba and Jabeel were already running for the encampment to begin breaking it down. Morgan trailed after Fox as he carried Beni over to the Jeep, her gaze moving to the small hill that was really a temple in disguise.

Maybe Fox was right; maybe this was the end of the trail. They had found something beyond their wildest dreams, something that would take years to excavate and decipher. It was the end of the papyrus, the end of the rainbow, an ancient temple with a mummy that contained a scroll mentioning Isis. She couldn't imagine it was anything else but what they hoped it was.

The tomb of Isis.

Kadin believes he knows what the Ape's Claw, referred to in the Lady of Heaven papyrus, is. He has not told me but he has intimated his awareness. Louis has packed all of our belongings and now awaits the ferry, which will take us back to Cairo and then back to England. But I fear that I cannot go; my choices may be selfish, but I am determined to find the tomb of the goddess.

~ FS

TWENTY-FIVE

WHEN THE GREEN fields of Edfu came into view, Fox nearly wept with relief. The entire drive back along the Marsa Alam road, he kept waiting for men with guns to jump out of the hills and take Morgan away from him. He kept running the scenario over in his mind, planning what he would do in such a case. Anything he could come up with would most likely end his life, so he kept praying that nothing would happen on the barren road, miles from help. Now that they edged to the outskirts of the city, it looked like they were going to be okay.

Morgan sat quietly against him, scrolling through the images on the camera of the temple, the mummy, and the few shots they had taken of the Manjam Hamsh dig. They came to the dusty intersection where they had filled up the gas cans a few days before and Jabeel pulled in to fill up the tank. As he popped off the gas cap and shoved in the nozzle, Fox and Morgan got out of the car to stretch their legs.

The day was warm and a balmy wind blew steadily across the fields. Fox removed his sunglasses and wiped the sweat from his eyelids, turning to see his wife folded over in the middle, stretching her back and legs as she touched her toes. All he could see was her great butt, smiling at her when she straightened up and caught him looking at her backside. She grinned and shook her head reproachfully.

"Anything I can help you with, Henredon?" she asked.

He wriggled his eyebrows and looked away as if thinking about her question. "It's possible," he said. "I'll let you know tonight when we go to bed, with what exactly you can help me with."

She laughed, cozying up to him and shoving her hands into the pockets of his jeans seductively. One hand was in his front pocket, one in his back. The hand in his back pocket squeezed a butt cheek and he growled.

"Don't you dare tease me, you wicked woman," he rumbled. "You know what happens when you do that."

She looked up at him playfully. "Yes, I do," she said. "You and I will have to find a bathroom somewhere."

He snorted, trying not to let the sensation of her hand in intimate places make him crazy. He saw the fruit stand across the street, the same one they had patronized a few days before, and it diverted his attention.

"Do you want to get some fruit before we move on?" he asked.

She laughed at his obvious attempt to change the subject but dutifully looked to the shop across the street. "I ate all of my oranges and grapes," she said. "But what I could really use is a diet cola."

He nodded his head in the direction of the gas station with a little mini-mart inside. "You get the soda and I'll get the fruit."

She grinned and skipped off in the direction of the mini-mart, passing Allahaba as she went. He was on his cellular phone, smiling and waving at her as she went by. Allahaba's gaze followed her as she disappeared into the store, his smile fading as he turned to search for Fox. He caught sight of the big man crossing the street toward the fruit stand. Saying a few words into the cell phone and hanging up, he made haste in Fox's direction.

He caught up to Fox just as the man was putting a few oranges in a plastic bag. Fox glanced at him.

"Want some oranges?" he asked.

Allahaba shook his head. "No, thank you," he lowered his voice. "Fox, I must speak with you."

Fox looked at him, tying up the bag and heading for the cashier. "What about?"

Allahaba waited until Fox paid for the oranges and they were heading out of the stall. He paused before they could cross the street, causing Fox to pause beside him. Allahaba's expression was serious.

"I just spoke with Ziva," he said quietly. "I wanted to let her know that we were coming home tomorrow. But my wife was hysterical, Fox; there is no easy way to tell you this so I will simply come out with it. Fanny passed away in her sleep last night."

Fox just stared at him for a long, painful moment. Then, it was as if an unseen fist hit him in the gut. He exhaled sharply and pulled off his glasses, looking at Allahaba with shock and grief.

"Oh, no," he murmured. "God... are you serious?"

"Of course."

He looked shaken for a moment as the full force of the information settled. "Bloody hell," he breathed. "I... I don't even know what to say."

Allahaba put his hand on the man's arm. "Ziva said she was very peaceful," he said. "It was simply her time, Fox; she went to sleep and did not wake up. But the bad part is that my elder daughters went to prepare Fanny for breakfast this morning and found her stiff and cold. Now my girls are distraught and Ziva doesn't know what to do. I must go home tonight."

Fox exhaled again, looking to see his wife coming out of the shop across the street. He ran his fingers through his dark hair and put his glasses back on, reconciling himself to the news. He hurt deeply on behalf of his wife but as he thought on her impending grief, he also thought of Allahaba. He put a big hand on the man's shoulder.

"Of course," he said. "And I'm very sorry for you and your family. You took care of Fanny for many years and I know you were fond of her. On behalf of my wife and her family, thank you for being so gracious and generous to an old British woman who broke up your grandfather's marriage. You could have thrown her out in the street but you didn't. That says volumes about what kind of a man you really are. Not many people would be as generous as you."

Allahaba smiled weakly. "She was family. There was never any question."

"I know."

Allahaba's gaze trailed across the street, watching Morgan's blond head as she climbed into the Land Rover.

"You must tell her," he said.

Fox was watching Morgan, too. "I will," he replied quietly. "She's going to want to go home with you. She won't wait, either, especially if you're burying Fanny soon."

Allahaba nodded and began heading back towards the car. "I would not expect her to wait," he said. "We must call the airport and see about a flight back to Cairo tonight."

Fox followed the man across the street, his eyes never leaving Morgan. "Call the airport right now while I tell Morgan," he said softly. "Give us a few minutes, okay?"

Allahaba nodded, moving off to conduct his business as Fox

approached the car. He handed the bag to his wife but remained outside of the car.

"Hey," he said. "Come with me, would you? I need to talk to you."

Morgan pulled an orange out of the bag and climbed out of the car. She wasn't on her guard in the least, peeling the orange as she followed Fox to a spot several feet away from the car. They were standing alone near the corner of the gas station as cars whizzed by. Morgan tossed the orange peel to the ground and began pulling the orange apart.

"What's up?" she asked.

He watched her pop a ripe piece of orange in her mouth. "Love, let me ask you something," he said gently. "Do you feel as if you've written the end to Fanny's story?"

Morgan cocked her head with thought, swallowing the orange in her mouth. "Almost," she said. "We followed the clues and found what she attempted to find ninety years ago. I feel like we've completed her quest for the most part."

"For the most part?" he repeated. "What more is there?"

She shrugged as she pulled out another piece of orange. "I want to tell her about what we found. I want to describe it well enough so she can visualize it in her mind. After that, I think the quest is over. I did what I set out to do. Why do you ask?"

He reached out, stroking her arms with his big hands. His manner was tender, gentle. "I think Fanny had other ideas," he said. "She went to sleep last night and when she woke up, she was young and beautiful again, and Kadin was by her side. Her journey, on earth, has ended and eternity, for her, has begun."

She stared at him, orange piece halfway to her mouth. He watched the emotions roll across her face as she lowered the orange segment; curiosity, confusion, and, finally, realization. She dropped the orange and wiped her hand on her jeans, her brown eyes wide with shock as she looked up at him.

"Fox," she grabbed him with her sticky hand. "What are you telling me? Is she... did she...?"

He nodded. "Fanny passed away peacefully in her sleep last night."

Morgan stared at him, digesting the information for a moment. As he watched, her features crumpled and she fell against him, her face in his chest as soft sobs filled the air. He held her tightly, rocking her gently as her grief bubbled over. She sounded so pathetic that it brought tears to his eyes.

"You were so lucky, love," he murmured into the top of her head. "You got to meet a remarkable woman you never believed you would ever know. You got a second chance with her that very few people ever have the opportunity for. Fanny was so thrilled to meet you, to know you, so when I told you earlier than you had already finished her story, I meant it. You brought her life full circle. You need to remember that."

Morgan was sobbing pitifully. "It... it's not that," she wept. "You... you said she passed away last night?"

"That's what Ziva told Allahaba."

Morgan burst out in fresh tears. "She waited," she sobbed. "She waited until we found the tomb. We found it last night and she passed away last night. It's like... like she waited until we found what she had dreamed about all of her life and once we found it, she must have sensed it and knew it was time to let go."

He rocked her gently. "She knew you had written the end of her story," he agreed. "There was no longer any reason to hang on."

"I really wanted to tell her what we found."

"Love, if you believe what I believe about heaven, then she already knows."

Morgan nodded, deeply devastated by the news. Fox let her cry for a few minutes before going in search of a napkin or a Kleenex so she could wipe her nose. Jabeel saw them coming and, knowing what had happened thanks to Allahaba, ran out to greet them with an offering of a roll of toilet paper. Fox took it gratefully, pulling off a length of it to wipe Morgan's face off. But she was still crying so he loaded her up into the Jeep and climbed in after her, pulling her close and holding her tightly as the vehicle sped off towards Luxor.

"Allahaba is finding out what flight back to Cairo we can take tonight," he told her, trying to give her some comfort. "We'll be back in Cairo by tonight."

She sobbed, wiping at her nose. "Wh... where is she?"

Fox caught Allahaba's attention; the man had been listening even though he discreetly pretended otherwise.

"She is still at my home, Morgan," Allahaba said quietly. "If she has not yet been already, she will be washed by Ziva and other relatives and placed in a shroud."

Morgan looked at him, her lovely eyes wet and a tissue to her nose. "She's not at a funeral home?"

Allahaba shook his head. "No," he told her. "She will stay at home, peacefully, and be buried tomorrow morning where we will offer the *Janazah* prayers. They are ritual prayers for the deceased before burial, much like a Christian funeral mass. After prayers, she will be placed in the grave next to Kadin, facing Mecca, where we will offer more prayers for her soul."

Tears were spilling out of Morgan's eyes. "Are you sure she died peacefully?"

Allahaba nodded gently, watching Fox kiss Morgan's temple. "Great peace, Morgan. In fact, Ziva said she died with the journal in her hands. You know that she had not let it go since you gave it to her. She slept with it. It brought her great comfort."

Morgan closed her eyes, tears spilling down her neck as she turned her face into Fox's chest again.

"Can... can we bury her with it?" she whispered. "I think she would have liked that."

Allahaba nodded. "Of course," he said. "We will lay it on her chest, next her heart."

"And the papyrus?" she murmured. "It meant so much to her... I'd like to bury her with a copy of it. Maybe we can get a color copy made so she can have that, too. The papyrus was really what started all of this."

Allahaba nodded, a smile on his lips. "Fanny and Kadin can chase the clues in the afterlife to their hearts' content."

Morgan nodded, unable to speak further. She held the tissue against her mouth, struggling with her grief. Her tears faded, mostly because she was too exhausted to cry anymore. Fox held her closely, feeling her eventually go limp against him. He was grateful for the fact that the woman could fall asleep anytime, anywhere. This time, it would give her a reprieve from her grief.

"Al?" he asked quietly. "Did you find us a flight out of here?"

Allahaba nodded, glancing at his watch. "There is an EgyptAir flight tonight at eight o'clock," he said. "We do not have to go to the airport right away. We will take you back to the hotel and I will return with Jabeel to off load his car. We must also pay Jabeel."

Fox nodded. "I'll write him a check before we go," he said. "Call the Hilton Luxor and see if they have any rooms available for the afternoon. I want to get Morgan into a hot tub and give her a chance to rest before we head home."

As Allahaba got on the phone again, Beni sat in the back seat, silent as the grave. He had heard what was going on, the plans that were taking place. He didn't exactly understand all of it, but Fox's wife was greatly distressed over someone's death, so much so that she mentioned burying the journal with this person and a copy of a papyrus. Beni could only deduce that she meant the papyrus that was translated in the journal. He and Alia had speculated if Fox had the mysterious Lady of Heaven papyrus with him; based on the conversation, Beni was fairly certain they did. Now, they were all heading back to Cairo, away from the Manjam Hamsh Wilderness and away from the drug lord and his men.

Truth was, Beni wasn't feeling warm and fuzzy about confessing everything to Fox. He had expected praise and rewards at the very least. What he received was a bottle of water and a plane ticket back to Cairo. It was frustrating for a man who had tried to do the right thing, now disenchanted by his noble intentions.

Alia was insane, of that he had no doubt, but he had history with her. And after Fox left, he would still have to live with the woman. She controlled so much at the museum and within the antiquities arena that even if he left her, he would probably not be able to get another job. His sense of justice, his disloyalty to Alia, would cost him.

As the car approached the lush lines of Luxor against the blue ribbon of the Nile, Beni began to rethink what he had done. He could fix it, of course, but it would be for a price. Always for a price.

When Jabeel and Allahaba dropped Fox and Morgan off at the hotel, Beni got out of the car and disappeared.

He had a flight to meet.

Fox paid for a room for one night at the Hilton Luxor even though they would only be using it for the afternoon. Morgan was exhausted and his primary concern was calming her down before their flight to Cairo that night. With their luggage reclaimed that they had been storing at the Hilton, they checked into the only room available for an early check-in, a junior suite.

It was early afternoon by the time they checked in. Fox carried the luggage in and laid it on one of two queen-sized beds in the room. Pale and weary, Morgan dug through one of her massive suitcases, pulled out some clean clothes, and stumbled into the bathroom.

Fox began unloading his duffle bag, listening to Morgan run a bath. As he shifted around the items in his suitcase, preoccupied by his wife's grief, he also checked the papyrus, which was in its case and shoved into the lining of his suitcase. It was safe, secure, and he pulled it out, opening the case and reading over the ancient hieroglyphics that had meant so much to Fanny. He could hardly believe the ancient symbols had actually told the truth.

As he unpacked his duffle bag, a small scroll inserted in a sock came forth and he pulled it out to make sure that one was all right, too. The small bit of linen that had been rolled up in the mummy's hand greeted him and he gazed at it a moment, wishing he could have told Fanny about it, too. To him, it was confirmation that the Lady of Heaven papyrus had, indeed, told a true tale. He felt like a black market smuggler with two ancient papyruses hidden in his suitcases and knew he'd have a hell of a lot of explaining to do to his superiors. At least until they understood the entire story. Then they'd probably build a shrine to him.

By the time he was finished unpacking his duffle bag, repacking his suitcase including the folded up duffle bag, the bathroom was quiet so he went inside to see what Morgan was doing. He found her up to her neck in bubbles and hot water, eyes closed as she lay against the side of the big Roman tub. She looked positively ashen. He took a few steps inside the room.

"Are you all right?" he asked.

She opened her eyes, half-lidded, to look at him. "I'm fine."

"Would you like anything? Something to eat or drink?"

She shrugged. "If you're hungry, then you can get me something, too. Otherwise, don't bother. I'm okay."

He smiled at her and left the bathroom, going to phone and calling room service. He ended up ordering a couple of sandwiches, cake, and four bottles of good Egyptian beer. After hanging up the phone, he stripped off his dirty clothes and stepped into the shower, a separate fixture from the big Roman tub. As Morgan lay in the tub and enjoyed the warm bubbles, Fox scrubbed himself down and shaved. Then he turned the shower off and walked, dripping wet, over to the tub.

Morgan's eyes were closed when the water suddenly surged and she ended up with bubbles in her mouth. Fox slid into the tub, grinning as he picked up the floral-scented shower gel and began to lather it up on a wash cloth.

"I haven't had the pleasure of doing this for a few days," he told her, seductively. "I've missed it."

Morgan smiled weakly, shifting so he could slide in behind her. Seated between his massive legs, she lay back against him as he soaped her arms, her shoulders. His kisses were gentle on the side of her head as he soaped her neck with one hand and pulled out the clip holding her hair up with the other. He wanted to distract her from her sorrow and he was slowly succeeding. Morgan let him pull her head back, his lips seeking hers. After that, things got amorous.

Forty minutes later, Morgan was limp and dozing in Fox's arms on one of the queen-sized beds. There were damp towels on the bed, on the floor, and the two of them were wrapped up in the sheet. Morgan was snoring softly against him, exhausted both emotionally and physically from the past few days. As Fox began to doze himself, there was a soft knock at the door.

His eyes popped open as he remembered the room service

he'd ordered before things got heated in the tub. Carefully disengaging himself from Morgan, he threw the bedspread over her to shield her from prying eyes as he wrapped the towel around his waist and went to the door. Peering from the view hole, he could see a young Egyptian man dressed in a uniform with a tray in his hand. He opened the door and let the kid in.

The young man didn't speak English; he quickly and efficiently set the tray down and handed Fox the invoice, which he signed for. When the man left and Fox shut and locked the door behind him, the phone suddenly rang.

Morgan's head popped up and she grabbed at it, groggy and grumpy at having been woken up. She put the receiver to her ear.

"Hello?" she asked, voice hoarse.

"Yes, hello," came a man's voice. "Dr. Henredon has a visitor. Shall I send her up?"

Morgan heard the "her" part and her eyes opened, more alert. "Who is it?"

"A woman by the name of Mrs. Aziz. Shall I send her up?"

"No," Morgan snapped. "What does she want?"

"She is here to see Dr. Henredon. Shall I send her up?"

Morgan sat up, irritated and suspicious after everything that Beni had told them. "Not unless you tell me what she wants," she said pointedly. "Ask her and call me back."

She hung up the phone and looked over at her husband, who was taking the heat lids off the sandwich plates. "Someone named Mrs. Aziz is here to see you," she said. "Does that name ring a bell?"

He brought the plates over to the bed. "No."

Morgan took the plate he sat down next to her on the bed as he went back for the beer. She had taken a big bite of her sandwich when the phone rang again. This time, Fox answered.

"Yes?" he nearly demanded.

It was the same nervous young man on the other end. "Mrs. Aziz says she has business with Dr. Henredon. Shall I send her up?"

Fox was on the same page as Morgan; given what Beni had told them, he wasn't so inclined to greet strangers, especially when no one should know he was staying at this particular hotel.

"No," he said flatly. "Ask her what business."

The young concierge could be heard, muffled, asking someone what their business was. A few unintelligible words were exchanged and the young man got back on the line.

"She says that she will speak with Dr. Henredon later," he said.

Now Fox was thoroughly perplexed. "Who was that woman?"

"Mrs. Aziz, sir."

Fox just shook his head. They weren't getting anywhere. He just hung up the phone and went to sit down on the bed beside his wife. She was already halfway through her sandwich.

"Who in the hell was it?" she asked.

He took a massive bite of his sandwich. "I have no idea," he replied. "It makes me nervous, especially after what Beni told us."

Morgan shrugged and took a big swallow of beer to wash down the food. "Assassins don't usually come knocking on the door asking for an audience," she said, eyeing him. "Maybe it was a call girl."

Fox smirked. "I've got my own call girl, thank you very much."

Morgan giggled. "Maybe it was a wedding present to spice up our honeymoon."

He laughed. "From whom?" he wanted to know. "My brothers have a fairly dirty sense of humor, but even I wouldn't expect them to send me a call girl on my honeymoon. A box full of lubricant and condoms, yes; a call girl, no."

Morgan just laughed as she started in on the second half of her sandwich. "I'm looking forward to meeting them."

Fox rolled his eyes. "God, they'll love you," he shook his head, taking a drink of his beer. "Chase is the one I'd worry about. He's almost as tall as me, a big bloke, with flaming red hair and a red goatee. He looks like a pirate. And he loves the ladies."

"I can hardly wait."

Fox just shrugged, secretly wondering if he'd have to kill his brother because he knew for a fact the man would find Morgan extremely attractive. He downed the rest of his beer and opened up a second bottle.

After their meal, they lay down to sleep for a couple of hours before rising and preparing for the flight to Cairo. Morgan, true to form, refused to wake up at the appointed time so Fox got up, showered and dressed before pulling her out of bed and depositing her into the shower. Yawning, Morgan finished cleaning up. She was wrapped up in a big towel as she finished brushing her teeth and putting on makeup.

Fox was finished with everything by the time she began blow drying her hair and he stood in the doorway, watching her. From the moment he had first met her, all he seemed to want to do was watch her. Morgan was chattering on about wanting to visit the pyramids before they left and visit some other sights, but as he watched her style her hair, it suddenly occurred to him that it was nervous chatter. He knew she was dreading Fanny's funeral and trying to distract herself. He leaned up against the door jamb and just listened. He thought that was what she needed most.

He moved to sit on the bed as she left the bathroom and began dressing. He watched her drop the towel and put on a lacy bra and panties, proceeding to dress in jeans and a beautiful flowing top that was sweet and sexy.

All the while, she continued talking as she put on jewelry, her beloved wedding rings, and her shoes. Fox just sat back and enjoyed the view; what was it she had said to him once? That she wondered what she had ever done to rate such an amazing guy. He thought the same thing, of her, every minute of every day.

When she was finished dressing and talking, she zipped up her suitcases and Fox hauled them both to the door as she made a final sweep of the room to make sure they didn't forget anything. She had her big designer purse in hand as she met him at the door.

"And that's another thing," she went on. "Since this whole venture has taken less than a week, are we planning on leaving Egypt early? We really need to talk about what we're going to do when we leave. Are you going to fly back to Los Angeles with me so you can meet my parents? They want to throw us a party, you know. And I'll need to go home and pack up all of my stuff to ship to England."

He opened up the door for her and she sashayed into the hall beyond. As she held back the door for him, he collected the luggage and followed her out into the hall.

"I'll change my return ticket and fly back to Los Angeles with you," he told her. "You're not going anywhere without me and I'm not going anywhere without you, so it makes sense for me to go back to California and help you pack. And in answer to your question, I can see us leaving Egypt in the next week. With those two sites that we discovered, I really need to get in contact with the Supreme Council for Antiquities to stake a claim for the Bolton Museum. But before I do that, I need to speak with my bosses and see how they want to proceed."

She nodded as the door closed behind them and they

headed down the hall. "How does it usually go in something like this? We weren't digging legally, so does that mean we don't have claim?"

He nodded. "Technically," he said. "The SCA will take over the digs regardless but the Bolton Museum will offer to sponsor it, making it our dig as well. We'll have equal claims to artifacts. It gets a bit technical and political, but we'll make it work."

She fell silent as they waited for the elevator. "What are you going to do?" she asked. "You're going to want to excavate, aren't you?"

He looked at her. "You asked me that already, remember?"

"No, I didn't," she shook her head. "That was before we found the temple. You said you didn't want to speculate about it, so I'm asking you now. Are you going to want to return to Egypt to excavate the temple?"

He shrugged as the elevator door opened and they went inside. "I don't know," he said, hitting the button for the lobby. "What do you think about it?"

She looked surprised that he would ask her. "What do *I* think?" she repeated thoughtfully. "I think I would be very happy living at Heaven's Gate with you while you work at the museum and I do whatever it is I end up doing. But on the other hand, we've followed clues on an old papyrus that has led us to two pretty substantial finds. You found them and I think it's only fair that you be in charge of excavating them."

He watched her as the elevator came to a halt, trying to deduce how she really felt; was she being truthful or was she simply telling him what he wanted to hear? "But you're not thrilled about spending years in Egypt while I dig," he said quietly.

She looked at him, a smile on her face. "I'll be happy wherever you are. Except for your crazy ex-girlfriend, I like Egypt."

He lifted his eyebrows in understanding as they left the elevator, dodging a few people who were getting in. "You like the hotels and the spas," he pointed out. "You didn't like camping out in tents and in digs so remote, that's exactly what we would be doing for months on end."

She looked at him with an exaggerated pouty face. "Are you trying to discourage me?"

He laughed. "No, love, I'm not," he said. "I'm just trying to be realistic with you."

She went into more of an exaggerated pout mode. "No way, buster; I'm on to you," she said as they pushed open the lobby doors. "You're trying to get rid of me so Mrs. Aziz, the call girl, can join you in the wilds. I'm telling you right now that your evil plan isn't going to work."

He laughed heartily as they moved through the lobby doors but his reply was cut short when a firm female voice suddenly interrupted their light repartee.

"And I hear my name," the voice said. "I am Mrs. Aziz. Hello, Fox."

Both Fox and Morgan turned, startled, to the source of the voice. The woman had been sitting on a bench right outside the door and Fox's blood ran cold when he saw who it was.

Alia was smiling back at him.

JANUARY 15, 1924

Last night, someone broke into my room and tried to smother me. Had it not been for Kadin, they would have succeeded. Perhaps it was a thief at random, for this country abounds with them, but Kadin seemed to know who it was. He would not tell me but I am increasingly fearful as we proceed on this quest. Louis continues to beg me to return to England but I cannot; not when my heart is in Egypt.

~ FS

TWENTY-SIX

AFTER A MOMENT'S SHOCK, it was Morgan who found her tongue first. She wasn't burdened down with heavy suitcases like Fox was, making it easier and swifter to move. She charged Alia and bumped up against the woman, causing her to stumble back. When Alia grabbed the bench to steady herself, Morgan was in her face.

"Listen to me, you crazy bitch," she snarled. "I don't know what your problem is or why you're so obsessed with my husband, but it ends here and now. Do you hear me? He belongs to me and I swear to God that I'll kick your ass if you come anywhere near us ever again; got it?"

She was snarling and vicious and Fox, very quickly, set the suitcases aside and went to Morgan, pulling her away from Alia before it could explode into a physical confrontation.

But as he moved, unbeknownst to either woman, he hit the speed dial on his cell phone and put it in his shirt pocket, hoping the person at the other end would answer the call and understand that Fox needed help. He needed a witness to whatever conversation was going to take place and he wasn't going to take any chances.

Alia, startled by Morgan's charge, struggled to come off with some dignity. "Mrs. Henredon," she stood up, straightening her mussed scarf. "You must learn to control yourself. You are coming off like a typical American."

That only served to inflame Morgan more. Fox had her around the waist or he was sure she would have ripped Alia apart.

"What do you want, Alia?" he asked calmly.

Alia looked at Fox, her big green eyes soft and adoring. "Want?" she repeated. "Simply to speak with you. I understand you've been doing some digging."

Fox's expression was like stone. "I'm not talking to you about it. You'll hear about it through proper channels just like everyone else."

Alia snorted loudly. "You speak of proper channels yet you did not go through proper channels before you began vandalizing the Egyptian wilderness," she shook her head slowly, her eyes glittering fiendishly. "One well-placed phone call and you, and your museum, will be banned from Egypt permanently. Is that what you want?"

"You can't prove anything."

She looked amused. "Is that so?" she shrugged lightly. "I have witnesses."

Fox's brow furrowed impatiently. "Who? Those thugs you hired to kidnap my wife?"

Alia shrugged nonchalantly. "The robbers didn't get her, unfortunately. She seems to be good at defending herself."

"So you really did hire them?"

"I did what I had to."

Fox snorted with disbelief, with irony. "And Beni? You've got that bloke so beat down that he'll say anything because you've threatened him so many times. He's afraid of you."

Alia didn't lose her confidence. "Beni will support my claim, of course."

She pointed to the end of the curbside area where the taxis were lined up. There were people milling about and gas fumes from idling engines filled the air. But there was no mistaking Beni standing at the edge of the curb, watching the conversation.

Beni looked nervous and edgy, and Fox's heart sank when he realized what had happened. He didn't say what he was thinking; *he played us. He earned our confidence and then he played us.* It was apparent that Beni had run to Alia with everything he had heard or been told over the past several hours. It was the only explanation since Alia would not have found Fox any other way. Fox felt sick; he couldn't even look at Morgan.

"I don't care who supports your claim," Fox tried not to sound too angry or too betrayed. "It will be your word against mine."

"We'll put your wife and friends under oath," Alia countered. "I wonder if they will lie."

Fox began to lose his temper. "Is this really what you want? To ruin me just because I'm not romantically interested in you anymore?"

Alia eyed the people who were coming in and out of the hotel, people who could overhear their conversation. She mulled over his question.

"Perhaps we should speak of this privately," she said quietly. "I tried, you know, but you would not see me."

"I still don't want to see you, but here you are," he countered, like a slap to her face. "Whatever you have to say, you can say it here."

Alia's confidence began to waver. She shook her head as if in sorrow. "You really should have more respect for our friendship," she said. "You came to me for help and when I provided it, you ran off. You took advantage of my knowledge, Fox. All I wanted to do was to continue to help you."

Fox was losing his patience. "We had this discussion. It was a mistake for me to have asked you for help in the first place because it made you delusional," he lowered his voice. "I told you before that if you couldn't control whatever you were feeling for me that I would cut you off. Consider yourself cut off."

He whispered something to Morgan who, eyes still blazing at Alia, turned to collect one of the suitcases. Alia watched as Fox reclaimed the other three as he and Morgan prepared to move out to the curb.

"Fox," Alia took a few steps towards them, her voice firm and in control. "If I were you, I would listen to what I have to say. I understand you have a papyrus with you and with one call to Customs I could have you arrested for smuggling artifacts out of the country. I wonder how that would affect your career and the Bolton Museum's reputation."

Morgan froze, her big eyes on Fox. He looked at his wife, calculating the situation, before turning to Alia. "It belongs to us."

"Can you prove it?"

"Can you prove it doesn't?"

Alia shrugged. "It will not harm my reputation in the least to try," she said. "I will look like a crusader for Egyptian culture. But it will destroy your reputation to fight it and you know it."

His jaw began to tick as his patience slipped. "All right, then," he said with strained temper. "I'll ask the obvious question; what is it that you want?"

Alia smiled. "Let us speak of this in private."

"We'll speak of it now. What do you want?"

Alia's smile wavered. "Why are you so rude to me? What did I ever do to you that would make you treat me so poorly?"

Morgan grunted and rolled her eyes but Fox stopped her from saying anything. He struggled to remain patient. "What do you want from me?" he demanded. "Hurry up; I have a plane to catch."

Alia's smile vanished completely as she came to realize he wasn't going to get into a deep conversation with her. It began to feed her psychosis. "You're going to a funeral, I'm told," she said coldly.

Fox nodded, not wanting to tread on fragile ground with this line of conversation, fearful of how Morgan would react. "Yes," he replied. "You still haven't told me what you want from me."

Alia began to grow incensed, hurt and rejected all rolled into one. Her gaze moved from Fox to the small woman beside him. The woman who had everything Alia wanted. The mere sight of her fed Alia's unreasonable jealousy.

"You will tell me what you were digging for," she lowered her voice. "Were you following the clues on the papyrus? Were you truly looking for Isis' tomb?"

Fox could see she was slipping and it bolstered his confidence. "By the way, it was very professional of you to steal the journal from my wife's bag," he said with disgust. "Pretending to help us search for it was quite a performance when you knew where it was the entire time."

Alia cleared her throat. "Nothing happened to it. It was returned safely."

"Then you admit you stole it."

"I borrowed it."

He sighed heavily. "If I had wanted you to know everything, I would have told you. You had no right to steal something that didn't belong to you."

Alia shifted on her feet, increasingly uncomfortable. "Just tell me if you found what you were looking for. Did you find Isis' tomb?"

Fox shook his head without hesitation. "I'm not telling you anything. We need to go."

Alia's jaw began to tick and she stomped a foot. "Give me that papyrus. I want it."

"Why?"

"Because it belongs in Egypt. You have no right to it."

"And you do?

"Give it to me or I'll have you arrested for stealing artifacts."

"But I didn't steal it," he countered calmly. "It belongs to my wife's family. I can get an oath of affirmation from the dealer who sold it to her family that it is legally ours. He has the sales records to confirm this. I can prove everything, so do you really want to drag me through the dirt?"

Alia was growing increasingly unsteady. "I should have been assisting you," she seethed, looking at Morgan. "We should have done this together, you and me. But instead, you married this... this stupid American woman. Why is she better than me?"

Morgan had had enough. She began to roll back the sleeves of her jacket. "Sister," she growled, "do you really want to go there with me? I'll take you apart piece by piece."

Fox found himself calming his wife down before she flew at Alia. Hands on Morgan's balled fist, he looked at Alia.

"Alia, I want you to listen very carefully to me," he said, his voice low. "What I do and who I do it with is none of your business. I do not have any feelings for you, nor did I ever. The three months we spent dating was just a fling. It didn't mean a thing to me. There is no chance for you and me, now or ever. Even if Morgan wasn't in the picture, there wouldn't be a chance for me and you. I am not interested in you. I don't have feelings for you. I never will. So do what you have to do, but Morgan and I are leaving for Cairo now to attend a funeral and I don't ever want to see or hear from you again. Is that clear?"

By this time, Alia was staring at him with an ashen face. "You'll be sorry, Fox," she hissed. "I want that papyrus."

He just stared at her; very little about what he had said had made an impact, or so he thought. He finally shook his head.

"I'm not going to have this discussion with you," he said. "If you really want it, we'll be in Cairo."

"Then I'll get it in Cairo before you can leave the country with it," she snarled. "I will make your life miserable, do you hear me? I'll pull the authorities in on this and I'll ruin you!"

Fox just stared at her. Then, he reached into his pocket and pulled out his phone. Turning the display towards Alia, he hit the speaker button.

"Did you get all of that, Mrs. Moberley?" he asked.

The phone crackled as a voice came through. "Everything but the first couple of sentences, Dr. Henredon," the faithful old secretary said. "The entire conversation was recorded. What do you want me to do with it?"

Fox continued to stare at Alia, who had turned a sickly shade of white. "Forward a copy to the General Director of the Cairo Museum, Dr. Mohammed Abdel Hamid. Also forward a copy to Dr. Trenton Dawes St. Héver, Director of Antiquities at the Bolton Museum. Tell them that this is a conversation between Dr. Fox Henredon and Dr. Alia el-Shabheen and let them know that I'll call them both later to clarify."

"Will do, Dr. Henredon. Are you at least enjoying your trip to Egypt?"

Fox smiled, his gaze still fixed on Alia. "Very much," he said. "I'll call you later."

With that, he hit the disconnect button and put the phone back in his pocket. He cocked his head at Alia's stunned expression.

"And with that, my wife and I will be leaving," he said

quietly, urging Morgan towards the curb. "Have a good day, Dr. el-Shabheen."

Alia was so angry that she was weaving unsteadily even as she stood there. Morgan couldn't help it; she gave the woman a triumphant cock of the eyebrow as she moved for the taxi stand. The next thing she realized, a roar of sorts was coming up from behind and Morgan turned in time to see Alia bearing down on her, claws bared.

Startled into a defensive stance, Morgan lashed out a hand and caught Alia in the nose, sending the woman onto her backside. As Alia lay prone on the concrete curb, hands on her face and blood pouring down her cheeks, Morgan bent over her without a hint of remorse.

"I guess this stupid American can kick your butt," she hissed. "Stay down. It's safer for you that way."

Fox gently pulled her away, not so much as passing a glance to Alia wallowing on the ground. A taxi pulled up several feet away and Fox began loading their luggage into the trunk. He opened the door for his wife and got in after her without a hind glance. For them, it was over and done with. The taxi pulled out of the driveway and lost itself in the dense Luxor traffic.

As a couple of the valets moved in to help Alia, still bleeding on the ground, Beni watched the entire scene from several feet away. He had no intention of moving in to help her. In fact, the more he thought on it, the more he realized he'd burned his bridges with both Alia and Fox. Perhaps it was time for him to find another line of work. He wasn't as distressed about it as he thought he would be. Perhaps there was more for him out there than being subservient to a madwoman.

Shoving his hands into his pockets, he faded into the crowd and wandered away, perhaps to better things.

We are prepared to move south to find the first clue of the papyrus. Dear Kadin has made the arrangements and Louis continues to beg me to return to England with him. As much as I love my homeland, something about Egypt beckons me and I cannot refuse. The quest is dangerous and I understand this, but if it claims my life, then I will not be sorry. It was something I had to do. My life, my heart, is here... in Egypt.

~ Frances Sherburn

TWENTY-SEVEN

FOX STOOD SEVERAL FEET AWAY, under the shade of an ancient olive tree, watching his wife as she stood over Fanny's newly covered grave. There were thousands of purple flowers, a color that had been Fanny's favorite, blanketing the fresh earth, and the noon sun was gentle overhead. It was a peaceful, perfect day in the old cemetery where generations of Allahaba's family had been buried.

Morgan had a white scarf over her head and around her shoulders as a sign of modesty and respect. It was the same white scarf that Fanny had worn to Morgan and Fox's wedding. Ziva had given it to Morgan that morning along with many of Fanny's other personal belongings. It was such a bittersweet moment for Morgan, collecting her great-grandmother's possessions that had meant so much to her. But the one thing that had meant a great deal to both of them, the journal, now lay buried under several feet of dirt.

A gentle breeze sang through the cemetery, lifting the edges of the white scarf. As Morgan stood there and gazed at the grave, lost to her thoughts, Fox walked up beside her. He slipped his big arm around her shoulders and kissed the top of her head.

"Are you okay, love?" he asked gently.

She nodded, sniffling delicately; tears were close to the surface, as they had been all morning. "I'm okay," she said. "She did look peaceful, didn't she?"

Fox nodded. He had been one of the pallbearers who had carried Fanny's tiny body down from her bedroom and to the waiting processional. Then he'd helped carry her into the cemetery for burial.

"She looked... happy," he gave her a gentle squeeze. "I'd be happy, too, if I was finally reunited with the love of my life."

Morgan gazed up at him, looking like an angel with her sweet face and white scarf. "Do you think we did the right thing?"

He kissed her forehead. He knew what she was referring to, something they'd talked about all night before finally acting on it when morning dawned. Given Alia's threats and the potential for something very ugly and damaging, he wasn't at all disturbed by their decision. His dark gaze moved back to the mound of purple flowers.

"I think so," he said. "It was hers, after all."

Morgan's gaze moved to the purple flowers as well. "If she has it, Alia and the Egyptian government can never get it," she said. "It'll be safe forever."

Fox nodded faintly. "If we buried Fanny with not only the journal but the papyrus as well, then its safety is assured. We have photographs and the translation of the papyrus and the Egyptian government can have that if they want. I can always make more copies. But the papyrus... it belonged to Fanny. Besides, like I said last night, I wouldn't put it past Alia to have alerted Customs in spite of everything. If they got a hold of it, we'd never see it again. This way, it's where it belongs."

She gazed up at him again. "And the other thing?"

He fell silent, still staring at the mound. "When Allahaba translated that tiny linen scroll, the first thing I thought of was Fanny," he said. "I don't know why, but I just did. She never found what was at the end of those clues. She never had the chance that we did. So by burying the scroll with her... to me, it's a piece of what she was looking for, the one tangible proof of a quest that changed the course of her life. She has her journal, her papyrus, and the scroll that was found at the end of that papyrus. Her story is finally finished."

There were tears in Morgan's eyes. "But it's valuable artifact," she whispered. "Maybe the most valuable artifact ever found."

Fox shrugged. "It meant more to a one hundred and five-year-old lady," he winked at her. "I have a translation of it and pictures of it. She deserves to have what she wanted so badly. She's earned it."

Morgan laid her head against his chest, her arms around his narrow waist. "What if the Egyptian government wants that, too?"

"Then they'll have to dig up an old woman to get it and we know that's never going to happen. Whatever is buried with Fanny is safe forever from crazy curators or greedy government officials," he stroked her back affectionately, comfortingly. "But I particularly like the fact that the scroll's translation will be on Fanny's headstone. It fits her perfectly."

Morgan agreed. "It made sense. It's a beautiful epitaph, don't you think?"

"I do."

Morgan wiped delicately at her nose as she released her husband and bent down to pick up one of the many purple mums adorning Fanny's grave. She gazed at the flower a moment, pensive.

"So now we have some things to do," she turned to Fox. "I need to call my parents and tell them all about this crazy adventure, about Fanny, and about our future plans. And you need to call your bosses and figure out how to proceed on those two digs we left out there in the desert."

He nodded, putting his arm around her and gently pulling her away from the gravesite. The cemetery was a beautiful one, with tasteful headstones and lush grounds. As he gazed up into the sky, he felt like he was embarking on a whole new life with a woman by his side, whom he adored more than words could express. All he could see was a bright, wonderful future.

"There's time for that," he said. "Can I at least enjoy the remainder of my honeymoon for the next few days before I'm forced back to reality?"

She grinned up at him. "Sure you can," she said. "What more did you have in mind?"

He met her smile, so in love with those big, baby doll dimples. "Lots of things," he told her. "Pyramids, romantic river cruises, maybe even the Valley of the Kings. And spending every night with you."

"And then?"

He simply grinned as they headed from the cemetery gate and towards the waiting car where Allahaba sat, ready to drive them back to his home for a big meal. Fox spied his friend in the distance, a man who was now, thanks to Fanny, family. He felt incredibly blessed, on many levels.

"And then we do whatever the Fates have in store for us," he told her. "They've been pretty good to us so far."

"I'm looking forward to it."

He gave her another hug, heartfelt and sincere. "I love you, Mrs. Henredon."

"And I love you."

"Enough to spend the next thirty years of your life living in a tent and digging in the desert?"

She laughed as they reached the car and he opened the door for her. She paused before climbing in, her wide brown eyes intense on him.

"Enough for that," she murmured. "More, even."

The car sped away from the cemetery, heading back into the ancient city that was as alive now as it had been a thousand years ago.

Back in the old cemetery, the purple flowers covering Fanny's grave blew gently in the wind, as beneath them a very old woman dreamed everlasting dreams of days when she was young and beautiful. Kadin was in her dreams, kissing her gently, so glad to see the woman he hadn't seen in twenty-five years.

As she eternally slumbered, in her arms she clutched her precious journal, the last page finally written by her great-granddaughter. Morgan had finished Fanny's story with the words from the tiny scroll, the same words emblazoned on her headstone:

Worship of Her, Who is Pure Being, Consciousness, Bliss.
Lady of Heaven, Who Exists in all Forms of Time,
And All That is Therein,
Who is the Divine Illuminatrix in All Beings,
Mother Isis, as she sails to Her final Rest,
May her Story be Told in Sanctuary,
and Know she is One with the Heavens

THE END

AFTERWORD

What's fact and what's fiction? The Manjam Hamsh Wilderness and Mt. Nuqrus are fact. There really are gold mines at Mt. Nuqrus as well as Roman ruins; if you look on Google Earth, you can see the ruins quite clearly. Ranthor is fiction as is the Lady of Heaven papyrus and the Isis scroll, so the contents of those scrolls are purely from the author's imagination. Edfu exists and so do all of the major landmarks in Egypt. Bolton and Bromley Cross, as cities, exist, but Heaven's Gate does not. This book is a perfect example where fact and fiction intermingle to produce a blockbuster storyline.

ABOUT THE AUTHOR

ABOUT KAT LE VEQUE

KATHRYN LE VEQUE is a critically acclaimed, USA TODAY Bestselling author (having hit the list over 30 times), an Indie Reader bestseller, a charter Amazon All-Star author, and a #1 bestselling, award-winning, multi-published author in Medieval Historical Romance with over 150 published novels. Kathryn also writes Romantic Suspense as Kat Le Veque.

Kathryn has received praise for her writing and has won several awards for her work, including two nominations for the Holt Medallion. Her books have topped bestseller lists, and she has gained a loyal fan base that eagerly anticipates each new release.

Kathryn is a talented author who has made a significant impact on the world of historical romance fiction. Through her captivating storytelling and meticulous research, she has enchanted readers with her tales of love, adventure, and the enduring power of the human spirit.

Kathryn loves to hear from her readers. Please find Kathryn on Facebook at Kathryn Le Veque, Author, or join her on Twitter @kathrynleveque, and don't forget to visit her website at www.kathrynleveque.com.

ALSO BY KAT LE VEQUE

The Unholy Angels

Hour of Surrender

Trent Chronicles

Valley of Shadow

The Eden Factor

Canyon of the Sphinx

The Eagle Brotherhood

The Sunset Hour

The Killing Hour

The Secret Hour

The Unholy Hour

The Burning Hour

The Ancient Hour

The Devils Hour